Emily A. Beaufort

Egyptian sepulchres and Syrian shrines

Including some stay in the Lebanon, at Palmyra, and in western Turkey, VOL. I

Emily A. Beaufort

Egyptian sepulchres and Syrian shrines
Including some stay in the Lebanon, at Palmyra, and in western Turkey, VOL. I

ISBN/EAN: 9783741194566

Manufactured in Europe, USA, Canada, Australia, Japa

Cover: Foto ©Andreas Hilbeck / pixelio.de

Manufactured and distributed by brebook publishing software
(www.brebook.com)

Emily A. Beaufort

Egyptian sepulchres and Syrian shrines

EGYPTIAN SEPULCHRES

AND

SYRIAN SHRINES

INCLUDING SOME STAY IN THE

LEBANON, AT PALMYRA, AND IN WESTERN TURKEY

BY EMILY A. BEAUFORT

IN TWO VOLUMES

VOL. I.

SECOND EDITION

LONDON
LONGMAN, GREEN, LONGMAN, AND ROBERTS,
1862.

TO

R. E. B.

MY FRIEND AND SISTER,

WHO SHARED IN EVERY SCENE DESCRIBED IN THESE PAGES,

AND WITH WHOSE KIND ASSISTANCE THEY WERE WRITTEN,

THIS BOOK

IS AFFECTIONATELY DEDICATED

PREFACE

THE FIRST EDITION.

———•———

CIRCUMSTANCES having rendered change of scene and climate imperatively necessary for my sister and myself, we hastily determined, at the close of the year 1858, to leave England for Egypt, believing that we should find there an endless store of deeply interesting subjects for thought and study, unfatiguing travelling, and no society: our hopes of the two former were more than realised, but solitude is difficult to obtain on the now fashionable and crowded Nile. I had no presumptuous intention of writing an account of our travels over such well-trodden ground, but, when I found that our long residence in the mountains of the Lebanon and at Jerusalem, as well as the unusual visit we had made to Palmyra, had given us opportunities of observation that did not fall to the lot of every traveller in those countries, I could not but wish to share our experiences with the public: since that, the horrible Syrian war having fixed the attention of England for some time upon that unfortunate country,

I have been glad to add my small offering towards appeasing the general desire for further information.

It is impossible for any one who has no personal experience of it, to understand the physical difficulties and impediments under which one's journals, &c., are written amidst the fatigues of such travelling: mine has had the further disadvantage of being re-written in a foreign land, without books or help of any kind: my work is, therefore, only a faithful, unornamented record of what we saw and heard; — the scholar will learn nothing by it save a few facts which I have recorded in hopes of his drawing deductions from them of which I am myself incapable. I have, in fact, written chiefly for those who, compelled to stay at home, would fain now and again draw their chairs to the cheerful coal-fire, shut out the grey sky and dripping rain of England, and follow in fancy the footsteps of those who have enjoyed the realities of travel; with these I not only love to share my pleasure, but I earnestly trust that many may be incited to similar enterprise, by showing them with what ease and security ladies may travel even alone, in those countries which have been frequently supposed to be open only to strong and energetic men. In this hope I have endeavoured to supply them with some practical information as to routes, points of interest, &c. &c. gathered from our own experience.

The chapter on Thebes may be useful to those travellers who cannot afford time enough to study the subject for themselves in deeper and more important

works : that on ancient Jerusalem contains notices of
some facts and recent discoveries which bear on the
topography of the ancient City, — for which I am
indebted to an able and intelligent gentleman, Signor
Pierotti, Captain of Engineers in the Sardinian army,
who is now Architect to the Pacha of Jerusalem, — an
office which has afforded him several opportunities of
studying ancient remains accidentally brought to light ;
the results of this study, on which he has been engaged for six years, will be found in his admirable
plan of Jerusalem, published in Paris, — a small and
rough sketch of which I have given upon the map that
accompanies this book.

The general map is taken from Van de Welde and
the recent Admiralty surveys of the coast of Syria by
Captain Mansell of H.M.S. " Tartarus." I have endeavoured to give the names of places in phonetic
spelling, or, at least, in spelling more in accordance with
the habits of English ears and lips than the now often-
adopted rule laid down by Sir William Jones, — as
experience has proved to me how very rarely names so
written are pronounced by travellers with even an
approximation to the Arabic ; and, therefore, in the
hope of making my book practically useful to them, I
have preferred this attempt to following the other,
perhaps more elegant, but, as I have found, generally
unsuccessful plan.

Valencia: April 1861.

EGYPTIAN SEPULCHRES

AND

SYRIAN SHRINES.

CHAPTER I.

FOG AND SUNSHINE.

A DENSE wet fog, varying from every shade of
yellow to brown, which continued with few inter-
missions for about three weeks, and a heavy frost of ten
days' duration, which, however, persuaded the fog to give
us some glimpses of the sun, and enabled us to distinguish at a hundred yards off the skeletons of that black
species of tree peculiar to Hyde Park, — such was our
preparation for a draught of warm, delicious air, heavily
laden with the scent of orange blossoms, which, exactly
seven days after we left London, rushed in at our cabin
window, when we dropped anchor in Valetta Harbour,
at one o'clock on the morning of the 1st of December,
1858. A few hours more and we were basking in the
hot sun, under the orange trees, thankful for *limonade
à la neige*, and forgetting the black bricks of London
among the magnificent marbles of the church of the
Knights Hospitallers of St. John of Jerusalem, besides
enjoying the cordial kindness and hospitality of our

VOL. I. B

friends at Malta. Still a few days more of the same
cloudless blue sky and unruffled sea, and we landed on
the dirty quay of Alexandria, on the 10th of December.
A boat and a janissary had been kindly sent to deliver
us from the noisy crowd of loud-voiced Indian passengers, and gratify our impatience to tread the soil of
old Egypt, though we only exchanged one scene of
noisy confusion for another, as we were greeted by a
mass of screaming Arabs, *in* and out of the water,
tumbling and fighting over each other, to seize possession of each member of the party, for his own donkey
or carriage, or his master's hotel; and glad enough we
were to mount into the carriage prepared by our stout,
grave, silver-sticked janissary, and to settle into a good
hotel in the Grande Place. Here we found it nearly
impossible to do anything but look out of the window
at the motley crowd, which filled that baking hot, sandy
place, with men of every colour of skin and garment
that the most vivid imagination could conceive : Arabs
of every tribe in Africa, from Morocco to Egypt, and
from Abyssinia and Dongola to the Delta — Syrians,
Turks, Greeks, and Italians — dozens of open carriages
in every degree of shabbiness, driven by black Nubians
in their white gowns, called *sudeyree*, with some bright-
coloured stuff wound round the head for a turban,
thrashing their fiery black steeds — strings of tall, dust-
coloured camels, slowly carrying their burdens of stones,
winding round corners, while every one waits for the
file to pass, or pushing their long necks over the heads
of the passers-by — hundreds of donkeys, each with a
horrid-looking goat-skin filled with water on his back,
the four legs sticking up into the air, with an uncomfortable dead-alive look — more donkeys still, each
carrying a snow-white oval-shaped balloon, with a huge

flapping canary-coloured leather boot at each side—these
are women, as you may know by the unceasing, shrill,
screaming chatter which comes from under the white
garment (called an *eezār*), to which the donkey driver
never seems to pay the slightest attention, — Turks,
Greeks, and Egyptian gentlemen, in various degrees of
semi-costume, but all agreeing in the invariable red
tarboosh, mounted on fine but small horses, sometimes·
richly caparisoned — and lastly, handsome European
carriages, always preceded by a running saïs (who is
really necessary to clear a path through the crowd),
dressed in graceful white robes, with red or dark blue
silk sashes, and sometimes a long stick — the carriages
containing ladies dressed in the newest French fashion,
or in black silk *hābarahs*, with white muslin veils across
the face, leaving nothing to be seen but large sparkling
black eyes painted with khohl. As Arabs always appear
to be in a violent passion when they speak, and they
are endless talkers, it is not possible to describe the
noise that rose to our windows from the Place, nor how
harsh, shrill, and intensely guttural the various languages of Africa and Turkey sounded to our English
ears.

The noise without seemed to us pretty well balanced
by the confusion we immediately fell into within ; ladies
travelling alone were certainly a legitimate prey to the
hosts (I use the word advisedly) of dragomans, old and
young, experienced and inexperienced, from the master
of eight or ten languages to the stammerer in all but
one, natives of every country within three thousand
miles, and of every degree of intelligence or stupidity,
who obtruded themselves on our notice, at all hours of
the day, walking into our *salon*, or, not finding us there,
coming straight into our bedroom without knocking ;

as well as cooks and waiters, each with his packet of dirty, thumbed, faded, torn letters of recommendation, which each entreated us to read on the spot, à l'instant, — all these creatures besieging us one after another, all day and every day during the whole time we remained in Alexandria.

We found several kind, though new, friends in Alexandria, and were induced by their advice to change our plans, and to take a boat at once, instead of waiting till we reached Cairo, which is by far the pleasantest plan; but we had fixed our minds upon securing a dragoman of whom we had heard much in England, Achmet Adgwa, and he would not separate himself from his own boat, or leave Alexandria until it was let to some one else; for the latter contingency we could not of course wait, and we therefore put an end to the hopes of all our besiegers and closed with him at once, after inspecting every boat on the Māh'moudīeh Canal over and over again, until we were too glad to be obliged to decide finally. And a beautiful boat our *dahabieh* was; from first to last we thought her the best and most comfortable boat on the Nile, and only two were larger. She had six cabins: first, a saloon, fifteen feet by twelve, with two divans, fitted with presses underneath them along each side, two book-cases, and a large table; four sleeping cabins, large enough to contain comfortable washing apparatus; and a good-sized back cabin, which we used as a storeroom, and a sitting-room for our maid. We had nine windows at each siee of the dahabieh, with glass, green wooden shutters, and curtains; and plenty of shelves, cupboards, and drawers enough to house everything. We saw other dahabiehs, the interior of which were prettier and more tastefully fitted up than ours, but none more comfortable, bright, and airy. In front of our saloon, on the lower deck, were two seats, and the table for the servants' dinner, and an enormous *goolleh* (a jar of porous clay used for filtering, from which the water was always deliciously fresh), enclosed in a lattice-work of wood prettily painted. On the upper deck we had a comfortable sofa on each side, and the raised skylight of the saloon made a table; there was, however, room for half a dozen tables besides. Beyond the mast, which is placed quite in the bow of the boat, the mysteries of cooking are conducted over a small stove, the sailors cooking their own food at a queer little fire made at one side of the mast, which, about twenty-four feet high itself, supported a lateen yard, 163 feet in length, slung on in a curiously clumsy manner, but which slewed about in the prettiest curves in a high wind. Our great sail was the largest on the river, and I never wearied of watching its graceful motions. There was a small sail on the little mast at the stern, and a platform over the stern cabin, where the sailors performed their ablutions at sunrise and sunset. The dahabiehs on the Nile are all very gaily painted, and have fanciful names, which some keep from year to year; ours we chose to change, and, after much consideration, we had the words " *Wandering Maiden* " painted on her sides, — a name, the appropriateness of which we found afforded much amusement among our fellow-travellers. We hoisted the British ensign at the stern; and a white fleur-de-lis (the symbol of maidenhood) on a dark blue ground, floated from the end of the long yard, together with a very long streamer of red and white, depending to the water, the best distinguishing mark at a long distance. This naming of their boat is an important affair among Nile travellers, and the odd fancies of people come out sometimes rather

amusingly: some names have become hackneyed into
cockneyism on the Nile, but certainly the "Ibis" or
"Lotus" seems more appropriate as a name for such a
nineteenth century affair as a dahabieh, than raking up
the ashes of a dead Pharaoh, since the pretty white bird
that still flies over the Nile is a living, though degenerate, descendant of the sacred Ibis of ancient days, and
the flower is said still to grow there; but we were rather
astonished at meeting two English gentlemen floating
down the river inside the mummy, gaily painted blue
and red, of Sesortasen III.! and it was truly puzzling to
imagine what that long-buried hero had to do with the
blood-red banner of the Cross, or the French motto
that floated from his (mast-) head.

Our crew consisted of the Reïs, or captain, the Mes-
tähmel, or steersman, fourteen sailors, and their cook-
boy; besides which our dragoman had his own servant,
a boy called 'Ali; and these, with our cook, our own
maid, and German man-servant, amounted to twenty-
three persons on board our fair Maiden.

Two or three days were occupied in filling her with
the stores required over and above what we had brought
from Malta, and in getting the canteen, &c., in order;
but we were rather glad of the delay, that we might
see the lions of Alexandria—the quays, the two harbours,
Cleopatra's Needle (as it is absurdly called), and her
fallen sister, and the various gates of the city, one or
two of which are picturesque. Then we had several
pleasant drives along the acacia-shaded roads all round
outside Alexandria. Very pleasant they are, the trees
forming a cool, green barrier on each side between the
road and the sandy desert; and along the bank of the
Mäh'moudïeh Canal, by the pretty villas of the Alex-
andrian merchants, each with its luxuriant garden,

throwing clusters and tangles of magnificent, gorgeous
coloured creepers over the walls, such masses of scarlet
poinsettias and convolvuli of all colours, with blossoms
of four and five inches in diameter, so delicious and
strange to English eyes. Here and there one comes
to a small stone terrace built on the edge of the water,
and shaded with bella-sombra or acacia trees; these are
kiosks, where people come out from the city to lounge
away the afternoons, smoking and drinking coffee or
sherbet. One or two huge palaces are also to be seen,
which presented no beauty externally; but we afterwards
visited the Rās-e-teen Palace, belonging to Saïd Pasha,
and built by Muhămmed 'Ali, which stands on the
north-east side of the principal harbour, that is, on the
island of Pharos, which is connected with the shore by
the ancient causeway called the Heptastadium. The
rooms are furnished with divans, and ornamental tables
of great elegance and richness, but all entirely European, except some fine pieces of gold and silver damask
on the Viceroy's couches, the *chef-d'œuvres* of Con-
stantinopolitan looms. The best thing in the palace are
the parquet floors, which are of various woods inlaid
with ivory and mother-of-pearl, exquisitely done, and
different in each room; the palace is also worth visiting
for the sake of the fine view from the balcony of the
old harbour, Eunostus.

Another day we drove along the shady, sandy roads
to see the Pillar erected in honour of the Emperor
Diocletian, probably on his taking possession of the
city of Alexandria, A.D. 296, which is vulgarly called
Pompey's Pillar; and in returning, we passed through
an encampment of Bedoueen tents, which certainly did
not realise any idea I had formed of them. "Black
as the tents of Kedar" they were indeed, but far from

"comely;" oblongs and squares of the darkest brown and black skins of rudely tanned leather, with *flat* tops, and only from two-and-a-half to three feet high! Men and women, wild, dirty-looking, half-naked Arabs, were crawling in and out from under the tents, gathering up their dirtier rags, or attending to about a thousand donkeys, goats, and sheep, all of them nearly black, which were standing in the encampment.

Sunday afforded us the opportunity of service in the very handsome church which the Alexandrians have lately erected, a pleasure all the more valuable, as many a week was to elapse before we should enter another church; it is prettily built of white and pinkish stone, adorned with arcades and pilasters, and a semicircular apse. In the afternoon every road and street seemed filled with promenaders; but French fashion predominated, to the destruction of all orientalism or picturesqueness.

At last, our preparations were completed, and we took up our abode on board the Wandering Maiden: one day more was allowed to elapse, on account of the Wednesday, a day of ill-luck, on which the sailors refused to commence a voyage; but on Thursday the 16th, at daylight, we started before a good breeze, down the Māh'-moudīeh Canal. About five P.M. we passed through the lock at Atfeh, and were at last floating on the bosom of the grand old Nile! I shall never forget that evening, when we slipped out of the long, narrow, high-banked canal, on to the wide, swiftly-flowing, smooth river,—the low, flat banks making it seem even wider than it was, almost like a sea, and the setting sun throwing a flood of rosy glory over the horizon, gilding the mud-houses of the tarboosh-making town of Fouah opposite, resting on the palm-trees towering

above the villages, and tipping the graceful white
lateen sails of a score of khandjehs and little boats,
going down to Rosetta. We stayed on deck till it was
quite dark, enjoying the new scene, — our last, for a long
time, of such weather — one or two tremendous down-
pours in Alexandria had warned us of what our fate
might be, but from that evening, for eleven successive
days, we had constant storms of rain and wind, the rain
threatening to drown us, as it leaked through deck,
door, and window, and the wind making us pitch and
roll, until we were nearly sea-sick. Once, when looking at the magnificently blue sky in Alexandria, so new
to English eyes, I made some remark to a gentleman
residing there on its beauty: " Ah," he said, " you
have not learned yet to *loathe* this cloudless sky! We
have not had one drop of rain here since the middle of
last February, and you cannot understand how one
wearies, mind and body, of the changeless expanse,
longing for the ever-varying clouds we think so beautiful, because we so seldom see them, and because they
bring us so much refreshment and vigour." We had
enough of them now, however; so much so, that to
some people, our voyage to Cairo might have been
tiresome, but to us it was not so. We were glad to rest
after the long journey from England, — we had books in
plenty, — our boat dried in the first rays of sunshine,
and sometimes, when the wind forced us to lie thumping on a bank, we could manage to find a sheltered
walk in the country, making acquaintance with castor
oil and gum-arabic trees, cotton plants, and the ever
graceful palm groves. Sometimes we examined the
*shadoofs** and *sakiyehs**, both on the banks of the

* The shadoof is the very simple machine used for lifting the water
of the Nile up to the height of the bank: a man, almost naked and

river and in the fields, or ventured into the tents
and mud-huts of the fellaheen (from sing. *fellāh*), from
whence we never failed to bring away many lively
and unpleasant *souvenirs*. The men seemed to have
nothing to do, but to stand lounging about, leaving
all the work of house and field to the women, whom
we always found busy; they were lively and good-
natured, though not by any means *engaging* in person
or deportment. They wear but one garment, a long,
dark-blue gown or chemise, thrown round the body,
in an untidy fashion, exposing generally the legs, always
the arms, and sometimes the neck, but drawn over the
head, and across the face, when any one is near : their
unkempt locks are thrown back and roughly plaited,
their eyelids are painted black with khohl, and their
grinning white teeth are set off with stripes or circles on
the chin and forehead, of blue tattooing. A large silver
ring stuck through the flesh of one nostril, ear-rings, a
dirty silver bracelet or two on each arm, and generally
one on each ankle, complete their costume, which is as
ugly as it is simple. I do not think I saw two women

with his head uncovered, holds a long pole balanced horizontally on
a perpendicular stick, with a palm leaf or wooden basket at one end and
a weight at the other end; he dips the basket into the river and then
throws it up expertly, making it empty itself into a hole or trough, cut
to receive it, above his head. If the bank is high, another or two more
men stand above him with repetitions of the same contrivance.

The sakiyeh is a huge wheel with earthen jars fixed all round it, which
fill as they pass through the river, and empty themselves into a trough
as they reach the top. It is turned by a couple of oxen, who pace round
and round to the screeching groaning music of the ungreased crank.
This creak of the sakiyeh, with the eternal melancholy song of the
shadoof men, half wail, half screech, is the true *sound of Egypt:* no hour
nor half-hour passes without hearing one or the other, and the very
name of the country brings the echo of it as distinctly into one's ears, as
the remembrance of the yellow sand, or of the broad river, floats before
one's eyes.

in Egypt, out of Cairo, whose appearance did not more
or less disgust me. When we went near their huts
they always invited us in, and generally insisted on
shaking hands with us, laughing all the time, and
expressing their wonder at our *riches*—the only reason
they could devise for our putting on so many clothes
one over another : and sometimes they would offer us
their dhourra bread, or milk, or show us how they
were grinding corn, between flat round stones, or
making cheese by leaving the milk to drain through
mats, made of plaited palm leaves; always asking
about how they do the same things in the Howadji's
country.

It is certainly a much less expensive plan to go from
Alexandria at once by railroad to Cairo, and there en-
gage your boat; since though you *may* reach Cairo in
four days' sail, you may also occupy fourteen, as we did,
and we heard of persons having been twenty-one days
on the way! But at the same time you have the advantage of knowing your boat, and finding out her
deficiencies before you come to the last place where you
can buy stores, or get anything altered or improved, and
you have also some amusement and pleasure in your
voyage, while the line of rail is wholly uninteresting and
ugly. I contrived to find something for a sketch every
day, and doubtless there would have been plenty more
subjects to be found with better luck than the unusually
bad weather we fell in with. For a sportsman I should
think the boat much pleasanter than the land journey;
as game is immensely more plentiful in the Delta than
above Cairo, and much less wild. The sand banks are
covered with thousands of wild geese and ducks: and
there are wild boars to be hunted in several localities.
If, however, people are likely to weary of a long quiet

voyage, it is better to go by railway, and have the dahabieh sent up to Cairo to meet them, stipulating that it *must* arrive within a certain number of days. The dahabiehs are decidedly better and nicer at Alexandria than at Cairo, but also proportionably dearer.

At this time we were slowly tracking against head winds; and at Kefr el Aesh, where the railway crosses the Nile, the wind increased so much that we were moored two whole days on the east bank. On the second day, when we had lost all patience, and, in spite of our dragoman's remonstrances, were going to insist on making an attempt to shoot the opening left in the bridge now building for the railway, an unexpected ally came to hand: the superintendent of the station, Ismaen Effendi, — may his shadow never be less! — arrived in a well-rowed boat alongside, saying, that on hearing there were English ladies on board, he had come to see if we stood in need of any assistance. He assured us that it was quite impossible to shoot the bridge, unless by the chance of an exactly favourable wind. " But," said he, " you English people always want to eat dinner together on your Christmas-day, and you must be in Cairo for that, — I will give you two hundred men to *pull* you through, if you like it." Of course we gladly accepted so obliging an offer, and while his men went off with his orders, the Effendi sat chatting in very good English with us, sipping his coffee and smoking his shibouque. He told us he had been educated at King's College, London, and afterwards lived a year or two in Kent, and that the English had been so kind to him, and made him so happy, that it was an especial pleasure to have an opportunity of assisting any English person who came to his country. The Effendi has since, I believe, left this station.

His pleasure was, however, frustrated: for, just when the men were all ready, the wind, which had been unsteadily bearing about for the last hour or two, suddenly settled into the precisely right point, and blew us through the opening with the Effendi on board, and all the two hundred workmen standing ready to assist on the bridge, gesticulating, screaming, and shouting quite as much as if they had really been doing the business themselves.

Our good friend sent us in the evening some excellent milk and turkeys; on one of which, in conseqence of the still unkind and cruel winds, we made our Christmas dinner, moored under a palm grove in the hot sun, the turkey stuffed with pistachio nuts and dates, and a "plum-pudding" of biscuit, citron, and dried apricots.

Two days afterwards, as I was watching the rich hues of the setting sun upon the sands and trees, I saw two small triangles, distinct and hard, on the western horizon, which my heart suddenly leaped up to greet — there stood the Pyramids at last! I saw them many times afterwards, in various ways and at various times of day, but they never impressed me more than on that evening, painted in the exquisite lilac hues of sunset, yet golden tipped, over the straight, flat green bank of the river, far away over line after line of sand — far away, standing up, straight and clear against a background of coloured clouds.

CHAP. II.

WE landed on the west bank, before we reached Bou-
lak, on the morning of the 29th of December,
scrambling over a forest of dirty boats to make our first
essay upon the Arab saddle of Cairo donkeys: the latter
are most excellent of their kind, as lively as they are
small, and the saddles are not uncomfortable; they are
simply cushions mounted high on the donkey's back,
with a round hump across them in front, and they are
generally made of gay red leather, while the saddle-
cloth is worked in colours with bands of cowrie-shells
sewn on in strips: a charm, enclosed in a triangular
silver box, is hung round the animal's neck.

Our road, which lay along a high causeway shaded
with fine trees, brought us into the Esbeykiyeh, at the
Shoobra corner, close to Shepheard's Hotel (where we
entered the name and distinguishing flag of our boat in
the Nile Howadji's book), and then went on to the
English Consulate, and into the Turkish bazaars to
buy sugar, sweetmeats, &c., which we wanted in the
dahabieh.

Shall I here confess the truth? that my first view of
Cairo absolutely disappointed me! In our second visit,
when I became better acquainted with it, I learned its
full beauty and interest; and now we constantly wish

that we could return there to gratify the unsatisfied
feeling of not having had enough of its charms; but
just at first,— whether my expectations were too highly
exalted, or that one reads the result of every traveller's
enthusiasm after they have had time to enjoy it, and to
think about it,— whatever it arose from, I certainly was
disappointed with the poorness and raggedness and
want of all handsome solidity in the houses of Cairo;
the gay wares in the wooden shops of the bazaars are
bright enough, but the shops themselves are of rough,
unpainted boards, uneven in size and height, and
covered in from the sun with only ragged old palm-
leaf mats, torn bits of carpet, and broken planks, "rags
of rotten wood," which give one a feeling of squalor,
perhaps all the more *mesquin* from its contrast with
the variegated hues, like a brilliant flower-garden, of
the crowd below. Then the contrast is continued
between the wooden and mud-built houses, and the
beautiful public fountains; the water, enclosed in circular walls, roofed over with a sort of dome, flows into
brazen mouth-pieces placed in compartments of exquisitely carved stone-work, divided by pilasters of
coloured marbles, with gilt capitals, and borders of
Arabic in gilt letters, recounting the names of the
benevolent Pashas who built them; sometimes (but
these are almost always in the courts of the mosque)
they are fountains open to the air, when they are surrounded by a marble trough, with a wooden roof
supported by pillars, very gaily painted, but tattered,
torn, and dirty, under which the Moslems perform
their ablution of face, hands, and feet all day long.
Nor do the mosques strike one at first as handsome on
the exterior; the high flat walls are unrelieved by
window, column, or any architectural ornament, save

one invariable line of cornice along the top of the wall, formed of simple pendentives of three bricks in the upper row, two bricks in the second, and one brick below these; simple as it sounds, its effect is very pretty, and even rich-looking. The mosque walls are always coloured in horizontal stripes of red or brown paint, roughly daubed along the courses of the stone, and it is wonderful the lively and handsome effect produced by it.

The Esbeykiyeh is a very large irregular-shaped " *Place*," planted with a pleasantly thick wood of orange, acacia, and many other trees intersected with walks, and dotted round with wooden kiosks for the enjoyment of coffee, lemonade, and narghiles; the houses round the broad road might make the Esbeykiyeh handsomer than any European *Place*, had any two of these buildings uniformity in height, colour, or kind; but they are so different, and mostly so shabby in exterior, that one loses all idea of the Esbeykiyeh being the Grande Place of a great city. Shepheard's Hotel and one of the Pasha's palaces occupy nearly all one side, but they are both of them ugly and common-looking buildings.

But whatever may be its shortcomings, when one's brains have become a little accustomed to the din, bustle, and noise of the streets, Cairo is essentially beautiful and excessively charming; it seems as if one could never weary of the endless, ever-changing sights and sounds of the multitude who throng its ways (street is too western a term for them); a thousand times brighter and gayer than the Grande Place at Alexandria, which seems tame after a single street of Cairo.

Let us stand aside for ten minutes, while this fine

old fellow with a snow white beard, white and gold turban, a purple silk robe and dark red trousers, lays down his long shibouque, and weighs out for us an oke of delicate rose leaf *confiture* (having first held out a little *dig* of two or three kinds on the end of his finger, for us to taste!), and watch the crowd pushing by our donkey. This bazaar is for groceries, and the shops are heaped with loaves of sugar of every hue except white, and palm-leaf baskets of dates, dry and fresh, nuts of all kinds, spices, roasted Indian corn, figs, olives, and innumerable sorts of dry sugar-stuff, pink, brown, yellow, and white, in sticks and lumps, which the Arabs are always eating; they are thoroughly nasty to our taste. Every shop is tenanted by a figure, rolled up cross-legged on the counter, in parti-coloured robes and white turban, smoking and chatting (or screaming rather) to their fellow-shopmen; while the donkey boys in their dirty, ragged, blue cotton shirts, and other idlers, sit down to rest on the edge of the booth, and join in the conversation right merrily. The way is quite full, and the beggars demanding " Baksheesh, howadji! baksheesh, ya sitt!" push by you as they go; while every second minute, a ragged Arab jingles his brazen cups, and offers you fresh water out of a black goat-skin which he carries under his arm, or a sherbet-seller bends down before you, while the brass jar at his side spouts forth a stream of sweetened water or lemon-ade into a cup, for which you pay two or three parās, if you wish to taste its sickly sweetness. A blind man is sure to stumble over you, and a dozen women, en-tirely enveloped in white wrappers with a couple of holes for their eyes, stop to peep up under your hat, or to feel the texture of your dress, while you are intent upon inspecting that Bey or this Effendi going by on a

fine chestnut horse, with a saddle-cloth splendid in gold
embroidery, himself in bright coloured silks, satin, and
cloth, smoking his long pipe as he goes,—or this Turk
of high degree, on a tall white donkey, whose bit and
bridle are strings of gold cord, hung as thickly as they
can hold them, with heavy gold sequins, and whose
saddle is of cherry-coloured velvet embroidered in gold
and pearls. You are bending forward to look at the
jewels on his sword sheath, when you suddenly see a
camel's ugly nose just over your own, and you start
back while he lazily pushes on, flattening you to the
'wall with his huge burden of green fodder, or stones,
or bales of calico. In another minute half a dozen
men, carrying on their shoulders a deal box, daubed
over with red paint, saunter by, chanting a discordant
song, and your donkey boy looks up with a grin, and
says, "Dead man in there;" and you turn away to
decline a quantity of sweetmeats in smoking hot pastry,
suddenly thrust up to your mouth by a boy in rags,
trying not to seem to see or hear the score of brown
hands thrust out on whichever side you move your face,
while the owners scream out "Baksheesh! baksheesh!"
till you are glad to move on, though every third person
assails you with the same wearying word as you pass.

   We stayed in the bazaars till we were perfectly be-
wildered and were glad to go back to our dahabieh,
which had in the meantime moved to the palm-grove
opposite Cairo, leaving the rest of our shopping to be
accomplished on the following day, when we had the
pleasure of making acquaintance with the Rev. Mr.
and Mrs. Frankland Hood, who kindly offered to
"keep company" with our boat, as we were strangers,
and they were spending their fifth winter on the Nile.
We moved on a little way the last day of the old year,.

stopping at sunset opposite the island of Rhoda, and looking back at a view that few things of the kind can surpass. The vast city, studded with graceful domes and still more beautiful minarets, rises up loftily from the flat, monotonous surrounding Desert, partly placed on and partly backed by the bold white Mokuttum cliffs, while, at a little higher elevation, the Mosque and Tomb of Muhammed 'Ali, with its white alabaster walls, dark blue roofs, and delicately slight minarets, stands, like a watchman guarding the city; in the foreground, the river-bank is lined with large palaces, some white and some red, adorned with graceful arcades and handsome balconies, each with its own garden and orange-grove, meeting the gardens of Old Cairo and Rhoda. The forest of boats, of every size and form, with brightly painted masts, red and blue awnings, flags, and streamers, form a gay fringe to the wide grey river. On the other side, far away over the fields of green crops, and the wide expanse of desert sand, the Pyramids raise their grave, calm, solemn triangles, cutting against the cloudless sky, clothed in strangely beautiful sunset colours of violet and gold, all too gorgeous for any paint-box to depict.

We were joined the next morning by Mr. Hood's dahabieh and another; on the following day we overtook a third; while a fourth joined us two days after. The five boats made quite a pretty little fleet; and during the ten days that ensued of slow tracking, we found plenty of amusement in efforts and stratagems to outstrip each other; this, however, is against all ideas of propriety among the crew, and our Reïs invariably apologised to the other Reïses at sunset if we had gained any advantage over their boats during the day; rather exasperating to our feelings when we were chuckling

over the accomplishment of a quarter of a mile beyond
our neighbours. It is amazing how these great dahabiehs do get on in the tracking; although they get
aground twelve times in a day, yet they absolutely
float on in safety, when the men are walking all round
them with the water reaching only just above their
ankles : and sometimes so close to the banks, that one
may touch the trees from the decks. They carry no
ballast, in order to keep them light, and they require a
directly fair wind to sail tolerably. We thought ourselves singularly unlucky in the strong head winds,
which blew perseveringly for ten successive days after
we left Cairo, fearing that any long detention below
Thebes would render our reaching the Second Cataract
impossible under our three months' contract for the
dahabieh. Our own boat was very heavy in tracking,
though she outsailed all the others, and we were naturally anxious to benefit all we could by her virtues.
Delicious as this Egyptian life was, we could not bear
to think of being disappointed of seeing Nubia; and
so we fretted from day to day about our progress, very
unnecessarily as it turned out, and were not a little
annoyed at our being obliged to put in at Beni Souef
for provisions, while the rest of the little fleet took
another passage for the sake of a short cut: but a
favourable breeze sprung up in the night; we sped on,
and in the morning could only just distinguish some
of the red and white streamers of our disappointed
companions behind us. The Florence, however, caught
us up the next night, and we sailed on gallantly, with
the pleasant little excitement of racing each other, and
enjoying the scenery of long, low mountains of rugged
shapes, at some distance from the river,—blue and
purple by day, pink and golden in the evenings, under

the ever-cloudless sky. We passed Minyeh with its pretty minarets and gardens—it is one of the prettiest towns on the Nile,—and reached Siout on the 15th of January.

Siout is chiefly remarkable for its many miles of roads, lifted up above the reach of the inundations by wide causeways; they are shaded by trees, and give one a fine idea of what can be effected by persevering labour. Beyond the town, which is thoroughly amusing with the oriental life in its good bazaars, are the catacombs of the ancient Lycopolis, the City of the Wolves : they are very extensive, excavated in the side of the Libyan mountains, with high vaulted roofs, and the walls covered with figures and hieroglyphics, which are, however, so much faded and defaced as to be nearly indecipherable : one vault is still pretty, with gold stars thickly painted on a bright blue ground. They are worth a visit, from their size, and as the traveller's introduction to hieroglyphics ; but perhaps the labour of mounting is best repaid by the very fine view seen from the entrance to the largest catacomb, called the *Stabl Antar* by the natives. The town, with its twenty-six minarets, stands in a rich plain of meadow, intersected with canals, and shaded with lofty trees ; as far as the eye can reach, north and south, it is all the same bright and beautiful green, but on the east it is bounded by the broad Nile ; while beyond that is the yellow desert to the foot of the Arabian mountains, fading away in the blue distance.

We rode back through a pretty Mooslim cemetery ; each tomb, arched over in stone or stucco, and shaped like a huge bolster, stood in its own plantation of acacia trees, and frequently a fountain, for the benefit of weary passengers, is added to the little building ; most

c 3

of the handsomer tombs being walled in and roofed
over. The wind was blowing a gale, and the sun was
very hot,—so hot that we were right glad to get back
to our shady cabin, although during the night before
and the night after, the thermometer showed some
slight frost! The mornings, indeed, till an hour or
two after sunrise, were always very cold and fresh until
quite the end of the month; but the cold is never disagreeable, even when the thermometer is alarmingly
near 32°. Travellers, however, should always be provided with warm clothing, although after half an hour
of sunshine one forgets one has ever been chilly.

My idea of the Nile, before I came to Egypt, had
always been of flat, shallow banks, and a palm-tree or
a mud hut here and there, such as it is in the Delta: I
was therefore most agreeably surprised with the beauty
and variety of the banks after Siout, which I, for one,
never wearied of watching. On one side or the other
there are *always* hills at no great distance from the
river bank; sometimes the Libyan chain, in various
tones of grey, shading into lilacs and purples at sunset,
advanced on the western shore, or receded into delicate
blue distance; more often the Arabian hills mounted
up in cliffs, sometimes very boldly and grandly out of
the water, leaving only a strip of castor-oil plants or a
narrow track for passengers. And their colour was always so charming: a peculiar rosy yellow, more nearly
resembling—if I may be allowed to use a very un-
poetical simile—fresh Cheshire cheese than anything
else I know, which forms the prettiest contrast to the
fresh cool greens of the banks, and to the glorious
gentian-blue sky, darkening in the strongly marked
lines of stratification, and in the abrupt, rugged ravines,
into indescribably rich shades of colour: the cliffs, too,

are dotted all over with caves cut out of old by the
monks of the Thebaid. Though I thought them beautiful on first landing in Egypt, I came to love the graceful palm-trees more and more every day : singly, or in
groves, they are always lovely and elegant, and even the
most matter-of-fact mind could scarcely help indulging,
I think, in a day dream of fairy-land delights, while
reposing in the pleasant shade of a grove of fine palms,
waving in the cool sunset breeze.

Then the villages, though entirely built of mud, are
not ugly as seen from the river, for the Nile mud is of a
rich brown yellow, which glows in the sunshine, and looks
rich in the shade ; and the flat-roofed houses are often
topped with white stones in a way that makes them look
something like fortifications from a distance. Each
village has scores of tall dovecots, the mud walls of which
are striped with whitewash, and thatched with Indian
corn-stalks : they are quaint and almost pretty objects,
while the minarets are always more or less elegant.
These and the palm or acacia groves, with the endless
variety of picturesque groups in bright-coloured costumes, white turbans, and long pipes, form a constant
succession of dissolving views passing into one another,
with some fresh and interesting, though always changing
charm as one glides slowly by.

A complete change, indeed, from all European *com-
monalities* is this river life—the proximity of those
around one is so strange and new at first ;—not as on
board ship, where the confusion of loud and inharmonious voices only gives one a sense of discomfort and
isolation ; whereas here the voices are close to one, by
day and by night, with only a thin plank or a glass
between, yet are neither inharmonious nor disturbing ;
then the faces are not merely individually strangers, but

c 4

of an unaccustomed kind; while the scenery changes all
the accustomed current of one's ideas with the many new
interests and new sights on each side, leaving scarcely a
trace of one's former self, or of the every day thoughts
that have been one's companions for years past : you
scarcely realise *what* you were and *where* only three or
four weeks previously, until the silent darkness of night,
hiding the engrossing sights of the present, enables you
to think back into the past; even then, the water trickles,
gently singing, past your pillow—Mooslim prayers are
heard whispering on the other side of a plank, within a
few inches of your ear—Arab snores come from un-
English noses—jackals squeal, shriek, and howl on the
shore,—and one starts up to peer out of the window, so
strangely close to one's face, whence one sees wild-
looking Arabs crouching round a crackling fire of
dhourra sticks, and the glorious clear moon shining
through palm trees, unlike anything one has ever seen
before but in the fairy-land of a bright dream.

As we every day improved our Arabic by a few more
words, we soon began to try to string them together
into sentences ; these we bestowed chiefly on our Reïs,
Abou Nour by name, and they invariably afforded
him the greatest delight and amusement. Our Reïs,
who was as good as he was handsome—unlike nearly
all the other Reïses whom we saw sitting, smoking,
or sleeping all day long, and only giving an occasional order with slow and solemn gravity, seldom *doing*
anything themselves—was up and about from daylight
to dark, and all night too if we were sailing, seldom
taking more than an hour's sleep, and even then having
one ear open for every sound of difficulty in the manage-
ment of the vessel. And what he did, he did with an
active energy, very different from the sailors, who

seemed only to move each muscle exactly as little as they
could possibly help; while Abou Nour was always flying
about here and there and everywhere, scrambling like a
cat up and down the rigging, and dashing into the
water, clothes, turban and all, pushing the dahabieh
from the shore or shoals, guiding the little felucca with
the towing rope, which he often held in his teeth while
his hands were employed in rowing or dragging the
vessel athwart the stream by his own powerful strength,
always with the same merry laugh and happy face, and
a joke or an affectionate slap for each one of his sailors,
who seemed to be all as fond of him as soldiers are of a
successful general.   Sometimes he assembled them in
a group, and gave them a solemn lecture or a scolding
with uplifted hands.   Then when an hour of quiet sailing came, with no sudden turns of the river, and a
tolerably deep channel, they would collect on deck at
the stern, lying or lounging round him while he laid
aside his pipe, and with all the eloquent gestures of the
Arab, recounted to them some adventure, or told them
a long story which elicited rapturous applause: and
sometimes we used to laugh too, his face was so infec-
tiously merry, and the changes of his voice so expressive;
but their greatest delight of all was when I sketched his
portrait, or that of one of the sailors,—how eagerly they
came to see it, and then how merrily they laughed over
the grinning brown faces and white turbans on the
paper, telling me approvingly it was "taïb keteer," or
"quïyis," (very good and pretty), and then each one
begging to be drawn too.   Sir G. Wilkinson says, "that
no modern Egyptians, of any rank, can understand
pictures;" but our experience everywhere was of the
liveliest interest in all we showed them : our Reïs would
point out immediately which of my portraits was most

like, and would catch at the accident in the dress or attitude for the sake of which I had taken them: while of the passing dahabiehs or kandjehs which I sketched almost daily, he was always ready to point out any want of proportion, or to detect what ropes I had omitted, or how the sails had been changed when he had passed too quickly for me to seize them accurately. A friend afterwards photographed him for us: but Abu Nour had specially prepared himself in his gala attire — a very . handsome one it was, of Damascus silks and embroidery —and he was grievously disappointed at finding his rich dress metamorphosed into one dull grey colour: even the gilt frame did not reconcile him to the shadowy picture, and whenever he saw it afterwards he always signified to me how much he preferred my rough, coloured sketches. He sat like a statue to have it done, only rolling his eyes in a way that made them come out *no how* in the photograph: and when it was finished he was allowed, as a reward, to put his head under the curtain of the photographing instrument: I was standing in focus at the time, and it was worth anything to see his face of astonishment and hear his "Mashallah! Wullah!" when he saw me standing upside down! he was too intelligent to think it magic, but I am sure he made many a long story about it afterwards. How much I wish I had still any sketch of him, in his beautiful white and coloured silk vest, his long khaftan of rich brown satin bound with black braid, his white turban embroidered in yellow silk, and over all the wide blue cotton shirt, which was his badge of Reïs-hood. He was physician-general also to the sailors, and bound up their scratches or gave them their physic, whenever any little accident took place, as tenderly as a nurse (though, to be sure, the Arabs have barbarous remedies for their maladies — such as dipping a cut finger into boiling oil, and setting fire to gunpowder on a wound); and we always saw him go to comfort any of them when they were in trouble, giving them affectionate squeezes, or shakes, or long consolatory conversations.

Achmet told us that the Reïs was under a vow of virtue, which bound him to abstain from all lies or dishonesty, or from using bad words — to have but one wife, and to take no notice of any other woman, &c., &c., and that he had kept it most religiously, punishing himself by two or three days of rigid fasting and abstinence from smoking (a terrible privation to an Egyptian), if he had failed by any shortcoming : and no one could be more steadily exact in the performance of his prayers, five times every day, during which, except occasionally in the telling of his beads, which is only a rapid repetition of the name of Allah, he seemed to be absorbed in the most earnest devotion. Some people object to this and call it fanatic, but we felt it far more satisfactory and pleasant to have the services of a conscientious man, acting steadily up to his own light, even though that light was darkness.*

* I hope I shall not be misunderstood, by using the word *darkness*, to wish to characterise the religion taught by Muhammed as darkness, save in comparison to that clearer light of Christianity which has been given to us in revelation; the Mooslim knows not Christ as God, and therefore, however far he follows the light that he has, it will not bring him to the foot of that Cross, wherefrom, as a glorious privilege of the sons of Christ, we have received complete salvation; he knows but in part, and can but see through a glass darkly; but in as far us a religious Mooslim has sought after God, be sure he will have found Him—"he who seeks Me shall find Me," saith the Lord; and He is near to *all* that call upon Him, yea, *all* such as call upon Him faithfully. It is shocking to hear those Judo-Christians, whose hearts are full of anything but the infinite Love which alone unites us with God (the Love which *loves goodness before all*), condemning to eternal damnation all those who, not knowing the law of Christ, yet have " showed the work of the law

Our pleasant course was now varied for two days with sandstorms, which, to use the mildest expression, are very particularly disagreeable : we moored for one afternoon, because we could not see 300 yards before us, but the wind lulling at sunset, we sailed on slowly by the light of a magnificent full moon (such moonlight as one has in Egypt!) until we neared "*the* mountain," of which the Nile sailors have so much terror, Jebel ez

written in their hearts," who have "done by nature the things contained in the law" (Rom. ii. 14); who have striven with self-discipline and self-restraint, with fastings and with prayer, with earnest humble sincerity, to keep the truth as they knew it,—are they to be eternally punished by a God of justice (not a God of vengeance) for not keeping a law they knew not? or, rather, is there not to be "glory, honour, and peace to every man that worketh good, to the Jew first, and also to the Gentile?" These unchristian Christians, who believe themselves far more enlightened than the inquisitors of old who condemned both body and soul, turn away their eyes from what is *good*, because, forsooth, it is not dressed in the costume in which alone they choose to see it, and which they call religion; as if good feelings, and purity, and self-denial, and devotion to a Supreme Being, when made the ruling principle of life, are not religion, even though the man who acts up to them may never have heard the name of Christ,—an incomplete religion, indeed, but true in its own integrity, whether it be of Osiris, or of Bouddha, or of Muhammed; strangely different is this from the announcement of the angel to the heathen Cornelius, "Thy prayer is heard;" and from the "truth" that St. Paul learned from the divine vision, that "in every nation he that feareth Him and worketh righteousness, is accepted with Him." "Faith," says one of the clearest-minded among our modern divines, "is no new, strange, peculiar power, supernaturally infused by Christianity alone," but the essence of Divine nature, implanted in *every* immortal soul (which may indeed be choked), without which we could have no part in the eternal salvation promised by God to *all* who serve Him faithfully, and without which our life can never be "hid with Christ." In the day when God shall judge the secrets of men by Jesus Christ; when the Pharisee, who kept the law by the letter, and thanked God he was not as other men, "shall be humbled;" and the Publican, who kept the law by his heart, "shall be exalted," the God-fearing earnest Mooslim may be found ready for the wedding-garment which the proud, unloving, so-called Christian will seek for on his own shoulders, and will not find there.

Zaïd; it is a very wicked mountain of sudden blasts and
gusts, that make one's sails seem bewitched, and which
baffle the most expert of crews. Gliding on smoothly
with the wind behind us, it was startling to be suddenly
seized with a violent blast ahead, and the great lateen sail
in an instant reversed with a shock that sent one's books
spinning off the tables; but we held on steadily, the
Reïs calling up every sailor, and himself taking up a
perilous situation on the long yard, where no one else
would venture; while Achmet stood watching and
counting the minutes between the blasts, and, as each
one came whizzing past, saying his prayers with a very
remarkable rapidity, and calling on the Sheikh ez Zaïd,
the Mooslim saint to whom the mountain is dedicated,
to assist us out of the difficulty. Achmet counselled
mooring, but we insisted upon trying to proceed, until
finding that in four hours we had not made a yard, we
gave it up at midnight, remaining on deck, however,
for the amusement of watching the five dahabiehs of
our little fleet, whom we had not seen for two days, and
two or three native boats, come sailing smoothly up in
the bright moonlight, unconscious of what was awaiting
them, and calling out to us to know " what we were
stopping for," while one after another each was seized by
the blast, and taken aback, and we heard the exclamations of astonishment and wrath proceeding from each.
We left them all behind early the next morning, passing
pretty Negādeh in a sandstorm that filled eyes, mouth,
and nose with unpleasant pertinacity, descending upon
one suddenly, like a December fog in London, obscuring
everything in a thick brown cloud, penetrating everywhere. We came into Luxsor on Friday morning, the
21st, but, alas for our racing triumphs ! the *second*, by
one hour, of our little fleet, for the Selima had passed

us in the night, and we had only the consolation of
hearing that the three other boats were "nowhere;" we
had been ten days doing the seventy-seven miles between Cairo and Beni-Souef, chiefly tracking, and now we
had sailed the three hundred and seventy-eight miles
between Beni-Souef and Thebes in only ten more.

We expected great delight in our first view of Luxsor
and Thebes; but the river was already too low, and
Karnak must be seen in detail first to be appreciated at
a distance : nor could the Sitting Colossi of the plain
be seen at all. We had determined to follow Sir G.
Wilkinson's advice of seeing the temples of Nubia before
examining Karnak, and accordingly devoted ourselves
to the bundle of letters we found awaiting our arrival;
but an invitation to join a party going to see Karnak
by the light of a full moon, such as we then had, was
not to be resisted, and we started at 8·30, six of us on
donkeys, attended by sailors and donkey boys *ad libitum*
to guard us from jackals, and headed by the obliging
Consular Agent Mustapha. The more fortunate chance
would be to have a fine moon *after* becoming well
acquainted with the plan of the ruins; but even under this disadvantage of seeing what we did not properly understand, it was a scene that impressed itself
upon the mind for ever : the deep black shadows concealing much of the brokenness and decay, and the
splendid light illuminating, with a sort of tender glory,
the massive columns, immense pylons, and slender obelisks ; by this light it was only and altogether beautiful
and lovely : one needs the sunshine and blue sky to
bring out the stupendous proportions of these unrivalled
ruins. Perhaps few spots on earth could be more
solemnly beautiful than the centre aisle in the Great
Hall, with the six gigantic columns between the sixty-

one attendant columns on either side, the moonlight
lighting up the open clerestory of delicate tracery
against the dark sky, turning the obelisk at one end of
the aisle, ninety-two feet high, into a silver needle,
rising with a stern grace against the ruined temple
behind it; and at the other end, illuminating a single
column, standing alone in the centre of a vast square,
between giant pylons and huge walls, with its capital
complete, its shaft uninjured, seeming almost livingly
sorrowful in its loneliness.

The howling of the jackals gave a wild dreariness to
the scene ; but we very unwillingly remounted our
donkeys and turned back towards Luxsor, through the
avenue of sphinxes, which, broken and defaced into
almost shapeless masses by daylight, became impres-
sively grand by moonlight. What must have been the
magnificence of Karnak, when all these splendid
avenues of sphinxes were still perfect in their mighty
limbs, leading up to the still more magnificent walls !

At midnight we glided smoothly on, feeling on the
morrow as if one needed *rest* after even that slight
view of Karnak, and glad to fall back into the quiet
sameness of Nile life : a sweet calm monotony it is, but
yet a monotony of pleasant little changes—dream-like
and hazy, but a waking day dream, without the sudden,
kaleidoscope changes of a sleeping dream. From day
to day, from night to night, you sail calmly on, watching the golden and rosy-tinted mountains advancing
or receding on either side, offering, indeed, but little
variety of form, yet of colours so lovely, that I think
no Egyptian travellers say half enough about them :
the same brown villages with their minarets and dovecots, and their luxuriant acacia groves ; the same ever
varying, yet ever graceful palms ; the same picturesque

Arab boats, with their burdens of dates, cotton, or
donkeys ; the same wide, smooth, rapid river, dark
brown in one's hand, yet blue in the distance—a deep
grey blue,—contrasting finely with the invariably bright
and cloudless sky, which is broken only by the flocks of
birds, which, hour after hour, rise whirling and wheeling
in the air in gracefully curving lines—vultures flying
singly at intervals like minute guns—millions of wild
geese and ducks—hoopoes, hopping about on the banks,
with their handsome brown coroneted heads—zikzags,
with their pretty black and white plumage—the snow
white ibis, like a winged star, dazzling in the sunshine—
more rarely, rosy lines of lovely flamingoes, worth coming
a long way to see : and from first to last the tiny black
and white " Solomon's bird," with its yellow cheeks—
the robin of the Nile—hopping about the deck, picking
up crumbs from one's hand, and saying all manner of
pleasant things with its little graceful nods.

Dreamy, too, is the Nile life, because we see then
with our real eyes the scenes we have all thought of
till we fancy we have already seen them ; now, in flesh
and blood, yet dreamily still, they stand before us—
Joseph talking to his brethren in the field, or the sons
of Jacob journeying with their asses and their sacks of
provender to buy corn in Egypt—Boaz sitting at the
gate, and saying, " Ho, such a one ! turn aside, sit
down here ! "—the two women grinding at one mill,
and the unmuzzled ox treading out the corn—Rebekah
carrying her pitcher on her head, or " letting it down
upon her hand " to give drink to the wayfarer—
Rachel coming out at even to water the flock—and
the blessed Virgin Mother sitting on the ass, holding
the young child in her lap, while Joseph, staff in hand,
leads them on.

No one seeking much excitement, or any exercise
beyond walking, should come to the Nile; for it is altogether dreamy and calm : you look on at life ever
moving before your eyes — you hear ceaseless sounds of
men on the banks, women washing at the river's edge,
melancholy Arab songs droned out, donkeys continually
braying, and the hoarse scream of the wild geese over
your head : but you yourself lie dreamily and silently
on your divan, and see it all pass by like pictures in a
diorama; and yet you never feel shut up or inactive,
for you know you are moving on and on; everything
changes around you each hour, and all the while your
mind wanders away — now, to the far south before you,
where you fancy you must come at last to the younger
days of the great river you have been passing up so
long — then back to the tideless sea, into which you saw
him pouring weeks ago — now, among the nineteenth
century of travellers like yourself — then back to the
countless generation in the almost infinite history of
Egypt; and so you look up at the everlasting hills on
each side of you, that stood there, already old and time-
worn, before the faintest light dawned on historic truths,
or even poetic fables, that your furthest-seeking per-
spicacity can discover, — and you are so weary with the
long search, that you only care to lie still and think.

Then, slowly and silently down sinks the sun, and
evening closes round with a delicious fresh sweetness,
which you must cross the Mediterranean to feel; the
boat is generally moored early to the bank, where the
sailors light a fire of Indian corn-stalks, and immediately fall asleep in every imaginable and unimaginable
attitude around it, or in heaps on the deck: voices of
prayer come from the next village, until all is hushed
but the howling and whining of dogs and jackals, and

generally half-a-dozen frogs holding an evening gossip, in stentorian croaks. A few hours after you hear the Reïs' beads pattering on the deck as he kneels at his prayers, and with the first rosy glow on the beautiful starry sky all the crew are up and the sails are hoisted, and the flags stream behind you; or the men jump ashore and your pretty boat goes lazily thumping along the bank as the file of sailors pull her slowly on, only stopping to make a rush at some neighbouring sugar-canes, which they greedily devour all the day after, or, to buy the more important "leben" (milk), for your own breakfast.

Perhaps, the sound *most* peculiar to Egypt, rivalling even the groans of the Sākiyah and the Shadoof, because it is so often close to your ear — is the "Hay-a-lee-sāh! Hay-a-lēe-sah! — (the emphasis on the last, or last but one syllable, according as the action of the moment is quick or slow) — sung by the sailors in chorus; a sound which I shall always consider, however rough in itself, as some of the sweetest music I have ever heard. I never got a satisfactory explanation of the words: our drago-man told us that Leesa was a daughter of the Prophet, whose aid they invoked; but this was, I believe, entirely nonsense; sometimes, but seldom, they called on other saints, — usually only in some locality espe-cially dedicated to a dead saint whose wely was in the neighbourhood, or to some Fakir or hermit living there; and sometimes of an evening the sailors would sing a long descriptive song, the translations of which were always very vague indeed. It is pleasant to have a good singing crew, but they are generally engaged for Pashas' private boats; and if your own is a very small boat you are apt to wish a crocodile stuck in their throats before they have half done a long song; but if you keep their singing within bounds it is sweet and harmonious, and an agreeable break upon the monotony of the downward drifting.

We met with but one instance of dishonesty on the Nile among the sailors : we left our things lying about all day, both in the cabins and on the deck — we dropped small coins on the floor — we were out whole days, leaving the Reïs in charge, though any of the cabins might be entered by the windows, unseen from the others, and we never missed so much as a pin ; every single thing was picked up and brought back to us with a simple straightforwardness, that showed it was their natural habit to do so : I heard the same from every one else on the Nile ; your dragoman may eat up your stores — the rats may abscond with your dearest treasures — and the mice may breakfast on your new English gloves — but with the sailors you are perfectly safe.

We reached Esneh in twenty-four hours after leaving Luxsor, the only incident of the day being an ineffectual effort to capture a crocodile ; but the wary monsters, though lying asleep on the spit of a sandbank at least half a mile long, wakened at the first step of a man on the other end, and after one or two yawns and stretches, waddled down into the water.

The bank at Esneh was very gay and crowded ; we were amused with seeing the costumes of the Ghawazee or dancing girls, generally a bright cherry-coloured silk robe, quite long, only just showing a pair of loose, pink gauze shintyān below, their heads covered thickly with gold coins strung together into a kind of cap, and a white gauze veil thrown over all. They wear quantities of gold coin necklaces and other ornaments, but we never saw a single really pretty face among them ; some seemed to be only eight or ten years old.

We had the good fortune of meeting here Mr.
Harris, the Egyptian antiquary, and his amiable
daughter; and they were so kind as to accompany
us to the Temple, and to read some of the hieroglyphics
to us. The portico of this temple has been excavated,
leaving the rubbish as a wall of its own height beside
it, so that you descend into it from the level of its
capitals. Though comparatively modern, having been
built in the times of Tiberius and Trajan, it is well
worth seeing for its massive elegance (an expression
which can only be realised in Egyptian architecture),
and for the harmonious symmetry of its proportions;
it is pleasanter, too, to study than most of the Temples,
as it is walled off from the town, and you can sit
enjoying your sketch in perfect silence and solitude :
the stone of which it is built is of a rich yellow-brown,
that tells well in a picture. We afterwards walked in
the orange-groves of the Kashef (or governor's) palace,
the Kashef himself paying us a visit in our dahabieh ;
he made himself as agreeable as any one can do through
the medium of an interpreter, even though Achmet was
a first-rate translator, and gave us a good deal of information more interesting than that in the conversation
between the Pasha and " The Member for Mudcombe,"
famous in Eōthean annals. He descanted largely upon
a map of Egypt, quite proud of being able to point
out each place, though he could not, of course, read
the names, and he criticised my drawings as freely as a
drawing-master. He afterwards sent his daughter to
see us, but we were unfortunately on shore when she
came ; and he was much disappointed at her not being
able to see the novel, and to him incomprehensible
sight of a *hareem belonging to nobody*, travelling in
blissful liberty by itself on the Nile.

Our crew had a *soirée* in the evening, and entertained us with deafening music and dancing; the
latter, which consists only of placing the body in
awkward attitudes, bending backwards, and balancing
upon bent knees, is as ungraceful as possible; and we
were thankful when they were pleased to desist from
the noisy darabooka (drum), clapping of hands, coffee
and pipes, with which they amused themselves till ten
o'clock: we sailed on an hour afterwards, determining
to allow no more balls in our dahabieh. The mountains became more varied in form as they changed into
the sandstones of Jebel Silsilis, and the cliff on which
Koom Ombos stands so finely; but darkness came upon
us, and we saw no more till we reached Assouän at
10 P. M. on the 26th of January, forty-two days after
leaving Alexandria.

CHAP. III.

"Oh, mighty Jove!
Forgive this monstrous love for a barbarian,
That knows not of Olympus!"

OUR eyes opened the next morning on a gay and pretty scene; instead of the yellow hills and smooth sandbanks of Egypt, strange, black, shining rocks popped up in the very middle of the stream—an old Saracenic wall or fortification stretched down to the river's edge on the north, as if to shut out Egypt from our sight—while in the narrow channel between the east side and the green island of Elephantine, four dahabiehs besides our own were moored, — the Arrow and Nenna, the Gertrude and the Pharaoh,—and the Pasha's steamer, which had towed up Lord Dufferin's boats. The high sandy bank was shaded with palm trees, and covered with gaily saddled donkeys, riding camels, tame ostriches, and crowds of Nubians offering spears, daggers, bows and arrows, pieces of ivory and sandal-wood, ostrich-feathers and eggs, silver bracelets, clay cups and vases, savage-looking necklaces and head-dresses of shells, strips of rhinoceros and hippopotamus hide, leopard skins, mats and baskets of dates, for sale.

It was tempting to linger among them, but we had business to settle; besides which, a ride, our first ride in the desert, was more tempting still. Achmet had been to see the Sheikh of the Cataract, and learned that he was already engaged to take three boats up before our turn would come, and he stoutly refused to take up any dahabieh as large as the Wandering Maiden in less than two days; we might therefore expect to be detained five days at least before we reached the other side of the Cataract: and in returning we knew very well that she would be, proportionably to her weight, slower in descending the river. So we determined to see if any boat was to be had above the Cataract, and accordingly we started early in the morning for Mahatta, — a desert ride of an hour and half. But what a different desert from one's nursery imaginations! the flat expanse of yellow sand had no place here — two or three hundred yards of white sand strewed with white stones, with banks of stones and lumps of granite piled up loosely on each side, as if "put away" by giants playing at bricks and suddenly called home to supper, — strange, fantastic shapes, sometimes like cairns, sometimes like walls, chiefly white, and yet shading into delicate hues of lilac and pale grey, with now and then a dash of purple. Solemn and stern it looked, seeming to close down upon one's heart with an almost tangible pressure as we journeyed on, the only living things in the whole way, save one hyena and some black and white vultures, slowly sailing to and fro, some keeping watch while others picked at the bones of a dead camel, which it required no vulturine organ to scent at a good distance. A wely of some Sheikh was the only sign of man, save the remains of an ancient wall or dyke, built by the Romans, some say, or by an Egyptian queen in the days long gone by. After leaving Assouän, the road commences with a cemetery of the most ancient converts to Mahommedanism, with very

small stone slabs, bearing inscriptions in Cufic writing —
a pretty elegant character. Many travellers have
sought to carry away one of these slabs, but the people
of Assouān will in no wise consent to part with them,
even for the handsomest of baksheeshes.

The village of Mahatta looked more tropical than
any we had as yet passed; it was neat and flourishing,
every cottage having its enclosure of dôm palms, and
its heap of gathered dates for sale or winter con-
sumption; it was swarming with coffee-coloured children,
destitute of any clothing save a leathern girdle or a
shell necklace. Achmet fought a way for us through
the crowd, and we descended to inspect an Arab boat,
climbing over slippery, perilous rocks afterwards to the
bank opposite Philæ, where two of the Reïses of the
Cataract (there are eight of them) followed to make a
bargain for its hire. In two minutes a cane divan was
placed under a huge shady sycamore, two or three
carpets and mats laid on the divan, for us; and then
the bargaining began. The two Reïses were perfectly
black, with the woolly hair, negro nose, and turned-out
lips, characteristic of Nubia; each wore only a white
cotton shirt tied round the throat, without sleeves,
floating out in the wind from their tall black figures,
polished and shining with castor-oil; very fine they
looked, standing gesticulating with Achmet. In about
twenty minutes coffee was brought to us, and when the
Reïs received the empty finjans from our hands, he
made a salaam, and Achmet said, "He says, Now you
have drunk his coffee, you have *stepped upon his back*,
so he must let you have the boat for the price you say;"
while meantime the other Reïs opened the bosom of
his dirty gown, and poured out a quantity of dates into
our laps, along with a platter of roasted Indian corn,

of which we duly eat before the bargain was concluded by shaking of hands and fresh salaams.

We ended that day with a row up to near the foot of the Cataract, to enjoy the indescribable sight of that confusion of rocks, thrown about as if by hand, piled up and smoothed by the rushing water, shining and lustrous as coal and marble; the only two colours, the jet black basalt and the red porphyry, ornamented here and there with the vivid green of the little sont (mimosa) trees.

The Desert looked strangely gay the next morning, as we followed the same route from Assouān to Mahatta, for all the occupants of the six dahabiehs, then moored together, were on the same route, as well as four camels loaded with the furniture and provisions for our kandjeh, — beds, basons, baths and baskets, all piled up in confusion on the swaggering camels, while, hanging out over the top of one of them, a great wooden sofa, painted green, went wagging ludicrously along. Our friends bade us adieu with a ringing cheer on the beautiful banks of Philæ — ever lovely Philæ; and we sailed gaily on at 2 P.M. into Nubia, with eight of our own sailors under a Nubian Reïs. Our new boat looked hopelessly unpromising and dirty, but we determined to make the best of it; and having made her look as nice as her old boards would permit, we gave ourselves up to watching the lovely scenes through which we were passing.

It is Egypt no longer, but something wholly different: the river seems to run more rapidly in its far narrower channel, and is of a deeper, clearer grey; the rocky hills rise more abruptly on both sides, leaving on each bank only a narrow strip, but a few yards wide in many places, sometimes not even that, gay and bright with

the vivid green of young lupins; then a fringe of
palms, dôm palms, or castor-oil trees, a yard or two
wide, and the dark red rock rises immediately behind
them, or the sand of the desert closes upon the green,
as if sternly saying, "Thus far, and no further!" And
thus it is throughout Nubia: scarcely anywhere does
the cultivated land extend a quarter of a mile in width.
Often the rocks tumble down in heaps into the water,
scarcely a village is to be seen, and but very few of the
people, only occasionally one or two working singly
among the lupins; a silence, almost deathly, reigns
throughout the land, and the whole country seems,
by a subversion of ideas, to consist of the river only —
a snake like kingdom of blue water set in green and
yellow enamels. The boats with their singing crews
are all gone — the birds have stayed behind in Egypt,—
there are no villages for the jackals to howl in — and
the only sound that breaks upon the listening ear is
that of the creaking sākiyahs and shadoofs at intervals.

And yet, such is the beauty of the scene, that Nubia
is not melancholy; and so delicious is the air, that
breathing seems in itself a pleasure. The balmiest
European summer's evening, is raw and cold, in comparison with the perfection of those Nubian nights;
scarcely even cool, yet with nothing of the oppressive
heat of the day, the evening air moves round one with
a soft, sweet freshness, as it bathes every sense at once
in a dreamy but not languid feeling of pleasure, and
charms sight, taste, touch, and hearing with equal
enjoyment. We afterwards found two or three mornings, about sunrise, quite cool; but during our stay in
Nubia, the nights were always the same, bringing, as
Eliot Warburton expresses it, a sort of conviction that
existence is a blessed thing.

Not, however, that Nubian existence by day is particularly inviting: very black and very oily is the Ber-
beri, and your olfactory organs shrink from the wind
that blows from him to you; wild and fierce are the
men, noisy and naked the women, and, in contrast to
the resplendent polish of their skins, unpolished is their
manner.   One girl tried to snatch rudely from my
hand a dôm palm nut I had gathered, while her companion threw handfuls of sand at us: but we were
taking a long walk, with only the protection of one
sailor, and had we gathered as much of their slender
provision as its equivalent in England, the British
peasant would probably have expressed his disgust quite
as significantly and perhaps more disagreeably.

One word more of our nights in Nubia: when we entered
our boat at Mahatta we found her reeking wet throughout the inside: "She's been sunk all night, ma'am, to
clear out the vermin," was the explanation we received;
and, relying on Sir G. Wilkinson's assurance of the
purity of Nubia, we thought only of rats, and asked no
more about it.   That night we slept in peace; the sunshine of the following day, however, dried up the old
boat into its normal condition; but, in the bliss of
ignorance, we retired to rest, when, after a few minutes'
slumber, I awoke with a kind of impression that the
imps of Sheitan had got hold of me.   Oh horror! inside
and outside of my mosquito curtains files of bugs were
promenading — late suppers, fit for imperial bugs, were
being imbibed all over my neck and arms — and when,
with more than usual contortions, I had struggled out
of my Levinge's bag, I saw on beds, walls, ceiling, and
floor, only bugs — bugs — bugs!!   In Syria, you
can buy tiny little scraps of the Koran, folded up in
highly ornamented silver, or gaily worked leather bags,

which are worn round the neck, and which are infallible
preservatives against bugs; I thought of importing
them to England, but I remembered they could not
be expected to guard any but Islamist bodies.

After that night we slept on the deck; and much
pleasanter it was, with the glorious stars for our roof,
than in the stuffy cabin and cupboard, which was
all our kandjeh afforded us. And indeed it was well
worth while to sleep *à la belle étoile*, to have full opportunity of seeing the beautiful Southern Cross, denied to
European eyes. We used to lie awake between two
and four o'clock each morning, for the pleasure of
looking at the lovely constellation,—such a mysterious
emblem of Nature's holiness it always seemed — as if
the heavens came closer, *plus rapprochés* to one's heart,
in wearing the simple but well-known symbol of our
Faith; and that these lovely stars visibly glorified the
material image of the only path on earth that leads to a
sure home amongst those starry hosts of heaven. It is a
strange sensation, but an absolute fact, that the stars in
Nubia seem really and tangibly nearer to you than in
Europe : not that the sky seems nearer, for, on the
contrary, it is lifted up to an infinitude far above what
we ever see in our *cieux couverts* of northern latitudes,
— but that the stars themselves seem to hang lower
down, to *lean out* of heaven towards man, shining on
him with the marvellous glowing radiance that seems to
bring home to the heart a living testimony of the
inconceivably glorious heaven above them.

Thus much of the sky over Nubia; of the land itself
the produce is almost entirely confined to two vegetables,
the palm and the castor-oil; it is one long, almost unbroken palm grove from end to end : the palm trees are
all numbered, registered, and taxed; their fruit is the

chief, almost the only food of the Nubians; they have
nothing besides this but the beans whose flowers perfume
the air at this season. The dates are sent down largely
into Egypt, for no one eats an Egyptian date in Cairo
or Alexandria if he can get a Nubian date; and the
trade is increased by the dates brought in the caravans
from Sennaar, which are much prized in the more
northern latitudes. The second product of Nubia is the
castor-oil, of which an immense quantity is consumed,
externally, by the Nubian; the woolly hair of both sexes
is soaked and matted into a stiff paste with the oil, and
their bodies are rubbed over with it till they become
polished and shiny. The oil keeps the skin from blistering or burning in the hot sun, which is the more necessary from their wearing no clothes; it likewise protects
them from the attacks of mosquitos and other insects.
The plant is extremely pretty; you have fruit and flower
on the same branch, like the cotton tree which bears
the pretty yellow blossom along with the silky, white,
cotton tufts of the dry open pod, both at once; the
castor-oil is red-stalked and of large, deeply cut leaves —
the young ones, dark crimson-brown and purple, the
old ones a bright green; the berries, like small chestnuts,
of two shades of green, and the flowers white. I have
heard of red and white flowers on the same tree, but we
never saw them. The ugly, stunted-looking dôm palm
every one knows by pictures, with its strange fan-shaped
leaves, like bunches of green paper strongly electrified;
and its fruit, large, dark red, deformed-looking apples.

On nearing Korosko the colouring of the scenery
changes marvellously; the river winds so much as to
appear frequently like a succession of lakes, enclosed
by hills or mountains which have all become of a dark
deep purple, sometimes quite black, while the sand

which creeps up their sides, and over the plains beyond
them, is no longer white, or even yellow, but a full
rich apricot colour.   About Korosko and Ibreem, the
mountains are singularly beautiful, and still more
strange; their dark purple tints and the bright coloured
sands contrasting finely with the luxuriant palm and
the green beans, while the mountains themselves begin
to assume the fantastic shapes which give to the whole
land, more especially about Abou Simbil, such a weird
and bewitched appearance.   The idea irresistibly suggests itself, that the country has been lately burned, and
each hill roasted; it seems as if nothing but a general
conflagration could have given such a resemblance to
over-baked pies, which the flame-coloured sand around
them increases.   One felt that there *must* be a legend
of some such thing, and accordingly we were soon
told how Surya, the Regent of the Sun, descended on
the country one morning to say his prayers, when the
waters dried up immediately, the mountains took fire,
and the inhabitants were roasted to death.   Ibreem —
a lovely subject for a sketch — is a lofty perpendicular
bluff, with curious old caves cut in the face, and crowned
with a castle, now in ruins, which must have been of
great strength and size.

   We reached Wady Halfeh only four days after
leaving Mahatta, so that we had not exchanged boats
for nothing; 220 miles in four days, one of which had
been lost in tracking against a westerly wind, was not
bad.   It blew violently at Wady Halfeh, invariably the
case there, it is said: the place looks wind-worn and
desolate; not but that it was lively enough that evening,
for a caravan from Dongola and Senaar had just arrived,
and the shore was covered with camels, and bales of
elephants' teeth, bags of gum-arabic, and ostrich feathers;

and we were pestered with people offering us the veriest
rubbish for sale, as "Antika, antika!" even common
bits of stone from the beach; one boy offered us an
English halfpenny, and another some broken morsels of
glass; but the best thing was a man, a few days after,
picking up a button before the eyes of a gentleman
from whose coat it had dropped off, and holding it up
to him, crying out, "Antika! baksheesh, ya Howadji!"

There were no donkeys or any kind of rideable beast
to be had at the village, so we mounted very early the
following morning on rough baggage camels belonging
to the caravan, in order to reach the Hill of Abouseer:
we had no saddles or riding arrangements beyond a
carpet and a mat thrown loosely over the beast's back,
and how we stuck on is still a marvel to me, — but we
firmly declined, after a momentary trial, all invitations
to trot. After becoming a little accustomed to the discomfort of the situation, I liked the springy long step
and even swing of the camel, and one could not but feel
it in harmony with the scene around one. A marvellous
scene, indeed, it was; a desolate Desert of seemingly
endless sand, both white and deep yellow, with rocks
breaking through of pale green, red, yellow, white, and
purple; sometimes pieces shone sparkling in the sun, of
so pure and clear an amethyst colour, that one quite
started to tread over the seeming precious stone. About
half way we came to a solitary Sheikh's tomb in ruins:
no other sign of man or life met our view during the
whole five hours of the ride, not a man, nor a camel,
nor even a gazelle or a jerboa; all was utter silence
and space under the bluest of cloudless skies, and the
rays of a scorching sun.

In another hour we had climbed up the back of the
famous Hill of Abouseer, whose face is a perpendicular

cliff, three hundred feet high, rising directly from the
northern end of the second Cataract, or Batn el Hajar*,
as the Arabs call it. Many a fair land and many a
mountain panorama have I seen, but never has any view
made *more* impression on me than that wondrous, though
scarcely beautiful scene ; the rock stands almost isolated,
yet with hills and heights on the west side, and an immense plain to the south and east : and standing alone
on its summit I thought of that " exceeding high
mountain " whence " all the kingdoms of the earth and
the glory thereof" were surveyed. But how different a
view was this ! kingdoms, indeed, there had been in the
land laid out before me, with hundreds of temples, and
palaces, and pyramids,—but of the glory of these there
is now nought but ruin and desolation; " their memorial," even, has almost " perished with them," and
the scene is one of the wildness of Nature only. Far,
far away to the south and south-west rose the mountains
of Dŏngola and Kordofân, grey and blue in the distance ;
between us and them the great river wound through
thousands and thousands of low black rocks, shining
black like coals, extending nearly twenty miles, a
mazy archipelago, but all jumbled into a mass that
could scarcely be distinguished into islets — the black
tinted here and there with shrubs of tamarisk ; and as
the river came within a few miles of our hill, it dashed
and foamed into wider channels of white frothy waters,
which joined into a smooth swift river, and, passing the
base of Abouseer, flowed on past Wady Halfeh on its
northern course. On each side of these miles of black
Cataract spread the flat yellow desert, carrying on the
eye westwards to the mountains of Dongola, and eastwards to the far away Arabian range, clothed in the love-

* Core of the rock.

liest hues of exquisite pale rosy lilac, half hidden in a dreamy kind of mist.

We gazed and gazed, feeling as if we could never have enough; like prisoners from the window of their gaol, looking with longing eyes over the far " sweet south " we so ardently desired to explore, and over probably the most tropical scene in all the world that our eyes will ever behold. Turning back is often sad, but it never seemed so *triste*, or such starving work before, as when we set our faces northward to regain the boat— almost like a hungry beggar passing a baker's shop and turning away his head from the food he longs for and cannot have. But before we retraced our steps there was something to do,—to accomplish which I had armed myself with a hammer and chisel, not knowing in the least how to use them, but resolved to leave our names among the pilgrims who had rested on that narrow ledge of rock before us. A mighty company of names are gathered there, and a feeling of something awful came over one in the sight of the hundreds recorded on that unchanging stone — abiding there still like tangible shadows of those who carved them when in health and vigour, yet of whom so many are now already passed away! For only a few years—twenty at most — has that ancient river been open to travellers, yet already, like the Volume of the Great Book, that rock, the imperishable record of those who spent but one short hour of their brief existence there, is crowded with the names of the dead! Of those we personally knew, by far the greater number were gone into that land whence none return; and it was with a feeling of sad pleasure that we placed our names among them — thus making a sort of re-union in matter as well as in thought—a silent, half-living companionship. The sun was scorchingly hot, and, never having been a schoolboy, I found the stone-carving a very hard task, and was heartily glad when I had accomplished it: then we went slowly back to the kandjeh, with our heads wrapped in thick Scotch plaids to guard us from the midday rays to which we were not accustomed on shore.

The real wealth of the glorious old Nile is derived from its lowest affluent, called the Black Nile—a river that rises in Abyssinia, near the town of Gondar, and pours into the great Nile just above Berber. The inundation owes its value to the greasy black mud suspended in the waters of this branch; and it is doubted by some persons whether the annual inundation would even take place were the Nile robbed of the mass of water that comes down the Black Nile. There might be a very large rise annually, but the water would subside without leaving that peculiar sediment which makes the soil of Egypt so fruitful. It was from knowing this that propositions were occasionally made by the enemies of Egypt in olden times of cutting off this branch, by turning its waters, before they left Abyssinia, into the Red Sea, and thereby reducing Egypt to a desert, or at least a very poor land; and on this account the Abyssinians were reported, in an ancient tradition, to have the power of reducing Egypt to utter and irreparable ruin.

This thick, greasy-feeling mud is thought to act beneficially upon other substances besides land: it is largely exported, dried in cakes, to all the hareems of Turkey; and the mud, re-softened in water, is laid on the skins of the fair ones of Damascus, Constantinople, and the beauties of Circassia and Georgia, to give whiteness and lustre to their complexions. Certainly

the water of the Nile has the most charming influence
on the skin, especially during its thickest flow. When
we ascended the Nile, the water was of a deep rich
brown, which had cleared, before we returned to Cairo,
into a clear grey. It is the most delicious water in the
world for drinking, even when very thick; you have but
to let it stand an hour or so in a clay goolleh, and the
most refreshing sweet water runs off, as agreeable to
the taste as it is beneficial to the health.

The following evening we anchored close to Abou
Simbil, in the prettiest reach of the river, where it was
enclosed like a lake, between ranges of purple hills, and
dressed in sunset hues of lilac and gold. These hills are
most curious from their fantastic shapes, besides hundreds of others which rise suddenly from the flat, flame-
coloured sand, like huge round haycocks with steeply
sloping sides. We toiled up the steep bank of sand
very early the next morning, as it is only the newly
risen sun which can penetrate at all into the depths of
that world-famous Temple of Abou Simbil, or Ibsam-
boul, as it is sometimes called.

Everybody is familiar with the interesting account of
its resurrection from under the sand by the spade of
Belzoni — that lesson of noble perseverance grandly rewarded; and since that time the Temple has been too
often and too well described by able pens for me to use
my feeble one in portraying its wonders; nor, indeed,
can I hope here or elsewhere to do more than to render
in some degree the impression made upon our own
minds, rather than to give the actual description of the
magnificent ruins of Egypt in themselves.

Our entrance into the Rock-temple is in nowise
likely to be forgotten : the sand has now closed up the

doorway (which was quite open a few years ago*) within eleven or twelve inches from the top, so that it would
be impossible to enter it if the sand was flat, instead of
being, as it is, on a steep slope. We divested ourselves
of hats, &c., for the heat inside is intense, and we were
puzzling over what was to happen next, when Achmet
suddenly disappeared, shouting back directions to us
from the depths inside the hole, in obedience to which
we laid ourselves, one by one, flat on our faces, insert-
ing our heels into the aperture, where being instantly
seized on, petticoats and all, a few vigorous pulls drew
us each safely through! such a ludicrously unpleasant
operation that I could not help opening my mouth to
laugh, thereby receiving half a pound of sand down my
throat. Still more intensely ludicrous did it seem when,
half an hour afterwards, we, being still inside, saw a
gentleman undergo the same process—the feet first
filling up the hole, and then the body coming thunder-
ing down the steep sand-slope into the darkness and
silence within. It is needless to remark that "jupons
d'acier" are not in fashion at Abou Simbil.

After this very unusual exercise we required a little
rest, and Achmet left us for half an hour that our eyes
might become accustomed to the darkness within; and
we were thankful enough to be alone, for very soon the
light which pours through the little opening enabled us
to distinguish the features of that far-famed hall, which
sinks deeper and deeper into the heart the longer you
behold it. Four colossal figures stand at each side of
the middle aisle, as pillars dividing off the narrow and
dark recesses behind them; all the light there is falls on

* The temple was cleared out, by order of the Pasha, for the visit
of Lord Haddo; but since then the villagers have thrown the sand in
again out of pure mischief.

these eight figures of Rameses now become Osiris, imbued
with his almost superhuman strength and majesty, and
divine calmness—the swathed legs, and the unearthly
repose of the face, bespeaking the God of Death, as the
crook and the knotted scourge portray the God of
Judgment. There is little in accordance with our
modern ideas of beauty in his features, yet the mind is
more impressed with admiration — an admiration that
almost oppresses the heart—at the majestic, passionless
purity and perfect peace of that countenance, than at
the most exquisite Grecian model of all that is most
beautiful in man; something *more* is here, more than
mere symbolism, and far beyond mere human beauty,
however perfect; something that speaks to the mind
with an eight-fold voice, as clearly as the grave, sweet
mouth and the powerful arms crossed calmly on the
breast, clasping the divine emblems, speak to the eye of
the gazer—something which tells of the rest obtained,
not by inaction but by conquest — something that
whispers almost irresistibly to the mind, "When He
giveth quietness, who then can make trouble?" a quietness — a repose that is, indeed, almost unearthly, for
it comes from far away, — he is dead, but speaking from
beyond the earthly life he has quitted: it is not only
that he has passed through death, but that Death is no
more to him; he is now *living* — living again, but in
silence—not in action, but in the life of thought which
is eternal, — he is gone, not *into* Death, but *through*
Death into the Silent Land — the land of the great departed; and from that land, through the still silence
between us and him, through the deep darkness of in-
tervening ages of idolatry and ignorance, there seemed
to come softly to our living ears the spiritual echoes of
those voices, for long ages silent upon earth, yet whose

praises are still ringing through eternity in adoration of
the one same God Almighty — the same then as now to
the pure in heart — even to them and to us as children
of the same eternal and ever-present Father;—through
the long past ages these have stood there, and for long
ages to come they will still stand there, silently singing
their solemn, sweet chant, ever and ever the same, from
those crossed arms and those serene, passion-stilled
countenances, and those restful lips — " Children and
brothers, your burden is heavy, your cares many; but
be of good courage — strive, struggle, fight your way on
— conquer through all, and attain this calm, this peace,
this rest, forgetting all the trials, sorrows, struggles of
life in eternity."

> " ' Daughter,' they softly said, ' peace to thine heart!
> We too, yes, daughter, have been as thou art:
> Hope-lifted, doubt-depressed, seeing in part,
> Tried, troubled, tempted, sustained.as thou art.
> *Our* God is *thy* God; what He willeth is best;
> Trust Him as we trusted: — then — rest as we rest!' "

Besides this hall there are fourteen chambers in the
Temple, all perfectly dark, of course, though before the
sand had choked up the entrance the four small figures
which sit, as on an altar, at the furthermost end of the
adytum, facing the door, must have been dimly illu-
mined by the rays of the rising sun (the Temple faces
the east); and they must themselves have appeared to
look, with their stony eyes, along the whole length of
the Temple, and across the sacred ever-flowing Nile, to
the deep purple unchanging mountains beyond his green
banks. If the sacred hawk, the emblem of the Sun to
whom the Temple is dedicated, was kept at the feet of
these four statues, as some suppose, it must have been
worse than the " penalties of royalty " to him, to be wor-

shipped in the dark enclosure, instead of enjoying blessed
liberty on the hills he could just descry without.

On the walls of the outer hall are represented the
historic deeds and conquests of the great Rameses; the
other chambers are also sculptured all over, and two or
three of them have a stone divan extending along the
sides: but the pictures are so blackened with smoke
as to be very difficult to decipher, and the heat and
suffocation in the inner rooms are so intense, that it
became impossible to examine half of them; strong
lungs and head are absolutely necessary for a real examination of Abou Simbil in its present state; it was
with much vexation that we turned to hurry out, but
one was forced to retain strength enough in one's faint
and semi-suffocated condition for the exit — head
foremost — through the same little hole: an operation
still more disagreeable than the entrance.

We lay down in the shadow of the rock to rest and
breathe, and to feast our eyes quietly and thoroughly
on the four colossal figures of the façade: three only are
quite uncovered by the sand, and one of these has been
destroyed to the waist, while of the fourth only the
face is visible. These enormous figures — they are
sixty-six feet in height without the pedestals — are of
the great Rameses II. seated on his throne; his posture,
the hands on the knees, signifying his rest after his
many conquests — viz. those portrayed within the
Temple; these figures are as striking as the Osirides in
the interior, but even more beautiful in face. The
countenance is as grand, and perhaps more human, with
an expression of majestic sweetness in the mouth and of
triumph in the nose, which gives a sort of conviction
to the mind that they are portraits. Till I saw those
figures, I never could believe that features of such

gigantic size could express such *grace* and benevolence, so sweetly and grandly mingled; but here, in reality, one felt in one's heart that Rameses — the glory of ancient Egypt's many glories, and the terror of the then known world — must have reigned over a people who loved him, as well as over slaves who feared him.

Then we turned to the mountains, now deep in violet shades against the Eastern sky, which we had seen from the inside of the Temple, feeling that these, at least, had been beyond the power of man to change; and yet, strange to say, they seemed to have come within reach of a hand's grasp, as it were, across the almost immeasurable gulf between us and the thousands of centuries when these figures were fashioned by men's hands; strange to feel how Nature came close home to one's heart as man seemed fading away in such dim distance; how the

" sweet and potent voice " —

from

" within the soul itself " * —

answered back the whisper from nature's grandest works, and the inward life of man and of Nature met together in the same God-given thought; strange to recognise the links of that immortal chain which bound up the spiritual life of Nature, with the thoughts of those whose works of the Past were living still in the Present, — in those old Egyptians and in the children of the new West, — children of the same Father, with thoughts alike eternal in both.

We had hoped to have re-entered the temple in the afternoon, but we suffered so much from the effects of the vitiated air of the interior all the rest of the day, that we were compelled very reluctantly to give it up.

* Coleridge.

The small, but pretty Temple of Amada was the next at which we stopped; it is situated on the western bank, and commands a remarkably pretty landscape, and is in itself more picturesque than most of the ruins of Egypt: the sculptures are very lively and interesting, and in some places very fresh; but the little Temple is more than half buried in the sand. The next day a very high wind kept us moored to the bank — the only day on which we had imperfect weather in Nubia; but we found amusement in watching the brown children and girls who came down with butter and dates for sale: they were very shy, and screamed frightfully if ever we went near enough to pretend to touch them; but at any reasonably safe distance they would stand for an hour, even the tiniest of them, shouting "Baksheesh, baksheesh!" We went on in the night, but the wind continued to blow, and our old tub of a boat rolled so much, that — I grieve to say — we were both sea-sick!

Koofideena (or Maharrāka) occupied us the next morning; an unfinished Temple, looking still as if fresh from the hands of the builders, with its half-carved capitals, yet now in ruins: it is very pretty and worth seeing, though almost without sculptures, and not to be compared with the noble ruin of Dakkeh, which we explored in the afternoon. Here there is a fine view from the summit of the great pylon, I *believe*, but such a splendid mirage spread all around us during our stay that we never rightly distinguished between the truth and the pretty fable: the Temple itself is one of the most interesting. Then came Garf Hosseyn — a coarse travestie of Abou Simbil, nearly passing the "one step" from the sublime to the ridiculous: the clumsy giants, who are fast crumbling away here, bear little resemblance to the majestic figures in the other, reminding

one only of the monsters of ancient India. In the
beauty and dignity of Abou Simbil one almost forgets
that from such conceptions man could degenerate into
the darkness of idolatry—for there the spiritual life only
is represented, which was afterwards clouded over by
error and materialism; but in Garf Hosseyn the degra-
dation of heathenism is brought before one : in the one,
you feel instinctively that what is before you is the
human representation of what is divine — imperfect,
perhaps mistaken, as from the hands of men " seeing
through a glass darkly," yet with the aspirations of a
heart "desiring a better country," expressed in it; whereas, in the other, the form is *brutalisé* into the expression
of something utterly and only human, lower than
human, and gigantically hideous; but what can one
expect from a temple dedicated to the rude Vulcan?
The whole place is swarming with bats, and is very
disagreeable to examine; but the proportions of the
Temple, which is hewn from the living rock, are very
grand, and there has been a fine portico : it is nobly
placed too, and the landscape from it is very green and
lovely; as, indeed, were the views throughout this day's
voyage. We saw Dendour and Kalabshee — the latter
a magnificent ruin, but being only of the date of Au-
gustus, it is too modern to claim as much attention as
its size would otherwise command, and the hieroglyphics
are miserable ; it is, however, imposing and curious too
from its excessive ruin — it looks really as if it had
been chopped up ! and it is only by very active scrambling that one can see it at all.

But the gem of all the hieroglyphics of Nubia is to be
found within a mile of Kalabshee, beautifully situated
on a cliff commanding a long reach of the river and its
bright green banks, — this is the rock-hewn grotto-

temple of Beit el Wely. It is very small, consisting of
only an adytum and a hall, supported on two columns;
the sides are filled with representations of the victories
of Rameses II. over the Cushites (Ethiopians) and the
Shori. In many places the paint is fresh as ever, the
pupils of the eyes of Rameses still preserving their
sharply defined blackness, and the pattern of red and
blue embroidery on his robes still bright and clear; the
piece washed by Miss Martineau is cleaner than most of
the rest, and is of course pointed out by every dragoman.
Outside the Temple the two sides of the area or court
are covered with small, but most lifeful figures: — on
the one side Rameses is represented in the act of con-
quering the Ethiopians, with portraits of all the offerings
presented to him by the newly-conquered people; on
the other, the great king is seen besieging the fortified
city of the Shori, who make a determined resistance;
the conqueror is also represented engaging in single
combat with a chief of the Shori, and afterwards sitting
on his throne receiving a group of prisoners, conducted
by his son: they are certainly most living and spirited,
but they scarcely equal the highly-imagined description
given of them by some travellers.

One night more of delicious fresh warm air — though
at Kalabshee we had left the Tropic of Cancer — and on
the evening of the next day, by the glorious starlight,
we drifted swiftly and noiselessly down the narrow
stream, between the dark high cliffs which charmed us
still more in returning than when ascending the river,
and anchored by the shore of beautiful Philæ. Our
tent was already pitched on the sand, and we thankfully
enjoyed such a night's sleep as we had not once had in
our carnivorous kandjeh.

CHAP. IV.

WHO can describe Philæ? and what good would even
pages and pages of writing do to the minds of
our readers? nought, I fear, but confusion, since Philæ
is made up of apparently incongruous elements, each
beautiful in itself, though combining badly enough together in description, but which in reality melt into one
harmonious whole; stern and wild, yet soft and lovely
— grand in feature, yet exquisite in detail — calm and
silent in its deep repose, yet surrounded with life and
sound — the vast white of the desert, and the deep
grey of the river — the glowing purple of the mountains and the vivid green of the palm trees — the
lustrous black of the weird rocks in the water and. the
fiery orange and red of the infernal-looking rocks on the
shore, — the blue and pink granite, and the red and
purple porphyry, — the creamy yellow of the ancient
ruins, so grand and beautiful, yet so arid and unpictur-
esque, and the dry, cracked, and crumbling mud huts
around and all over them: — these are the various op-
posing features which combine into the one unique and
perfect Philæ; of all spots in Egypt and Nubia the one
to which, perhaps, one looks back through the vistas of
memory with the most love and tenderness.

Much of its magnificently planned Temple was still
unfinished when all was left to silence and ruin; what
would it have been in its complete beauty! what must
it have been even in its incomplete magnificence, when
the pagan priests of old sang their hymns of worship
along its sacred shore! Isis and Osiris, with their son
Horus, the type of youthful beauty, was the Triad worshipped here (Egyptian worship was always in triads),
and the interior of the great temple is filled with their
"domestic annals;" but the earthly history of Osiris did
not end here, for the oath, which has dreamily thrilled
through our minds, so ancient in history to us, was a
modern error among the Egyptians, and " He who
sleeps in Philæ," was really believed by them to have
been buried temporarily in Abydos.

The Temple and the buildings connected with it must
have once entirely covered the island, which was nearly
surrounded by a quay of smooth stone-work; only a
portion of this remains, and the chief parts of the
Temple are now connected only by piles of broken stones:
nothing, however, can lessen the grandeur of the enormous pylons and pyramidal towers in the centre; of all
the rest the effect is sadly spoiled, to our minds, by the
perverse irregularity and unsymmetrical arrangement
of all Egyptian architecture, which is nowhere shown
more broadly—I had almost said, rudely,—than at Philæ.
There are two splendid colonnades of pillars, commencing from a wall of rock rising at the southern end of the
island; but only a few of the pillars can be seen in true
perspective, as the line of each colonnade is almost un-
accountably crooked, following with unnecessary closeness the shore of the island; many of the columns too
are unfinished, with uncarved capitals, the grace and
elegance of the first score making one doubly regret the

vacancy of the others. After this and a whole heap of
ruin, among which lie the broken limbs of a gigantic
lion, you enter between enormous towers through one
court into another : every side of the second square is
different from the rest : one of them is occupied by a
corridor of richly ornamented pillars, while on the opposite side is the small but beautiful temple dedicated
to Horus. Beyond this is the gem of Philæ, " the ten-
columned court," as it is called, of the great Temple :
these columns are still quite perfect, and are almost the
only ones in Egypt where the colours *are really* as fresh
and bright as they must have been two thousand years
ago—unlike the descriptions of enthusiastic tourists :
their capitals are of the most vivid blue and green,
picked out with red, crimson, and orange ; the roof is
bright blue, with golden stars ; and the winged orb,
typifying the Sun, is here more elaborately portrayed
than usual. Then comes the adytum and several other
chambers, all in darkness — thick darkness, the abode
of bats and dismal odours — yet whose walls still hold
vivid pictures, in spite of dirt and decay, of the birth and
education of Horus, who stands between Isis, horned
and sun-crowned, and Osiris with the crown and mitre.
There are inner chambers, staircases still unbroken,
passages innumerable, and some smaller temples ; one
among them on the western side was dedicated to the
god of the Nile, and is full of pretty water plants, lotus
and papyrus, neatly and well sculptured ; whereas the
colossal sculptures on the pylons, &c., are very coarse and
ill done, unlike the really ancient hieroglyphics, for this
temple was built by Ptolemy Epiphanes and Ptolemy
Physcon, and was begun about 200 B.C. Turning to the
east side of the island there is one beautiful and very
graceful building : a quadrangle of columns, rising from

a wall of only a few feet high, support an architrave,
and again a cornice raised some feet above that; there
is no roof, and the pillars and walls are, with the exception of a single winged Sun, quite unsculptured ;
the intention of the building in its unfinished condition
is somewhat incomprehensible, but it is singularly elegant
and pretty, in spite of the efforts of vulgar and low-
minded individuals to deface it by the hideous scribbling
of their own paltry names on its walls.

On the west of Philæ, there is a small island, called
Biggeh, one huge heap of black and purple rocks,
thrown and piled upon each other in the most wild and
fantastic confusion; to the top of this we climbed in
the afternoon — not a very easy or pleasant task, but
worth achieving, as without seeing Philæ from its
summit it is hardly possible to understand the plan of
the ruins, through the thick crust of overlying mud
huts, built, it is said, by the ancient Christians ; or to
see how beautifully the great Temple was placed in the
centre of the river, which is here like a large oval lake,
closed at the southern end by the lovely mountains,
clad in soft Nubian colours : the river comes gliding
from their bosoms to your feet, and, flowing by in a
rapid deep current, hastens over the wild, black rocks,
past all the bewitched-looking piled-up islands, into the
north-west corner of the picture, from whence the
distant roar of the Cataracts, borne upon the breeze,
murmurs up occasionally into you ear.   Behind you it
is all black, burnt-up rock, like the outpourings from
a furnace — mountains of slag, with patches of flame-
coloured Nubian sand : at your feet lies Philæ, slum-
bering in calm beauty, and beyond that, the broad
white pathway through the Desert to Assouân.

We were soon surrounded by the black islanders, and

a number of little children, entirely naked, except a girdle of leathern fringe round the loins; one lovely little girl, with properly oiled and plaited hair, made great friends with us, insisting upon giving the support of her six-year-old arm to help even the gentlemen of our party to descend the rocks, or pointing out the way with her round, slender arms; nor would she quit us for a moment till we rowed away, leaving her graceful little figure poise on a pinnacle of rock, waving farewells with her little arms, and crying, "Ma es salâmé! ma es salâmé!" * nor did she once ask for baksheesh — a very remarkable circumstance in Egypt.

We devoted the next day to sketching in the beautiful ten-columned Court: a strange day for Philæ — for it rained unceasingly, small, fine rain, such as they said had not been seen there for twenty-two years, and the dark purple mountains and wild black rocks looked more eerie, and sad too, than ever, in the lowering un-Egyptian sky. A sandstorm came on in the evening, filling our tent to about eight inches' depth of sand in the course of an hour; and the sun rose on the morrow in a lurid heavy glare, soon shaded by rain, in which, however, we took leave of our dirty kandjeh, and sailed over to Mahatta in the boat of some friends who had kindly invited us into their dahabieh to see the shooting of the Cataract, as we were very anxious to enjoy that experience instead of riding again across the Desert to join our Wandering Maiden. We had no sooner reached Mahatta than a furious thunderstorm broke forth, the lightning playing round the rocks, and the thunder pealing away in thickening echoes, that seemed to gather up and give back the sound in

* "Good bye! good bye!" More literally, "Go in peace!"

hundred-fold majesty. The Arabs declared they would not pass the Cataract in such "weather of Satan," but after a couple of hours it passed off, and a cold sunshine having come out, we shipped about thirty Arabs, and the eight rowers took their places at the oars, tightening their turbans, and turning up their sleeves as though their work was to be done in earnest. We settled ourselves on the deck, admonished that the safety of the boat would be risked should we move hand or foot during the passage of the dangerous parts; and the Arabs squatted round, packing themselves tightly in the prow and on the upper deck, and carefully balancing the boat. Of course they all talked marvellously fast, but the voices lulled as we neared the Cataract; and, in something less than half an hour, silence fell on all save the rowers, who for once keeping good time with their oars, kept singing their "Hayalee-sah!" vigorously —the old Reïs of the cataract standing on the upper deck (a grand old white-bearded Nubian he was), shouting short, deep-toned words of command to the helmsman and to the Reïs of the dahabieh, who stood in the prow with a stout pole ready for action. Every face was turned to the narrow passage between the noble black rocks, down which we were to pass—every eye was fixed and eager—and here and there a hand was raised or the fingers tightened in a clasp, as if in mute appeal to the spirits of the rushing waters to bear us down gently and safely. On we went, swiftly and smoothly gliding through the labyrinth of rocks which seemed to fly past, scarcely a yard's distance on either side of us,—swifter and swifter in the rushing, boiling mass, till the dahabieh seemed to bend for a brief second, poised in mid air over the edge; then, down she leaped with one swinging bound into the white whirling foam

VOL. I.   F

at the bottom, spun half round in the eddy, sped away
beyond the strength of the rowers in a sideways plunge
— and the Cataract was passed! The Arabs all joined in
a shout of triumph, and the Reïs of the Cataract had
just time to snatch the turban from the head of the
dragoman (his invariable perquisite from the owner of
every boat which has safely passed the Cataract under
his guidance), into whose white lips the blood had just
time to return, when a reeling shudder shivered through
the vessel from stem to stern — she gave a sort of stagger
in the water — and bounded off from a pointed rock
which had knocked a tolerably large hole in her bow!
It was no great harm, however,— we passed another
smaller descent a few minutes after in safety, and soon
moored in a little cove, for the double purpose of getting rid of our host of Arabs and to put the vessel in
order, as all the chairs, divans, and spare spars, &c., had
been built up *en masse* in the stern to balance the boat
more perfectly. It was then just one hour since we had
left Mahatta.

Three hours after we found ourselves comfortably re-
instated in our pretty "Wandering Maiden," which
seemed a perfect palace after our miserable Nubian
barge; and we spent the remainder of the day in walking over that much be-praised island of Elephantine,
whose beauties, if it ever had any, are now hidden under
heaps of broken pottery of marvellous depth, among
which the ruins of one small gateway still remains, and
a few palms. The view, however, from the southern
end of the Nile, studded with black islets, with green
and purple banks, is very pretty. It was more interesting to ride out once again into the desert, winding
among the beautiful pink, white, and yellow rocks to
the quarry where the marks of man's work still linger

in a sort of ancient freshness, on the half-carved Obelisk, which lies unfinished and unremoved from the
rock, whence so many thousands of blocks have been cut
and conveyed down the Nile, to build up the unperish-
ing memorials of " a people terrible from their beginning and hitherto, a nation extending its limits, a victorious people, whose land is washed down by rivers !"

A heavy wind detained us within a few miles of Assouān for two days, the bumping of the boat against the
waves making us unpleasantly sick. On the third day
we made a long row in the little felucca to the beautiful
ruin of Koom Ombos, one of the finest in Egypt. An
enormous wall, raised on an artificial substruction, and
pierced with a lofty gateway in the centre, towers above
the river ; a grand hall once stood here, it is said, but
it is entirely ruined and fallen into heaps of broken
stone. The Temple itself, built in honour of two
divinities, — the god of the Temple, hawk-headed, and
that of Ombos, crocodile-headed, — is half buried in the
sand ; and the *two* sanctuaries, an arrangement peculiar
to Koom Ombos, have almost disappeared, but what
remains of the fine lofty portico is remarkably beautiful. The capitals of the huge but not clumsy pillars
are richly and most elegantly carved ; the sculptures
are well done and easily decipherable, and the painting
on the roof is still bright and fresh. It is the more interesting from being in some places unfinished, the
squares, drawn for the convenience of the copying
artist, being yet clearly visible. As the portico is almost perfect, within and without, it is a good example
of the smaller Egyptian temples ; and the finish of the
carving is the more easily examined from the overlying
sand raising one half way up the pillars. Yet how well

this beautiful temple would repay clearing, and how easily it might be done !

It was now midday, and the sun was very hot. We waited hopelessly long, as it seemed to us, for our boat, and scarcely knew where to look for her; for, far away, winding from beneath our feet, the Nile glided into a misty haze, which seemed only to end in sand; then, coming back from the dim horizon eastwards, came a long reach of the river, bending round towards us, and back again to the south. The banks were shaded with rich palm trees, and we fancied we could distinguish sails upon the blue grey water. We sat looking, and upbraiding ourselves for not having observed how much our course must have wound round in the early morning, when river and banks began to tremble; the sand seemed to rise in a faint hot haze, and on changing our point of view by a few yards in height, the whole panorama dissolved away into "the devil's water," as the Arabs call the mirage of the Desert.

We spent the following morning, the 16th of February, in examining the very ancient rock-hewn grotto of Hajar Silsilis on the eastern side of the river, with its most interesting and life-like sculptures, and afterwards had a scrambling walk over some of the gigantic quarries on the same bank. We hoped to have reached Edfou by daylight, but the sun sank, and a glorious moon arose before we moored at the bank about six o'clock. A boat belonging to the Mr. Jackson's came up at the same time, and we agreed to visit the temple by moonlight in one party, in consequence of Sir G. Wilkinson's warning to travellers that the natives of Edfou are apt to be troublesome, and sometimes to molest one impertinently. We determined to be extra prudent, and desired our dragoman to select six of the sailors, provided with stout sticks, to accompany us, headed by Achmet himself, and our man-servant; and, alas! we carefully took off our watches and rings, and the few trinkets and little valuables one cared for most, and put them by in our cabins, as we *thought*, in safety. Then we sallied forth *en masse*, without hats,— for it was a very sultry stifling night,—and had a pleasant walk over the fields for about three-quarters of an hour before we reached the magnificent Temple. It has gigantic pylons, and a huge square, with an interior peristyle of thirty-two columns; then comes a splendid portico of lofty and richly carved pillars, which looked mysteriously beautiful in the strong lights from the torches, and the deep black conflicting shadows thrown by the bright moonbeams: then we mounted on the roof, in order to survey the wide extent of the Temple, and looked down on the great courts, into which burning wood was thrown to show us, though dimly, their depth and width. The view thence, too, in the calm clear moonlight, was serenely pretty; from the lofty platform on which we stood we looked over the village, which lay in a hollow below us, over a mile or so of field between us and the river bank, and then across the river, shining in silver lustre, to the dark dim mountains on the other side. The bank was much too high to admit of our seeing the dahabiehs, but we remarked to each other that the sailors had lit a more than usually large fire on the bank, by the light of which our flags were gaily illuminated; but in another minute that seemingly trifling idea was forgotten. We lingered a little in the Temple, and then walked quickly through the village, stopping only to observe a circle of Derwishes performing a *zikr*, or sacred dance; about twenty of them joined hand in hand, jerking their

bodies forward with a short sudden start, as fast as possible, violently nodding the head with every movement,
first over one shoulder, then over the other, making
with each jerk a loud harsh grunt, exactly like a London
paviour, only that instead of being expressed with his
slow stolidity, this sound was flung out with passionate
excitement. Achmet, however, begged us not to loiter
watching them, as the Edfou people are very fanatical,
and might take umbrage at Frank inspection : so we
went slowly on through the fields, enjoying the quiet
silence of the hot night, and the bright moonbeams
playing on the picturesque figures of the sailors accompanying us : alas, this pleasant half-hour was but the
calm before the storm ! we were within but a few yards
of the bank, when the sailors in front made some loud
exclamations, and rushed up the steep slope—Achmet and
all of us ran forward . . . . .   and looked down
. . . . . on what had been our beautiful boat—our
little home—now a *mass of flame!* roaring and crackling with that terrible, long-to-be-remembered noise,—
the devouring tongues of flame licking round the sides
of the vessel—hissing in sudden quenchings upon the
water—running in fine darting lines up the ropes—clinging round the masts—and, over all, the gay flag and the
red and white streamer flying out in the fierce draught,
redder and prettier than ever, in a sort of demoniac
dance of triumph at his own illumination, till a higher
and still higher tongue of flame leaped up and shrivelled
it into black nothingness ! It is easy to describe it even
now—for I have but to close my eyes, and the whole
thing, living and horrible in its reality, comes only too
vividly before me, burned into my memory. The dragoman of the other boat, the Tayr el Nil, and a few of
our sailors, now that we were at hand to see them, were

throwing up some small basinfuls of water upon the flames, which could be of no use at all,—the others stood passively looking on, only exclaiming, "Mash-allah, Mash-allah!" except 'Ali, the sailors' cook-boy, who was crying bitterly. Not a single thing had been thrown out from the inside of the boat, except the sailors' own bread and their bundles of clothes; nothing of ours had they attempted to save, but, on the contrary, had held back our maid by force when she tried, with the courage of an English-woman, to rush into the burning vessel and save my sister's desk which was in the outer cabin, containing money and some valuables. Within a quarter of an hour after our return the masts had disappeared, and the flames sunk down with sullen satiety into the hull, where alone there was anything left to consume; and we stood upon that bank absolutely bereft of every-thing—without home, food, clothes, or money, among a strange and savage people, three thousand miles away from home, and at some five hundred miles from the nearest spot where any of our wants could be supplied, with no means of getting there, apparently without friends or help! Who could describe the forlornness of such a position, or the overwhelming feelings that rushed over our sinking hearts? Such circumstances must be experienced to be understood; and were I to try to tell of even a part of the present loneliness or the dim vista of future difficulties and dangers, it would but appear exaggerated to those who have not gone through something of the kind; God alone knows what it was to us; even as His Arm alone could support us under the trial.

But in this hour of direst need, help and friends were —God be thanked —close at hand. The Mr. Jacksons, whose boat had arrived at the same time as our own at

Edfou, insisted on our coming at once on board their
dahabieh, and immediately, with the most generous
kindness, devoted the whole of the inner cabins to the
use of ourselves and our maid, and placed their stock
of clothes, linen, stores, and all other necessaries, at
our disposal. With these, and other kind gifts received
from several of the boats we afterwards encountered,
and which were always pressed upon us with the most
liberal kindness, we managed to get through the seven
weeks that elapsed before we reached Cairo, not quite
in rags, and in some degree of comfort,—although, of
course, the want of constant change of clothes is a great
privation in a hot country, and necessarily there were
scores of things wanting which not even the kindest
ingenuity could supply in a boat and outfit originally
furnished only to supply the wants of two gentlemen ; to
say nothing of the distress of feeling to what discomfort
our intrusion must have reduced our kind hosts, exclud-
ing them from the principal part of the boat, and changing
all their own comfortable arrangements by the occupation of five persons in a dahabieh only adapted for two.
But from Edfou to Cairo no one effort was ever spared
by them to make us forget our own losses, or to assure
us that their comfort and convenience were not only
willingly but gladly sacrificed to ours, by those who were
comparative strangers, with whom we had only been
acquainted three or four weeks, by meeting occasionally
here and there on the Nile.

No fellow Christians, under the circumstances, could
have refused to give us an asylum in their boat at the
time, but the manner in which the hospitality was
rendered made all the difference in the world to us;
and, anomalous as our position could not help being, it
was a good deal to be assured that we were not looked

upon as intruders, but were really welcome. We
had hoped to have found at Thebes a boat of some
kind, in which we could have descended the river to
Cairo, with some of our sailors and our own dragoman; but there was not even an Arab kandjeh to be
had, and our friends foresaw that we might find ourselves very unpleasantly situated had the dragoman
taken the opportunity of our separation from Europeans
to demand promissory notes of payment for his boat;
we thought our man-servant was sufficient protection
against this, but they decided that it was better we
should not risk it: failing this we felt sure there
would be some large dahabieh at Thebes, with ladies
on board, willing to make a spare cabin for us; but
no such offer came; one young lady lent us all she
could spare of the clothes we so much needed; and
Mrs. Hood, who was still at Thebes, shared with us
everything she possessed with the most unselfish kindness; but from the boats then at Luxsor no other lady
broke through the formalities of lacking an "introduction" to Englishwomen in distress; and we found
our country*men* far more generous and thoughtful for
us than our country*women;* all *their* little stores of
handkerchiefs, brushes and combs, needles and threads,
&c. &c., were brought out and pressed upon us, and
one gentleman even sent us shawls and green veils!

There was one very large dahabieh with a small
party on board, which came down the river to Luxsor
while we were there: — they offered nothing of their
own accord, but in our utter distress for some of the
common necessaries that gentlemen could not supply,
we ventured to send our maid on board to ask for some
common materials requisite for making up the clothes
we had contrived out of Arab cotton; the reply to this

our first essay in the art of begging was — the gift of *one hook and eye!* We sought for nothing more from that boat.

In contrast to this, another lady who was at Assouân when the news of our misfortune reached her, immediately prepared with her own hands every article of clothing she could possibly spare, packed them up together and kept them ready in hourly hopes of overtaking us, or of finding some quicker means of sending them to us! Unfortunately their dahabieh was detained by the same winds that detained us, and it was not till her arrival in Cairo, a week later than ours, that we knew of, or could profit by, her true hearty kindness.

It was not at first that we fully realised how great our loss had been; our penniless condition, *forced* to accept the hospitality, however kindly bestowed, by our companions and friends, was painful enough; so was the heavy loss in money, clothes, &c., and the necessity of replacing the latter at prices three times their value in Cairo : but besides this, we had a really valuable stock of books on board, and — still more valuable to us because irreplaceable — all our journals, notes, and our little collections of antiquities bought at various places — all our drawings and sketches, and, alas ! many a dearly loved little treasure of past days, which neither time nor money can ever replace. Not then, nor for very long afterwards, did we really know the length and depth of our losses — losses which we still feel sometimes sadly enough.

The cause of the fire was briefly this : our maid, who had been left in the boat, went out, as she usually did in the evenings, to walk for a few minutes on the bank : she had been ironing till dark in the stern cabin, and had hung up a quantity of clothes on lines across it;

on leaving it she omitted to lock the door behind her,
and 'Ali, the sailors' cook-boy, seized the opportunity of
going in, with a light in his hand, to steal money out of
the man-servant's coat, which was hanging up inside, or
perhaps to pilfer the store-bags of nuts, raisins, &c.,
which were there also. We learned afterwards that he
had stolen money twice before from the servants, but
Achmet had always entreated that we might not be informed of this, saying that 'Ali (for whom, as well as
for all the sailors, he was answerable) must be caught
in the very act of stealing. He was strictly forbidden
to enter the cabins at all, but unhappily the fatal
opportunity was now afforded him, while the Reïs was
at his prayers, and the few sailors left on board were
performing their evening ablutions: the draught from
the open window probably blew the hanging clothes
into his candle, and seeing the flames all round him,
he rushed out screaming, "What will become of me!
I am undone, undone! I have set fire to the ship!" and
in another minute the flames burst out of the windows.
These words of 'Ali's were translated *at the very moment*
by Mr. Jackson's dragoman to our maid as she stood
on the bank: Achmet afterwards denied all this when
he got to Cairo, and gave out several stories, each one
differing from the other, to account for the disaster.
'Ali, who was a bad specimen of the lowest Egyptian
people, with a cunning, dishonest countenance, was
taken up three times for stealing before we left Cairo,
and we knew ourselves that neither Achmet nor 'Ali
were very particular as to truth.

Our dragoman and man-servant both sat up all night
to watch by the burned boat, and to keep off the
villagers; and with the first dawn another dahabieh (the
"Titania") came up; two of the gentlemen in her joined

our friends in superintending the digging through,
and the careful sifting of the ashes from the inside of
the boat; a party of Arab boys were organized for this
dirty work, who laboured intelligently and industriously
enough throughout the day, only stopping occasionally
over the irresistible temptation of a roasted potato, or
broiled fig, as they turned them up; or a pot of
marmalade, into which they plunged their dirty fingers
to suck off the jam, with great glee, ashes and all. A
few sovereigns and some melted metal were recovered,
and the works of my watch (of which the case was found
curiously enough at some distance from the works),
melted into a shapeless mass; a small box of silver
ornaments, tightly packed in cotton wool, which had
preserved them in perfect freshness, were the only other
things found — a melancholy mockery to us, in want of
all necessaries, was their silvery brightness shining in
the ashes, so prettily useless; complete and fierce
had been the fire, and rapid too — for the dry sun-
heated boat burned like paper; but a good deal might
have been saved in the first few moments, had any one
of sense been at hand; and the sailors would probably
have worked well and usefully had they been properly
directed.

We had not either heart or head enough to revisit
the Temple of Edfou, nor indeed had we much leisure
for anything but trying to repair our losses, as far as we
could, by adapting the various contributions we had
received to our use. Our boat, which looked like a long
green coffin with its painted hull just showing above
the water, all black and charred within, and the words
"Wandering Maiden" still gaily painted on the outside,
preceded us down the river, carrying our dragoman
and sailors; the owner of the "Titania" had kindly

given a passage to our man-servant, for there was not a
spare inch in the " Tayr el Nil; " and we stopped
at Esneh only long enough to make a report of our loss
to the worthy Kashef, or governor of the district, and
to obtain a quantity of miserable Arab calico, after a
long, weary bargaining in the bazaar. At El Kab we
also made a halt, and rode to the rock-tombs, but we
were so much worn out and stupefied that I can recall
nothing about them, beyond the general impression that
they were well worth seeing.

Early in the morning of Sunday the 20th we reached
Luxsor, where we had the comfort of attending the
Church service, read by two clergyman at Mustapha's
home, to a congregation of nearly forty English persons.
There were, I think, *ten* dahabiehs at Luxsor on that
day ; and it required some little courage to face that congregation, even in the wilds of Egypt, in our destitute
condition ; this was, indeed, fully attested by our soiled
dresses, half-burnt shawls, and old shooting caps — a
most useful contribution to our wardrobes, given to us
by one of the gentlemen we had met, and which we had
covered with muslin, to give them a somewhat more
lady-like appearance.   Alas, our nice large shady hats
had been burned : and only those who have been in a
country of hot sun can imagine how much we missed
them afterwards ; nor had I even a pair of boots or
shoes, — I had gone out that evening, for it was very
hot, in a pair of linen slippers, and I had nothing else
but these to walk in over the sands, stones, and rocks
of Egypt all the seven weeks that elapsed between our
fire and our reaching Cairo.

CHAP. V.

ETERNAL THOUGHT IN IMPERISHABLE STONE.

" With God's elect in every age
And every race — the Athenian sage,
And all those ancients who perceived
And lived the truth they had received,
In old Osirian mystery,
In Bouddha, Balder — holding pure
That Faith through man's self-will obscure,
And selfless ones for Hell decreed
By men, because they lacked a creed."
Hon. Roden Noel.

A BIRD skimming through the smoky sky of London, perching on this steeple or on that, here and there peering into a window, or picking a few crumbs in one street or in another, would have an endless tale of wonder to relate to the mate he left at home in his country nest; but the town-bred sparrow would not have much respect for the accuracy with which he described even the external architecture of the immense city—and of all that was " underneath the eaves," what would he know? Just as much as a traveller, lingering his longest possible on the green plain of Thebes, may fancy he knows of even the ruins of that ancient City, whose stones and walls are laid in desolate heaps upon the ground, whose statues and obelisks are now shapeless masses, and whose history is looked upon, but not read, by eyes that are unwillingly blinded by ignorance. The devotion of a long life is but sufficient for the understanding of a very little of what has gone before, — while much labour, much thought, and much study is indispensable for the comprehension of even the broken materials that lie there still. For only this latter object, we had endeavoured to prepare ourselves with some months of careful study, — although neither expecting, nor even hoping to have attained much; but the unfortunate disaster, described in my last chapter, cleared everything but its own troubles out of our heads, and produced such a numbing effect upon our minds and memories, that when, four days after, we began to examine the ruins of Thebes, we found it difficult enough to command our thoughts, and next to impossible to exert our memories of previous readings: present discomforts and small anxieties and awkwardnesses are sad hindrances to thought and study. A graver loss, both in itself and because they would have more than replaced our faded memories, was the loss of all our books, and the notes we had made in preparation for seeing the realities themselves, as well as various other useful maps, plans, &c., only intelligible on the spot, and with which we had been amply provided. From the want of books it was hard, more than hard, to profit even by what we saw; we were too much dispirited to recommence journals, &c., and we had no strength to spare for sketches of any kind, even had we had any materials. The shadowy memory of a bird's-eye view, is, therefore, all I have to offer to my readers; such as it is, I must let it go, trusting only, as I do for every other page I have written, that it may succeed in building up some faint picture of the reality before the minds of those who stay at home, — and, what is much more important, that it may induce others to go and see for themselves.

Ancient Thebes stretched across the whole plain
which we now see at each side of the river Nile; but
the principal part of the city was on the east bank, and
only the royal palaces and temples were placed on the
western side, which was otherwise occupied by the Tombs
of the dead. The city was never enclosed by walls, and
the "hundred gates" sung of by Homer, are supposed
to have alluded to the portals of a hundred Temples, if,
indeed, it was anything beyond a figure of speech.
Thebes is believed to have been a great city, even before
the invasion of that hated race of Shepherds, who ruled
the country for several hundred years; but about 1500
years before Christ, the Theban kings expelled the
Shepherds, and their city then became the capital of all
Egypt,.both Upper and Lower, and continued to be so
for a thousand years; this thousand years contains all
that is most brilliant and glorious in the most ancient
history of the world. The removal of the throne to
Saïs in Lower Egypt caused the decline of Thebes, and
the invasion of Cambyses, the Persian conqueror, in B.C.
525, threw her into ruins, the last magnificence of
which were crumbled into their present condition by
the siege of Ptolemy Lathyrus, in B.C. 116, when the
Thebans had revolted from the yoke of the Romans.
It is with the thousand years of the glory of Thebes
that we have to do in the examination of the ruins that
now lie upon the verdant plain; would we could rebuild
in our minds even a dream of their former splendour!

The enormous quantity of mud — the source of all
the riches of Egypt — brought down every year by the
river, gradually raises its bed: the water consequently
extends slowly but surely over the plain, and leaves
behind it a certain amount of soil; so, like the sand
gathering round the feet of the Desert Temples, the green

herbs wave higher and higher round the ruins of Thebes:
and thus, year by year, the two great Colossi seem to
be sinking gradually down among the young grasses of
the plain. These two, sitting, like the Sphynx, wrapped
in the silent mystery of unnumbered years, are the
first objects that attract one's view from the deck of
one's dahabieh: scarcely changing in the varying light
of morning and evening, they are always, and from
every view, the same—grand, calm, and almost sublime
—their very ruin making them more mysteriously fine,
in contrast to the perfect tranquillity of repose—not
idleness, but the rest earned by long labour—expressed
in their impressive figures. One's first and last impres-
sions of Thebes are hung upon those two broken but
noble statues. Both represent Amunoph III.* (the pre-
decessor by a thousand years of Rameses the Great),
whose virtues and greatness are thus emphasised, as is
always the case in Egypt, by reduplication and superhuman size. Behind them a stone causeway, of which
the two Colossi were the outer sentinels, stretched back
for eleven hundred feet, with pairs of statues and
sphynxes at every few steps, up to the palace-temple of
the same Amunoph; scarcely anything now remains of
it. The Colossus that was anciently so famous for the
sweet sounds emitted at morning, was destroyed to the
waist, it is said, by the barbarian Cambyses†: it has

* Other opinions are, that the one covered with Greek inscriptions is
that of Amunoph, but that the second represents his Prime-Minister,
whose magnificent tomb is shown in the Valley of the Dead: it contains two very grand sitting figures of himself and his wife, besides some
exquisite bas-reliefs of hieroglyphics. His name is said to have been
Shammar; the Arabs call the colossi Dammar and Shammar, and also
Balamât — salutations — an evident allusion to the musical sounds so
famous in tradition.

† Strabo says it was destroyed by an earthquake — the one seems as
probable as the other.

been rudely built up since with roughly hewn stones. The sounds are supposed to have been caused by a man, hidden in the huge lap of the statue, striking a hammer upon a stone which still lies there, and which rings like the sarcophagus of Suphis, and many other Egyptian stones. As the whole of this Libyan bank of the river was dedicated peculiarly to Athor, the Aphrodite of the Egyptians and the "president of the west," the Colossus, who surveyed the plain, could do no less than greet with a harmonious salutation the first rays of that sun, who was to sink at evening into the arms of his divine mistress. Standing, as it were, underneath his knees, are the figures of Amunoph's wife and mother, sculptured on the throne, as at Abou Simbil; the wife also re-appears between his feet; while, on the throne, the god Nilus is represented holding some of the plants that then grew in his bosom far away, but which he now annually leaves around the feet of the statue—like flowers laid upon a grave.

The great palace-temple of Rameses II. is the first ruin visited on this western bank; it has been commonly called the Memnonium, from a confusion caused by the title of Mi-Ammoun belonging to Rameses the Great, but it is more rightly called the Rameseum; the expression *palace-temple* does not, at least in this instance, mean that the king and his court resided in the Temple, but only that rooms were attached to it where the king may have retired in the intervals of his own devotions, or after receiving the offerings of his people; and he may also have held his receptions in the grand courts or halls of assembly of the Temple; the Rameseum was called by Diodorus the "tomb of Osimandyas" (Rameses); but it is not quite this, the dead king's actual tomb*

* No. 7.

was in the mountain side, towards the setting sun,
and this Temple is consecrated only to his *memory*;
and here, therefore, as in a few other Temples, there is
no sanctuary or adytum appropriated to the image of a
particular god. The Pyramids had each of them a small
Temple on their eastern side, consecrated to the dead
who lay beneath them; and the Rameseum bears the
same relation to the mountain Tomb of the king, as the
memorial Temple bore to the Pyramid.

The Rameseum is one of the finest and most complete
of all these ruins; the noble pylons are still standing,
with a good deal of the first and second courts, including
the fine interior peristyle of the latter, which once contained eight Osiride pillars, and two splendid statues,
the head of one of which is now in the British Museum;
besides these there is nearly all the beautiful hypostyle
hall, which, though small in comparison to that of
Karnak, is very fine. The sculptures here are more
than commonly interesting: they are boldly and well
executed, chiefly of battle scenes, some of them even
more densely crowded with figures than Tintoret's
famous "Paradiso" at Venice, but every figure is left
perfectly clear and distinct; they illustrate the different modes of warfare, the varieties of kingdoms and
peoples overcome by the great conqueror, with the king
returning thanks to the gods for their assistance, while
his deeds are noted down by Thoth: he is here given by
the gods the sword and the sceptre — the one for his enemies and the other for his people, while the goodness of
the king's character, which has rendered him the favoured
son of the gods, is indicated by the stream of "pure life"
poured upon his head by them; and so vivid is the interest raised in one's mind by these graphically portrayed
historic scenes, that one turns with double curiosity to

the mysteriously shattered colossal statue of the hero of
every incident graven there, which lies close by, un-
questionably a real, true portrait; it is about the same
size as those of the pair sitting on the plain, but cut in a
finer stone, — one cannot conceive how such a block was
transported here, carved or uncarved, from Assouân — it
is nearly as large and heavy as the famous stone still
lying in the quarry at Baalbek: but this huge mass once
wore the same noble and beautiful features as the giant
faces at Abou Simbil, and that of the fallen hero lying
in the mud at Mitrahenny (Memphis).

Then comes the beautiful old temple at Gourneh, of
the great warrior Sethi, or Osirei I., completed by his
son Rameses II., — perhaps the most venerable looking
of all the Theban ruins; it has a sad and melancholy
air about it, but the sculptures are very interesting.
There are two pylons, one beyond the other, from each
of which an avenue of sphynxes led to the temple, where
a corridor of very elegant columns bears the dedication
of the Temple to Amoun-Ra, the king of the gods, by
Rameses II., who appears afterwards introduced by his
father Osirei to the gods, among whom his grandfather
Rameses I. is standing, bearing the insignia of Osiris, as
a dead king now with, or absorbed into Osiris. This
Temple lies to the north of the plain. Far away at the
southern extremity is the magnificent pile of buildings
now called Medeenet Habou, the palace and temple
of Rameses III., who reigned about a hundred years
later than Rameses the Great. This is probably the
largest ruin in Egypt. There is here a temple with all
the usual pylons, courts, sanctuary, &c.; and then another mass of towers, pavilions, courts, halls, and pylons,
in one immense heap of confused ruin. The sculptures here, retaining the most vivid freshness of colour,

are perhaps, on the whole, the most varied and interesting
to be met with. Many pages would be required to give
even a faint idea of their subjects; one open court alone
with an interior peristyle, 123 feet by 133, is completely
surrounded with battle and other scenes depicted in the
liveliest manner possible. Every column also is painted
in beautiful patterns, and, although these columns are
but three diameters in height, the *tout ensemble* is one
of the grandest things in ancient art. At Medeenet
Habou, every thing connected with the king may be
seen and studied together; his leisure hours and his
amusements in his court at home, his state processions
abroad, are closely detailed in the walls of this palace,
while on those of the towers and huge areas are all his
noble deeds, and his religious ceremonials and duties.
Unfortunately, within the latter the Copts made their
cathedral, and the houses of their village filled up the surrounding ruins : much therefore has been sadly spoiled
and intentionally mutilated, though they happily preserved many of the sculptures in their original brightness by concealing them under a plaster of mud. One
cannot help fancying what grand cathedrals these beautiful hypæthral courts must have made, however incongruous the mixture of the past and the present.

Here Rameses III. dedicates all these buildings to
his great father the god Amoun-Ra, who calls him his
" friend," and, in company with other gods, presents
him with the scythe wherewith to conquer and cut off
all his enemies. The warrior king is then seen fighting
his battles, after which he returns in triumph, leading, or
rather dragging, his enemies by their hair, to show them
to the gods, to whom also he makes rich thank-offerings,
gratefully receiving their praises : his conquests have
been innumerable, and his god-given virtues are nearly

as many; his new subjects assure him that he " reigns like a mighty sun in Egypt," — that his " courage is like that of the griffin — our breath is thine, as well as our lives, which are for ever in thy power," — while he declares that he has but obeyed the command of Amoun-Ra, and conquered by the might of his god-given strength. The coronation of the king is also seen, and, while he offers incense to the protecting gods, carrier pigeons announce his greatness in all the four quarters of the world. The king also gains a great victory at sea, assisting his fleet of finely drawn ships by manœuvres on shore: to this fresh conquest he declares himself inspired by the spirit of Amoun-Ra, who has thus " laid the whole world at his feet."

Not far from the ruins of the royal palaces of Medeenet Habou, the remains of an artificially made lake are distinctly discerned like that at Memphis : across this lake the corpses of the king and of all the nobles of the city were ferried with grand processions of boats, before they were drawn on sledges along the dreary valley, opening in the mountain range at whose feet we stand, to their " eternal habitations." We will delay speaking of them till we have glanced over the rest of the city of Thebes.

Luxsor, being now a market town of some small dignity, has clustered its miserable houses within and without the once beautiful ruins of its Temple, and it is almost impossible to see them with any very intelligible understanding of their plan : one can only perceive that it is a fine and picturesque ruin. One beautiful obelisk (sister to that in Paris), still marks the site of the once proud city, — it is the oldest and most interesting of all the obelisks in Egypt, for it bears the name of Sesortasen the Great, of the twelfth dynasty, — (the king in

whose reign the wonderful tombs of Beni-Hassan were
hewn and painted) — and perhaps it stood there before
Moses refused to be called the son of Pharaoh's daughter
— perhaps even before Joseph was brought into the
land of Egypt by the Bedouin! yet the characters engraved upon its sides are as clear now as they were five
or six thousand years ago, and one may well be excused
for the fancy that the stone is as imperishable as the
idea conveyed on it. These two obelisks commenced
an avenue of *twelve hundred* giant ram-headed Sphynxes,
which led from Luxsor to the pylon of the first temple
of Karnak, each standing on a pedestal; hundreds of
these have been destroyed, but many, headless and
broken, still border the empty path down which the long
and gorgeous procession of priests, clad in panther skins,
passed daily, carrying the ram-prowed barge containing
the shrine of the god in whose honour the festival of the
day was held, before whom burning incense was borne;
several of these Sphynxes are at Turin — very many at
St. Petersburg — some in Berlin, and one or two in
England. Another avenue of Sphynxes led from the
front of this Temple to the bank of the river, overlooking Gourneh, and a third led in a southerly direction
towards Luxsor.

The first Temple reached at Karnak is a very complete
and fine one, approached by another Sphynx avenue —
but one cannot linger here in one's impatience to see
the grand Temple itself, a few minutes further on. Two
giant pylons open into a large court, with columns on
two sides, and an aisle of columns up the centre, leading
into the famous hypostyle hall, which Fergusson calls
" the greatest of man's architectural works;" the centre
aisle is formed of twelve columns, sixty-two feet high,
the largest if not the tallest columns in the world, with

sixty-one smaller columns on each side of them ; a beautiful clerestory runs along the top of each first row of the
lower columns, and may have supported a stone roof
over the middle aisle, as in the Rameseum : the rest was
probably hypæthral, — some suppose it to have been
covered in with hangings either of stuffs or of palm-leaf
matting, but as ample shade must have been found
beneath the very closely placed columns, even had it been
hypæthral, one cannot help hoping that the blue sky
was open to the worshippers within, — so beautiful is the
effect of the sunlight and the shade of the columns falling athwart the apparently innumerable pillars. This
is the place to see what a complete tapestry the hieroglyphics formed — here not an inch of wall or column
is left uncovered with closely sculptured figures, once of
brilliant colours — as complete a covering for the stone
as the marble inlay of a Damascene house, or the
brocade pattern of a modern house paper, — strange to
say, *every column* has the same set repeated in rings all
round it ! but though so subordinate a feature, their
sameness probably adds to the feeling of infinite space,
as the eye is not attracted by any change of object, and
therefore wanders on indefinitely among the mighty
forest of 6420 square yards.   Behind this and the
slender rose-granite obelisks, happily still erect, is the
fine hall and adytum of this Temple : then comes, within
the same outer enclosure, the palace of Thothmes III.,
where the hall is supported by alternate rows of square
and round pillars with reversed capitals; in one of the
many chambers behind it the valuable list of the sixty
predecessors of Thothmes was found sculptured, which is
now in Paris. Deeply interesting indeed are the splendid
sculptures that cover the great walls throughout this
pile of buildings, portraying the history of a thousand

conquests, — among them that of the land of Palestine,
with its name of *Canaan* and *Yooda Melchi* — the
Judah kingdom, conquered by Shishak or Sheshonk in
971 B.C.

Numbers of other ruins of great interest lie scattered
around this great Temple, in strange but picturesque
variety, among palm groves and verdant fields; and it is
pleasant to wander from one to the other, and rest one's
mind, oppressed with the stupendous ideas generated
by these ruins, so sublimely expressed in the stone and
pictured in the sculptures, while listening to the evening breeze among the palms, and the melancholy
chaunt of the fellāh, and watching the flocks of exquisite, tiny paroquets, with shining green feathers and
crimson bills, flitting about in the sweet air. And it is
right to linger — for this is truly one of the grandest
scenes that earth can show; Athens, with all the delicate refinements of comparatively modern days, stands
smiling like a white dove pluming herself on the summit of her noble rock, a pæan of war still echoing
round her white statues, — Palmyra, far away in the
silence and solitude of Nature's wildest and most impressive splendour, sings sweetly to herself the sad
elegy of her own dead glory, — but Karnak, with no
natural beauty save the ever cloudless sky and the
delicious air over the fresh green palm groves and the
yellow sand, closes down upon the mind with a grand
and almost awful solemnity; and the feeling comes over
one, that while in the others the chivalry and poetry of
life were solidified in stone, you have here the expression
of man's deepest religion. I have often thought since,
that Athens told of the bright and hopeful ardour of
the busy morning, — Palmyra of the lovely tenderness
of beauteous evening, — and Karnak, of the calm and

holy night, in closer communion with all beyond this world.

Let us now go slowly down over the fields, through the groups of trees to the river bank, and, crossing the wide grey stream, land on the western side, threading the green paths between the rich fields of waving dhourra, till we reach the low mountain range at the back of the plain: here, turning a little to the right, we enter a narrow defile which the Arabs call the Biban el Molook, or Valley of the Kings; it ought rather to be called the Valley of the *Shadow* of Death, for the *reality* of Death is further on. The winding ravine is an absolute Desert of loose stones, with steep rocky sides, broken, jagged, and crumbling, of bright yellow and orange cliffs, with here and there a blackened, burnt-up summit: it is not high enough to be very grand, but it is utterly and intensely desolate and dreary,—nothing can be more solitary and silent—not a bird nor a moving insect is to be seen—not a sound of any kind heard; it is generally painfully hot and glaring, and forms a fit passage to the Land of Death beyond.

After a ride of about an hour, the valley opens to a somewhat greater width; here every rock and hill-side is honeycombed with excavations, receding back to the extent of from two to four hundred feet—chamber succeeds to chamber, passage to passage: nearly all slope downwards as they recede; some have staircases cut down to much lower levels, as if to sink the body of the deceased lower and lower under the crust of the mountain,—but the reason was probably to avoid faults in the rock. The larger chambers are supported on pillars left in the excavation, but smoothed over for the reception of hieroglyphics; some have divans round a few of the chambers : the sarcophagus rarely remains ; in some it was buried in a pit, and carefully covered over.

The tombs in this valley appear to have been entirely devoted to kings and royal personages, whose bodies were probably concealed in secret passages, lest avarice should lead to the plunder of the tomb, and the sacred person of the King be discovered : the Egyptians seem to have considered that the body might at some time be reclaimed, and, at any rate, they regarded what had once contained the divine spark of any man as sacred ; it was therefore carefully embalmed and laid by with some of his regal ornaments, a list of his possessions, and a roll of prayers written on papyrus. This set of tombs are all of the Theban Kings of the XIXth and XXth dynasties : sometimes a king of later days has taken the place of one of his predecessors, when his name is seen to be marked in a different style to the rest of the sculptures. Near Medeenet Habou is a small valley, containing the Tombs of the queens ; while beyond those of the kings are the Tombs of priests and rich men, in a place called the valley of Assaseef. It is believed that among these Tombs some were excavated and ornamented with sculptures appropriate to the solemn place — with the lessons for the living drawn from the life of the Dead, and the hopes and fears of the future : blanks were left for the names and peculiar titles or biography of the individual who afterwards bought the Tomb, which were filled up at the time of his death,—some remain still unfilled, and some tombs are supposed never to have been occupied, save by the bodies of the modern dead, thrust in, in after times. The roofs of these Tombs are generally lined with crude brick, and covered with stucco, as are the walls on which the hieroglyphics are painted. Over the portal of each is painted the great red disk of the sun, signifying that the soul of the deceased is gone down into the darkness with him, and, after traversing the shades, will ultimately rise up with him again. Near the entrance you find the scarabæus (the emblem of the resurrection), and the crocodile (the emblem of darkness); while *beyond* the sarcophagus you come to the young Horus, son of Osiris, the Divine Man, who again signifies the resurrection.

It is impossible to give an idea of the immense variety of the sculptures which tapestry the walls of these tombs, and, happily, it is unnecessary to do so, as so many excellent descriptions are already published of them : suffice it to say, that they illustrate every trade, profession, manufacture, occupation, and custom of the ancient Egyptians, besides the religious and royal ceremonials, and the minutest details of the burying of the kings and the nobles : the tombs of private individuals are still more generally interesting.*

The chief thought made present to one's mind in examining the Temples and Palaces of the Egyptian kings, is their (natural) pride in the extension and glory of their conquests : the next is the perception of how invariably every triumph and every blessing was acknowledged as bestowed by the supreme God, the Father and Giver of all good. At every moment throughout his life we find the king honouring, reverencing, and, per-

* The tombs best worth seeing among those of the kings are Nos. 17, 11, 6, 14, and 9; the magnificent tomb of the priest Petumunap, in the valley of Assaseef; that of King Amoun Toonh : Nos. 5, 16, 17, 31, 34, and 35, of those at Goorneh Murraee ; and another among these latter, inhabited by a family of Arabs, and very difficult to crawl into, containing the most varied and lively representations of all kinds of hunting.

haps, propitiating the gods to whom he daily pays his
grateful homage, and to whom he offers up his prayers
for virtue and life, as well as for the throne and power
they have conferred upon him. In death he is portrayed in still closer communion with the gods; the
short and varied term of earthly life appears over, and
the spirit, parted from the body, commences a new and
still more important life, the entrance to which is attended
by the most rigorous difficulties, for the overcoming of
which he has been preparing throughout his earthly
career. And truly to us, this Life in Death seems almost
more comprehensible than that which has come before;
here there are but few signs of ruin and destruction —
we know that all have equally passed away, but the Life
after Death seems nearer to us than the Life before
Death, — the idea of the grave and of judgment is closer
akin to our minds than the old-world customs of the
past, — Death seems a link binding us into one brotherhood, and is, in truth to us, more living than Life.

The awfulness of the future judgment began with
the ancient Egyptians even upon earth [*]; a type of it
was enacted over the dead body, carried across the lake
for burial, by forty-two judges, who each examined the
testimony given of the candidate's innocence or trans-
gression in each of the forty-two sins most common to
man; if the dead man was proved to have been of
an immoral character, whether king, priest, or peasant,
he was refused burial. [†] The mummy is everywhere
entitled "the habitation of Osiris:" it is carried to the
tomb in his boat — his symbols precede and follow it in
procession, and the high priest offers incense to it. The
soul was supposed to sleep during the forty days of

[*] Champollion. Martineau's Eastern Travel, p. 194.
[†] Osburn, Mon. Hist. vol. i. p. 427.

embalming; it then revived again and accompanied
the body to the tomb, where it received liberation. In
the "Book of the Dead" (the Turin copy), Isis and
Nepthys are thus addressed : — "Oh ye liberators of the
souls of them that are built into a house of Osiris"
(that is, made into a mummy), "liberate the soul of
M—— whom ye have made into a house of Osiris :
he sees as ye see, he hears as ye hear, stands as ye
stand, sits as ye sit." The soul is then directed to pay
adoration to Ra, the rising sun, and Athom, the setting
sun. In the illustrations that occur here in this papyrus, the soul * is seen entering the bark of the sun
in the twelfth hour of the day : the disk of the sun is
seen passing the portals of the west, which are opened
by male and female guardians : then the orb of day is
seen to have entered into the cave, where he is received
into the arms of Athom, his human impersonation, while
eight apes shriek forth the impurities of the soul that
accompanies him; after this the soul is seen, arrived in
the world of spirits underground, adoring the souls of
his deceased ancestors, offering them incense and liba-
tions. Afterwards, the adventures of the soul in Hades
are described : they consist of transmigrations into the
forms of many divinities, all of them of the family of
Osiris, who is styled "son of the sun," "the lord of the
cave of Amenti," &c.; the disembodied spirit still navi-
gating a river which represents the nocturnal path of
the sun. It at length reached the grand hall of the
judge of the dead, where his heart is tried in the balance

* The soul is portrayed under the symbol of a bird, usually the white
ibis: it was natural to think " these beautiful white, silent, ghost-like
birds, standing motionless and pensive on the sand-flats, might be the
souls of the departed, waiting the completion of the funeral ceremonies."
— *Osburn.*

(upon which a cyno-cephalus, the emblem of Thoth, the scribe who has recorded his good and evil deeds, is sitting) by Anubis and Horus against the feathers (the emblem of truth and justice), and the sentence is pronounced by Thmee, the goddess of justice, in the presence of Osiris enthroned and holding the emblems of supreme judgment, the crozier and the scourge. The dead were instructed to make deprecations to the divinities presiding there, to the assessors who wear the feathers of truth and justice, and also to the forty-two avengers (represented in the tombs with various heads), who sat with knives ready to inflict torments on those that failed at the balance : thus he says, " I have neither done any sin nor omitted any duty to any man; I have committed no uncleanness; I have not prevaricated at the seat of justice," &c. &c.* If the soul was found really wanting, it is seen sent away in the form of a black or white dog, driven by the servants of Typhon down steeply sloping paths, descending in a Dantesque manner, deeper and deeper, according to his guilt. If the soul was found worthy of acceptation, the goddesses Hathor and Nutpe, deputed by Amoun-Ra, the Creator of the world, poured over him the water of eternal purity and life, and he was believed thenceforth to be reunited, if not absorbed, into the spirit of Osiris, — to have become a part of Osiris †; and in all future offerings made to the god, the soul is remembered as dwelling in Osiris, and, therefore, partaking of the gifts offered to him. At some future time, long after the judgment, three thousand years according to Greek tradition, the justified soul returned to the earth and resuscitated the body; but after many cycles, the final

* Translated by Osburn.   † See page 53.

doom was probably rest with Osiris, the divine lord of spirits and of the spirit world, in whose person they arrived at the indescribable happiness of the presence of Amoun-Ra, the "hidden one," the lord of heaven, from whom he had emanated.

In the Egyptian religion every principle was embodied in some recognised type, under which form it was worshipped as partaking of the Divine nature: thus, the generation of life, the most important, and, to their naturally reverent minds, consequently the most sacred fact in creation — a fact *in* this world but not *of* it — a mystery utterly incomprehensible, and therefore to be the more venerated, — was worshipped in the persons of several gods and goddesses, such as Khem *, the god of generation *par excellence*, Kneph †, Maut, Pasht, Neith, Hathor, Isis, and many others — for each and every god and goddess had a share, as it were, in the Divine power; the vulture, the cat, the lion, the cow, and others, each and all were supposed to typify some Divine attribute, and were therefore considered sacred as *types*, not gods in themselves; probably they were to the Egyptians the less perfect manifestations of the things typified, partaking of the same one Divine nature, and thus truly Divine in themselves : yet it was only that peculiar attribute found in each which united them to Divinity, or had a Divine origin; just as the life which animated them must have been Divinely given. Thus the crocodile was sometimes worshipped

---

* In the 18th dynasty, Khem was erased in the hieroglyphic names, and Amoun-Ra (generator) substituted : Amoun-Ra was not worshipped earlier.

† Kneph is most frequently seen standing in the boat which Horus steers; he is the vivifying *spirit* of God, " brooding over the face of the waters." The serpent is stretched above him, and the ram is peculiarly sacred to him.

as the type of strength; but he was usually consecrated to Typhon as one of the types of evil things, such as darkness. It is somewhat hopeless to determine the *reasons* why the sacred animals were made respectively typical of certain principles, as they occasionally represented contrary ones : the ignorance of natural history at that time may sometimes account for the choice.

There were also deities of each nome or division of the land, and local deities in great variety : but we see signs of the united empire under the great dynasties, in these deities having each other's attributes, while, as Herodotus tells us, Osiris was universally worshipped. The principle of Triads seems to pervade every form of the worship, and is a subject well worthy of study; it is difficult to ascertain the precise idea of the Father, Mother, and Child, but the Triad principle runs through all mythology, and, together with the worship of a God-Man, dying in his strife with Evil, and rising triumphant as the Judge of the Dead, is one of the remarkable evidences that God has been speaking to Man everywhere, and in every age : instead of being, as the school of Volney represent it, an argument against Christianity, such a coincidence is one of the strongest evidences of its truth.

The worship of the king is another instance of the worship of the Divine attribute; he was deputed by the Gods in heaven to rule on earth for them; he was divinely appointed and divinely assisted; a portion of the Divine essence dwelt in the king, *as king*, and was so completely a *part* of the god from whom it came, and so separate from his human nature, that he could offer worship—not to himself, but—to the divinity in him; although, of course, this Divine essence can only be materially pictured by the temporary habitation of his

own human body, holding or wearing Divine symbols.
For this reason the king bore the title of "the son of
the sun"—a title which has been roughly rendered in
our Bible as "Pharaoh,"—*Ph* being the article *the*—
Ra, the sun. The king was High-Priest, and the princes
were necessarily of the priestly order, while the queens
were priestesses to the goddesses. Joseph and Moses,
from their distinguished positions, must have been
priests; and taking what St. Paul says of Moses, that
"he was learned in all the wisdom of the Egyptians,"*
with the fact that Joseph married Asenath, daughter of
Pet-ph-Ra, priest of On†, we may infer that they were
both initiated into the mysteries of Osiris, On being one
of the principal places of the worship of Osiris.

The Egyptians found a spiritual meaning in everything natural, and inculcated this with the deep religious poetry of their grave, calm minds : thus Osiris,
the Father Nile, and Isis, the Mother Earth of Egypt,
were brother and sister as well as husband and wife ;
their life, they taught, is one of perfect, divinely-given
happiness (because perfectly pure and holy), until Evil
or Typhon—that is, all the noxious powers of Nature,
sterility, darkness, and scorching heat—arrives and
murders Osiris, who descends into the nether world,
while the earth remains widowed under the dominion of
Typhon,—that is, dry, burnt up, and sterile. Horus,
the son of Osiris and Isis, the fruit grown upon the earth
after the annual inundation of the river, grows up into
manly strength, struggles with Evil, and, overcoming
him, spreads fertility and blessing once more upon the
soil ; Horus is therefore entitled, "the great deliverer,
the support of the world," and is invested with the

---

* Acts vii. 22.   † Gen. xli. 45.

signs of power and life; his face is as the hawk's, he wears the royal head-dress, and holds the *anch*, the sign of pure life, in his hand.

To mention — for the assistance of travellers — a very few of the chief and most frequently repeated figures, we may speak of — AMOUN-RA the Creator, distinguished by the red disk of the sun, winged, and the feathers on his head: he is the great god of Thebes, the capital of Egypt, which was probably one of the reasons for his being the chief god of all; many others take his name as a prefix. As the name meant *hidden*, he would in his own character express one of the highest religious Ideas, and other divinities would be merged in him, so that, amidst the endless complexities of this idolatrous system, we have a glimpse at times of the Truth of the Divine Unity underlying all. The hawk, signifying omnivision, and the scarabæus, chiefly typical of creation and of the world, were sacred to Amoun-Ra; the complete ball of mud with which the latter surrounds its egg, and which it fashions and rolls away so ingeniously, might well suggest creation: and they seem to have had a fancy about all the beetles being males. It was also distinctly a type of the resurrection, and with this meaning its images were bound in a hundred ways upon every corpse, and painted upon every coffin as the pledge and token of a future life. Still more strongly, and by a beautiful figure, the scarabæus is seen *, as it were, leaning out of heaven, and helping the mummy over the difficulties of the entrance, which, indeed, looks as if they expected the body to be included in the resurrection.

PASHT (corresponding to the Grecian goddess Diana) was the " mother of the gods," and had the vulture

---

* In the Harper's or Bruce's tomb.

H 2

sacred to her as the emblem of maternity, because she was supposed to feed her young with her own blood: this was changed in later times to the pelican. But Pasht in the Tombs is the goddess of fire, and presides over punishments: she is seen standing over souls enveloped in flames, with the sword of vengeance in her hand, and spitting fire upon them; she has a cat's head usually, but sometimes that of a lioness.

Osiris is known by the scourge of punishment for the wicked, and the crozier of acceptance for the righteous; the crozier is often seen held out by the kings to supplicants, just as Ahasuerus held it out to Esther.* He is called the "manifester of good, the lord of life, the lord of spirits," &c.; his legs are swathed, to represent the repose of one who has passed through death.

Isis (whose face is, like that of Osiris, always full of sweetness and dignity) has the sun's disk as the mother of the earth; and, in the character of Athor, the horns of the cow on her head, as the provider of nourishment (milk) for all the world. She is continually represented with the attributes of other goddesses; but as the great goddess, "the mother of the child" (Horus), she is distinguished by the throne as her head-dress, which is one of the hieroglyphs in the name of Osiris: in fact, her name is written similarly to his, but with the female sign, the egg; she has often the vulture as a head-dress, with the asp, and sometimes water-plants, as "the bride of the Nile." She corresponds, when in the Amenti, to Proserpine, but usually her character is that of Ceres.

Neith (corresponding to Minerva) is goddess both of wisdom and of war: she wears the crown of Lower Egypt, and sometimes holds a bow and arrows, but

* Esther iv. 11.

more frequently a sceptre of flowers; while her face is green, signifying the verdure of the fruitful earth. Her great Temple was at Saïs, and over the portal was this remarkable inscription: "I am all that was, is, and shall be, — I proceed from myself, — none have lifted the veil that covers me." The great mysteries of the burial of Osiris were performed on the lake at Saïs by torchlight, with those of Neith as Isis, — whence, says Herodotus, came the Greek Eleusinian mysteries, and the "Thesmophoria."

NUTPE, — wife of Seb, and mother of the gods, — the heaven or firmament; this is the Divine origin of Osiris, from the primæval Mother, the ineffable Darkness, and Time, his father. The figure of Nutpe within the sarcophagus, means that the soul is become as Osiris. In one Tomb *, she surrounds the whole ceiling of a chamber like a winding river, giving birth at one side to the Sun, the form of Day, who is led away by a group of gods along a path which grows shallower till it reaches a lake on the other side, through which he passes, and thence in solitude and darkness returns to the side whence he commenced his course.

SEB corresponds to Saturn as Chronos, Time; an inscription reads: "Saturn, youngest of all the gods, is my father, — I am Osiris;" so the Divine children of Seb constitute the *third order* of gods; for there were three of these orders: 1. the eight Great Gods (according to Herodotus), Amoun, Kneph, &c.; 2. Ra, and his family; 3. the Osiride.

SET † represents Evil: he is brother of Osiris, and the son of Time; he and Horus are sometimes seen pouring the anointing oil over the king, — Horus embraces him,

* No. 9.
† Possibly from this name comes the Arabic *Sheitân*, the devil or Satan.

and Set gives him weapons of war; the king also offers
to, and propitiates the destroyer Set, that he may be
induced to favour the king, and make him his instrument.

One of the most interesting subjects of all in these
Tombs, both for examination and thought, is that of
the Serpent, which meets the eye at every step, and which
evidently speaks a language of deep meaning, which one
longs to hear and understand; it is one, however, about
which, I believe, little is as yet known. These animals
form the most conspicuous and important feature in
every representation of a mystery, or of an unearthly
ceremonial: frequently drawn as in nature, and as
frequently with human heads, male or female; sometimes with many heads, with human legs, some turned
one way, some another; occasionally with lion's paws;
sometimes with a head at each end of the body, and
some growing along the back, or ranges of mummies
supported on it; sometimes — and these are always
grand, giant serpents — they have vulture's wings, and
bear a sun's disk. They are seen in battle with the
gods, and in the end, overcome by them, they lie
wounded and bound. Sometimes there are long rows
of them, each one enwreathing a headless human body,
forming grotesquely-shaped rings; they are painted of
all colours, beautifully striped, mottled, or scaled; they
are also seen lotus-crowned, with human legs, as the
symbol of Kneph, the good spirit, the paternal and
spirit-giving deity. In some Tombs the Serpent commences at the entrance, and winds in countless folds
throughout the whole Tomb to the very end: sometimes
he swallows his own tail in a circle, as the symbol of
eternity. One can only say that they *usually* represent
Evil, and perhaps more peculiarly Moral Evil than the

god Set does.   Coleridge takes the Serpent as symbolis-
ing the understanding; and in some cases this may be
the meaning — " Now the Serpent was more subtle than
any beast of the field."

But with the most accurate knowledge of the meaning
of the hieroglyphics, the scholar still gropes in the dark
respecting their less tangible translation; little more
than has been already read historically from the walls
of Temple and Tomb will probably ever be educed by
the mere hieroglyphist; there is but one method by
which we can ever hope to attain to their spiritual
meaning; the old Greeks — rude, untutored infants in
the days of Egypt's glory — drew from her the first
sparks of that fire which they afterwards refined and
beautified into models for all the world; from the days
when the little band of Egyptians left the mouth of the
Nile to plant a new kingdom on the fair shores of
Greece, down to the thirteen years that Plato studied
at Heliopolis, every Grecian superstructure will be
found to have its foundation in the Egyptian faith :
and only by the light of those who taught the deepest
and highest philosophy of the Greek school, can the
parent principles ever be solved.*   The very gods
bear all the same attributes and functions: Zeus is but
Amoun-Ra, keeping, indeed, his Egyptian name; Seb
turned into Chronos; Phthah into Hephæstos; Pasht
into Artemis; Thoth into Hermes; while Athor, the
lovely lady of the West, the Morning Star, became the
queen of beauty, Venus-Aphrodite.   True, the Greeks
threw a poetic veil over them, and re-created them, as it
were, with a new and fresh beauty which made them
peculiarly their own; yet not the less is every deep

---

* Doubtless the Greeks owed much also to the Phœnicians; but it is
impossible to say how much the Phœnicians owed to the Egyptians.

and holy idea of the Grecian mythology essentially and
originally Egyptian.

> There came a day in Egypt's shadeless land,
> When, floating on the bosom of old Nile,
> We stood between the walls of ancient Thebes
>   And noble Karnak's stately pile.

> The " hundred gates " of Thebes are crumbled down,
> And nought remains of all her splendid ways,
> Save some few mounds with green and waving corn —
>   (The veil by Time laid o'er her glorious days)—

> And endless ruins, in sublime decay,
> Of Palace-Temples rich in sculptured strife,
> And Tombs — where closed in everlasting rock,
>   Death now outliveth human life.

> Across the swiftly flowing stream we passed
> To gaze on Karnak's many-columned hall —
> That vast hypæthral fane, whose beauty proud
>   Never on thoughtful mind can pall.

> Slowly the silent, ruined splendour sinks
> Upon the heart, while gathering shades *will* throng
> Of Past and Present time, confused in one
>   Imaginative memory strong.

> The living heart recalls in mortal guise
> The ancient hearts that throbbed and fluttered there,
> Their sorrow and their joy, bright hope and fear,
>   Their calm and strife, faith and despair.

> While still those mighty columns proudly stand —
> Outpassing human lives, yet lifeless things —
> In grand disdain of those whose names they bear,
>   Long buried dust — once mighty Kings.

> Three thousand years lie o'er each silent grave —
> The shroud alike of evil and of good,—
> And Death is but the link that binds us all
>   In one long chain of brotherhood.

> And now *we* come from then unpeopled isles,
> With hearts as apt to throb as those of old;
> The same brief joys, bright hopes, and dark despairs,
>   The same long strife for victory cold.

We strive to cast the Present day aside,
And live again with these bright pictured shades,—
The insolence of Life o'ercomes the Past —
    We grasp them — as the vision fades.

But higher links unite eternal souls,
Remembering how th' Egyptian loved to pray,
Where God's own sky his grateful vision met,—
    Sublime by night — more grand by day.

For we too kneel beneath that unchanged sky,
That same Jehovah from our hearts adore,
Our Judge and theirs of evil and of good —
    Saviour and Friend to us still more.

On storied walls their kingly strife we see
God-ordered, and their victories God-given,
While all alike their deathless souls prepared
    To gain th' unpictured joys of Heaven.

Oh ye who linger 'neath the welcome shade
Of this time-honoured and time-ruined fane,
Unite your living souls with these of old
    The eternal rest of peace to gain.

Kneel down and pray the Spirit of our God
Will seal your brow with token of His love,
Your little place in that vast Heaven to find
    'Midst deathless multitudes above.

The Temple of Denderah should be seen in ascending the Nile, as it loses all interest of detail after the Temples and Tombs of Thebes, the hieroglyphics broadly testifying their modern age by their poorness of outline and bad arrangement; its nearly perfect preservation, however, renders it a good explanation, in its plan and general construction, for the more ruined but more interesting Temples farther on; the great square court succeeding the pylons usual in the larger temples, is here wanting, but the magnificent Portico makes up for the loss. This portico, leading to the fine hall and lofty adytum within, has scarcely even a chip on the stone, — it

is supported by twenty-four grand columns with square
capitals, to which the colossal face of Athor is affixed
on each side, — very sweet and dignified is the head,
however singular the adaptation of a small pylon which
is inserted below the abacus as her head-dress; the
whole front is richly covered with hieroglyphics. There
are a number of other buildings near this, much ruined;
one is a Temple of the class that Champollion calls
" mammeisi," where the child of Athor is supposed to be
born — this is Ehu, the young god of day or light, born
of Ra, the sun, and Athor, the morning star : — this
Temple is covered with representations of Typhon, the
god of darkness, with whom Ra is in continual combat,
and to whom the birth of the child is a fresh disaster.
Outside the wall of the large Temple is a portrait of the
famous Cleopatra, — she has a fat, chubby face, and is
not very much prettier than the lion-headed gurgoyles
which surround the roof, as grotesque in form as any
mediæval monsters.

For the study of hieroglyphics, there is no place, after
Thebes, to be compared to Abydos; and in descending
the Nile, the difference in them, to the eyes that have
looked on Kalabshee, Philæ, and Denderah, is very
glaring ; there is a neatness and precision here, an evident meaning vigorously expressed, even to those who
cannot read them, which strikes the most cursory glance ;
while in some of the late Ptolemaic Temples they seem
only pictures stuck on as ornament; they are here conveyed, too, by a fine medium, the walls of the now ruined
sanctuary and chambers being lined with slabs of
alabaster and finished with all the princely richness and
fine execution of Rameses the Great. I remember three
most living figures, larger than life, sculptured on one
wall with something like chain mail over the head and

the dress; and the plaited hair and embroidery all conveyed with the utmost delicacy of finish. The other
building—the Temple-palace of Seti (or Osirei) I.—was
last year uncovered ; it was finished by his son Rameses
the Great, and is very rich and large; the bass-reliefs
are the most beautiful in Egypt,—indeed, there is
nothing equal to them in Egyptian art, except the
paintings in the Tomb of this same king Seti at Thebes.
In earlier periods art was far more *naturalistic*, some of
the statues found by M. Mariette being really as natural
as Roman art; but what we may call Egyptian art
proper was in the reign of Seti the most perfect of all,
—it is beautiful, living, and highly picturesque, although
completely subject to the arbitrary rules imposed by the
Priests on the artists, in accordance with that elaborate
theocratic system of government that extended through
all the minutiæ of life. Here at Abydos stood, it is supposed, the city of This, the birth-place of Menes, and
the capital of Upper Egypt long before the rise of
Thebes, and at least 1300 years before the time of Rameses the Great, who lived about as long before Christ.*
I think the ride to Abydos was the prettiest and
pleasantest we enjoyed in Egypt; we had good little
donkeys, who took us there in about three hours and a
half, through green fields of flourishing sugar-cane, bean,
and dhourra crops, with every here and there a grove of
shady trees, and buffaloes in large herds feeding on the
plain. The sun was hot enough without being fierce,
and there was only too much of a cool breeze, delightful
in the fields, but very disagreeable when we reached
the ruined city, which lies under many fathoms of loose
sand. The path was gay with passengers, all of a very

* Wilkinson's Chronology.

dark swarthy brown, and in the village we found troops
of pleasant-looking women, and naked shining-skinned
children, who seemed more obliging than usual, offering
us dates and water as we passed by.   Then there were
camels old and young, feeding round a pretty little
natural pond shaded by palm trees.

We were very much detained by contrary winds the
whole way down from Thebes to Cairo — day after day
the same head wind blew, with only the cessation of
three or four hours now and then, and frequently with
so much violence that it was impossible to proceed ; then,
after enduring a variety of unpleasant collisions with
the small waves, we hauled to and lay bumping on the
bank.   The process of drifting down is not an agreeable
one, — the boat generally gets near the middle of the
stream, and spins slowly round and round and round as
it goes on, and in any wind it drifts with a kind of
heavy ground-swell motion, which makes many people
qualmish.   The sailors row a good deal, but in head
winds it is labour thrown away.   We sometimes found
pleasant walks on shore, especially in the lovely gardens of Siout and Minyeh, but the wind was often too
high even for walking.   We had intended to stop in
coming down, to see the Red and White Convents, and
many other things, but we were now, in truth, only
anxious to get on.   One morning very early, however,
we started to see the Cave of Diana, the Speos Arte-
midos, by no means to be missed by any traveller : it
lies in the midst of a wild desert ravine of broken rocks,
and is excavated from the mountain side, leaving in
front a portico of eight square pillars, with an inner
chamber containing a large niche, probably for the
statue of the goddess Pasht, " the beautiful lady of the
cavern," to whom the excavation was dedicated by

Thothmes III. and Seti (or Osirei) I. Lions and cats, the animals sacred to Pasht, have been buried in numbers of grottoes hollowed out in these rocks, and some of the larger Tombs in the ravine contain a few hieroglyphics.

From this the deeply interesting Tombs of Beni Hassan are soon reached, but they occupy a long time in examining; they are, next to the Pyramids, the oldest records in Egypt, some of them being of the time of Osirtasen I. and II., with the name of Suphis, the builder of the Great Pyramid, introduced in one of the inscriptions. Yet no colours anywhere in Egypt are fresher, and no paintings more vigorously and admirably executed : they contain vivid representations of every trade, occupation, amusement, and mode of life known to the Egyptians, besides a hundred other subjects far too numerous to describe or even to mention. The porticoes of two or three of the southern Tombs are ornamented with polygonal columns, the representation of the stalks of plants, bound together, with a lotus bud for the capital; and one is considered to be the original from which the Doric Temple at Corinth was copied; in others the column is the same, without any capital or fillet beneath the abacus. It is pleasant to linger among these Tombs, and to examine them narrowly; my own feeling is strong that they should be studied in ascending the Nile, for the sooner the eye is accustomed to *good* hieroglyphics and the *best* Egyptian art, the better : after becoming even only a little familiar with them, one's enjoyment of the finest and oldest Temples is doubled and trebled to what it is if the eye has not learned to distinguish easily between the ancient reality and the modern imitation. One should never lose an hour of favourable wind in ascending the Nile, nor stop for anything (even the all-

important daily milk!) should there be a chance of a
good breeze: but the few, very few miles gained by a
whole day's tracking, are worth nothing in comparison
to the knowledge thus gained in preparation for the
Nubian and other Temples: Thebes, indeed, on both
sides of the river, should be left till the last of all —
unspoiled by even a glance in ascending: and after it
has been seen, the slowest downward drifting without
landing, is scarcely enough for arranging all the knowledge one has gained there clearly in one's mind.

The last excursion we made before arriving at Gheezeh
was to visit the site of Memphis, the first city of which
even a legend still exists in Egypt: it is believed to
have been built by Menes, the first king, whose date is
given between 3640 and 2700 before Christ, and some
hundreds of years prior to the building of the Pyramids:
it continued to be the capital of Lower Egypt throughout
the glory of Thebes and long after its fall; in fact, until
the rise of Alexandria robbed it of its commerce. It was
still a city in the time of the Mohammedan conquest, 600
years after Christ: but, unlike Thebes, not a trace remains of its magnificent Temples, and only a few green
mounds, and some broken statues, guide the antiquary
to its long-forgotten site.

A short ride from the village of Bedreshayn brings
the traveller to that called Mitrahenny, where, prone
on its face, lies the statue of Rameses the Great, forty-
three feet high, and finely carved in a hard limestone, which was probably polished: the beautiful
features (which can fortunately still be seen, from the
ground sloping away from under the face) are in perfect
preservation, and recall their brother portraits at Abou-
Simbil to the mind. There is also a broken statue
further on, about eight feet smaller, of another Rameses,

and many fragments and broken bits of sculpture lie
scattered about, besides smaller pieces arranged with
some care by the villagers in a little mud enclosure.
We could not loiter under the fine trees that shade the
village, nor even by the ugly ruin of the Sakkāra
Pyramid, for we were hastening on to the Serapeum,
the happy discovery made by Mariette in 1851, of the
enormous tomb of all the Apis bulls. This remarkable
excavation is one long winding passage, sixteen feet
wide, and fourteen feet high, with large recesses on a
level of some four or five feet lower at each side; in
these recesses we counted thirty sarcophagi, only a very
few were empty. It is almost incomprehensible how
these sarcophagi, each thirteen feet by eight, and eleven
feet high, could have been drawn along the passage; they
are all of fine granite, some reddish from Assouān, some
of a dark green nearly black,—the stone is said, I
know not on what authority, to come from the mountains
of the Dead Sea, which does not seem likely. One sarcophagus was of basalt—the hieroglyphics were remarkably small, and delicately cut, and the granite was in
some of them polished : they are, I believe, the finest
sarcophagi ever discovered, and they are, indeed, wonderful masses. No Apis bones have been discovered in
them ; all that have been opened were found filled with
stones, as a mark of contempt. Apis was called "the
living image of Osiris,"—his name is probably an
adaptation of a Coptic word meaning "conceal,"* as
Osiris was concealed under his form; his body was
black, Plutarch says, but he had a white triangle or
star upon his forehead, the spot where the spirit was
supposed to enter into him : on his back there was the

* Osburn.

mark of a vulture, a beetle under his tongue, and his tail was double,—all which was, of course, managed by the priests. In fact, this Apis-worship shows what a monstrous system of priestly imposture the religion had become: how hard it must have been for the spiritually-minded, in these later times, to get at the ground-work of deep truth that underlay many of the myths with which the priests had covered it, and changed it, as far as the ignorant and vulgar went, into a degrading and gross idolatry!

But these are things to sigh over, and to think upon with an earnest, grave attention; what people find " so amusing" in the "bulls and cats," I never could understand; one would think that even the most frivolous would be sobered, and the most trifling impressed into something like reverence after a few days at Thebes; yet even in the silent solemnity of the Valley of the Dead Kings, one's mind is jarred and worried with the strangest and most disagreeable contrasts; one may be lost to all the realities around one, and then be interrupted, as we were one day, by a voice close to one's ear, calling to the unhappy dragoman, "I say—you there—awsk that feller oose tomb this is!" Being answered "Belzoni's tomb," the owner of the voice says he believes "that was the name of the king who built Abou Simbil;" and then he goes back to his dahabieh and his dinner, and confidingly remarks to his neighbour, after his champagne, "I say — wawt a bawr these tombs are! Egypt's quite a sell for a man like me!" in which latter sentiment we agree with him.

CHAP. VI.

"Nay, certainly, I have heard the Ptolemies' pyramises are very
goodly things: without contradiction I have heard that."

SHAKSPEARE.

A S we knew we should not have much time at our
disposal for sight-seeing when once we had
reached Cairo, we determined to visit the Pyramids from
Gheezeh, this being a quieter and shorter ride than
from the city. The heat was becoming greater every
day, and those who wish to examine them in any
degree of comfort, or see the view in bright tints,
should leave their dahabieh before sunrise, taking
breakfast with them : we did not start till 9 A.M., and
only reached the Pyramids towards midday, when all
the beauty of colouring had faded into the hot white
glare, which is as painful as it is ugly. The path was
for some way fresh with pleasant verdure, and crowded
with Arabs, laden camels and donkeys ; then at last we
emerged on the dry loose sands, and had neither thoughts
nor eyes for anything but the Pyramids. Their appearance, however, is very disappointing as one approaches
them—I was not at all prepared to find how much so :
the deception caused by every line sloping away from
the eye is inconceivably great, and not even a column
raised beside them would correct the natural error,
since the pyramidal form would still give the idea of

something foreshortened; I had to keep repeating to myself that the tower of Strasbourg Cathedral might stand beneath the apex, and I found even then I did not quite believe my own reasoning about it.

We were soon in the usual mob of fellaheen anxious to be chosen as assistants for the ascent, on account of whom we had previously determined to forego a visit to the Pyramids unless we could join a party with gentlemen; for they are an unruly and turbulent set, and only a very short time before a most unpleasant attack had been made by them upon a couple of gentlemen, and some blood been shed; the fellaheen had probably been roughly treated, as the gentlemen in question were Americans, and I believe that a little quiet firmness, with the declaration that you are English, and the determination not to be put into a passion by their noisy and extortionate demands, will soon secure the comparative comfort of the traveller. But one must make up one's mind to purchase the interesting result of examining the Pyramids, by a thoroughly disagreeable process in every way; I am most glad to have *done* it, but nothing would induce me to repeat the operation, and I would earnestly dissuade any and every lady who is not entirely sure of her own nerves and self-control, and who is not very strong, from attempting it. Gentlemen who go to Egypt on account of delicate lungs or imperfect circulation, probably do themselves as much injury by the effort of visiting either the outside or inside of the Pyramid, as the delightful climate is calculated to do them good; still worse if they indulge in the absurd school-boy emulation of who can get up first.

The only right way to get through the ordeal is to be

quietly passive in the hands of the three Arabs ap-
portioned to each visitor. When once you have commenced the real business, they are good-natured and
careful fellows, proud of their knowledge of half a dozen
sentences in half a dozen languages, and anxious to
please you; they know best how to tie up your garments
so that they shall not impede your progress, and how to
lift you with least exertion or disagreeableness to yourself, and the sole piece of advice I give to my country-
women is, to *let* them lift you, and — to leave your
crinoline in Cairo. Many of the stones are four feet
in height, but the Arabs lift you at one jump with
more ease than a stool or any other contrivance will
afford you; sometimes, too, they appear to mistake
you for a doll or a swaddled baby, and you find yourself seized by the ankles as well as by the arms! Even
thus passively impelled upwards, the ascent is an
enormous fatigue to both blood and breath.

The now broken summit affords a platform of thirty-
two feet square, with stones upon which and beside which
you can rest comfortably; the view is fine, and interesting as being characteristic of Egypt, and should, I think,
be viewed at the commencement of the traveller's stay
in the country, thus taking in, at one glance, what you
learn by slow degrees afterwards. Cairo, with its un-
countable minarets, the most varied in form and the
most picturesque in the world, rising upon the steep
slope of the Mokuttum hills, up to the citadel and
the mosque of Muhammed 'Ali, is a remarkable view in
itself; still more so the clearly-marked boundaries of
the wide sandy Desert, so melancholy and bare-looking,
from the verdant, smiling plain studded with palm trees
which adjoins it: while the pyramids of Abouseer, Sak-
kara and Dashoor, to the south, give a sort of still life

to the scene. In the early morning or evening, doubtless, the view becomes as beautiful as it is striking, when
even the featureless, desolate sand of the Desert gains
for a few moments the hues of a wild, stern beauty
peculiarly its own.

An American gentleman arrived on the summit, while
we were there, and breathlessly informed us that the
English Ministry was entirely changed, that England
had declared war against nearly all Europe, and that
the Old world was soon going to pieces. Those who
never stir beyond the reach of some kind of newspaper
or letters, can hardly imagine the excitement with which
one greedily seizes on all the news one can get, after
three months of perfect silence from the civilised world ;
but the feeling was still more curious of realising the
vivid interest one felt in a thing of to-day,—whether
one man or another was living "his little hour" in the
new history of a tiny island 2000 miles away,— in comparison with that singular scene actually near to our
eyes, but which we seemed to be looking *through*, with
apparent clearness and almost personal interest in the
men of such hoary antiquity as to be far beyond the count
of Time. I *felt* the incongruity, but I could not *think*
on the burning fiery furnace of that platform ; my mind,
too, was nervously fixed upon the horrors of the descent
that awaited me. I found it by no means so difficult,
but infinitely more disagreeable than the ascent. It
was a very happy moment to me when I reached the
bottom and found my sister standing, with the full
complement of her limbs, in peace and comfort beside
me : one had not felt one's legs or arms one's own in
either the up or down ordeal.

We rested some minutes in the shade before we
entered the Pyramid. I think not less than eighteen

Arabs went in with us; and it is impossible to describe the stifling feeling in the narrow passages, filled with noise, lights, heat, and smoke. I did not perceive in myself any sensation of horror or fear, so frequently felt by even the strongest-nerved travellers, but I confess that, according to the proverb of the "burnt child," the dread of fire came strongly upon me. We were above a score of persons, obliged to crouch quite on all-fours for many yards together, the flames of our candles flaring about in the draught which we made in passing, and my sister and I wore Arab cotton dresses, on which one spark alighting — and many flew about — would have put us in a blaze, while any rush in those stifling passages must have been fatal to some one. The steep angle in which they dip, and their smooth surface, oblige one to have recourse to the barefooted Arabs for support, and their close company is considerably more disagreeable here than in the open air outside. But the passage is soon done; and after visiting a small empty chamber, nearly square, called the Queen's, — which is only interesting because it stands directly under the apex of the Pyramid, — you pass through a gallery twenty-eight feet high, the walls meeting at the top by progressive steps, and enter the King's chamber, an oblong room nineteen feet high. There are small holes or tubes in the walls of this chamber to admit ventilation, and over it are four large spaces, one above the other (which Sir G. Wilkinson naïvely calls *entresols*, in spite of their eternal darkness), intended to relieve the weight of the mass above them. In the two uppermost of these chambers the two stones were found on which the workmen had painted the names of the kings for whose mausoleum the Pyramid was built, — Shofo (or Suphis, commonly

called Cheops) and Nou (or Nef) Shofo, two brothers
who reigned together, the one for fifty years, and the
other for fifty-six years; their cartouches have been
found in the rock-cut tombs close by, as well as the
gold ring of King Suphis.

The chamber is formed of blocks of granite, cut
smooth*, which sparkle in the torchlight, so exquisitely
joined that the seams are almost imperceptible, and
at one end is the broken sarcophagus of the king, it is
supposed, made of red granite, and still emitting a
bell-sound when struck. It was a fine idea of those
old Egyptians, as Herodotus tells us, that of admitting
the waters of the life-giving Nile to enclose the dead
body of the king, who in life "called the Nile his own,"
in its watery arms, thus insulating it from all earthly
contact; but antiquaries have ruthlessly declared the
tale to be less than a fable—a total impossibility. The
overpowering feeling of immensity, while thus descending lower and lower into the interior of the Pyramid, is
certainly very great and never to be forgotten; it is
doubtless very much increased by the quickening of
the pulse, in the hurried rush down passages and up
again, and by the difficulty of respiration. I felt something of the same kind afterwards in the cave of
Adullam (near Hebron), the perilous path leading to
which naturally hastens one's circulation a little; but
there the habitual confidence of man in Nature and her
glorious works has a soothing, strengthening influence,
while inside the Pyramid one finds a vague feeling
of fear steal involuntarily over one, as one calculates
the giant mass of human-raised Titan blocks around
and above one. I am sure the man who invented

---

* The rest of the Pyramid is built of limestone.

the horrible tale of the prison whose walls gradually
closed in day by day on the unfortunate prisoner
confined between them, had once stood inside that
King's chamber; but I remember comparing myself
mentally to the little almond I had seen so gently and
quietly cracked by the wonderfully regulated power of
the giant "Nasmyth's hammer," which but a moment
before had pierced holes through a massive bar of iron
as easily as a needle passes through fine cambric — the
monstrous mass above me, however, remained unmoved,
and the fate of the small almond was not mine.

The next half-hour was pleasantly spent resting
under the shadow of one of the enormous blocks of
which the lower tiers of the Pyramids are 'composed.
Of course the finish given by the triangular stones,
which made the surfaces of the sides smooth, must
have added much to their appearance, but they are
more picturesque as they are, with their rugged steps.

We saw the Sphynx in her very worst light, the glare
of 2 P.M. : then all colouring is spoilt, the poetry of
Nature silent, and the surrounding scene rendered as
ugly as it can be.   And yet it impressed me as much
as anything I have seen : like the Pyramids, it is impossible to form any idea of its size, from the fine proportion kept in all its parts, until the Arabs climb like
ants over the neck and head.   The features *have been*
beautiful, but they are now so much destroyed that the
mind must be full of those perfect faces seen in Abou-
Simbil, &c., to fill up the gaps for oneself : like them,
it is more than wonderful how such exquisite harmony
could be preserved in the 172 feet long of the figure and
the 28 feet of the face cut out from the natural rock.
In spite of fractures and discolourments it still retains
its "mild and bland" expression : unimaginably grand

it must have been when the bearded chin overhung the
temple and the altar between its paws, and the group of
lions crouched in front.   It is believed to have been executed by Thothmes III., who was fond of architectural
caprices, but we must all be thankful to him for a
" caprice " as grand and enduring and noble as this.
It is a marvellous mystery, keeping its own secret behind those wide-open eyes and within that serenely
smiling mouth, and one wanders round it, vainly
searching for the key to what one feels instinctively is
full of meaning, but which is now, and perhaps for ever,
locked beneath the eternal veil of sand.

   That evening we went on to Cairo, and arrived at
Shepheard's Hotel on the 25th of March, and for the
next ten days we were employed in a ceaseless labour
of shopping — wearisome enough anywhere, but at Cairo
really dreadful: one hunted the whole day for some
indispensable trifle, seldom having the slightest idea
where to go to, and at the end of the day found the
thing in the first shop one had been in.   We were soon
in despair at the invariable answer to all inquiries for
articles, that they had none; but a Cairo lady, who was
so kind as to help us very much in our difficulties,
assured us that meant only laziness, and at last we
learnt to answer " We will help you to look for it," and
by dint of opening drawers and searching for ourselves,
we sometimes found what we wanted.   But one never
could guess where to look for anything: for instance,
we found books and trunks at the tailor's, boots and
shoes at a watchmaker's, a French dressmaker behind
a butcher's stall, and some strong, useful dresses at a
warehouse for glass beads.   Many things we never
found at all, and we had to get on as best we could till
they were sent out to us from England after some

months of small discomforts. Everything European
was, of course, enormously dear, and our wardrobes,
even the very queer medley they were, cost us certainly three times their real value. We were, of course,
constantly in the bazaars, which, though very amusing
to see, are tedious and provoking to the last degree
when one wants to get any real business done, and excessively fatiguing. The sirocco and heat became very
oppressive ; the noise and bustle of the city after being
so long quiet on the river was very trying to nerves
that were already a good deal shaken. The hotel was
very full of passers-by, and the few friends we had
came and went without being able to help us ; the
unjust demands of our *quondam* dragoman grew daily
more annoying, and we soon perceived that the proceedings of the Arab court regarding the loss of the
dahabieh might be far worse than the misery caused by
any Circumlocution Office ever set up in a civilised
country, where truth, honour, and honesty are at least
words understood by all : they do not seem to exist in
the modern Arabic used in Cairo.

Of the city, which we were longing to examine, we
saw little or nothing ; only once or twice, by way of
rest after our weary work, we went up to the splendid
Mosque of Muhammed 'Ali, to enjoy the magnificent
view. The famous view of Damascus is far more really
beautiful, but there is a singularity and a grandeur
about Cairo, the mingling of the works of man in the
thousand domes and minarets with the desolate face of
Nature, the verdant cultivation beside the barren waste
of sand, that is unspeakably impressive. One day we
paid a hasty visit to the four finest Mosques of the
city, those of Sultan Hassan, Touloun, El Azhar, and
Hassaneyn : they are well worth seeing, grand, simple,

and interesting, with bits here and there of admirable
richness and beauty. We found most of the persons
who admitted us civil as showmen and tolerably intelligent, and we were careful to show the decent attention due from one worshipper to another ; so, not
being provided with overalls, we walked through the
mosques in stockings,—a not very comfortable proceeding, but one must have very little of the spirit of
Christianity in one, and still less worldly good-breeding,
if one refuses such conformity to their notions of
reverence.

The minarets of the Mosques of El Azhar " the
splendid," Barkook, Nasr Muhammed, and Hassan, are
beautiful ; the domes, too, are sometimes elaborately and
elegantly worked. But the buildings which charmed us
most were the Tombs of the Mamlook Kings outside
the town, full of variety and of singular elegance : they
stand in the loose sand, and should be visited early or
late to avoid the heat of the sun, but they will well
repay a visit at any time, and artists would find among
them subjects for many months of drawing.

One Sunday morning we got up an hour or two before
sunrise, having arranged with a Copt dragoman to take
us to the Coptic service, which was celebrated in a small
old church while their large one was being enlarged
and repaired : it commences always at the first dawn
of day. We found an oblong room with latticed
windows, cleanly whitewashed and hung round with
pictures of saints, some of which were not bad, and a
part of it latticed off at one end for the women. On the
north side there was a recess the whole length of the
Church, like an aisle, but nearly dark : one half of this
was the chancel, enclosed within a screen ; in front of the
other half stood the Patriarch's chair and the reading-

desks. As each Copt came in he crossed the Church, and, going into the back of the recess, washed his hands in a little running fountain in one corner; then returning into the Church, squatted on the floor among the rest of the congregation. At first the service consisted of short readings of the Gospels, each portion read first in Coptic, then in Arabic, by little boys ten or twelve years of age, dressed in a kind of surplice over crimson silk, with caps, embroidered in gold, on their heads; these were the deacons. There were also several priests who wore crowns with gilt crosses on their heads, and robes of various coloured stuffs. There was chanting besides, and bells chimed in now and then, which sounded like cymbals. After about an hour of this, the Patriarch,— the successor of the Apostle St. Mark, and the spiritual head of the Egyptian Church,—entered the Church from behind the chancel, clothed in a magnificent mantle of green and gold tissue, with an enormous hood of the same, which almost hid his face; he held a beautiful patriarchal staff in his hand with a silver crozier on the top, surmounted by the figure of a knight slaying a dragon,— that universal legend, found in nearly every country where any "ancient story" existed, typifying, each according to the local colouring in which it was found, the triumph of pure-hearted courage over brute wickedness. In his other hand the Patriarch carried a small gold cross, jewelled, and wrapped in a handkerchief of gold tissue, which each person who passed him stopped to kiss.

The readings continued for some time with many short prayers and sentences, the people responding with uplifted and waving hands, often repeating "Kyrie eleeson, Kyrie eleeson." After this the Patriarch preached a short but very energetic sermon, stopping

continually, both in the reading and the sermon, whenever he saw anything amiss in the congregation; calling out very loud orders to them, " Oh ! ye donkeys,
don't make such a noise ! " " Give more room to each
other ! " " Oh ! ye pigs, attend and listen ! " the people
also frequently expressing their approbation of what he
said in his sermon, with a loud murmur of applause
and the words " taïb, taïb." Then he retired into the
chancel, and seemed, with the priests, to make processions round the altar, and to consecrate the holy Elements; after which small cakes, circular, and stamped
with the name of Christ, a cross, and some other words,
were handed about, and bought by many (for five paras
each) to take home. These are not consecrated, but,
having been prepared for the Eucharistic bread, are
considered semi-sacred, perhaps lucky. After a pause,
some members of the congregation went to the door of
the chancel, where the Patriarch gave them the bread
and the wine together in a spoon from a glass he held
in one hand, at the same time laying the edge of his
hand across the eyebrows of each while he gave his
blessing. The people made numbers of responses in
this part of the service, not one having any book, and
they recited together the Creed, the Sanctus, and the
Lord's Prayer, the service seeming, as well as we could
make out, to be arranged very much the same as our
own. The whole service was exceedingly *chaleureuse,*
not merely a duo or quartett of priests, with the
congregation as audience, according to the fashion of
some of our Churches at home, but all the people
joining in very frequently, and with apparent devotion. At the end of it, the kiss of peace was passed
round, each one to his neighbour, the Patriarch kissing
the priests and blessing them. The women did not

enter any part of the Church but that screened behind
their lattice; two of the priests carried the Sacrament to
them; and they joined in the responses very frequently.

The service is read in Arabic as well as Coptic, because
very few of the people readily understand the latter now;
but the liturgy and all their religious books are written
in it, and they are instructed at school to pray, both in
church and in private, in that language. The Copt is en-
joined to pray seven times in the course of each day, and
Mr. Lane says he believes there are very few who do not
practise the rule; and the educated Copts repeat in
their prayers the whole book of Psalms *every* day; they
also keep long and rigid fasts. We heard afterwards
that the Patriarch is much beloved by the people *; he
is still a young man, and has a fine countenance, with a
very black, thick beard, and bushy eyebrows, which he
knit ominously when he scolded them. We were told
by those who knew him well, that the present Patriarch
is an earnest, energetic man, bent on reform, which
he is endeavouring to carry out, as well as, by means
of judicious and enlightened education, to elevate the
minds of his flock. He entered frankly and earnestly
into an elaborate argument, or rather explanation, of
the difference between the Coptic and Anglican faiths,
with a friend of ours some time after, and seemed as
much interested in the details given him as he was
evidently pleased at the impression made by the Coptic
service on an Englishman. We thought it one of the
most interesting services we had ever attended.

The Coptic creed is very similar to that of the Eutychians (who were condemned as heretics by the Council
of Chalcedon in A.D. 451), with some admixture of the
tenets held by the Jacobites and Monophysites; their

* He died a few months ago.

rites and ceremonies have been preserved with but
little alteration for the last fourteen hundred years. The
Copts are undoubtedly descendants of the ancient
Egyptians, says Mr. Lane, but they are very far from
being a pure race, having intermarried, long before the
conquest of Egypt by the Arabs, with their Christian
brethren of Abyssinia (who were Jacobites), Nubians, and
Greeks. The name of Copt is thought to be derived
from the ancient Greek name of Egypt, Ægyptos, or
else from the city of Coptos in Upper Egypt, to which
numbers of Christian Egyptians retired in the time of
the Roman persecutions; the word is pronounced Gkubt
or Gkibt, in the singular Gkubtee or Gkibtee.

After a fortnight's stay in Cairo, during which the
examinations of our English servants and of the sailors
were constantly repeated, each repetition bringing out
some new variety of absurd falsehood in the history of
the boat-burning, we learnt one morning from the
English Acting-Vice-Consul that the story next to be
adopted was that our maid had set the boat on fire, and
that on this plea the dragoman Achmet Adgwa, owner
of the boat, intended to sue us for 900l. damages.

On first arriving in Cairo we had been strongly advised to institute proceedings against Achmet for the
recovery of our losses, which we estimated at considerably above 300l., since our contract with him included our safe conduct and indemnity from accident
during the three months of our voyage. Many said we
owed at least the form of instituting such a claim, to
future Nile travellers, the safety of whose persons as well
as property is at the mercy of their dragomans and
crews, who should, therefore, be made fully aware that
they are held responsible for injury suffered by one or

the other, unless caused by the traveller's own fault. But even the knowledge that we need not enforce the payment in the end, did not reconcile us to the appearance of harshness against a fellow-sufferer; and we felt more disposed to exert ourselves to effect some compensation for his losses, with which experience had taught us so well how to sympathise.

But now the case was changed; from what we heard, Achmet seemed to be restrained within no limits in the false and injurious stories he was spreading everywhere about us; we knew him, from his own account, to be possessed of property in land and cows, unusually large for one of his class, and we heard now that he had expended much of this (as well as money begged and borrowed for the "maintaining of his cause") in bribing the members of the court from whom he hoped for a decision in his favour.

Under these circumstances the Consul was so kind as to step somewhat out of the course which he would have felt to be right in his public capacity of Consul, as he said, in consideration of our being ladies alone in a foreign land and among such a people, and he advised us to leave Cairo as quickly and as quietly as we could; he assured us that the final decision of the cause would not be at all affected in this country by considerations of truth or justice, and would probably be protracted to the very utmost limit that ingenuity could devise, or during which bribes could be supplied, detaining us thus prisoners, during many a long month of summer heat, in Cairo, to the great risk of our health, which had already suffered much from the shock and subsequent anxiety.

Unfortunately for us, just at this time there was really no Consul either at Cairo or Alexandria; our ex-

cellent friend Mr. Green had gone, and his successor
had not yet arrived, and there was the same transition
state of affairs in the Consulate at Cairo; and thus,
while everybody was acting for some one else, nobody
liked to take any responsibility on himself, or to come
forward in an affair not very simple, and not very distinctly his own.

We therefore lost no time in paying to our dragoman
all that we owed him for the hire of his boat, and his
wages up to the last day of our stay in Cairo, as if he
had still been in our service there, which of course he
could have no claim to ask: the sailors we paid up to
the same day also, as we learnt that in the prison
their supply of food depended on their own funds;
and then, after passing the night in packing, we left
Cairo by the early morning train for Alexandria, feeling even then how little pleasant it was for Britons to
flee! especially when they had truth and right to stand
on; but remembering also that " prudence is the better
part of valour," especially when the Britons happen to
be ladies.

But rest was not to come yet; we had a very
fatiguing journey of thirteen hours (something was
amiss in crossing the river which detained us far beyond our time), and we hoped to remain a few days in
Alexandria to obtain the rest which had become so need-
ful for us. However, a friend who was so kind as to act
as our deputy in announcing our arrival to the Acting-
Vice-Consul early the next morning, chiefly as a matter
of precaution, brought us back a most emphatic message
of advice to quit Egypt *immediately;* — he was aware
that an order for our detention had arrived in Alexandria, though it had not yet reached his office; and
though the preferring such a claim on us, to use his

own expression, was "simply infamous," there was too
little hope of justice in an Arab court, not to make it
most important that we should not be exposed to the
exercise of its power, and therefore his advice was,
that we should go immediately on board any vessel in
the harbour whose steam we should see up, without
waiting to ascertain its destination; and he added
significantly, "I trust the ladies will be gone before
I am in my office." So advised, we lost not a moment
in driving down to the harbour, leaving even the con-
veyance of our baggage to the kindness of a friend, who
brought it after us to the Austrian steamer, which, fortunately for us, was just starting for Smyrna; nor
would it be easy to tell the immense relief we felt, after
so much anxiety and turmoil, when the screw beneath
our feet began to revolve, and Egypt—with all her inex-
haustible and high interests, her indescribable beauties,
her manifold charms, and, to us, her many troubles—
was left on the far horizon.

CHAP. VII.

WHERE HOMER LIVED AND SAPPHO SANG.

THE "Arciduchessa Carolina," though a fine little
boat and very clean and comfortable, did not prove
a berth of roses to us; a terrible storm on the second day
blew us back a considerable distance towards Egypt,
as if our evil destiny would force us into the jaws of an
awkward position, and, instead of a three days' passage,
we had the benefit of five. On the evening of the third
day, however, we were able to enjoy the exceeding
beauty of the islands after passing between Scarpanto
and the southern end of the island of Rhodes. On
the following morning our eyes opened on a grand
mountain mass of violet hue, — an *awful* colour, deep
as the ripest autumn plum, mysteriously dark; solemnly
the huge rock rose from the sapphire sea, which folded
it round in waves of indescribable blue, while heavy
masses of savage clouds now swooped down the mountain side, now rose and tore themselves asunder on the
summit, leaving bare to view, ever and anon, the calm,
pure snow lying in loving mantles half-way down the
rock, and answering to the glistening white masses and
wreaths of surf thrown up again and again in ever-
changing beauty at its feet. I saw this island twice
again; but never again did its sacred rocks impress me
with such solemn beauty as then in that wild April
storm-sky, when I came up with my mind full of the

grand old idols of Egypt, and remembered that *there*
the Disciple whom Jesus loved, — he who taught us that
God is Love, and who showed to us that love whereby,
when made perfect in our own hearts, we dwell in Him
and He in us, — that *there* he dwelt in tribulation, but
in patience, when the Spirit of the Lord came upon him,
and he saw, with spiritual eyes, the "great city, the
new Jerusalem," and wrote that heaven-born prophecy
which, "blessed is he that readeth;" — for this was
Patmos. A large cave, in which the Beloved Apostle is
supposed to have lived, is still shown; a solitary and
spacious grotto about 700 feet above the sea — it is
very probably a true tradition. Nikaria, Samos, and
Khio (Scio) were passed successively, while the mainland
presented an ever-changing outline of cliffs and bays,
richly coloured and in some parts wooded. They were
beautiful enough for any eye, but doubly beautiful to
those accustomed to the monotonous yellows and the arid
white rocks and sands of Egypt, however beautiful the
colours in which sunset and distance sometimes array
them. Lovely the Bay of Smyrna looked on the fifth
morning when we landed at the quarantine very early
in the day, and willing were we to be pleased with the
clear water and the shining pebbles on the beach,
the green vines and meadow-land around us; but the
quarantine itself filled us with dismay. The dirty Hajj
pilgrims who had crowded the deck of the "Arciduchessa
Carolina," poured into the courtyard of the wing appropriated to us, which looked forlorn enough with the
iron-barred windows and doors, and the bare stone walls
and floors of our prison; the three English gentlemen
who had come in the same steamer were shown into one
little room together; and to us, with our maid, was as-
signed an upper room with a staircase to ourselves, not

so bad in itself, but that every room and the whole place was pervaded by the most horrible smells one could imagine. We passed the whole day sitting on the dirty floor, with nothing to do or to look at, or, what was worse, to eat, till sunset, when a boatload of beds, and food, &c., arrived from the hotel; and we were then allowed to have our luggage, which had been kept from us all day, in order, I suppose, to see whether the plague would burst out of the locks and straps in a visible shape.

We fortunately enjoyed a pretty view of the bay from the window of a front room, and once we walked in a paddock of long grass under the guardianship of a soldier, but it seemed bitterly cold and damp to us after Egypt, and we counted the hours of our very long five days most wearily. We were always expecting a visit of inspection from the Turkish medical officer, but no one came; and when we had fulfilled the law, the five days concluding at the very same hour as that of our arrival, we were allowed to embark in a little boat which carried us across the lovely bay to the city of Smyrna on the 15th of April. After this we never had any reason to complain of the cold, for the spring changed at once into delicious summer heat and sunshine.

We spent a pleasant fortnight enjoying the beauties of Smyrna. The town is beautifully situated at the end of the thirty-six miles of winding gulf, the sea washing the very walls of the houses, whose bright red roofs, mingled with pretty trees and gardens, rise up a very steep hill, finishing in a forest of the finest cypress trees in the world, not excepting those at Constantinople : it is really almost worth going to Smyrna only to see these trees. From the summit, which is crowned by an ancient castle and is the site of the martyrdom of

Polycarp, a noble view is obtained; the town, with its
bright colours and numerous Churches, sweeping round
at one's feet, and extending partly along a creek at the
right, while sloping up from the water's edge are rich
meadows and fig groves, dotted here and there with the
summer residences of the wealthier inhabitants of
Smyrna, and with a few villages. On the north, across
the creek, the fair and lovely mountains rise, backed by
Mount Sipylus, of ancient fame; on the south, the bay
curves round westwards under the gloomy grandeur of
fine dark purple and brown craggy mountains, on which,
at this time, the snow was lying in light shrouds. All
around the eye discovers remains of aqueducts and other
ruins, through which the new railway steers its unwavering, narrow line. I should think that there are not a
great many cities in the world that can boast a much
prettier panorama than Smyrna.

As to the town itself, it does not possess many fine
buildings; some of the bazaars are handsome and
solidly built, and there are a few pretty Churches. The
streets are wide for an oriental town, and many of them
are lined with European-looking private houses, which
remind one of a French town; they are interspersed
with trees and little gardens, and pretty *cafés* beside
running streams. The bazaars are very amusing; there
is nothing like a Levantine town for the jumble of languages one hears, and at Smyrna no one seems to think
of troubling himself to select all the words of a *whole*
sentence in any one language. Your true Smyrniote,
being accustomed to think in all the eight or nine he
knows, mixes them up at once into an *olla podrida* of
language without the fatigue of separating them, for he
is sure that to whoever he speaks one or other word
will be intelligible. You ask the price of a thing—the

coin will be in one language, and the number in another ; you ask what o'clock it is, and the hour will be told in one tongue and the minutes in another, and so on.   In a sentence of twelve words there are certain to be four or five languages mixed up, forming a jumble which is truly astonishing, and not a little perplexing at first.

We found the town well supplied with European goods, chiefly German, most delightful to us in filling up our many wants of the things not purchasable in Cairo ; and the change was very agreeable from the cold, listless impassiveness of the oriental shopkeeper, who does you the favour of bestowing his goods upon you to his own entire ruin, as he assures you, though at double their value, and the brisk anxiety of the civil Levantine merchant pressing his goods on your notice. Almost every shop is wreathed with strings of sponges of every variety of size, quality, and price : some nice little sponges are sold for a few halfpence, but a really good, fine sponge fetches almost as large a price in Smyrna as in England.   The Broussa silk and embroidery bazaar, which is handsomely built of stone, is exceedingly gay and pretty ; but the gayest of all the bazaars is that for made-up garments, — the stalls are filled with many-coloured cloths, gay waist scarves, embroidered turban stuffs, striped and flowered silk robes of the most brilliant colours, and gold-embroidered jackets, varied with antique arms, little glass cases of delicate porcelain and amber beads, Persian carpets and shawls, and table-covers of needlework ; the sellers almost attack the unwary traveller, rushing at him with the articles generally bought by strangers, and shrieking to him on all sides, " Howadji ! Señor ! Ingleez ! Franja ! Monsieur ! Signor !" &c. &c.   Strings of camels

pace along the streets — large, untidy-looking beasts,
with long thick hair hanging down from their necks,
very unlike the trim, closely shaved, and more lively-
looking camel of Egypt. Numbers of mules, and most
gigantic donkeys, meet you at every turn. But the day
for seeing Smyrna is Sunday, when all the inhabitants
of the houses, high and low, sit outside their doors in
groups, on chairs placed in the carriageless streets. You
walk through the Armenian quarter after midday, and
you have thus an opportunity of seeing whole families,
of three or four generations, dressed in French fashions,
but with the large, soft, lustrous eye of the East, and
the languishing, graceful gait of the South; in the
Greek quarter, blue eyes and more regular features
make a pleasant variety, while each and all have
coquettish flowers, freshly plucked, twined with an
Eastern *abandon* in the dark tresses of both maid and
matron. The Jewesses, alas! do not exhibit themselves
in the same manner to the admiring passers-by; they
are said, by those admitted to their houses, to be very
remarkably beautiful.

We made one pleasant day's excursion to Bournabat,
a village of the citizens' summer residences; each house
has its own nice garden, but every one is enclosed in a
high stone wall, making all the streets seem blind, and
preventing any kind of view of the lovely mountain
scenery to the inhabitants within them. But we
learned that this had been, till within the last four or
five years, a matter of necessity, not choice; since without these high walls no Frank was safe from insult
from the Turks, even in their own gardens. The only
exception to the rule was in a new iron-railed wall,
just completed, round the garden of a Mr. Whittal,
an English merchant of half a century's standing in

Smyrna, and who is much respected and beloved by all classes. His house is the handsomest of the numerous good houses about Smyrna, and the garden is very large and charming; it has cost a large sum of money, and is still a costly luxury, from the enormous expense of keeping it watered: in dry seasons the water has to be carried out from Smyrna for weeks and weeks together, and of course the thirsty soil requires a vast quantity to keep gardens of such extent in order. Seeing us at the gate, the hospitable owner was so kind as to invite us in, strangers though we were, and to show us the house and grounds, and a small but handsome Church which he has just built at his sole expense for the English community of Bournabat. In the course of the following summer, Mr. Whittal entertained Prince Alfred with a fête in his pleasant grounds.

We wandered about the village for some hours, peeping into a pretty Mosque, and a beautifully clean bath watered by the river Meles, on the banks of which the " divine Homer " sat and sang for all the generations of the world after him; and after resting in a *café*, and being refreshed with coffee and hot bread which we took from the baker's oven — like all the shops here open to passers-by — we rattled back in the rickety *char-à-banc* which had brought us from Smyrna: such a pleasant hour's drive, the lovely meadows between the fine mountains clothed in the richest and brightest spring greens, beds of wild flowers on all sides, and the hedges filled with hawthorn, dog-roses, and acacia blossoms, filling the air with their sweet perfume, and the Judas-tree, with its tall spikes of bright and lovely lilac flowers on the leafless branches.

The next day a friend kindly called to invite us to accompany his family to the Armenian Church in the afternoon, as it was Maundy-Thursday, on which day,

at vespers, the Patriarch washes the feet of twelve
Bishops to commemorate our Lord's act at the Last
Supper. The Church is spacious and lofty, half Italian,
half Saracenic, built partly out of the ruins of ancient
Churches, and having itself twice fallen down, each time
immediately after its completion, to the great delight of
the enemies of the Armenians. It has no architectural
beauty in the interior, but it is pretty and gay, like the
temples on the top of a confectioner's cake, all pink and
white paint and gold, with numbers of pretty silver
lamps hung from every arch. The galleries were filled
with women in bonnets and hats instead of the old-
fashioned and more graceful black silk scarf; the floor
of the Church was closely covered with tarbooshed Armenians squatting, — and as a great favour a bench was
brought in, and placed for us near the altar. The service
commenced with half an hour's singing, performed by
twenty or thirty little boys and lads, dressed in flowered
white muslin tied with riband, and each holding a lighted
candle as tall as himself; *such* singing ! — screamed at
the top of their lungs with so much exertion that they
all got red in the face in five minutes, each one on a
different note and in a different key, following his own
fashion and fancy as to tune, only getting in the words
to something of the same time and swing, and keeping
the nose steadily shut. Then came in the Archbishop,
clothed in black with a great black hood (which, however, he soon threw off, and then appeared in splendid
robes of green and gold brocade), accompanied by twelve
Priests or Bishops, each dressed in a different-coloured
velvet robe embroidered with gold, and a large circular
crown of the same colour as his dress, hooped with gold
and surmounted with gold crosses.

After some more singing the Patriarch changed his
robes before the altar to still finer ones of white satin

covered with heavy gold embroidery; he put on a fine
gold mitre, and advanced towards the people, holding a
beautiful jewelled crozier in one hand and a gold cross in
the other; he then preached a short but seemingly very
earnest sermon in the harsh, nasal Armenian language.
After this a huge silver basin was brought, which the
Archbishop blessed separately with the soap and towels;
he then seated himself in a squatting fashion on the
floor beside it, while one by one the twelve Bishops sat
for a few moments in a chair opposite to him, and placed
one foot in the basin, over which the Archbishop poured
some drops of water from a silver flagon; they then
bowed and retired, kissing the Gospels and the Cross in
his hand as they went. The service was then concluded.
We had been involuntary witnesses of the preparatory
process to the ceremony; for, while standing about, before
it was time to enter the Church, we had seen the twelve
Bishops previously washing the twelve legs which were
to be afterwards exhibited, in a very ordinary wooden
pail in a small back room! They had incautiously left
the door open, and we had reason to think the preparatory and more thorough ablution not at all unnecessary.

On Good Friday afternoon there was a grand procession from the Patriarch's Palace to the same Church,
the Bishops, dressed as on the day before, bearing
pictures to excite the adoration of the people. We also
went to several Greek Churches, where crowds of people
were streaming in and out to kiss some favourite
picture in each; in the Church of San Giorgio the
popular favourite was St. George, but as no one
could reach the saint comfortably, they kissed the
dragon with as much complacency and doubtless with
as much benefit. There was a very good performance
of Rossini's "Stabat Mater" at the French Church,

but the crowd was so great that we could not even get
inside the door. The prettiest and most interesting
sight to me of all the gorgeous ceremonies, was the
Greek " announcing the Resurrection " on Easter morning; places were kindly obtained for us at the windows
of the Greek Patriarch's Palace, to which we went at a
little after midnight. The crowd was then assembling
in the court between the palace, the Church, and the
belfry (which was separated from the Church, a tall,
dazzling white building, like a tower of filagree sugar
on a supper-table), and service was going on in the
Church. The crowd at last was packed as densely as
it possibly could be, every individual bearing a long
lighted candle, and nearly every one a pistol of some
kind or other. Expectation and impatience got higher
and higher, and the noise louder and louder, until about
2 A.M. the Patriarch and clergy came from the Church
in procession, carrying a huge silver cross wreathed in
artificial flowers, and mounted a low platform; after
some singing there was a pause, and then, in distinct,
solemn tones, he announced " *Christ is risen!* " In an
instant all the bells burst out in loud peals, the people
shouted like mad things, and every one waved his candle
and fired off his pistol again and again: the waving
candles had a beautiful and quite indescribable effect —
it seemed like the wind passing over a field of fiery ears
of corn, burning the brighter as they bowed their heads
to the breeze. Then the people separated, and the
strange sight was over, and the acacia trees were left
in silence and darkness: they might well wonder over
their own fantastic, fairy kind of beauty during the
ceremony — their white blossoms, illuminated with a
soft, bright light by the thousands of candles underneath
them, against the dark sky of night above their heads,

looked like a white cloud bending down gently in
fragrant blessing over the people. Despite our fatigue
we had little sleep that night; for the whole population
was in the streets, firing pistols, squibs, and crackers,
without one moment's cessation, throughout that night
and the next day.

Another but a sadder sight passed our windows on
Easter Sunday morning, — the funeral of a young girl,
the only child of a widowed Greek doctor, who is rich
and much respected in the city; the funeral was therefore conducted in the grandest style. The procession
commenced with a score of little boys, dressed in scarlet,
carrying crosses and candles; then thirty priests, all
robed in the richest brocades and the peculiar black
cap of the Greek Church, one of them singing a sweet
and solemn chant; then came the Archbishop, robed in
brocade and mitred, carrying a gold crozier, a boy
bearing his train; and after him the coffin — uncovered
— painted white, and supported by bands of white satin
riband: within it lay the young girl (embalmed, they
said), and the face painted enough to conceal the terrible colour of Death, the body dressed in white satin,
with a wreath of orange blossoms on her head, and
strewn over with white roses, buds, and leaves. About
a hundred gentlemen followed, wearing white hat-
bands, foremost among them the poor father, bowed
down with grief — and no wonder, for the girl was very
lovely; one could fancy her sleeping to the measured
sounds of the sweet chant sung by the boys who preceded her and by the rich-voiced priest —

"A dirge for her the doubly dead in that she died so young!
For her, the fair and debonnaire, that now so lowly lies;
The life upon her dark brown hair, but not within her eyes —
The life still there upon her hair, the death upon her eyes!"

The whole scene was touching; but there is a horrible ending to it: at the grave, the corpse is taken out of the coffin and stripped of all its fine clothes and ornaments, for which a regular scuffle then ensues among the gentlemen, and happy is he who can secure the white shoes, or the wreath, or any other morsel of the finery! The corpse remains in the grave for one year, when it is taken up, and the bones put into a small bag, which is buried inside the Church, the tombstone remaining as before.

All the shops in Smyrna were shut for the next few days, the people making holiday with every imaginable noise, and eating quantities of little pastry baskets filled with gay-coloured eggs; while at every door a lamb was tethered, all through Easter Sunday, decked out with flowers or ribands, as on this day everybody gives everybody a lamb, and as few can afford one for each family of his acquaintance, the lambs just accepted are passed on in fresh presentation until they have changed owners through a score of hands : even so, the custom is a great tax upon the purses of the inhabitants.

As we found that there was no steamer going to the coast of Syria for another ten days, we determined to pay a flying visit to the island of Mitylene, where our friend the English Consul, the far-famed excavator of the Mausoleum of Halicarnassus, had offered us the use of his vacant house for the summer months. We started at midday, in a dirty French steamer, bound for Constantinople, enjoying the lovely views of the gulf ending with the dark, bold promontory of Kara Bouroun, which contrasted well with the yellow and red cliffs on the mainland. The wind freshened enough to make the passage very unpleasant, but we reached the island in

less than eight hours. The day, however, had ended in.
rain, and the night was as dark as pitch. The steamer
stops outside the harbour, nearly two miles from the
shore : if a boat has been pre-engaged to come out for
you, well and good; if not, the chances are, that you
must go on to Constantinople, as, after dark, a Mitylene
boatman would never think of an excursion on specu-
lation. I was sorry to have missed the view of the island
from the sea, as some travellers describe it to be "as majestic as it is graceful." We had, however, fortunately,
an introduction to one of the few Mitylene gentlemen,
M. Pinto, a fellow-passenger on the voyage, and he
kindly landed us in his boat. The air on the island felt
warm and balmy, perfumed with the fresh spring flowers,
and we almost enjoyed groping our way up to the English Consulate, where we were received by the French
Consul, who had kindly prepared supper, &c., for us.
The house, is spacious and comfortable; we found a
good library, and all we could desire : our only per-
plexity being, that as neither of us knew a syllable of
Greek, we had to send the servants to the French Consulate to get our wants and wishes explained to them,
whenever we required hot water, or dinner, or anything!

The English Consulate commands a good view of this
lovely island. The bright-coloured town curves round
the little bay from which the mountains slope upwards,
clothed in the rich hues of orange groves, pomegranates,
figs, and mulberries ; grey rocks cropping out sternly at
the tops among the dark shades of purple heather. An
old castle on the left, and two quaint lighthouses on the
right, add something to the beauty of Nature, while
the eye travels on across the calm blue sea, caught here
and there by a graceful latteen sail till it reaches the
beautiful coast beyond; and truly there can hardly be

a more beautiful coast view than that of these time-
honoured mountains of Mysia, blue and hazy with light
wreaths of white mist and snow; while rising straight
up from the gulf of Adramytium at her feet, stands the
noble and graceful peak of Mount Ida, clouds resting
lightly on the summit, and shadowing the eternal snow
on her crest: truly a fit resting-place for Jupiter and his
attendant gods, for the noble mountain—now de-poetised
into the " mountain of goats"—was once covered with
pine forests, in a lovely glade of which " Beautiful Paris,
evil-hearted Paris," adjudged the apple to Aphrodite,
" new-bathed in Paphian wells; " and I never looked
at the grand old mountain without fancying I heard
the sorrowful chant of " Mournful Œnone, beautiful-
browed Œnone," repeating —

> " O mother Ida, many-fountained Ida,
> Dear mother Ida! hearken ere I die ! "—

while one had but to walk through half a dozen of the
streets of Mitylene or the villages near the town, to see
girls beautiful enough for all the heroines of ancient
song — even " the Greek woman " herself — with figures
like statues of Phidias, and draperies that a sculptor
would go wild to reproduce.   Broken pieces of fine
marble figures are frequently found beneath the soil on
this classic ground : we saw two fine heads which had
just been dug up, in one of which, the gems placed in
the eye-sockets, to represent the dark iris of the eyes,
had fallen out, leaving round empty holes, shadowing
the eye with a softer expression than the original
gems could have done.   A little patience and money
would soon be repaid in collecting some valuable remains, — broken, of course, but well worth having for

private collections. The natural marbles of various
colours, found in the island, are also said to be valuable.

We saw a new hospital building with the stones taken
from the ruins of a Temple of Apollo, which was discovered in digging the foundations: it is a pity that
some of the friezes could not have been secured for the
Mitylene museum, — a praiseworthy institution which
ought to be supported by strangers, the European community being far too small to accomplish much, though
they have acquired a wonderfully admirable collection of
scientific instruments for their college, into the uses of
which the Lesbian youth of the present day, we were
told, enter most heartily and readily. The institution
appeared to us, in our hasty glance, to be superior to
many of the institutions of the same class in England.

A good many things are produced in the island,
beginning with the delicious little beccafigues, of which
a hundred may be shot in one tree, in a few minutes of
the first hour of a spring morning; then the figs,
which are small but luscious, though not as far-famed
as their Smyrniote neighbours; abundance of olives,
the chief commerce of the island, and some tolerable
wine; besides the innumerable *confitures*, on the manufacture of which the Mitylene matron prides herself, and
of which every visitor invariably partakes, the mother or
daughter of the house bringing various kinds on a silver
tray before the inevitable coffee. An amusing story is
told of the consequences of the rhapsodies written by
Lamartine on the confitures he tasted in visiting the
hospitable house of M. and Mdme. Pinto; a few weeks
after the publication of the " Voyage en Orient," letter
after letter arrived by each succeeding mail, containing
" *orders* " from Parisian confectioners for " Pinto's confiture," with special directions for its being exactly the

same as that M. Lamartine had described; and for some
months these letters continued angrily reproaching the
astonished and indignant M. Pinto for not attending to
their "commissions!" There are also abundant truffles
in the island, and, it is said, "unequalled oysters."

Another product of Mitylene is the needlework of
the women, which is really ancient and beautiful. It
is rarely to be met with now, Lord Stratford de Red-
cliffe having bought up all the best in the island, so
that we thought ourselves fortunate in obtaining a few
specimens of the pretty manufacture, which no modern
Lesbian can imitate: at present the islanders do
"*broderie Anglaise*," and despise the tasteful colours
and elaborate patterns of their ancestors. If poor
Sappho — " violet-crowned, pure, sweetly smiling
Sappho " — had only stuck to her needle instead of
meddling with the Muses and Aphrodite, "the fatal
fire" in her heart might have remained for ever un-
kindled by the rejuvenated old Phaon, and the rocks
of Leucadia would not have been immortalised by a
myth which I insist on believing, despite a whole
library of commentators. By-the-bye, her marble coffin
is shown in one of the Mosques here, which, they say,
she had prepared for herself before the fatal leap was
determined on.

As we wanted to see something of the far-famed
beauty of the Mitylene women, we gladly accepted an
invitation to a Greek fête, given in honour of St.
George at a small village on the other side of the harbour. It did not seem to our ideas a very lively fête;
the large gardens were filled with groups of men,
women, and children sitting in family parties, eating
dinners which they had carried with them, and listening
to very barbarous music: there was no dancing or

games, and we were disappointed at seeing no costumes
except among the men, who still look picturesque. The
women are altogether dressed in gowns *à la Européenne*,
of the brightest possible colours in thin sarsenets and
muslins, and their pretty heads adorned with natural
flowers. It is said that within a hundred years ago, the
women wore only a very short petticoat, and an embroidered handkerchief over the bosom—the smallest
modicum of a costume possible! They wear a great
many jewels—strings upon strings of pearls most commonly, very often with diamond clasps and ear-rings,—
and are certainly beautiful women, with very fine lustrous dark eyes, and graceful movements: but their
sweet mouths are sadly spoiled by the effects of the
rouge which they all wear from their earliest childhood,
the mercury in which so affects the teeth that there is
scarcely a girl in the island above the age of sixteen
with any front teeth left in her head.

We took a most delicious ride one day to the Porto
d'Olivieri, the second large harbour in the island, in
itself large enough to contain the whole English navy,
even if half our ships were Great Easterns,—Port Callone
is still larger. We ascended the mountain behind the
town, on our good mules, enjoying as we went the most
lovely and ever-changing views of the island itself, the
sea, and the opposite coast; our road was a good one,
well paved and not broken into holes, sometimes steep
enough for broad shallow steps. The whole way over
mountain and dell was a continual variety of rich colours,
forests of pine and white cypress, thick sad-coloured
olive groves alternating with the fresh green of the
newly leaved fig-tree, in pretty contrast with crowds of
luxuriant juniper, dwarf oak, hollies, oleanders, myrtle,
and many shrubs we did not know; while our mules

stepped through the thickets of gum-cistus, both white and pink, growing in huge tufts everywhere; and every morsel of flat ground, or "smooth swarded bower," was carpeted with the most brilliant beds of flowers,—"the crocus brake like fire," and all the mountain slopes seemed striped like gay-coloured silks, with ribands of the brightest yellow, lilac, pink, and blue. Sometimes the rocks overhung the path in perpendicular bluffs, but in general the character of the island scenery is more lovely and fine than stern and grand.

We descended in about two hours into the olive groves on the sea-shore, and alighted at some ancient Baths, now used for a *café.* The shore, perfumed with flowering shrubs, is interesting from the multitudes of shells, sponges, and beautiful Medusæ of all colours and sizes; and the view of the tranquil water of the harbour, like a lake, from which there is apparently no outlet, surrounded by the beautiful mountains, is very lovely indeed. The ancient towns of Hiera and Pyrrha stood at the lower end of the harbour. Passing thunder showers threw a thousand colours and changing lights over the scene, so that we forgave the wetting we got in riding back, for the sake of seeing the beautiful mist-wreaths carried in haste over the opposite shore, —and the sun soon dried our garments. A short detour in returning brought us by the Leper colony, encamped among the caves of a wilder and less cultivated valley : there are a great many of these poor creatures in Mitylene ; they marry among themselves, and we saw two or three very pretty young girls in the group who begged from us ; sooner or later, however, it is said that the taint invariably shows itself, and the inevitable disease slowly but surely eats into the whole body, till limb after limb drops off. It is not thought to be so very painful

a complaint, as its horrible appearance would seem to
imply.

We returned into the town by the sheds where the
Slave market used to be held, and made our way into a
small Church filled with some splendid wood-carving;
it is of a different style to the Venetian chef-d'œuvres
of Brustolon, but quite equal to them in execution. A
transparent screen stretched across the Church, composed
of arabesques and wreaths of natural flowers; pulpit
stalls and reading desks were all alike made of the
same exquisite workmanship: we heard there was a
great deal more in two or three other Churches, and
that it was all the work of native artists of the olden
days; it would be priceless to many a collector in
England of such antique beauties, and I hope the
pretty island may some day be robbed of it. Wood-
carving is still a favourite employment here by the
peasantry during the winter months: and we afterwards
heard that the peasants in the island of Scarpanto also
excel in this work. We may hope that Mitylene will
one day regain her place in the commercial world: an
island so easy of access, and possessing such harbours
and so fruitful a soil, with an active, intelligent, and industrious population such as they are, ought indeed to
be prosperous and important; but her vicissitudes have
been many, though her name has been great, and at
present she is under a thick cloud, called Turkish dominion. The birthplace of poets, musicians, philosophers, and historians,—a stout member of the Grecian
confederacy, — she passed under the Romans, and long
afterwards to the Venetians, under whose sway, probably,
her fine castle was built: in 1465 she gallantly resisted
the siege of the Ottoman Sultan Muhammad II.,
aided by a band of the Knights of St. John, until the

city was betrayed to the Turks by the treachery of the
Governor, who paid for his baseness by an immediate
execution : not a Knight remained alive after its capture.
A good half of her inhabitants were destroyed in the
Greek War of Independence, and in the horrible massacres of that period, which were nowhere conducted with
greater brutality ; but now, after a long interval of peace,
one longs to see the beautiful island repopulated and
prosperous, as some day — inshallah — she will be.

The "Euphrate" steamer, in which we took our
passage from Smyrna to Beyrout, is one of the finest and
most comfortable of all the Mediterranean steamers, not
excepting even those belonging to the P. and O. Company. We had the ship nearly to ourselves, except for
the addition of the Hajji to Jerusalem — the inevitable
nuisance in every Levantine voyage during the spring
and summer. The pilgrims, who are continually going
to, or returning from every port in the Levant, live
upon the deck, which is generally divided like a sheep-
pen down the middle ; they are expected to keep to
their own side and within the railing ; but, even if they
do so, the sights, sounds, and odours proceeding from
their locality are unpleasant to the last degree. They
lie all day huddled up on their mattresses, presenting
every variety of costume and Eastern language, — grand-
fathers, parents, and infants, all pell-mell together.
They bring their own provisions, and also plenty of small
companions, on whose unfailing activity neither open
railings nor ship regulations have the slightest effect.

The day after leaving pretty Smyrna found us threading the islands we had passed by before, — this time,
however, going closer in shore, so as to catch a glimpse
of Boudroum and Cnidus, and the glorious Cape Krio,
which rose majestically, snow-covered, from the blue

waters that foamed over its rugged feet. The evening brought us to Rhodes, whose busy little harbour looked very pretty, with its minarets and ships lighted up with lines of coloured lamps to celebrate the last night of Ramazān. We rowed on the following morning in the gig of H.M.S. Tartarus, to the inner quay, where we landed and found ourselves amongst crowds of gaily dressed Turks, hurrying in great state to pay each other visits on the close of Ramazān ; from the Beys on richly caparisoned horses down to the smallest child, all were in bright clean clothes, with natural flowers stuck in bouquets into nearly every one's turban or fez ; it was really gay and pretty ; but nothing can save the streets of poor old Rhodes from looking desolate and deserted, when one compares it in one's mind with its days of chivalry and splendour, the like of which has passed away for ever from the world. Passing by the Barracks of the Turkish soldiers, the ancient doors of which have been removed to Versailles, we found ourselves in the " Knights' Street," — once so grand — now so silent and sad. There are but few remains of the fine " Auberges," which belonged to the eight Languages of the Order : only some richly ornamented doorways and finely carved marble scutcheons in the walls, the armorial bearings on which are still very perfect ; but they are much hidden by the miserable balconies, &c., of old boards and broken lattices, which have accomplished the metamorphose of the palace of a monastic Knight into the hareem of a Turk. The once noble Church is now a heap of unintelligible ruin, to which state it was reduced by a singular accident : some rock-hewn caves had been used by the Knights as a store-house of gunpowder in the days of Rhodian glory, but they had long been forgotten, when, in November 1856, a flash of lightning

during a severe thunderstorm ignited the gunpowder
and blew the Church, the Palace of the Grand Master,
and a hundred other interesting remains, into utter ruin !
We were told by an English officer who witnessed the
catastrophe, that he saw the Church *lifted bodily* into
the air, from whence it fell with a shock that was felt
for many miles round ; every glass window in the town
was broken, and large stones wrenched from the walls
beyond the outskirts of the city. One might almost say
that by this powder Rhodes was *twice* lost : 330 years
before, the fortress was " heroically lost," and obliged to
capitulate to the Turks for want of the ammunition
they had buried and forgotten — and now, the last
memorials, even the skeletons mouldering in the tombs
of the gallant heroes of her siege, were utterly destroyed
by the very means which would have saved them in
their day of need !

The towers and minarets of the fortress-city mingle
prettily in the views round the harbours of Rhodes,
backed by the green hills and gardens which surround
the town ; people still amuse themselves disputing over
which harbour the famous Colossus stretched his
brazen legs, but the fact is, that he was placed on the
point of the rocky promontory *between* the two, called
now the " Arab's Tower," — but, in the time of the
Knights, St. Michael's ; it is still a massive square tower,
and was topped by the waist, bust, and head of a man,
covered with brazen plates, with an arm stretched out
towards each of the harbours, and holding a lamp in
either hand. He must have been a monster of ugliness,
but he figures nowhere so amusingly as in the chronicle
of the old British pilgrim Sæwulf, in 1182, who re-
counts how St. Paul addressed his " Epistle to the

Colossians " to the men of Rhodes, because they dwelt beneath the legs of the famous Colossus !

As the steamer allowed us but two hours of daylight, we could at this time see but little of Rhodes; but on returning in the following year we had the benefit of receiving much information from M. Salzmann — the best authority on the remains of Rhodes; and I therefore defer any description of it till that time.

Nothing can exceed the beauty of the coast scenery of Asia Minor from Cape Krio onwards : the mountains are rugged, stern, and grand, the savage wildness at times changing into varieties of luxuriant, many shaded woodlands, and green meadow-nooks — the snowy peaks in the spring and early summer rising behind the dark purple and red-browns of the nearer cliffs; and then the sapphire water — it is said by experienced sailors, that the water near this coast is of a deeper and brighter blue than any other in the world — and one can well believe it. The beauty which extends along the whole coast attains its highest loveliness in the Gulf of Makri, and the famous Seven Capes : the outlines of the cliffs and mountains are here both grand and graceful, and the blue distances on the other side of the Gulf lend much to the scene. Kastelorizo, Khelidonia, and Anamour, are each very fine, and all abound in historical interest to the scholar. This little nine days' voyage, in a fine steamer, coasting closely along under such beautiful scenery, is more than plea-sant : we had lovely, clear weather, and fortunately always a calm sea. The fifth day was spent at Mersina, where, however, we did not land ; and the sixth in the beautiful Bay of Iskenderoon, where the Amanus mountains come down into the water, clothed in rich woods, and the beach is fringed with thickets of oleanders.

The bay is enclosed by lofty mountains, the Taurus range to the north rising in the pale blue distance, covered with snow, which seldom melts even at the end of the summer. All these mountains are full of souvenirs of the misled but gallant Crusaders. Among their precipitous ravines, and in the hot valleys and plains between their heights, not hundreds, but thousands, lay down to die or ever they saw the Promised Land of their enthusiasm * ; and, of those who survived, many more passed along this great mountain road, called the "Iron Gates of Syria," though only to be slain before Antioch, Damascus, &c. Excessively hot is the Bay of Iskenderoon, and deadly the fever of the malarious plain on which the little town stands: but our walk on the sandy shore among the oleanders was delightfully pleasant.

Sunday we spent at Latakia, landing early in the tiny harbour behind a fine old tower, built on the rocks which rise insulated in the water; the shore was covered with something white, which I took for Tombs, — when, as we came nearer, I saw them move, and discovered that they were living women, wrapped in the white *eezar,* or sheet, with which we were afterwards to become so familiar throughout Syria. Their faces were covered entirely with the *mandeel,* a dark coloured cotton handkerchief of gaudy patterns, which is made at Manchester, and which we also now saw for the first time. The pretty town is surrounded with fine gardens, where we soon got quantities of roses and carnations. The streets are so frequently covered in with stone arches, even where there is no bazaar, that they are very shady and pleasant, and give a handsomer appearance to the

* The Crusaders frequently called even Northern Syria "the holy land of Jerusalem."

small town than a fuller acquaintance warrants : the long
vistas of arches are most picturesque, and great numbers of broken granite columns are still standing at the
sides of the streets.

There are also some ruins worth seeing : one is a row
of four columns with fine Corinthian capitals, still supporting a richly carved architrave and frieze; another
is a Triumphal Arch, or square of four arches, with fine
friezes and capitals.   Their beauty was much enhanced
in our eyes from their being covered with luxuriant
trailing weeds, springing from between the old stones,
instead of the severe aridness of the unstained Egyptian
ruins, to which we had been so 'long accustomed.   The
capitals and friezes are of very rich Corinthian, and well
cut; and the stone, which appears to be a soft one, is of
a fine golden-brown colour now.

It is difficult among the narrow winding lanes of
modern Latakia to carry its topography well in one's
head, at least in the visit of a day; but it would be very
interesting to map down the various remains still *in situ*
of ancient Latakia, or rather of Laodicea-ad-Mare ; there
is still, however, enough to show that a double row of
granite columns once made an approach the whole way
from the quay on the harbour up to the Corinthian
Temple, whose remains are now quite at the back of
the town, and at the distance of 1500 yards from the
harbour.   Numbers of these columns still remain, but
the greater part have been broken off and rolled down
to the sea, to be built into the foundations and walls of
the Castle in the harbour — the memorial left there
by the Venetians, and where many of them, with their
rough broken-off ends, are still to be seen.

From a large Mosque, on the hill behind the town,

a very pretty view is obtained : Mount Casius on the right, and the Lebanon on the left, — the graceful bays, where sponges luxuriate, sweeping into every imaginable curve on either side. From the gardens, on the south of the little harbour, the view is also very pretty. In short, this Latakia is a gay, pretty little town, subsisting upon its merchandise of tobacco, and sponges, and remarkably delicate silver-work; the bazaars are uncommonly good for so small a place; the tobacco is brought in from all the north of Syria to be shipped from the port, and is, when the duty on reaching home is added, very nearly as dear as in London; the sponges are gathered off the coast, chiefly from the rocks near a little bay to the north, which is occupied by the divers and seamen only. The cliffs above are filled with the rock-hewn tombs of the ancient Laodicea-maritima; they are very simple, and, of course, all of them quite empty.

Tripoli, where we spent the next day, is a handsome town, and beautifully situated on a narrow strip of plain, at the foot of the Lebanon range, which rises with abrupt loftiness directly behind the town — its strata most strangely and grotesquely marked, as if a boiling mass had been thrown out and suddenly cooled in its still seething commotion. Between the beach and the mountains are miles and miles of delicious fruit gardens — oranges, apricots, and figs, hedged with pomegranates, tangled over with clematis, and watered by thousands of tiny streamlets from the Kadisha river. Five old Castles remain: the largest of which, on the seaside, built by Raymond de Toulouse, was still occupied and fitted with cannon till 1840, when the English knocked huge holes in its ancient walls; the

Saracenic doorway and the interior vaultings are good,
and worth seeing. Another castle is situated in the
pleasant valley of the Kadisha, a picturesque ruin; and
a third crowns the mountain spur above the town, from
whence there is a splendid view of the town and gardens,
and of the river foaming through the rocks and woods,
with the Mosque and Convent of the Derweeshes in a
fine ravine.

We amused ourselves drinking coffee and eating ice
in a *café* beside the river, listening to Arab story-tellers
declaiming romances to large groups of well-dressed
Tripolitans, seated in rows on stone divans along the
streets, smoking nargilehs, and eating the sweet, fresh
oranges which are plentiful here. The little town is a
flourishing one, with good bazaars; its best production
is, however, but little known: these are carpets made by
the peasant girls in some of the neighbouring villages.
They are very slowly made, as for each carpet the
girls, or the family, gather, prepare, spin, and dye the
wool themselves, which is then woven in patterns of
their own design — very tasteful they are, and the
colours rich and brilliant; they are very strong and
thick, as well as pretty, especially the finer sorts. They
cost from 100 to 500 piastres *, according to their
size.

The eighth morning found us outside Beyrout, where
the swell— which is ceaseless in that bay — made every
one so sick, that we were thankful to get out of the
ship, and to settle into the pleasant Hôtel on the southern
headland below the town, at Râs Beyrout; this hôtel is
simply, almost barely, furnished, — the open corridor is
the only general sitting-room, but the semi-naked

* From about 1*l*. to 4*l*.

simplicity suits the climate, and we found it at all
times a delightful residence, the heat of Beyrout being
here tempered by the sea breezes which blow all round
it. Besides, it was the cleanest hôtel we had been in
since Paris : and it is an unspeakable comfort sometimes to get into a place where you can sleep in peace
without battling with scores of fleas, or worse, and
where there are plentiful signs of brooms and brushes.

CHAP. VIII.

THE "BEAUTIFUL GATE" OF SYRIA.

THE world must be very rich in beauty, if there exist half-a-dozen places on its surface much more beautiful than Beyrout; but I, for one, cannot believe that there are; its loveliness is of many kinds, and though different pictures may combine to represent its beauties, no one will contain them all. Tripoli, Saïda, Hhaïffa, Smyrna, Mitylene, rightly lay claim to many charms,— but they do not surpass Beyrout. The amphitheatre of mountains, clothed in every hue, which change with every passing hour; the snowy summits towering up behind them; the rugged headlands of rocks, over which the sea dashes in ceaseless wreaths of foam; the city rising from the water's edge, and climbing up the slopes of hills, adorned with gardens, minarets, domes, and mosques, castles, and palaces; the scattered palm-trees, and the bright colours dotting every street and quay,— make a *tout ensemble* which fascinates the eye in the first moment — grows upon you under every changing light and sky — and rests in the mind an everlasting memory of loveliness.

To the north one blue headland stretches out beyond another, till the Theoprosopon (which forms one side of the Bay of Tripoli) arrests the view; from this the mountains reach back with majestic beauty to the far East, the various heights covered with every variety

of green, from meadow to pine forest; tiny white
streams dash down the sides, while crags, grey, white,
purple, and yellow, break out from between them, and
nearly every crag is crowned with the towers or walls of
a monastery. In magnificent loveliness Sunnîn rises
up behind them, the saddle-shaped summit covered
with a thick mantle of snow, and the barren creamy-
red sides stratified into terraces; then Kunîsyeh, more
peaked and but little less lofty, snow-covered also; and
then the mountain ranges gather round southward, still
more richly clothed in wood, — and, sloping down towards Saïda and Sour in blue distance, meet the clear
blue sea again at their feet. Râs Beyrout, to the right,
throws out bold rocks to greet the waves, over which a
coast-road in front of rich gardens speckled with
houses leads into the town: lifted above all are
the fine barracks, standing proudly on a hill in the
midst, while a hundred palaces of the European residents and merchants of Beyrout attract the eye, each
house surrounded with verandah-terraces of fantastic
Saracenic arches, in various coloured marbles; in the
foreground the once strong Castle of Beyrout is to be
seen among the houses, and, on rocks jutting out
into the little harbour, two other Castles, now picturesque ruins, pretend to protect the crowds of oddly-
shaped feluccas, stout merchantmen, and scores of
little boats painted all manner of bright colours, that
are jammed together in struggling confusion at the
custom-house quays. Some way out of the town lies
the white Lazaretto, among mulberry and fruit gardens:
while the golden-sanded shore curves round from
beneath the old seven-arched bridge over the river, and
sweeps away past myrtle-edged villages into the smiling
little Bay of Jouneh.

In the early morning sun how clear and bright and
beautiful it is!   Later on how busy the gay boats, and
how graceful the white sails flecking all the bay!   At
midday how refreshing and delicious the green woods
and gardens!   In the afternoon how tender and indescribable become the tints, and how enchanting the
perfumes that spread through the air!   And in the
evening, how unearthly the hues that steal over mountain, sea, and sky — dyeing the sea into a full larkspur
blue, and the mountains into a soft grape-like purple,
which seems, although so dark, to be semi-transparent,
with deep crimson shining *through* the purple in some
mysterious union; while the more distant summits
become transfigured in a tender spiritual rose-colour,
pure and lovely as a real, living, fresh-blossomed rose;
and the white snow softens into a kind of pale glow,
and seems ready to float away and dissolve in the rose-
coloured and golden floods above.   What scene on earth
can be more exquisitely lovely than this?   For many a
month I watched all this day by day, with a thousand
other changes; and, looking back through all I have seen
before and since, nothing surpasses it in loveliness but
the Great Desert and the Dead Sea (and they have
much less variety, though not less glory of colouring),
and one view of Broussa.   Then at night, when the lights
twinkled through the town, and the moon came
out and seemed to turn the marble arcades and the
minarets into molten silver, and illuminated the snow
on the mountain tops, — when the stars swam in liquid
light over all, and the cool refreshing night air came
gliding by laden with sweets — silent messages of
whispered fragrance — and faint music stole up from
the town, and the sea murmured below in soft plashings
on the rocks, — then one sat and listened and looked,

and longed to have it always night, until the glory of
the dawn made one feel that joy is better than sadness,
however sweet, and one's heart sang, " The earth is the
Lord's, and the glory thereof ! "

Behind all this, unseen from the sea or the town, is
the delightful Pine-forest, made famous by the rhapsodies of Lamartine; it is a charming place, for though
the trees are nearly all quite young, yet they throw
a cool and refreshing shade upon the hot sand beneath them, and nothing can be pleasanter than an
early morning or late evening gallop along the wide
open glades, occasionally stopping at one of the quaint
cafés for a glass of snow-lemonade, or pacing slowly
under the sombre, fragrant trees on foot. The sand
from the beach had blown over this part of the plain,
rendering it quite a desert, until these trees were
planted to prevent its drifting; and it is to be hoped
that the forest will be very much extended, to form
shelter for the town and gardens on the rest of the
plain from the south winds.

The hot season was now beginning, and it was time
for us to secure a summer residence; Beyrout, however
enchanting, did not suit us, as we did not choose to
remain long either in a town or in an hotel, and except
in the charming palace-houses of the residents, or in the
Râs Beyrout Hôtel, it is too hot a climate to be healthy
for European strangers in the summer; we were longing too for mountain air and a quiet home, — so we lost
no time in making inquiries and preparations for attain-
ing both. First of all we engaged a dragoman, Habeeb
Soma, the best of those at Beyrout, and whom we afterwards found, during the year he remained in our service,
more honest than most of his class, invariably obliging,
and particularly well-informed concerning the country;

he was a mountaineer from near Bukfeyia, and used so
guttural an Arabic that we found our very limited
Egyptian vocabulary of little or no use to us; but as he
spoke excellent Italian and tolerable French, we had
no need of anything else, and he afterwards made great
progress in English under the tuition of our maid.
Guided by him we mounted some ugly but good
Syrian nags, and proceeded to some of the neighbouring mountain villages.

We were informed that the abode most likely to be
convenient to us would be apartments in one of the
numerous convents which are strewed over the Lebanon
mountains; we, therefore, first bent our steps to the
Convent of Mar Ronkas, where we knew a European
family of ladies had spent the previous summer.   At
first we followed a pleasant road among gardens and
fields hedged with prickly pears, and two large plantations of cactus (on which some one was trying to culti-
vate cochineal), the scarlet blossoms of which looked
splendid; after fording the stream and pushing through
thickets of lovely oleanders, we begàn to ascend the
mountain, and the path became as bad as the scenery
was beautiful; the horses scrambled over rocks like cats,
with occasional bolts, jumps, and struggles that really
astonished one; for this was one of the very vilest paths
I ever saw, and we were quite *new* to such undertakings;
the beauty of the scenery happily consoled one, and
we reached the convent at last.   It stands on a little
horn of the mountain very low down, but high enough
to overlook the rich and lovely plain.   We pushed the
gate open and found ourselves in a little court-yard full
of fowls, from whence we made fruitless efforts for
about half an hour to waken any of the monks — they
were taking their siesta.   At last one of them appeared,

and learning our wishes, sent off for the superior, who soon came panting up the steep, with his black gown turned up in front, and the under skirt carefully folded out of harm's way during his digging and pruning. He made himself tidy and then joined us, sitting in a pleasant window-seat, while we sipped lemonade, — only one of us at a time though, as they possessed but one glass. The rooms he offered were tiny white-washed cells, about ten feet square each, with a hole for the window and one little shelf, and a saloon commanding but little view, and which was then filled with silk-worms; we did not fancy the *gîte*, especially as we fore-saw that the good monks would inspect us from morn-ing till night, as if we were beasts in the Zoological Gardens, and that it would be impossible to have the cloisters to ourselves; the monks seemed good simple-hearted creatures, employed in cultivating their silk-worms and little herb garden, and in prayer; we heard they were very kind to the few peasants who lived near them, helping them in the mulberry grounds, &c. They were very anxious to have us as their guests, but our bodies being already immensely impressed with the as-tonishing concourse of fleas in their little court, we departed, determined to look a little further.

Another day, therefore, we clomb the mountain to the village of Beit Miry, of whose charms we had heard tell even in Egypt; the road lay in the same direction, but instead of continuing to the left to Mar Ronkas, we went straight up the mountain, through brushwood and thick beds of bright flowers and shady trees,—then came a pine-wood and a long delicious hill covered all over with a low forest of myrtle just bursting into blos-som and perfuming the air, as we trod through it, most enchantingly. Next we wound up through mulberry-terraces to another pine-wood, from whence paths branched off to the two horns of the mountain, one leading to the fine convent of Deir el Kulah, the other to the village of Beit Miry*; here, under the pine-trees, is the spring, trickling down the rocks, and giving birth to lovely branches of maiden-hair, and other ferns sprouting from every little crack in the rock over which the water passed. Not knowing the path, which, indeed, had little to mark it, save all the biggest and roughest of stones turned out of the terrace walls, we rode in a steeplechase fashion through the mulberry gardens, till we arrived at the Emir or Prince's house, which had been twice occupied by English families. Four very small rooms, built of unplastered stones, surrounded a little court, with the village chapel and priest's house; they were little stone huts and no more; they asked a high price for the rooms, and we felt exceedingly dismayed at the prospect of spending the summer in those dirty little holes. The Emir was very civil, and his wife, the Princess, came out to stare at us; she had been lying in one of the rooms on a couch covered with rich white silk, but was herself dressed in common cotton; she was old and very ugly, and wore the disgustingly open costume of the Maronite women. This Emir was not one of the highest rank, but we were told by several people that he was very much loved and respected, and very kind in sharing his small wealth with his poorer neighbours; the meaning of the name of the village is " the house (Beit) of Emirs (Miry) or Princes."

Seeing a better looking house in the middle of the village, we rode on and asked if we could have it; it had a pleasant arcade-terrace, but was too small for us, and was not to be let till later, as it was then filled with

* Pronounced Bayt Mēēry.

silkworms, who would not *cocoon* for another month. The owner, a Druze woman, came out and invited us in to see the darkened rooms filled with the trays (made of mud mixed with straw) in which the silkworms were feeding, placed on a light wooden framework; the worms were still young, not being more than an inch long, and they were awake and feeding, but we were requested not to speak loud or to disturb them, and we beat a hasty retreat, as the silkworm nurseries have a very disagreeable smell, and are horribly lively with fleas. The mistress wore the black serge veil, supported by the long silver horn* peculiar to the Druzes, and her face was of course hidden. They draw the veil across it so as to leave only one eye uncovered, and generally hold it in their teeth, a style that is more convenient than pretty; but, indeed, nothing can be more ugly than the horn itself; it might add some dignity to the figure if it was worn standing upright like a steeple from the head, but it is fixed on the top of the forehead at an acute angle, looking like the signpost pole over a barber's shop door, and is worse than grotesque. Once put on, at marriage, it is never removed from the head, even at night.

All this time we had seen at the opposite extremity of the village a very large palatial-looking house, which we concluded belonged to some Sheikh or Emir of high rank, but on inquiry we found it had but just been completed, and was the property of three brothers, native merchants. We thought we would at least try if we could see it, and rode on to the door, where we found a large collection of horses, — seven Russian officers, having ridden up the mountain, were smoking and chatting in one of the rooms. The house was large

* Called the *tantour.*

M 3

and very handsomely built; it contained six lofty rooms
(one of which was thirty-six feet long), and a delightful
arcade in the centre; the front windows had double
arches with stone mullions, with deep recesses in the
thick walls; there was a second terrace at one end, and
a nice little garden attached to it. The view from the
house was superb, overlooking the road up which we
had ridden, with the whole of the exquisitely rich little
plain of Beyrout spread out at one's feet, the river
winding along in the midst like a silver ribbon, the
town glittering in the sunshine, the beautiful Baruk
mountains opposite, and a wide expanse of blue sea.
Immediately behind the house rose a nearly perpendicular grey crag, two minutes' scramble up which led to
the brow of the mountain, and opened out the magnificent wooded valley, or rather ravine, of El Metn, on
the opposite side of which rose snowy Sunnîn in all his
majestic grandeur.

We were not long in making up our minds about this
delightful spot, and the price, 21l., was soon settled
over lemonade and coffee; another half hour was spent
in paying compliments before we descended the abominable path back to Beyrout: people said afterwards that
we had given too much, but we were afraid of losing the
house by hesitation. The canteen furniture belonging
to the dragoman, which we had engaged for our future
tour to the South, was sufficient to furnish the house
enough for one's simple wants in that climate, with the
addition of a table, Turkey carpets, and divans which
already occupied the sitting-room. We took it for three
months from the 23rd May.

Meantime we employed ourselves in seeing Beyrout
and the neighbourhood. There is little to see in the
town. We visited some Greek, Armenian, and Maronite

Churches not particularly worthy of notice, and entered
one pretty Mosque with delicately painted arabesques
covering the walls and roof of the interior : service was
going on, the congregation chanting and praying in
unison — the music of the chant was wild and harmonious. The bazaars of Beyrout are not by any means
handsome, but they contain a very fair variety and plenty
of goods : one quadrangular court surrounded with arches,
where silk cord and tassels are manufactured, is exceedingly picturesque, and parts of the cotton and silk bazaar
would supply endless subjects for sketches. Beyrout is
famous for its gold and silver work, in which the jewel-
lers display a great deal of taste and tolerable execution;
but they do not produce the best things at the first
asking. There are also some very good German shops
for housekeeping articles, situated near the Marina,
where it was always a pleasure to go on account of the
lovely view from the quay of the mountains and castles.

One day, in order to save a long ride by a short cut
across the bay, we hired a small boat, and taking advantage of a fair breeze, set sail for the Nahr el Kelb —
Dog River; St. George's bay, however, is not a pleasant
one for boating, and the heavy swell had a very unpleasant effect upon our party, though it broke up
finely over the rocks at the entrance of the river and
over the foot of the fine promontory ; the surf ran high,
tossing up over the volume of fresh water which poured
down to meet it, and we sped gallantly in on the crest
of a wave, not however without getting a very sufficient
wetting. This *embouchure* is really very pretty ; the
convents perched on the summits of the hills give
much life to the scene, and the indecipherable tablets
carved on the cliff-face by ancient Assyrian and Egyptian conquerors (supposed to be those of Sennacherib

and Rameses II.), add historical interest to it : the fine
bold rocks and the winding ravine, with the full, clear
river, and the little Khan with its group of bright-
coloured figures, and probably a mule or a horse and
rider fording the stream instead of going round by the
steep, single-arched bridge in the middle of the picture,
—unite into a very pretty scene. But the glen increases in sternness and grandeur as it winds back, a
few olives and mulberries finding scanty standing-room
on the edge of the river, while just beyond the bridge
are the romantic-looking arches of an old aqueduct now
filled up with tangled masses of luxuriant ferns, sweet
hawthorns, the splendid leaves of the Arab sweet-potato,
and trailing creepers hardly distinguishable from some
long pendant stalactites, gemmed with bright drops from
the water trickling through. The stream was bordered
with flowers, among which flourished a numerous family
of enormous green frogs, who were croakingly admo-
nishing each other that some one would soon come to
catch them for his dinner. I have no doubt they are
very good, but we declined making our luncheon on
them, and preferred coffee and lemonade ; after which
we returned to our boat, and, tossing up on the top of a
wave of river water, slid down the sloping surf on to the
sea, and went slowly back to lovely Beyrout, which
everybody should linger one whole evening in the bay
to see.

We would not put ourselves again at the mercy of the
swell in that bay, so we took horse the next day and
proceeded to the same place by land in the morning.
The road passes by the fine old bridge over the Nahr*
Beyrout, and the place where St. George of Cappadocia
killed the " mighty worm " and rescued the Syrian
prinæess ; an indubitable fact, since it is witnessed by

* River.

the stain of the blood which still remains on the spot
where the holy warrior washed his hands, after finishing
the dragon with a knife. Then we wound through
some lanes and came out on the sands, taking a brisk
canter along the edge of the waves till we reached the
promontory of the Nahr el Kelb: the pleasant sands
were strewed with the remains of vessels driven ashore
during the past winter, two of which were English.
Several ships are lost every year in this bay. After
crossing the beautiful river, we rode a good hour further
along meadows and gardens to the village of Zouk
Mehayl, where one of the chief *fabricants* of pretty silk
and gold stuffs had been requested to make us welcome.
He took us to his house and spread piles of mattresses
for us in the guest-room, his mother and pretty sister
bringing snow-sherbet and coffee, and nargilehs for
some of our party. We reposed for some time, for it
was very hot, before we went up the village to see the
fabriques; nearly every house or even hut in the place
had its loom, sometimes many were at work together.
The cloth is a woof of bright-coloured silks on a warp of
thick cotton threads, gold or silver thread being laid in
with the colours of the pattern: it is shaped in pieces for
cushions, slippers, bags and caps, which are very pretty
and durable, but somewhat costly, and they asked more
for them here than in Beyrout. Some were also weaving
silk scarfs and shawls—a poor imitation of the Damascus
manufacture. Zouk is a thriving town, and very prettily
situated on the side of the mountain sloping down into
the lovely little Bay of Jouneh. We came home at a
great pace in the cool evening air, thinking how charming a winter residence this bay would make for an
invalid; it is a pity that this coast is not more sought
by those who are obliged to seek a warmer climate than
our own; there are many places on the coast which

combine the advantages of the most delicious climate and magnificent scenery under a clear sky, bright sunshine, and sweet, but not relaxing air. Beyrout is said to be somewhat damp in the winter, but then the winter seldom lasts six weeks, and is not severe enough to render a fire necessary, though a brasier of hot coals in the evening may sometimes, but not often, be agreeable; and with a little notice and some pre-arrangements, houses might be found at Latakia, Beyrout, and its neighbourhood, Saïda and Hhaïffa, all most charming places; and living is certainly less, with a tolerably honest dragoman, than at Naples, Nice or Malta; they are easy of access by frequent steamers, and the necessary comforts required for invalids can be had at Beyrout or from Alexandria, while, with a good dragoman, you have as little trouble in housekeeping as in an hotel. Of course these native-built country houses do not look very grand; but our experience can testify that a very little trouble taken, with the help of a dozen nails and a few yards of coloured flannel or cotton, will make the room not only comfortable but pretty also. The coast of Syria is at least worth thinking of by invalids for whom the ascent of the Nile is too expensive an affair: while Cairo is very damp in the early part of the winter, and feverish; and few people like Alexandria; Corfu is said to be dull; and many persons are tired of the regular Italian watering-places, and are unwilling to encounter the enormous expense of a winter there. Of course, with the exception of one or two families at Beyrout, there could be no society, as the Consuls are the only European residents at each place; but to some persons this would be a minor objection.

There are innumerable charming expeditions to be made from Beyrout; and while waiting for our house to be ready, we determined to initiate ourselves into the mysteries of tent life in an excursion to Deir-el-Kamar*, the capital of the Druze country, which generally takes two long days' riding; but as we were *new* at mountain riding we determined to devote four to it. The starting day of any excursion in Syria is one that calls for extraordinary patience and good temper; even with these it is immensely wearying and provoking. We were ourselves dressed at 5 A. M., and our mules arrived soon after, but they were not finally loaded and despatched till near 11 A. M., and we followed at mid-day; we had eight mules, and a donkey to carry their master, and we took a cook, canteen, and three tents. This was our kit throughout Syria: — a large tent for ourselves with double carpets, beds, dinner-table, and two folding arm-chairs, with another tent for our maid, and the kitchen tent; our personal luggage, which was packed in two tin travelling-baths in stout wicker coverings (a luxury with which I recommend every lady-traveller in this climate to provide herself), and a couple of portmanteaus, went on two mules, one of them surmounted by a little wooden cage or carriage, in which the Maltese dog, our inseparable companion and faithful little night-guard, was carried; he used to distinguish us at an almost incredible distance, and his bark of recognition, his voice of welcome in answer to our footsteps, was always the glad sound which announced that the tents were nigh and the dinner ready, at the end of a long weary day's ride; every one, even Mooslims, petted the pretty little thing wherever we went. His ancestors, of the noble Lion family of Malta, had some time ago settled at Smyrna, where this small scion of the house

* Alas, thirteen months after, the scene of horrible and sanguinary atrocities.

was given to me. He has long white hair, large black eyes, and a knowing little black nose.

Our road lay through the Pine-forest, thence it turned off through many winding lanes, hedged with prickly pear, pomegranates, and hawthorn still in blossom, towards the mountains; in the gardens a few palm-trees are growing, but they look very stunted, sickly, and small, and give but a melancholy *souvenir* of Egypt. Leaving the olive-groves about Hadith, the road crosses a narrow sandy plain and then begins to wind up the mountain. The beauty of the scenery compensates for all the *désagrémens* of the path. But before we ascend further let me try and describe what is called a road in Syria, without understanding which no one can by any means fancy what travelling there really is like; how much it adds to the fatigue; how much it must necessarily occupy the attention, and still more, how much time is consumed in its difficulties. The *best* of all the mountain roads are staircases of paved stones, made chiefly by the Emir Beshir; these are all very well in going up, but in coming down most horses give you a kind of jolting bang on each step, which makes one feel sea-sick in a long descent. I had a dear old horse afterwards who used to come down quite gently on the step, but it is at the best a disagreeable jogging process: very frequently these steps are broken or missing, and then one gets down as one can; more usually the path is the dry bed of a torrent, full of stones and big boulders, brought down and left by the rushing sream, loose and awkward to tread amongst: worse than these are long places like an old stone quarry, or as if the side wall, originally built of large blocks, had fallen down. Over these sharp edges, deep holes, and uncertain footing, the horse feels his way as

cautiously as if they were burning hot, and in descending it is somewhat dangerous. Nothing, however, is so
bad as the dreadful smooth rocks at an acute angle,
with perhaps a horrid cleft at the bottom, down which
the unfortunate animals slidder in a way that is apt to
excite a very unpleasant sensation in the region of the
heart and throat, — in excuse for which it must be remembered that as all these paths, except the staircases,
are made by mother-nature, they are of any conceivable
slope, and of course the worst bits of path are always at
the most perilous spot, — a winding turn at the edge of
a ravine, or overhanging a yawning chasm; then no
one likes to feel the horse under him gathering up his
fore feet for a jump or a drop, which, overdone by an
inch, will precipitate you, if not him also, to the bottom
of the mountain. True, the horses are extraordinarily
sure-footed and cautious, though they seldom seem to
have a good point about them, and they climb like
cats; but accidents do occur sometimes, and a lady's
seat has a strong feeling of one-sidedness about it when
both her feet are hanging over a precipice, and only
one shoulder seems really over terra-firma. The Arab
saddles save some fatigue in this continual ascent and
descent, and where it is very steep indeed, and your
horse feels as if he *must* topple back or fall on his nose,
they give support and steadiness better than the English saddle. Most gentlemen bring their own saddles,
but I believe those who do not, get on quite as well as
those who do. We had English side-saddles sent out
to us, and our bridles were of anything, bits of rope or
leather, often adorned with fine tassels and amulets,
fringe and shells, &c. &c., over the head and neck of
favourite animals, and excessively pretty the harness
often is when they are fresh and good. Well, we have

wandered far from our present road, but this description
is really necessary, and having been thus given once, it
applies to nearly *all* the paths throughout Syria.

The road to Deir el Kamar, however bad, is charm-
ingly beautiful. After resting a little at a fine fountain called 'Ain Bsâba, we wound round a richly-wooded
gorge on a path about two feet wide, and through a
pretty village called 'Ain Anoob, full of sweet geraniums,
where we looked up to the great English silk-reeling
factory of Shumlan, belonging to Mr. Scott, and down
over all the road we had come from Beyrout; then turning up a breezy hillside, we found our tents pitched in
an olive grove outside the village of Anâb, commanding
splendid views of the plain of Beyrout spread out like a
map, the miles of olive and pine-woods and gardens
contrasting with the white town and the red sands, the
blue sea, and the ever beautiful mountains. All the
valleys on this road are richly wooded and luxuriant
with flowers; every stream teams with oleanders; the
pines perfume the air; and. every height, if not covered
with a village, is topped by a convent.

Our day had been a short one, but we were very
much tired, and went to bed at once, after dining by
lantern-light under an olive tree. The next morning,
somewhat appalled by the difficulties, not to say dangers of the road, I remarked to the dragoman that I
hoped to-day's would be better: "Mademoiselle," he
solemnly answered, "'la route devient toujours pire;"
and with this consolation in my mind we started. Our
way led over a hill that was literally rose colour with
wild flax; the old terrace walls were studded with
cyclamen, and every here and there the wild hollyhocks
shot up in spikes of fine lilac flowers, over a truly
atrocious path, which soon opened on the Wady el

Kâdy (the Valley of the Judge), a magnificent valley
running N.E. and S.W., with a fine dashing river
at the bottom ; but before we had sufficiently enjoyed
it we were descending. the most fearful winding track
through a pine-forest, throughout which, much as I
have climbed and descended since, it is still a marvel to
me how any one of us stuck on our horses * ; however
we reached the bottom in safety, and crossed a picturesque old bridge over the foaming river, and began
to ascend the other side, amidst ilex and thorn, juniper,
myrtle and cypress, tangled over with wild vines: but
we lost the track, and finally had to clamber up an
almost impossible place, where one of our horses fell
and threw his rider, but happily without hurting him.
The summit gained at last, we looked over the sea on
the right, with the bright red-sided mountain terraced
with figs and olives, and noble cliffs of cold grey limestone ; and on the left, down the fine valley of Deir el
Kamar, Druze villages on every hilltop, the town itself
standing out white and shining on a mountain spur,
and at the head of the valley, the famous castle-palace
of the Emir Beshir, Bteddeen. We were soon in the
town, which struck us as handsome and lively ; the
houses all built of smoothly-hewn stone, frequently with
arched and mullioned windows, each with its little
balcony of flowers, among which we noticed several
white lilies; we passed through some tolerable bazaars
and a fine convent, from whence the town takes its
name, there having been anciently a figure of the
Virgin standing on the Moon, carved on a stone outside

* The "Times'" correspondent gave (September 21, 1860) a detailed
account of all this road, in which we were amused to recognise each particularly " bad step " that had horrified us when, like him, we took this
path on our first Syrian excursion.

the convent wall *; it had a small dome surmounted by
a cross, and seemed well built. There were also one or
two minarets and a gaily-painted Serai, or Turkish
Governor's house for business †: but we did not stay to
see much, as we wanted to reach Bteddeen early. The
descent, however, from the town was so terrific (we
took the wrong road where no horses go, I believe),
that we did not get to the bottom, and up the long,
steep, zig-zag staircase leading to the palace, till 2 P.M.

Bteddeen has been often described, but yet another
description still may perhaps be pardoned ; it is a
pleasure to me to linger over the memory of its many
beauties, all the more as probably ours were nearly the
last European eyes that beheld them.   We entered by
a gateway under a succession of dark arches leading into
a spacious square, the right-hand side of which was
built on arches, forming the stables of the Emir's stud
(usually of 500 horses it is said), over which was a
terrace looking out on the glorious valley ; this square
had been the tilting or parade ground in the Emir's
time : we crossed it into another square of the same
size, in the midst of which stood a fountain in a bower
of acacias in blossom, and at the opposite end the
beautiful palace front itself, with an arcade to which a
wooden staircase fantastically formed and gaily painted
and gilt, was attached ; the walls were panelled entirely over with medallions of various-coloured marbles,
and the doorways and windows adorned in the same
way, the whole frontage being thus, with the floorings
and balustrade of the terrace, a mass of marble mosaic
in the most exquisite arabesques — in fact the patterns
and execution of the Bteddeen mosaic are superior to,

---

* *Deir*, convent: *kamar*, moon.
† Afterwards the scene of the most atrocious part of the horrible
massacres here.

and more varied and elegant than the best things of the kind in Venice, not excepting even the flooring of St. Mark's. In the centre of the terrace, against the wall, a beautiful little fountain still played, but some of the bits of mosaic had dropped out here and there and were replaced by delicate sprays of light and tender maiden-hair fern, bending down to the crystal stream, which seemed to brighten up under the smiles of the green fronds — a mark of ruin certainly, but sacrilegious would have been the restorer's hand that should pluck out those graceful wreaths that hung there, hiding the decay of past splendour in their own sweet freshness. Off this terrace were several rooms, the ceilings, doors, and shutters of which were most elaborately painted in bright patterns, the gilding sadly dimmed, but enough remaining to show what charming little bowers, fit for fairy princesses, they had once been. From this we passed into the inner apartments, and went through the bath-rooms : they were considerably finer than any other thing of the kind we saw in the East, excepting one or two of the principal houses in Damascus : they were entirely of mosaic in marble, everywhere, except under each fountain where porcelain tiles of a very fine make were used : there were plants — oranges, lemons, roses, &c.— growing in every room except the hottest, and fountains trickling or playing everywhere ; and the large siesta hall was divided down the middle by slender, clustered columns supporting a hundred vaultings. Many of these rooms opened into gardens of lemons and oranges that once were doubtless very charming, but they showed the want of care and the rude hand of the Turkish soldier more than the palace itself.

The colonel of the ugly soldiers quartered there was gone to Damascus, but after we had reposed some time

on the terrace, a lieutenant, dressed in a complete suit
of primrose silk, brought us a pressing invitation from
his chief's wife to enter the hareem; she sent the eldest
son of the colonel, a boy of about ten years old, and an
old black slave to conduct us there. We were shown
first into a hall, full of marble columns, with a square
gallery at each end, ornamented with marble and
gilding, through which we entered the hareem court,
where a large fountain was playing in the hot sun; in
this court a number of immensely fat women and slaves,
each dressed in a single loose garment of coloured
muslin, were romping violently, throwing water at each
other, and jumping in and out of the fountain, upon
seeing which, the boy who had come with us tore off
all his clothes, save a small pair of drawers, and jumped
in with them. Not any of the women were pretty;
they took very little notice of us, and only left off their
romps now and then to come and stare at us for a
minute. We were taken into a small richly divaned
room, where the favourite wife of the colonel was nurs-
ing a fat baby of which she was very proud, as it was a
son. She was young and pretty, but her features were
more like those of a boy than of a young woman, and
her dress of yellow Manchester cotton was very ugly;
her hair was cropped in a straight line on the forehead,
as Mooslims generally wear it, and hung down behind
in one long plait; afterwards she put on a blue velvet
jacket embroidered with gold, and a dirty tarboosh.
Two Christian women who were paying a visit like
ourselves, and who were both very pretty, looked beautifully neat and clean beside the Mooslims. The wife
asked innumerable questions, all of which we answered
to the best of our Arabic powers, when we understood
them, and then she showed us the other rooms, of

which the ceilings were equally beautifully painted;
they all had plenty of mattresses spread on the floor,
but the wife's room had an iron bedstead with mosquito
curtains round it. We saw little to admire; they wore
no jewels, and the only pretty thing was a hand-
mirror, in a finely worked filagree silver frame, which
we wanted to buy, but she would not part with it.

We were glad to have been invited into the hareem,
if only to see the view from the windows, so romantically beautiful in the long narrow ravine up which the
Castle windows look, due west, with the sea at the end;
hill after hill bordering the valley on each side, the
nearest one crowned with another small palace built for
the Emir's mother, and the pretty white town further
on at the other side; both sides richly clothed with
mulberry terraces and fruit gardens, while from the
stream at the bottom the steep zigzags up to the Palace
are so well seen, that a knight of yore might have
mounted the whole way without once losing sight of his
ladye's eyes shining on him from her latticed bower, the
rest of the fortress proudly and sternly guarding the
narrow pass below the lofty cliffs. It is, indeed, a place
for dreams of chivalry and fair ladies; but from such
dreams, certes, nothing can awaken one more completely than the sight of the rows of Turkish soldiers,
round, fat, and short, in tight blue trowsers, little close
jackets, and small red fezs over their ugly heads,—nor
can anything be less romantic than the stout, coarse
females of the hareem. These soldiers blew a fine
flourish of trumpets and stared at us immensely when
we left the fortress; they were probably the same garrison who butchered the unfortunate Christians in the following summer (June 19, 1860), and were ill-looking

enough for anything; too horrible it is to think of the
beautiful place, with the gnawed and mangled remains
of human bodies scattered through its courts, and the
snowy marbles of those delicately ornamented floors
"pallid with horror, while the red darkened with blood." *
The Turkish soldiers had done much to spoil its beauty,
but the plundering Christian peasants are doing much
more, and if we regretted then that we could not transport the whole place bodily to England, one is more
than ever sorry now that ruin and desolation and a horrible memory has laid its heavy hand upon the once
lovely and smiling spot.

The children of the town regularly mobbed us after
dinner, bringing bouquets of flowers as we lay upon
the sward outside our tents, enjoying the beautiful view,
the twinkling light, the large shining stars, and the
multitudes of fire-flies that danced round us. Now and
then a faint sound of singing rose from the valley, or
a bird trilled a little evening strain; but the boys
would chatter; for the American mission schools have
done much work here, and not a few could speak both
French and English, which they were too glad to exercise upon the strangers. One of them had impudence
enough to beg we would *lend* him fifty piasters, which
he assured us he would certainly repay if ever we came
back to Syria !

Every house in the little town had its flower garden
of roses, lilies, geraniums, &c.; among them we noticed
a splendid double sweet-scented moss-rose of a fine
deep lemon colour, which would make glad the heart
of an English gardener. The inhabitants were nearly
all Christians — chiefly Maronites, with a few Greeks

* Ruskin.

under the Mutsellim; but the valley is full of Druze villages, as it is close to their chief stronghold Mukhtārah,
and their Kūlwehs are seen everywhere, generally
perched on some lofty or nearly inaccessible crag. The
Kūlweh is their place of worship, there they meet
every Thursday evening, and feast after service upon
raisins, figs, &c.; but the meetings are conducted with
such entire secrecy that little is known about them,
and any one hardy enough to venture too near has
invariably been put to death; but from what is known
they seem to be more political than devotional assem-
blies, only the Akhals (or initiated) are admitted, and
the affairs of the community discussed; a wonderful
system of rapid and thorough communication is kept
up, and the most perfect organisation and discipline
reigns among them, — this is one of the things in which
they are so far superior to their Maronite neighbours.
They buy and sell much in the town, and are far neater
and cleaner in appearance than the Christians. The
Bazaars were lively, and the people crowded round us
with antiques, coins, &c., to sell, and sweet snow-
water, which they pressed upon us and for which they
seemed unwilling to be paid. We got a fine antique
bronze lamp, and a bronze ornament of two rudely
sculptured but very lively bulls, for a few piasters;
they closely resemble some of the Phœnician bronzes
in the fine collection at Turin.

The sun was too hot for us to linger, so we started off
at 9 A. M. over the hill-top; there the fresh sea-breeze
met us, as we looked down on the winding Da'mour, the
ancient Tamyras, and retraced our steps through the
Wady el Kādy, till we reached our tents placed beside
the fountain of 'Ain Bsaba among thickets of honeysuckle and wild geraniums; as the sun sunk over

the sea I went up and bathed in the bright spring,
which is shaded over by noble trees. Late in the
evening a terrible khamseen set in, and we had a wild
night, the tents every now and then coming down over
our heads as we lay panting and suffocating on our
beds; they had been badly pitched on soft ground,
where the pins would not hold, and two of them had
been unwittingly placed on an ant-march, so that the
unfortunate occupiers were swarmed, over the whole
night through, by countless multitudes of the black
beasties. The khamseen brought up thousands of
sand-flies, who operated vigorously upon our faces,
for we had no mosquito curtains then, and we became
so ill with the unwholesome air, that we got up at three
o'clock to dress, in hopes of getting off by daylight, —
but, *pour comble de malheur*, I was incautiously washing upon the grass, when a big black scorpion, astounded
at the apparition, walked up to one of my feet and
stung me, and I fell into such pain for some hours that
dressing or moving was out of the question. We sent
off to Beyrout for ammonia, but by the time it came I
was better. The khamseen began to abate, and we
reached the hôtel at mid-day, very ready for breakfast
and thankful it was no worse, for the black scorpions
are the least venomous of the race. The yellow ones
sting terribly, and cause fearful agony and swelling,
but the wound is seldom fatal.

We found a large party of our Nile companions
arrived at the hôtel in readiness for the French home
steamer; it was pleasant to meet with even such slight
acquaintances in this distant land, — but the change
effected in them all since we had met in Egypt was
more or less appalling. The nose of each one had been
skinned once or twice or thrice; several were in the

most brilliant process of excoriation, and every face below the forehead was painted in turkey-cockian hues! It was perfectly absurd to look round the table at the indescribable varieties of RED that graced the board.

Two days after this we rode up to Beit Miry and took possession of our house, which we found perfectly charming and comfortable in every respect; the balconies were filled with carnations, the terraces bordered with hollyhocks and belle-de-nuit, and everything looked smiling; while just as we set foot on the threshold a volley of cannon sounded from the town barracks and from every ship in the bay! resounding back in peals of thunder from the mountains all around us. We were a little astonished, and the villagers believed it was to welcome the English ladies, — but in reality it was a royal salute on the landing of the Grand Duke Constantine of Russia.

CHAP. IX.

OUR MOUNTAIN HOME.

THE village of Beit Miry runs along the top of a mountain ridge, something more than 2000 feet above the
sea, which curves round in the form of a semicircle:
the peasants' houses slope down on either side of the
ridge, the Druzes mostly occupying the west, and the
Christians the east end. Our house was planted on the
end of the western horn, while the Christian Emir's house
and the Maronite chapel faced us at the end of
the eastern horn, just above a beautiful little pine-
forest, — the whole of the circle between being filled up
with curving mulberry terraces and a few of the best
houses. Beyrout is so charming till the end of June,
that the *season* of Beit Miry had not then commenced,
but by July eight or nine European families had taken
refuge from the heat of the town and arranged themselves somehow in three peasant houses; they were
miserable *gîtes* in themselves, only one other in the
place besides our own house being really a good one,
and that was not half as pretty as ours; but from
standing at the western extremity of the village it commanded the view in the northern valley as well as the
southern view of Beyrout, and in this respect was
certainly one of the finest spots in the whole of the

Lebanon, indescribably beautiful. Beyond this another smaller semicircle curved out from the ridge towards the south; this was covered with a forest of pines, planes, and some magnificent oaks, while, like a fortress crowning the summit, the large Convent of Deir-el-Khŭllah, proudly surveyed the glorious country, itself a landmark for many miles.

Immediately above our house, on the top of the crag, stood a collection of Druze houses; about half an hour's steep descent below us was the palace of the Maronite Bishop, called Madrāss. When the Europeans had come up, we used to think what a curious variety of creeds had met in that one small village — Druzes, Maronites, Roman Catholics " united " and ununited, Greeks, Lutherans, English Protestants, and a few Mooslims. Perhaps the constant communication of the villagers with Beyrout, and the annual stay of so many Europeans among them has done a good deal to improve the inhabitants of Beit Miry, but we certainly found them an honest (honesty, *bien entendu, à l'Arabe*), simple-minded, and industrious set; the Druzes are more industrious, the men much cleaner, and immensely finer-looking than the Christians, but the Druze women, on the contrary, look filthy and frightful beside the mountain Maronite women, many of whom in Beit Miry were really very pretty, and were always gaily, and generally cleanly dressed. A bright-coloured cotton gown, with usually a thick red woollen shawl wound round the hips, white muslin appearing at the neck, (though the gown is always left wide open to the waist in front,) a white apron sometimes, and invariably a white muslin veil, often very prettily embroidered in colours, — such is the costume of the Maronite woman, to which must be added string after string of gold and silver coins wound round the throat, falling over and below the bosom, according to the wealth of the owner, and among them perhaps two or three little triangular silver boxes containing charms, scraps of the Koran written on parchment. Her headdress is a red tarboosh edged with coins, a piece of bright-coloured crape or gauze tied round it, and then *the* Christian head ornament, viz. from 100 to 200 strings of black silk cord, about two feet long, into which are woven at intervals little bits of gold shaped thus; each string ending in a solid tassel or knob of gold or silver; I have seen as many as 3000 bits of gold on one headdress, but usually they carry from 1000 to 2000. These strings, which are all joined into one mass at the top, and are called the "*saffah*," are fastened to the back of the tarboosh, the long silk tassel of which hangs over them; an ornament of filagree gold, called the *koors*, is generally worn at the top of the tassel also; while from the front of the head, on one side only, a very pretty festoon ornament, of eight or ten chains of gold or strings of pearls, is added, each one strung with larger bits of gold than those on the *saffah*; a brooch of diamonds, &c., or a bouquet of natural flowers, is stuck in on the other side. This headdress is extremely pretty and graceful.

In this land of constant petty warfare and bloodfeuds, it is no wonder that the wealth of every family should be reduced to a portable form; nor is it any wonder either that a husband should heap ornaments on his wife's person year after year to the utmost of his power, since, at his death, she retains no other possession, all the remainder of his property being divided among his children. It is thought unseemly for a man to propose marriage until he has funds

sufficient to bestow on his bride a massive gold necklace
of a peculiar pattern — *de rigueur* throughout·Syria —
and which costs at least 24*l.* In times of distress one
of the coins, or if these are gone, a piece of the necklace is cut off and sold, but to be replaced as soon as
possible.

The Druze women wear a long dark blue cotton
chemise like the Egyptian women, and a square of the
same stuff which is drawn over the head and face, and
over the tantour, if one is worn. The Christian women
are generally very fair, though with dark eyes; the Druze
women are dark, skinny, and ugly, and grow old much
earlier than their Christian neighbours, because they do
more hard work, and are more exposed to the weather,
with fewer clothes to cover them.

Our housekeeping was soon arranged; we had eggs,
milk, and fowls from the village, and meat, vegetables,
and groceries from the town for the first month; after
this, we had abundance of meat and fruit, &c. from the
village. Three or four Druzes went down every morning early to Beyrout with their mules, and brought
back their commissions duly performed in the afternoon. We seldom had occasion to find fault with them,
but we had a great grievance in having every little
package or parcel turned over and searched by the
douane at the gate of Beyrout, even if our dragoman or
cook accompanied them; and, like Frank in the story,
who would look, then touch, then smell, and finally
succumbed under the temptation of tasting, large pieces
of our sugar, coffee, and fruit were mulcted by the
soldiers, and very provoking it was to have one's
peaches and figs arrive looking like *moulds* for their
curious and presumptuous fingers. We applied to Mr.
Moore, the Consul, to have a ticket of exemption given

to us as consumers, not dealers, but nothing was ever
done about it, and the food was too simple and good
to admit of our hoping it might disagree with the
soldiers.

It is not easy to say how happy we were in our
mountain home; we were perfectly indifferent to
society, as we had plenty of books (thanks to our
friends), and many other occupations besides reading;
our maid was still sewing hard to replace the burnt
clothes; and, in truth, we found very close attention to
study remarkably difficult with so beautiful a prospect
ever enchanting and fascinating our eyes: hours and
hours that I intended to spend in reading found me
looking and looking at the view, with my book in my
hand, — and yet we never could decide, all the months we
stayed there, whether the landscape was most beautiful
by morning or by evening. In every light and under
every circumstance I longed to sketch its many
beauties, but we had not been able to replace our
paint-boxes since the fire, and it was not till ten days
before we left it, probably for ever, that paper, pencils,
or colours arrived from England. Our days passed in
monotonous pleasantness, every little variety seeming
only a fresh pleasure. We were up with the first
streak of dawn, between four and five A.M., and if
Paradise is to be found in this world, it must be in the
feel of the air early in the morning on those mountains.
How the birds sang — how the fresh air came up, stirring
with fragrant perfumes all round one — how the night
clouds floated softly away — how the sunlight strode with
majestic steps down the mountain side and over the
plain — how the sea deepened and brightened from red to
blue — how the sun caught the white line of foam on the
rocky shore, and tipped house after house and village

after village with gold! Truly this was what Hood
calls :

> "that breath in the air
> A perfume and freshness strange and rare,
> A warmth in the light and a bliss everywhere,
> All sweets below, and all sunshine above."

Then we sat in the balconies among the flowers, or
under our shady arcade, watching the villagers making
very brief toilettes as they rose from their beds on the
housetops (the children, like dogs, seemed only to shake
themselves for their toilettes, while the family washing
was invariably deferred till after sunset, when one bowl
of water would be brought up for a couple of women or
half-a-dozen children),— or we watched the goats going
by to fresh pastures,—or the cows, of which there were
not many, and the sheep on their way to be fed in the
mulberry-terraces on freshly gathered leaves,—or strings
of mules departing to some distant place,—or the crowds
of women going down in the cool early shade to the
fountain to fetch up the water for the day, before the
sun came on the spring; while we sat eating basketfuls
of figs gathered before the dew was dry on their yellow
skins, or of fresh, cool, golden prickly-pears. About eight
o'clock a row of little round clouds, like tufts of cotton
wool, rose up in a white line along the horizon of the
sea, and the heat soon after became too great to bear
out-of-doors,—but the little clouds rose and rose and
spread, whitening broadly on the sky, and by 9·30 or ·45,
as punctual as a watch, up came the delicious breeze
from their bosoms, and seemed to whisper, "Never
mind the sun, I'm here, and I'll keep you cool;" and
so it did; every day unfailingly it came, and every day
it died away between 4 and 5 P.M., when the sun was
going down, and the mountains beginning to cast long

shadows on the plain. Then we used to go out and climb a new height, or dive down into a new glen or ravine each day; every day we found a fresh path, or no path, to take, but some fresh object to interest or some fresh beauty to admire, so enticing that we never came home till after the sun had sunk behind the resplendent sea, and the purple night clouds had come up, and the villagers were rolling themselves up in thick blankets on the housetops; then sometimes the moon would shine with such loveliness, shedding floods of silver over mountain, sea, and plain, that we could not but pace our terraces till quite late, too full of admiration for sleep,— even when sleeping nature seemed near one; for as glass panes were unknown articles in Beit Miry, our windows had only iron bars to keep out animals, and wooden shutters in case of a storm; these, however, we never shut, and the fresh air of heaven blew over us while asleep, without a chance at this height of bringing fever or cold, or any other ill, so delicious was the climate by day and by night, never too hot and never too cold.

Even our little village had its legend of love and death. There was a small house, consisting chiefly of a large verandah, half hidden among the mulberries between us and the Pine-forest, which was occupied some few years ago by a half European and half Arab family; the great beauty of the daughter had attracted many suitors for her hand, one of whom was most assiduous in his attentions; these were at first accepted, but after some time the affections of the fair one were bestowed on a more fortunate object, and partly in order to escape the unwelcome assiduities of the first lover, the family came up to the mountains for the summer. The inconsolable deserted one could not, however, resist the temptation of following his beloved mistress, hoping at least to gladden his eyes with the sight of

her; tying his horse in the wood below, he stole through
the trees near the house, and beheld her standing
in the verandah with his hated rival; the bright moonlight shone down on both, and the expression of her
face revealed to him how hopeless were his own pros-
pects with regard to her. In a transport of jealousy
he drew a pistol from his pocket and levelled it at his
rival; but, alas, the mad passions of his soul had
unhappily been beating in his hand, and the ball
pierced the heart of the unfortunate girl, who fell,
bathed in blood, into the arms of her more favoured,
but not less unhappy lover, maddened with horror and
despair at the sight, the miserable young man dis-
charged another pistol at himself, and in another second
lay dead at only a few yards distance from his murdered mistress!

We had rigged a flagstaff soon after our arrival, and
there we hoisted a grand red jack above the house. Of
course we had no kind of *right* to do so (as only Consuls
are granted the privilege in Turkey), but we had carried
our flag in Egypt, and intended to pitch it before our
tents in travelling, and we had an idea that it might be
of use to us in the mountains. Time proved the idea a
good one, and we had reason to thank the kind friend
who had provided us with the means of carrying it out.
It led to an amusing consequence, for we found afterwards that every individual peasant who came down
from the mountains, and all strangers from other
villages, invariably stopped and asked who the great
person could be whose house was ornamented with such
brilliant colours: and that our dragoman and Arab cook,
who were both mountaineers, and, consequently, tremendous gossips, for their own aggrandisement as well as
ours, enlarged greatly upon how these English princesses
had come all the way alone over the wide sea and

through kingdom after kingdom to let their greatness
sojourn for a while in the highly honoured village; the
which history was received with innumerable "Mash-
āllahs," and usually produced an amazing number of
compliments.

The first Sunday after we arrived there, the dragoman announced that the Maronite priest of the village
wished to pay us a visit, and after the morning service,
he and a companion priest, or curate, arrived. They
were dressed in long black robes of serge, with a scarf of
the same wound round the waist, and the elder wore
the regular mountain-priest's headdress, a large globe
of black serge: he had a fine open intelligent face and a
long white beard; the other looked commoner, and
wore only a red tarboosh with a black scarf tied round
it. They congratulated us on our safe arrival in their
village after the innumerable perils of which they had
heard travellers tell, and invoked all manner of
blessings on us while we sojourned near them. The old
Priest was pleasantly communicative as far as his limited
subjects of interest and few words of Italian would
admit: he told us that every Priest must be seven
years in the college at Artourah before he is ordained,
and that in the act of ordination the Bishop places one
had upon the candidate's forehead in blessing, while
holding the chalice over his head with the other: they
are supported by the voluntary contributions of their
flock, but if this is not sufficient the Bishop provides
them with a small allowance. Each Priest has a little
garden which he cultivates for himself, but he is not
permitted to labour elsewhere for gain; but we heard
of many instances where the Priest helped a sick or
unfortunate parishioner in his labour, and they seemed
to be generally much beloved and respected in all the

villages: everywhere we were told of their being dili-
gent visitors of the sick. They marry generally the
daughters of a Sheikh or Emir, some one a little above
the common peasantry; marriage being one of the pri-
vileges which Rome was obliged to concede to the Maronite Church, and the peasantry are very particular in
having married Priests for the confessors of their wives
and daughters. We had not many subjects of conversation, but an "Illustrated London News" and some
portrait photographs seemed to interest them very
much, and they asked a great many questions. The
Convent bell sounded mid-day during their visit, and
both Priests stopped even in the midst of a sentence,
and bowing the head said a short prayer, which they
told us they repeated at every third hour in the day.

Some of the friends we had known in Egypt, who
came up to see us before they embarked at Beyrout on
their homeward voyage, and many of the richer Arabs
in the village, came begging to see the English ladies,
and were enormously pleased to examine us and our
clothes, and our books and pictures, &c. &c., and they
really seemed so much delighted that we had not the
heart to send them away, however much they bored us;
the woodcuts in a copy of Lane's "Modern Egyptians,"
representing the costumes of their Arab brethren, were
viewed with clasped hands and many "Mash-āllahs!"
but they said if we had such good pictures why did we
come so far and take so much trouble to see them?
After my paint-box arrived I used to get repeated
messages entreating me to take their portraits for them;
one very pretty woman, very rich in gold ornaments,
came up early in the morning and sat till the afternoon,
imploring to have her picture done, until I was really
forced to do something like it, with which she was quite

enchanted, the colours being very bright and the bad
drawing quite immaterial to her. That woman became
a perfect torment to us afterwards, for having happened
to see a pair of stays lying on the table she became so
mad to have them, that day after day she returned to the
house with new and pressing entreaties, offering me at
last coin after coin from her head-dress if I would only let
her have the much-coveted articles to make her figure as
enchanting as a European lady's! We generally found
them very quick and intelligent in taking in new ideas,
several of the girls learning to play "solitaire" after
once seeing our maid do it, and more than one succeeded
in accomplishing the triumphant one-remaining ball,
much to their own delight and our surprise. Perhaps
our favourite walk of all was along the back of the
village, and through the cool, delightful shade of the
wood, up to the Convent of Deir el Kulah. There was
a little chapel half way along the path, shaded by a
group of lofty evergreen oaks, under whose sombre shade
we rested many an early morning and sunset evening;
after passing which the path wound up the hill, with
the loveliest views of Beit Miry and the coast, through
the wood and over the roughest of paths; for all this
wood has grown over the ruins of an ancient town, the
smoothly hewn stones of which would appear to have
belonged to well-built houses. Then came the great
square of the Convent, where some civil black-robed
monks bade us welcome, and conducted us to the corridor. Here we loved to sit, for the view, framed in the
mullioned double-arched window, is as beautiful as the
heart of man could desire: the deep, richly wooded
valleys at each side, the cheerful villages, the green
uplands, the blue and purple ranges of distant hills, the
wide expanse of sea, and Sunnîn, rosy and snowy, rising

up a giant wall, beyond all. Many an evening we
lingered here, sketching or chatting with the monks,
and wondering if any earthly view could be much more
beautiful.

This Convent is built over the ruins of a very large
Temple, of which some huge columns and stones are
still standing; a great many Greek and Latin inscriptions have been fixed in the modern walls (most of
them upside down), all mentioning the god of sports,
or *Bal-markos*, the god to whom the Temple was
probably dedicated. Doubtless the Greeks, in building
the Temple, adopted to themselves the god to whom this
"high-place" was originally dedicated by the Phœnicians, whose chief god, Baal, was invoked under various
names and emblems added to his supreme name (as
Baal-pheor, Baal-Berith), instead of translating or
changing the divine name into their own Apollo or
Jupiter: it is exactly the kind of spot which the ancient
idolaters would have chosen for making a "grove," and
a "high-place," whereon to perform their mysterious
rites.

Close above our house there was a threshing-floor, —
a little circular bit of smooth ground in the midst of a
wild conglomeration of rocks; and often in the earliest
sunbeams we used to wander up there to watch the
bullocks dragging the board round and round over the
ears of corn, on which sometimes the three pretty little
children of the Emir would sit, helping to press down
the rollers on the straw, the under side of the board
being covered with sharp stones fastened on securely.
In some parts of Syria they use knives or short scythes
which chop the straw while they press out the corn;
and, on a windy morning, they would all be busy flinging
up handfuls of it into the air, that the wind might

blow away the chaff ere the corn fell back upon the
threshing-floor.

Beyond this a rough path led through a deep, romantic,
wooded glen, where, bending low under prickly oaks,
terebinth, and hedges of juniper and clematis, we used
to come out upon a luxuriant vineyard, truly " a very
fruitful hill," and sit on the edges of an ancient wine-
press of hewn stones, which had probably been there
since the days when the Prophet Isaiah sang songs of
the spiritual vineyard in the deaf ear of the Jews. There
were three or four of the receptacles for the grapes
built up of stones, and hollows for the juice to run out
of them into a lower place, hewn out of the rock ; all
were now tangled over with unpruned vines, honeysuckle, and clematis, making a bower of shade for the
workman when gathering the rich juice, and the
mountain torrent dashing past wherein to cleanse the
vessels. There were several of these winepresses on the
hills close to us : the upper one had legends attached to
it, and stories of *jinns* and spirits and murders besides,
and close to it ran the aqueduct which brings water
down from Sunnîn, and, descending into the valley,
used to carry a stream into Berytus, it is said. It is a
pity it is not still kept in order, for water in Beyrout
is very bad and very dear, and the aqueduct works to
this day at Beit Miry, where we used to see a stream of
pure water trickling through the interstices of the displaced stones.

One Sunday afternoon we descended the hill till we
reached Madrass, the Bishop's Palace, to whom, on a
hint from one of his attendant priests, we announced
our intention of paying a visit ; he sent word that he
should be delighted, &c. &c., and we walked through his
pleasant gardens and into the well-built, commodious

house, part of which is a residence for priests. It was a plain but well finished building, with a good open staircase, on the balustrades of which crowds of snow-white doves were perched. The Bishop received us at the door of his apartment, — a good room, with a pink and white bed at one side, handsome carpets, and a large writing-table piled over with innumerable papers and letters and a few books. He was a very fine, noble-looking man, with bright intelligent eyes, an intellectual countenance, and a venerable white beard ; he seemed in the prime of life, and perfectly conversant with the affairs of the day in Europe. He asked many pertinent questions about England, but considered her evidently a half heathen land a very long way off, whose only importance lay in her influence on the great European powers ; but he really knew more of the details of the war then going on between France and Austria than we did, and had fresher intelligence : in fact, it was very remarkable, as we often had occasion to observe, how closely the Syrians watched the events passing in Europe, seemingly beyond their personal interest. Here, and further up in the mountains, it was the same thing : they knew as much, and more than we could tell them, and the Druzes seemed absolutely to have the news of each engagement in the campaign, before the Europeans themselves had had notice of the affairs of the very countries they represented !

The Bishop was very busy, but he talked a great deal, and begged us to come back soon ; he asked many questions about English ordinations, and how and whence we got bishops, &c. &c., and seemed very much interested when we told him of our great cathedrals, and his eyes brightened up as he said he wished he

o 3

might go to England to see them. We promised to pay
him another visit, and to show him some "Illustrated
News" pictures; but the very day we had appointed
to go there was, alas! the day of our forced departure
from Beit Miry, and we never saw him again.

Notwithstanding all the beauties and delights of our
quiet mountain home, we became impatient to make
some excursions from it, before the summer had become
quite too hot for travelling among the higher mountains; especially we determined that we must scale that
snowy Jebel Sunnîn, whose rosy crest was ever before
our eyes in every walk. So we sent down to Beyrout
for horses and mules, packed up our tents, &c., and set
forth very early on the morning of the 6th of June,
leaving the little dog to keep house at home with one
of the men-servants, as we knew it would be too cold
on the mountains for him.

The guide-books and travellers' accounts of the district
we visited are so insufficient that we were obliged to
trust entirely to the guidance of our dragoman, to whom
every path was familiar; and we were not disappointed
in the route he selected. Of all the wanderings we
made, from north to south of Syria, no other seven days
showed us such a vast variety of ever-changing pano-
ramas of glorious and magnificent scenery as these did.
The Cedars of Lebanon have a grave, majestic beauty
about them which nothing else can equal, — the wild
and wooded sides of the Litaany,— the soft, sad tenderness of the Lake of Tiberias, — and the flowery forests
of Mount Carmel, each have their own peculiar loveliness; but the Kesrouân combines every variety of
scenery in its stern grandeur and gentle grace, its rich
colouring and wild contrasts, to say nothing of the ex-
hilarating mountain air, cool, refreshing, and so fragrant

with perfumed sweetness, that Israel, in the perfection of
his blessedness, might well be said to " smell like Lebanon."

The blue morning mist was still veiling the valley
with its beautiful bright haze when we skirted the valley
of El Metn, passing through the pretty village of Brumâna (where the Emir has a nice-looking house actually
built with a sloping roof and glass), and turned up over
a sea-blown mountain brow into a pine forest, where the
rocks looked as if they had been burned like those of
Nubia, and the path was, as we always observed it was
under pine trees, abominable. On the left hand the
Convent of Mar Ishayr, the highest of all the convents
seen from the mouth of the Nahr el Kelb, stood perched
on an insulated peak — a fine situation, but they have
no water, and are obliged to carry every drop they use
up the toilsome ascent. Then winding round two sides
of a deep valley we reached the large village or town
of Bukfeyia, where we alighted to see the French *fila-
ture* or silk-reeling *fabrique:* nearly all the workers
were boys, each with his bundle of cocoons hopping
about in a pan of boiling water before him; after
brushing off the coarse outer silk, the ends of the fine
silk from three cocoons were instantly attached to a
spool on the edge of the table, whence it passed to the
huge wheel that wound off the large skeins. The silk
is sorted into yellow and white — the productions of a
different variety of worm — and looked exquisitely fine
and glossy: it is not, however, considered quite equal
to the silk of Broussa. The refuse silk is used for tassels
or other coarse articles. The boys were mostly ugly
enough — one was precisely a Thibetan Mongol, with
sloping eyes and eyebrows, high cheek-bones, and a
melancholy mouth with thick lips. Bukfeyia boasts a

fine palace, where the late Emir Hyder resided, and where the Emir, who is governor of the whole Lebanon, ought to reside; but it was then empty: the reigning prince, being very unpopular among the Bukfeyians, was living at Beyrout. Bukfeyia is full of pretty gardens, and commands an extensive view overlooking several valleys and picturesque villages : the wood about it is more than usually varied, the pine and oak being mingled with poplar, willow, plane, ilex, arbutus, caroob, &c. &c.

At mid-day we reached the foot of the mountain cliff where the large, rich Maronite Convent of Mar-esh-Shouwyair stands proudly on the promontory looking up through beautiful valleys to Jebel Sunnîn. We mounted the path, hoping to make a comfortable rest; but the Superior was absent. Most of the monks had gone to a funeral, and the younger brothers seemed so dreadfully frightened at the idea of admitting three women into their salon or their chapel, that we compounded with them for permission to spread our carpets in the cloisters. They managed to bring the alarming daughters of Eve some cushions (upon which we immediately fell asleep), and when we left them they exploded into fits of laughter on seeing us jump up sideways on our saddles, and we heard them still laughing and laughing as we descended the winding path. Then came a long, narrow, beautiful ravine, on the opposite side of which, among thick mulberry terraces, we looked down upon the Greek Convent of Mar Hanna * Shouwyair, a very large building where the first Arabic printing-press ever set up in the Lebanon was made. This good work and the fine cultivation of the mountains all round these Convents speak much in favour of the monks; nor did we ever hear a single word said against

* St. John.

any one of the numerous Convents of the Lebanon —
nothing but respect and gratitude; and perhaps, until
the government of the country is in some degree improved and the peasantry protected, and civilisation and
education are in some degree spread amongst them,
these fraternities of single men are the best methods of
accomplishing any kind of cultivation in the unhappy
and wasted land.

From first to last, throughout Syria and Palestine,
the one great feeling ever present to one's mind, as one's
eyes journey on, mile by mile, is this deplorable *waste*
of land : — when one sees what the rude industry of the
ignorant and poverty-stricken peasant can accomplish,
— that smiling crops, delicious pastures, luxuriant fruit
gardens, and rich woods, result from the meagre,
clumsy work done by the mountaineer, unassisted by
modern implements or knowledge, — one cannot but
sigh to remember our half-exhausted homelands, and
think how small the capital, how slight the head-work,
and how short the time, that would turn the plains and
mountains of Syria again into "a land flowing with
milk and honey," and repay the workman, not tenfold,
but a hundredfold.   At present a little corn, mulberries
and olives, figs and vines, are repeated, generation after
generation, in the same terraces; but the amount of
work necessary to convert thousands of miles of mountain and valley into fertile ground would be but small,
and there are few crops to be found anywhere that could
not be cultivated successfully either on the uplands or
lowlands : while the climate is incontestably remarkable
for salubrity, and a life in the hill country would be
by no means too hot for even a Scotch Highlander.
Cotton would be admirably produced in the plains ;
and if the enterprise was commenced on a sufficiently

large and imposing scale, a very little firmness, resolution, and judicious conduct would undoubtedly insure
success. It is true that the Turks do not particularly
like or encourage European settlers, but the Christian
Arabs are delighted to welcome those who they know
will improve their condition, — will be their guardians
and protectors, — and beside whom they could in some
degree range themselves, against the rapacious and
dishonest cruelties of the government, and of their own
lawless sects and tribes.

A most atrocious zigzag ascent led over the crown of
the ravine, and we found ourselves suddenly on a small
meadow, where our tents were pitched beneath a group
of truly magnificent oaks, commanding a view on all
sides that was really sublime; Kunîsyeh, Nukh el Jurd,
and Sunnîn stood with numberless other heights majestically round us, — the feet of the two former clad in
thick woods, which we were told abounded in wild boars.
This place is called El-Merooj.

We went to bed very much tired, — to be awakened
from dreams of fine scenery and sunshine by torrents
of rain, — a very unusual circumstance at this season.
Long before morning our tent, which was not a double
one, had begun to leak; our clothes had got soaked
through in the night, and we had no alternative but to
remain in bed, as the only dry place, and to take our
breakfasts in waterproof cloaks under umbrellas. Alas!
the rain continued with unabated violence, and towards
the middle of the day we unanimously agreed that we
were not a little uncomfortable. However, at last a
bright thought occurred to Habeeb; at a little distance
there was a half-finished stone hut, built to shelter
mules, &c. &c., with a roughly made oven in one
corner; into this hut our three beds, which had been

kept pretty dry, were carried, and we followed them, conveyed on the back of a mule. The hut was unplastered and windowless, but dry; it seemed uncommonly like a dungeon, and I was in mortal fear of snakes, &c., but we lit a charcoal fire in the oven, and were sleeping comfortably enough, when — we were awakened by low, hoarse sounds, perfectly inexplicable, and very alarming. We were at some distance from the tents and men-servants, and were beginning to feel a little odd, when the strange noises waxed louder and louder, shriller and shriller, and at last burst forth into the unmistakable crows and cacklings of a lot of cocks and hens that had been placed by some peasants in the oven, and were becoming immensely astonished at the heat of the fire!

The rain, which is very uncommon indeed in June, continued to fall all night, but in the morning the sky cleared, and we mounted about eleven, and pushed on up steep paths, among loose rocks and crags of blue limestone of the most fantastic shapes, round the head of a valley tributary to the Nahr el Kelb, coming suddenly upon thickets of glorious and lovely rhododendrons growing in wild luxuriance among the rocks, with a beauty that made one forget cold and rain and everything disagreeable. Beds of purple lupines, too, were dotted all along the path as we turned up a short pass into the great valley of the Nahr el Kelb itself,— a most peculiar and magnificent valley, — the mountain sides of all manner of rich, bright colours, with trees and meadows of fine corn up to the very summits; while half way down commenced, on both sides, vertical walls of blue limestone, straight and smooth down to the very bottom : it looks as if the mountains had turned bottom upwards by mistake. This part of the valley can scarcely be

crossed anywhere, so unbroken are these rocky walls.
We passed along opposite the pretty, scattered village of
Biskinta, half hidden in woods and fruit gardens, and
then, having climbed up a very steep conical hill, we
stopped at a little hut, placed in a wild, mournful
solitude in the midst of a barren waste, where some
shepherds were eating their dinner. Here we took
shelter from a shower, and had but just rejoined the
road when the rain increased tenfold and a thick blind-
ing fog came up the valley, only breaking here and
there enough to give us glimpses of perpendicular
depths below, from so dizzy a height and so narrow a
goat-track, that perhaps it was as well we could see so
little of the perilous way. We were now passing over
the southern shoulder of Sunnîn, right up among the
snow, when Habeeb suddenly stopped, and jumping
down exclaimed that here, at last, was a piece of sandy
ground upon which we could pitch our tents, the ground
everywhere else being as soakingly wet and dripping
as we were ourselves. He spread a mat for us, and we
alighted, huddling under one umbrella until the pitch-
ing of the tent was with much difficulty accomplished,
a large fire lit, and our beds made, in which we immediately took refuge, and where we dined. We needed
the fire, for the wind coming off the snow was horribly
cold : we were now at least 7000 feet above the sea.

The morning proved fine, and we rode on enjoying
the sunshine along the ridge of the noble valley, catching once a most exquisite view of Beyrout, with the
curving shore and blue sea, until we came to the
famous Jisr el Hajar (bridge of stone), a grand scene
indeed. This Neba el Leben (fountain of milk) is the
chief source of the Kelb, and here the river rushes in
three tremendous cascades from the top of Sunnîn,

forcing its way through the limestone walls, under white masses of foam, and falls into a boiling cauldron just above the bridge, whence it tumbles down head-long into the valley in roaring torrents. The rock forms a natural but oblique bridge over the torrent, 163 feet span and 80 feet in height. The view from the bottom of the chasm is truly sublime, the moun-tains forming fine contrasts of browns and bright reds with the snowy summits and the stern grey crags; while all about the bridge and the cascades the loveliest flowers grow in wild profusion, including pink convol-vulus and blue forget-me-not. In a cavern under the arch, in the very midst of the deafening roar, some shepherds had made a home; the wife was churning butter from goat's milk in a very primitive churn, nothing more than a goat's skin, filled with milk, which was tied on the end of a long stick, itself mounted on a tripod of sticks stuck in the ground, between which the skin was swung backwards and forwards.

After this we continued along the side of the valley under the snowy head of Sunnîn, rolling clouds of mist occasionally wrapping him mysteriously from sight; and passing over some very perilous places by the Neba el Asel (fountain of honey), for we had lost our path, we began to ascend the very steep pass which separates the valley of the Nahr el Kelb from that of the Nahr Ibrahim. It was very difficult and severe for the mules, and Habeeb watched his canteen with great anxiety: one block they scrambled up was very nearly four feet high, and our horses made a great fuss about it, although we dismounted to ease them. We were, however, well rewarded on reaching the top, for the scene was superbly grand,—the snow all round us and under us, and a kind of glacier above our head. Then came a zigzag

descent, which it is pleasanter to remember than it was
to perform: the muleteers requested us to dismount,
and after riding for some way we did so, for the sensation was not a pleasant one, when looking down the
fearful depth as one's horse struggled over the masses
of rock at the edge of the very steep and narrow path.

The valley of the Nahr Ibrahim, the ancient river
Adonis, is wilder and sterner than that of the Kelb.
We had intended on reaching it to have gone direct to
Afka, the source of the river, but the inhabitants seem
to be as wild and stern as the valley itself, and our
dragoman declared himself afraid to venture without
further tidings of their politics at the moment, as war
had just broken out between the Metouaalees, who
chiefly occupy these mountains, and the Christians;
and some sanguinary murders had quite lately taken
place. We were not at all willing to give up seeing
this celebrated spot, when we had really got within
reach of it, and we felt pretty sure that as English
ladies we had not much to fear; so we told him to
settle it as he pleased, and do the best he could, only
explaining to him that we intended to go to Afka, and
go we would, somehow or other; but, to give him time
to gather tidings, &c., we agreed to defer the visit till
the next morning, and so we turned away westward, and
rode on for an hour or so till we came to a good camp-
ing ground, at a place called the " round meadow," just
opposite the village of Amhaz, on the other side of the
magnificent and savagely wild ravine. Immediately
above our tents were steep mountains, partly green and
cultivated, but with masses of white and yellow crags
breaking out on the side, some shaped like grotesque
statues; and on the opposite side of the valley uprose
stern walls, one above the other, of purple-grey rocks,

seeming almost vertical, yet here and there terraced
with narrow ledges lined with trees that seemed to
have no footing, and a thousand strange shades of
colour blending on the mountain tops, till lost in the
distant snow. We walked on a little beyond our tents,
and there, turning a corner, was the sun shining on a
mountain slope, one vast mass of glorious rhododendrons, "spreading their soft breasts, unheeding, to the
breeze," and seeming like a soft veil of tender, delicate
purple gauze drawn over the whole slope, so radiantly
lovely one could never forget it.

The cold forbade all sleep; perished and frozen
through the night, we gladly welcomed the morning
light and hot coffee. Meantime Habeeb had consulted
several peasants about our going on to Afka, and they
all declared that it would be very dangerous; however,
at last, by good fortune, we captured a peasant whom
Habeeb had known before, and believed trustworthy, and
who was himself a Metouaalee,—a fine hook-nosed dark
fellow, with a long beard and good teeth, armed with
gun and dagger, like every peasant and shepherd in
the district, — and he engaged to conduct us safely there
and back again. So we rode on along an excellent path
for about two hours, enjoying the magnificent valley and
the ranges of mountains before us (looking north-east),
reaching right up to the snowy Makhmel, the mountain
of the Cedars, until we began a steep descent into the
hollow where the source of the Ibrahim lay; the wood
increasing till it became quite like a park, — pines,
lignum vitæ, oak, terebinth, and fine lofty walnuts. We
were fully occupied with the delightful view, when — on
suddenly turning the brow of a cliff, we found the
narrow path closed by fifteen men, who started up
apparently from out of the rock, and pointing their

guns at us, demanded our business; a parley and explanation ensued, and we immediately became excellent friends, the secret of which sudden transition we did not know till the day after, when the dragoman acknowledged that he had informed them, not only that we were English, but also near relations of Mr. Wood, our late Consul at Damascus, who did so much for the Metouaalees and Druzes that his very name is a passport still among them. We were equally innocent of the relationship and of the falsehood, but we reaped its benefit.

The mountains now rose in a close semicircle to the height of two thousand feet from the bottom of the deep dell, their nearly perpendicular sides dotted over with tufts of prickly oak and other shrubs; the bottom itself filled with houses among gardens of pomegranates and figs, shaded by noble walnut trees; while rushing out from a cavern under the great cliff was the cascade and source we had come to see. There was not very much water in it at this time, but we did not regret it; the divided cascades were prettier than a larger single one, and the sheets of foam were quite wide enough to be very grand and beautiful. The wild luxuriance of foliage about the boiling waters much increases their beauty, and the dark cavern, with the monstrous black mouth through which they pour, is fringed with tremulous maiden-hair and other delicate ferns. A peasant told us that sometimes in summer the stream sinks into so small a compass that persons have crept into the cavern itself, where there is even now a small ruined building at the very back of the cave, probably a shrine or sanctuary for the most secret rites of the Greek worship. At the most picturesque part of the lower cascade, on a little cliff, are the remains of the old

Temple of Venus, one hundred feet by fifty; little of ornamental work is left, beyond bits of cornice, but all the stones we saw were of grey granite smoothly hewn. This Temple was a very famous and highly honoured shrine, for here, beside this foamy fountain, the beautiful Adonis was said to have received his death-wound from the boar, and here Venus is still heard, by imaginative persons, lamenting the untimely fate of the young hunter, — a victim to the cruel jealousy of Mars, who, distracted at the caresses lavished on him by the fair goddess, took the form of the ferocious animal he felt himself to resemble under such pangs, and pierced the youth with his cruel tusks. The despairing Venus metamorphosed his white and beautiful corpse into a white rose — a flower ever sacred to herself — which was afterwards changed into a red one, in consequence of a drop of her own rosy blood, drawn by the prick of a thorn, falling on the flower. Thus she still kept him beside her in emblem; but her grief was so great that the gods in pity permitted him to return to earth for six months of the year; the time of his departure from her side was announced by the sanguinary hue imparted to the falling waters which then

" Run purple to the sea, suffused with blood of Thammuz." *

At this moment, thus advised by Nature herself, the annual and solemn fête was celebrated, chiefly by women, who sat on the thresholds of their houses tearing their hair and weeping loudly. The statue of Venus was exhibited covered with a veil, the head leaning on her left hand, and the whole figure expressing sadness and weeping; on the day of her invocation,

* Milton.

it is said that a fire, bright as a star, invariably fell precipitously from the sky into the water *; this they believed to be Venus, but, probably, it was only an immense tear mingling in the blood of her lover. It is curious that the Jews should have adopted this Phœnician idolatry so entirely as to have carried its observance into the very courts of the sanctuary of the Lord God, where the Spirit shows them to Jeremiah " weeping for Thammuz," with their faces turned "towards the north †," offering to her cakes and incense and pouring out drink-offerings before her; the women during this festival wore men's clothes, while the men wore women's clothes, as was generally the custom where two persons (as Osiris and Isis, Venus and Adonis, Hercules and Hebe, &c.) were celebrated together, stores of dresses being kept in the temples for that purpose, — an allusion to which is made in Deut. xxii. 5, and 2 Kings x. 22, and possibly in Rev. iii. 4, in speaking of Sardis, a city consecrated to the double worship of Hercules and Diana. The celebration lasted two days : the first was spent in lamentations and wailings, as we have said ; on the second they danced, shouted, and sang for joy, as if Adonis had returned to life.

So runs the legend, — under which, as is almost invariably the case, one finds the natural fact of which the story is but the poetic clothing. Adonis, or Adonai — a Hebrew title signifying Lord — the friend and favourite of Apollo, was made the personification of the Sun, or summer, by the Phœnicians; the boar and the bear were both used as emblems of winter, whose rude onset signifies in the fable the departure of the summer sun-

---

* Nicephorus.
† Ezek. viii. 14; Jer. vii. 18, xliv. 17—28. It was, in fact, part of the Astarte or Venus worship.

shine, vanquished by the cold blasts of winter. So the
fable of the daughter of Plenty, carried off to dwell
beneath the earth for half the year, — so the Tyrians,
Romans, and Cappadocians kept some of their gods in
iron chains till the winter was gone; then the gods were
supposed to be re-awakened, and rose up endowed with
new strength and power. In the Syrian mountains the
winter is short, but the contrast must be quite terrible
between the blazing and scorching heat of the long
summer, and the severity of the winter, especially in a
place like Afka, surrounded by the loftiest and most
snowy summits of the whole range; they might well
consider it an annual death of Nature, and nowhere
would spring be more sudden, beautiful, and gladdening
than here — more completely the resuscitation of a dead
body. It is related, by an eye-witness *, that at the
end of the days of mourning a dead man's head was
thrown into the river Adonis, which carried it down to
the sea: this is in fact precisely the same legend as that
of Osiris, who, after being murdered by Typhon, the
Evil One, was cast into the sea, and his mangled remains
found by Isis on the Phœnician coast, — to celebrate
which mystery the priests of Alexandria used annually
to throw a head amidst great pomp into the sea, which
held in its mouth a letter declaring that Osiris had
come to life again. Both allude to the desolation of the
earth at one season, and the return of verdure and
fecundity at another.

The word Afka is said to be derived from the Hebrew
Apheka, meaning to hold or embrace, in allusion to the
embraces of Venus and Adonis; but, as it also means a
basin, it is more likely to describe the mountains sur-

---

* Lucian.

rounding or embracing the deep basin of the sacred glen, which is shaped precisely like the interior of a tea-cup, only with one side lower than the rest.

It is said that a good deal of these old ceremonials still remain among the wild people of Afka, but how much or what we could not learn; they were much more intent upon questioning and examining us than upon imparting any information, and possibly they might have resented any very curious inquiries respecting their religion, the peculiarities of which are, I believe, very little known. They are said, like the Shyites, to acknowledge 'Ali as the only true successor of the Prophet; but they have probably many other more peculiar doctrines of their own, besides their scrupulousness in what they eat, drink, or touch, all which is carried to the very highest pitch. They would die rather than drink from the same vessel that a Christian or a dog has touched; and it is in truth natural that a band of lawless and savage men, living in secluded and wild mountainous districts, should have adopted local ideas, especially such as were sufficiently exciting to fascinate their untutored minds. But that any traces of such rites and ceremonies should have survived the fifteen centuries since Constantine destroyed the temple at Afka, is at least very curious — if it is true.

Wild and savage as the Metouaalees are, they were civil enough to us, — the men assisting us to scramble up and down the rocks by the waterfall, holding our horses, &c.; the women, who had evidently never before seen a Frank lady, gathered round us with eager curiosity to examine our clothes, which appeared to be quite incomprehensible to them. Our large shady hats were subjects of great admiration, and they laughed long

and loudly over the size of our waists, which they
insisted on spanning with their hands, until their embraces became so troublesome that we mounted our
horses, and, with many lookings back at the beautiful
and romantic spot, re-ascended the hill into the upper
part of the valley, where the cool fresh air was most
refreshing after the suffocating heat of the pent-up
glen, as we retraced our steps of the morning and passed
on still along the south side of the Nahr Ibrahim (or
River Adonis) towards the sea. We were half way down
the very worst of all possible descents, jumping, slip-
ping, and struggling among huge rocks and impossible
crannies, when two of our horses took to fighting, and
before the attendants could reach them one horse had
toppled down part of the precipice and was lost to view.
We had many more miles to go, and the adventure was
somewhat dismaying. However, some stiff bushes had
kindly broken his fall, and the horse was picked up ; the
saddle, which had been a good deal broken, was patched
together somehow, the things tumbled out of the saddle-
bags re-collected, and we continued our tortuous way,
not pausing again till we reached a very beautiful spot,
where the tents were already pitched, called Wātr-el-
Jauz — the " country of walnut trees," but the walnuts
have now disappeared — and we sat under the shade of
a grove of fine willows, enjoying fresh views of the
beautiful mountains. No day's ride had given us a
greater variety of magnificent scenery than this one,
and very lovely it had been under a cloudless sky and
brilliant sunshine.

But the next day was almost more beautiful, for
after crossing the hill on which we had encamped the
sea was added to the still more extended and splendid
view. Habeeb averred that Hermon was visible, but

we could not distinguish its cone. And then came an apparently endless descent of deep and very narrow ravines of great beauty, one after another, filled with flowers and fragrant shrubs and pleasant villages, with weird and savage rocks and stern grey crags, and such an abominable path that more than once we had to dismount and scramble down on foot. At last we reached Ghazîr, a beautifully situated, large and thriving village, full of fruit gardens, roses and myrtles, and with a great number of convents and French *filatures*. We rested here for an hour in a hospitable merchant's house, and then continued our way, descending literally through fissures in the rocks, till we had reached the sands of the sea shore, and gladly found ourselves in the lovely Bay of Jouneh. Nothing could be prettier than the scattering of this bright-looking town over the steep cliffs, crowned with white convents behind it; the curve of the bay was so graceful, and the little gardens so rich and pretty, and the sea breeze so fresh and pleasant after the hot ravines we had come from. There were several ships in the bay waiting for corn. We turned off from the sea to pass through the atrocious paths of pretty Zouk Mehayl, and by the fine college for Maronite priests, called Antourah, most romantically situated in the bosom of a lofty gorge, surrounded by gardens of arbutus, ilex, pomegranate, &c. &c., which we should have liked to see, but had not time enough.

On leaving Zouk we found ourselves in an extensive pine forest on the upper side of the Nahr el Kelb, through which we descended by a winding path. Nothing could exceed the rich beauty of this narrow valley, the river winding at the bottom, and both sides clothed with wood. At the foot of the descent is one of the chief sources of the river, welling forth from a

cavern, round which the ferns hung in green wreaths
and garlands, as if veiling the source from common eyes.
We had to scramble on stepping-stones through a
swampy thicket of St. John's wort, rhododendrons,
myrtle, and oleander, in order to reach it, but it was
worth the trouble. There are much finer caverns with
stalactites at another source of the same river, somewhere higher up in the mountains, but these we never
reached, not having heard of them till shortly before
we left Beyrout: they can hardly be *prettier* than these.
It was half-past seven when we had regained the
summit of the hill side, for very steep and difficult it
was to our tired horses and our tired selves, and the
light was gone. We had still a long ride over the mountain, guided by a shepherd, and then came a descent to
the river side, which, in the darkness, was really most
perilous; it was terrific enough by day, and the shepherd seemed so shocked at the ladies having to descend
it in the night, that he offered to stay with us, and very
useful he was in encouraging the unfortunate horses,
who would fain have stood still instead of struggling
down the rocks, which in the darkness we could not
attempt on foot: and had not the moon helped us in
some parts we must have remained on the mountain all
night; so we were indeed thankful to reach the bottom
without any accident, and to find ourselves close to the
mouth of the Kelb, looking doubly lovely in the moonlight. We pushed through the oleanders, and forded
the stream (though the current was very strong for the
weary horses to withstand), finding our tents pitched
beyond the river at the edge of the waves, and very
gladly ate our dinners and went to bed, after being
thirteen hours on horseback; and late we stayed the
next morning resting, with the tent door drawn back,

watching the little waves curling up close to us, and the fishing boats lazily sailing over the blue waters.

However, we had still a long way to get home, so we mounted at eleven, and rode along the shore as far as Antélyias, where we turned aside into charming gardens, bowered and hedged with myrtle and clematis, both of which the horses greedily devoured, and then up steep mountains, thickly covered with myrtle all in blossom, perfuming the air delightfully; a lovely ride, but the path turned round and round till we began to fancy ourselves bewitched and fated "never to return." At last, at near 4 P.M., we reached Brumâna, and completed the circle we had been seven days in travelling; and in another hour we were very happy to find ourselves once more in our pretty home, where the little dog nearly went into fits, sobbing with joy at seeing us again.

CHAP. X.

ONE day early in July we had occasion to go down to Beyrout to despatch some business, and when there we found ourselves suddenly included in a hastily settled ride to Saïda, the ancient Sidon. The opportunity of accompanying some friends was too pleasant to be resisted, and the arrangements were so managed that we were not to be troubled with mules and canteen; a Saïda gentleman, Signor Pietri Santi, then in Beyrout, having offered us the use of rooms in his house. The heat in Beyrout was now very great indeed, and the mosquitos almost intolerable: we felt them all the worse as there are scarcely any at Beit Miry, the bloodthirsty creatures seldom taking the trouble of flying so high above the plains. We therefore settled to make our journey by night, and to rest by day. We had, too, a glorious full moon that lighted us through the narrow lanes of the town and the pine-forest, with a cool flood of silver-coloured light that was infinitely delightful, hiding much of the monotony of what is sometimes considered a tiresome ride, although there is really constant change, — the steep rocky shore, here and there dressed with olive groves, alternating with smooth curving sands. It is very wild and perhaps dreary by day, and to add to this impression, in one place where we were threading the broken rocks by the

sea, a hyena bounded past, so close as almost tó touch
my horse's nose : he had been lying on our track : the
kawass, and, indeed, all of us were much disappointed
at his escape, but the rocks were too bad to attempt a
chase in the darkness. Further on, where the Khan
Khulda marks the site of the ancient city of Heldua, we
came upon camels swinging along under enormous burdens that seemed like walking houses, almost concealing
the beast beneath, while at top of each lay the driver
fast asleep, tied on to his own goods ! — and we were
told that they will often go on and on in this way, almost without any rest or food, for a week at a time.
After fording the Damour, where we recognised the
richly-wooded valley of Deir el Kamar, we stopped at
Neby Yunus, the Khan of the prophet Jonah, and, dismounting, fell fast asleep on the sand over our coffee.
The light was breaking as we awakened half an hour
after, and found ourselves in a pretty sandy bay, at a
picturesque khan, beside a fine grove of tamarisk trees,
a sapphire-coloured sky over head, and the moon — one
large mass of glowing silver, most wonderfully dyed and
crimsoned with the flush of morning, — standing on the
very horizon of the sea, while behind us, above the
grove, the glorious " Daughter of the Morning " shone
with steady golden light, seeming to grow larger and
larger, when — all in a moment, up shot a flood of crimson and orange, lighting up the rocks and the sands and
the trees and the sky, like a marble statue transformed
into a living breathing mortal ; and the moon, after
lingering a few minutes as if to rival the red light of
day, sank down behind the waves, and when we turned
round a moment after the morning star was gone too.
It was one of the prettiest scenes possible — a perfect
vignette of beauty — and the show was not yet over ;

for now dark masses which we had taken for stones
and rocks on the sand, wakened up, stretched, shook
themselves and arose, and in two minutes their horses
and camels and mules were shaken up and mounted,
and they, with their bright-coloured burdens, rode off,
clearing the place, and changing it really like a magic-
lantern slide, or a double scene in a theatre. Then the
sunbeams streamed widely over the bay, and down
came troops of chattering girls, in huge scarlet trousers
and white veils, to fill their pitchers at the fountain —
the super-excellent fountain, for this water is sacred,
and *must* be particularly sweet, the spring having
appeared on the very spot where the good-natured
whale was so kind as to come to shore and vomit forth
poor Jonah (*Yunus* in Arabic) after his long and uncomfortable voyage in its stomach. It would be difficult to prove which of the reports is the true one, but
other people believe that the whale turned aside from
the Great Sea into the quiet bay of Iskenderoon, and
laid Jonah among the oleanders that fringe its shore, in
imitation of Moses in the bulrushes; and if the whale
was only careering about between Joppa and Tarsus,
one place is as likely as the other.

Many of the Jews consider the Book of the Prophet
Jonah to be only a parable, or moral story, written long
after the time of Cyrus, and intended to account for the
fact that the city of Nineveh was not so ruthlessly destroyed, or the inhabitants so cruelly afflicted, as the
Prophets had predicted: they say that it is full of im-
possibilities; as if *all* miracles were not, apparently,
contrary to Nature. Possibly they are less unwilling
to repudiate the book altogether than to acknowledge
so direct a type of the Resurrection of our Lord as is
contained in the account, or to read the judgment on

their own generation who "repented not," although "a Greater than Jonas" preached to them.

Another mile or so brought us to the brow of the last headland, and to our first view of Saïda — and a lovely view it was: there she sat at the edge of the deep blue water, pale brown and purple mountains embracing her in warm, giant arms, with battlemented walls and towers round her, — all white and glistening in the early sunshine — like a swan sitting by the sea-shore, or a white dove resting on the crest of the cliff. We turned down to the beach and continued our road on the soft, slushy sand along the edge of the wave, sometimes stopping to pick up some particularly pretty shell, oftener to watch the colours of

> "the last foam
> That trembled on the sand with rainbow hues " *

from the bright morning sun. The view grew prettier and prettier as we distinguished the high castle above the town, built by Louis XI. of France, and the other fortress, standing on rocks which run far out into the sea and are connected with the shore by a low bridge of nine arches. We entered the town about 8 A.M., and wound through the narrow streets and gay bazaars, and still gayer, thriving-looking people in bright, clean dresses, to the house of Signor Santi, where we were soon established in a pleasant saloon furnished with divans and mats : one expects nothing more in an Arab reception room, unless it be a tray of pipes and nargilehs. The heat and the mosquitos drove away all thoughts or hopes of sleep, and we could only lie still and pant till the cool breeze of the sunset hour enabled us to

* Thalaba.

visit some hospitable French Arabs living in the French quartier, or khan as it is called, a huge building as large as a London square, erected by the Emir Fakhr-ed-dîn for the use of the French merchants in the seventeenth century; a large tank and fountain occupy the centre of the court in a garden of banana, acacia, and lemon trees, which made the evening breeze come into the apartments laden with perfumes. Each family has its own suite of rooms, communicating with the rest by a wide corridor extending round the court on both storeys to walk and lounge in: it seemed to us a most pleasant residence, with a promenade on the house-top where one could enjoy fresher breezes and a lovely view of the city. Saïda is one of the prettiest towns in Syria; the Mosques and baths are particularly picturesque and almost handsome; the two Castles and the fine rocks with the breakers constantly dashing over them, and the rich fruit gardens all around the city, form a most charming *tout ensemble*. The view from the Château of St. Louis is equally pretty and more extensive, the headland of Sour (the ancient Tyre) bounding the scene. This castle is kept in good repair, and was originally a strong fortress; that on the rocks is very much shattered, but worth seeing : Saïda is a place for endless sketching both within and without the town, and would repay an artist for a stay of some duration.

Warned by the heat and closeness of the house on the first day, we established ourselves on the following morning inside a Wely or Saint's tomb on the sea-shore a little to the north of the town, — a spot to be recommended to future travellers, as we found the heat much less intolerable there than elsewhere; we were close to a spring and to the sea, with the lovely fruit gardens close to us. The tomb, which occupies one half of the building, is walled off, and locked up; the rest is a small square whose arched roof is supported by sixteen columns and is raised on steps at each side: such are most of the Welys in Syria, and they are often very agreeable resting-places. In the afternoon we rode through some miles of the gardens, the richest, we were told, in all Syria; for here were not merely lofty trees tangled over with thick bowers of vines laden with luscious grapes, — orange, lemon, fig, almond, and plum trees, fragrant with perfume and bending with fruit, — but banana trees also, rare in this country, with enormous clusters of the rich brown and orange fruit hanging down among the splendid leaves and beautiful purple blossoms above them. The prickly-pear hedges were full of fruit, and roses and honeysuckles grew everywhere. But the glory of Saïda are her apricot groves: from her — her sole commerce now — is exported the greater part of the *mish-mish* consumed in Egypt, Damascus chiefly supplying Syria; and there must be nearly as much mish-mish eaten in Egypt as we consume of oranges or apples in the whole of Great Britain. The fruit of all kinds grown at Saïda is considered of a better quality than any other in Syria.

Sidon was one of the most ancient cities in the world, and is one of the very few of those (such as Damascus, Hamah, and Hebron) on which a modern city or town, bearing the same name, exists at the present day; it was the chief port and capital city of Phœnicia, and the mother of a hundred other cities whose very sites have been forgotten in the dark ages of history. Six of the sons of Canaan *, the grandson of Noah, founded the principal cities of Phœnicia (Sidon, Arka, Sinna, Aradus,

* Gen. x. 15—19.

Simyra, and Hamath); hence their descendants were
called Canaanites, the Greeks afterwards giving them
the name of Phœnicians. Their coast extended from
Mount Carmel to Mount Casius, along which numerous
ports and cities were placed, the inhabitants of which
appear to have attained a high degree of civilisation and
even of luxury. Dismayed, however, at the extraordinary
success of the divinely supported arms of Israel, as
step by step they victoriously subdued nearly the whole
of Palestine, the Phœnicians emigrated in large numbers
— "fleeing from the face of the robber Joshua," as
they expressed it — and planted kingdoms and colonies
throughout the coast of the Mediterranean, founding
cities in Africa, Spain, Italy, Greece, and the isles of
the Ægean sea. They need not, however, have been so
much afraid, for Asher, to whom the land containing
Sidon fell, never took the city, or drove the Phœnicians
out of the country*; and God, in his anger against
Israel, permitted these and some other tribes to dwell in
the land in order " to prove Israel," and " to teach them
war."† Unhappily the Israelites not only profited by their
teaching in this and in other accomplishments‡, but
they also learned from them their abominable idola-
tries : from them came the worship of Baal, the Sun, —
the ruins of whose Phœnician-built Temples abound in
Syria, and especially about Hermon, whence arose its
name of Baal-hermon, although the Sidonians called it
"Sirion," or the "Breastplate," — and from them came
also the worship of Astarte (or Venus), the enticing
goddess, after whom even the heart of the wise Solomon
turned from the paths of virtue, and to whose honour
he erected an altar or "high place," on the Mount of

* Judges i. 31, 32.   † Ibid. ii. 20—23, iii. 1, 2.   ‡ 1 Kings, v. 6.

Corruption over the brook Kedron; and it was from Sidon, also, that Ahab, king of Israel, took the wicked princess Jezebel for his wife, the great promoter of Baal worship.

Sidon was in the height of her glory about a thousand years before the coming of our Lord; her colonies, of which Carthage was the chief, had then spread the knowledge of letters*, science, and art over all the then known world, and her ships had sailed round the southern extremity of Africa, in passing from the Red Sea to the Mediterranean.† Her daughter Tyre was still more flourishing and renowned than herself, — "perfect of beauty," "very glorious in the midst of the seas," — but she was slain, destroyed, "brought utterly to ashes;" and Sidon fell also, destroyed alternately by Assyrians, Persians, Greeks, and Romans. "Pestilence and blood" has been indeed "sent into her streets," and "judgments executed in her."‡ "Blush with shame, O Sidon! thou city sitting beside the waters, the strength of the sea; thou mayest indeed say, I have not travailed, I have nourished neither young men nor virgins; for now none remain unto me: it is as though I had never brought forth a child!"§

We left the city at 8 P. M., passing through groups of people sitting in clusters in the streets and on the beach, smoking and listening to gesticulating story-tellers — and had a delightful ride along the shore, in the sweet, fresh, warm night air by the light of the magnificent moon. Twice we stopped at the roadside khans to drink excellent coffee, and morning began to break as we entered the olive groves and gardens about Beyrout; they were gay with flowers — among them the colcynth

---

* Herodotus, book v. 58.　　† Ibid. book iv. 42.
‡ Ezek. xxvii. xxviii. 22, 23.　　§ See Isaiah xxiii. 4.

(coloquintida), a queer-looking creeping plant with a fruit like green pills, now (happily) so much disused in medicine, that it no longer pays to collect it. We refreshed ourselves with quantities of the cool, sweet prickly-pear from the baskets of pretty women, who were gathering them in the early dew; and as the blue mist cleared away, the mountains looked so lovely, that we felt well repaid for the fatigue of the nocturnal ride; we reached the hotel at 6 P. M. and found occu-pation for some hours in slaughtering the fleas we had gathered up in the khans *en route*, — and at midnight we mounted again, to ride up to our dear little home at Beit Miry,

One morning at Beit Miry, the Druze muleteer who had accompanied us to Deir el Kamar, came to request the honour of our presence at his marriage, which was to take place that day; and on our promising to go to it, he left a present of an oke of pine fruit kernels; as the Druze custom is to leave a gift with every guest invited to the wedding. We were summoned by a messenger, who said, " the feast was ready," at 2·30 P. M.; and on reaching the Druze quarter, a volley of muskets saluted us from a group of gaily dressed men surround-ing the bridegroom, attired in new clothes, and looking very sheepish and uncomfortable. On arriving at the house, which was at the further end of the quarter, we found the little outer court full of old hags, horned and veiled, cooking in stew-pans over fires made on the ground; the *cuisine* did not look very *appétissante*. The house consisted of only one large room, the roof supported by two pillars in the centre and quite full of women, to whom we were introduced by the bridegroom's father — a venerable and handsome man, with a long white beard; his dirty old wife made many salaams, and kissed our hands, as did nearly all the guests in the room; there were both Druzes and Christians in the room—the latter dressed in gay coloured coarse muslins and pretty white muslin veils, hanging down behind their heads, some of which were finely embroidered, with quantities of gold ornaments and bracelets; the former in dirty blue or brown serge gowns, and veils of the same stuff in black, which they held over their faces when any man appeared; nearly every woman had a small infant in her arms, and the floor was strewed with bigger infants — small and large squalling alike most of the time. The Druze women are usually less pretty than the Maronite women, and their costume makes them appear still plainer: but they are finely made and have good manners, though, like all Oriental women, they are far less charming than their husbands, whose open, free, graceful and polished bearing is remarked by all travellers. A place was immediately cleared for us and a carpet spread, on which we sat to take ever so many glasses of *eau sucrée*, which we disposed of to the children, much to the delight of both children and mothers, but the heat became so intolerable that another carpet was placed for us on a shady terrace: whence we soon saw the bridegroom arrive at his own house, escorted by his friends, who fired muskets all the way.

Our seat faced the whole of the beautiful ravine of El Metn, and we presently saw some bright spots emerging from the thick woods at the bottom of the valley, and winding up the steep zigzag ascent on our side; this was the bridal procession. First came three mules, carrying the bride's bed and a great box, painted scarlet, and adorned with flowers, containing her wardrobe; then her father, with a snowy turban, mounted on an ass, followed by a number of relations on foot; and lastly the bride herself, surrounded by women, but without her mother, whom etiquette keeps at home. As soon as she entered the district, firing began; after this a volley was fired at every zigzag on the road, the unceasing noise and shouting seeming much to annoy the horse on which she was mounted. She was closely veiled, first with yellow silk, then green gauze, and, over both, a white cotton eezar; and one of her hands, wrapped in a yellow cotton handkerchief, was held the whole time on the top of her head, in token of submission and obedience to her new duties; sometimes the weary arm was supported by a neighbour, but one or other hand was never taken down. When she came near the house the firing and shouting redoubled, and a score of persons went to meet her, among them the bridegroom, who bowed to her; then a very stupid sham battle ensued, one man on each side running into a vacant space alternately, and firing his musket in the air; this lasted about ten minutes, before she was allowed to proceed; her father lifted her from her horse, and the door was shut upon her and the women for a short time.

When we were summoned inside we found a gaudy shawl hung against the wall of the room, with her back to which the bride was standing on a pile of cushions, like an effigy in a church; she was unveiled, and proved very pretty, fair as an English girl, with light brown hair, the only Eastern characteristic in her face being the highly arched eyebrows, which are artificially formed in childhood. She was dressed in a red silk vest over a white silk chemise, and a green silk pelisse over that, fastened with large silver buttons, and several silver chains, to each of which hung a triangular silver case containing a *hezab* or charm, and a very massive and

costly gold necklace; a muslin handkerchief lay over
her head, but no *tantour*, the chief Sheikh of the
Druzes having just published a command, we were told,
that they should be given up by all but the old women.
Here the unhappy girl was to stand for three whole
days, with her eyes closed and her hand over the top of
her head in the presence of the guests; even in the
night, should any visitor come in, she must resume her
place ! the friends sometimes whispered in her ear, but
she is supposed to be incapable of speech or sight till
the contract is signed and her husband appears. During
these three days no man enters the room. She looked
very hot and tired, and flushed still more deeply as she
stepped down from the cushions to kiss the English
ladies' hands, in honour of whom she was allowed to lift
her eyelids for one moment, whereby we saw her pretty
brown eyes; after which her nearest relation, a very
jolly looking woman, stood before her, and, pushing
back the crowd a little, flourished each present brought
by the guests, one by one, over her head, screaming
out the name of the donor and the substance and value
of the gift; and, before she deposited it in the bride's
pocket, spinning round between each announcement in
a wonderful jigging dance, and giving the mountain
cry of joy or triumph till one was nearly deafened; it
is a very peculiar whistling scream, beginning on a
high note and then jumping to the octave above, something like the Tyrolese *jodl*, only simpler, and never at
any distance musical : we learned to know the cry well
and sadly afterwards.

Having stood this as long as we could and our hands
aching with squeezes and kisses, we bade them good-bye
and departed, sending our present of three dollars in
the evening, as we were told that was considered much

more aristocratic and dignified than giving it at the time. The bridegroom and all his friends were sitting in rows on the house-tops, eating an enormous dinner spread upon nice mats; the dinner continues all day long, giving them fortunately something to do in the long interval before the contract is drawn; the Druzes have no religious ceremonial of marriage. The bridegroom, a fine tall young man, seemed very anxious and curious about his bride, whose face he had never seen, and to whom he had never spoken; he was much pleased with the praises we bestowed on her, which, as Europeans, we could do; — an Arab could not have spoken to him of his wife.

We learned on this day something of the division of property among the Lebanon mountaineers. On the death of a man all his possessions are divided among his children, with no distinction of the first-born, the sons each taking twice as much as the daughters, who are supposed to be provided for by their marriage. Should the land-property be too small for division, it is sold, and the proceeds divided in the same proportions; if there is any choice in the lots, the youngest child chooses first, and so on, the eldest coming the last; and if there are any young children, the largest portion is reserved for them.

CHAP. XI.

THE BATTLE.

DURING the first six or seven centuries after the Resurrection of our Lord, a number of sects sprung up in the bosom of the Christian Church, nearly all of them finding birth in the North of Syria, and in Egypt. To say nothing of the Sabellians and Arians of Africa, or the Nestorians and Eutychians of Constantinople, the semi-converted Jews of Syria split into Nazarenes, Ebionites, and other sects, while among the Arabs of the north and north-east, Jacobites, Monophysites, Mariamites and Collyridians, Gnostics and Docetes, spread themselves over the mountains of the Lebanon, and the countries of Aleppo, Diarbekr, and Mesopotamia. These mountains, and the rocks of the Desert, were soon thickly peopled with hermits and recluses, singly and in bands, living in different degrees of asceticism. Those of the mountain tribes, who had been converted to Christianity, were united under a Patriarch (*Batrik*, in Arabic), as their spiritual head, and were governed by Emirs or Sheikhs of the different districts.

About fifty years after the birth of Muhammad, and before the Reformed Religion taught by him had made any progress beyond the immediate neighbourhood of Medina and Mecca, or the confines of Arabia, one of those Christians who had retired into a cave in north Syria, in order to pursue his studies and meditations uninterruptedly, made himself remarkable by the peculiar sanctity of his life, and the unusual depth of wisdom that fell from his lips. This man was called Hanna (the Arabic of John) Maroun,—the cave where he dwelt, was close to one of the chief sources of the Orontes, the 'Ain or spring mentioned in Numb. xxxiv. 11.

About this time, the quarrels between Constantinople and Rome, for the spiritual jurisdiction of the Christians in Syria, broke forth, and emissaries from each were spread through the country, for the purpose of influencing the people. Hanna Maroun was at once elected by the united voices of the mountaineers, as their adviser and leader : he immediately declared himself for the Latins, acknowledged the Pope as his spiritual master, and put himself at the head of a large body of followers. Those who acknowledged Constantinople as the throne of their spiritual and political Head, separated from the followers of Maroun, and gave themselves the name of *Melekites* from (*melik*, the Arabic for sovereign), which they bear to this day *, but they are more usually called the people of Roum, as members of the Greek Church, whence they then received their Patriarch and their tenets ; they are of course, now as then, equally with the Maronites, subjects of the Turkish Empire, but they hold the doctrines of the Church of Russia, and look to her Emperor as their chief Protector.

The tenets of the Maronites are simply those of Rome — their colleges and schools being presided over by teachers and priests sent from that city : they submitted more entirely to the Pope in 1180, giving up at

---

* They also separated in the same way from the Copts in Egypt, and took the same name of Melekites. See Lane's " Modern Egyptians."

that time the Monophysitism, which had till then
tinged their tenets, and obtaining in return the immense
concession of retaining many of their own peculiar
customs,—a very remarkable, and perhaps unparalleled,
concession on the part of Rome. They have a very
large number of monks, who of course take vows of
celibacy and poverty; but the parish priests are almost
always married : the people communicate in both kinds,
and their service is conducted in Syriac,—a language till
lately well understood by them, but now entirely disused, since only three villages are existing where Syriac
is still spoken,—the Gospels, and other parts, are read
also in Arabic. There are between 90 and 100 convents,
containing about 1500 monks, and 500 or 600 nuns :
the number of the Maronite population is differently
stated, but is most probably about 233,000 souls. There
are large numbers of them at Aleppo, Tripoli, Beyrout,
and Saïda, but they may be said chiefly to inhabit the
Lebanon, the Kesrouän district of which is almost
entirely occupied by them : the principal number of
their convents are placed there, and about the Cedars,
and in the Kesrouän they have their great Priest's college of Antourah.

Hanna Maroun died in A.D. 701, and was buried at
Hāmah, his tomb becoming at once, and for a very long
time after, a place of pilgrimage to both parties among
the mountaineers, — his remains were believed to perform miracles, and were visited by pilgrims from even
Egypt and all parts of Turkey. A Convent was soon
founded beside the tomb, the monks excavating cells in
the living rock for themselves, and building up loop-
holed walls overhanging the ravine below — as in the
convents of Mar Antoun and Khanobîn; to this Convent the Pope sent a present of a fine Library.

Among these monks, the belligerent leaders of the
Maronites for the future were found. At one time, in-
toxicated with some successes over the partisans of
Constantinople, the Maronites marched down to Jerusalem, when the Mooslims, taking advantage of their
absence, seized and pillaged the Convent, massacring
the unfortunate monks that had remained there; after
this the Maronites and Melekites wisely made peace,
having enemies enough to contend with, without fighting
their fellow-Christians.

The Maronites hastened to join the bands of the
Crusaders on their arrival in Syria, and did them much
service in replenishing their ranks, as hundreds and
thousands of gallant Franks were slain in the field or
died in the camp. At Damietta, in 1249, vast numbers
of the Maronites fell fighting under the banner of
Louis IX.; a fresh band, however, joined him afterwards
at Akka, and there exist still in Paris copies of a letter
written by Louis IX. to both the Emir of the Lebanon
and to their Patriarch, *assuring the Maronites of the
protection of France for ever:* it is dated May 21, 1250;
Henri Quatre, in 1620, was addressed by Sultan Suley-
man II., with the title of " Protector of the Christians
of Mount Lebanon;" and exactly 400 years after,
Louis XIV., and still later, Louis XV., repeated this
assurance in letters addressed by them to the Patriarch
of the Maronites in the Convent of Khanobîn.

Certain it is that the Maronites have a strong belief,
that as they are now under the protection of France,
they will one day be openly ruled by her; time will
show how near this idea is to the truth. But there are
plenty of facts which appear very like it; one thing is
quite certain, — and that is, that gradually, cautiously,
and silently the French have obtained a footing, a *pied-*

à-terre, throughout the Lebanon, and nearly throughout Syria; there is scarcely a single large village in the whole of the Lebanon without a mission of one, two, or three monks, and a school taught by Lazaristes; and these are all Frenchmen; they have also missions and schools scattered throughout Syria, especially in the country round Jaffa and Jerusalem; and the Lazaristes teach so well and work their missions so thoroughly, that they are not only an immense example to us, but they are sure ultimately of success; for the Arab appreciates education, — that is to say, they love money with all their hearts, and even the poorest mountain peasant is therefore glad to have his sons taught to count and to add up piastres, and to read and write; accomplishments which they acquire with remarkable facility. In the towns they teach French also, which is gladly enough learned to aid them in commerce, and to enable them to become dragomans. Unfortunately their French education usually renders the town Arab pretentious and impertinent; the best example of which are the people of Zah'leh, where this education has been in full force for very many years, and of whom Mr. Porter says, they "are notorious for their pride, insolence, and turbulence. Family broils are incessant, and scarce a month passes without bloodshed." *

The French have also found another method of gaining substantial influence in Syria. Wherever their Lazaristes tell them of an unusually intelligent Sheikh or person of influence, they send him letters of naturalization, and make him an *honorary*French subject: of course this includes, or would be found to include, the peasantry of whom each Sheikh is chief, whenever the occasion

---

* Handbook for Syria and Palestine, vol. ii.

needed. We learned also, on good authority, that the
French Consuls along the coast have an ingenious way
of recommending the crews of boats to *buy* a flag, bearing the Jerusalem Cross, which is blessed by the Superior
of the French Convent of the Terre Sainte, the Guar-
dian of the Holy Sepulchre; under which they sail in
double security, both spiritual as well as temporal.
France then claims them as *her subjects*, though of
course they are in reality only Turkish subjects, and
though all Consuls are forbidden to protect any but
their own lawful countrymen: and when France requires them they will be found all ready for her service;
our informant mentioned sixty-four well-manned boats
whom he himself knew who had done this.

Nothing can be more mischievous than the various
"protections" accorded by the European governments
to subjects of the Sultan, Mooslim as well as Christian:
they serve but to render them insolent when they have
nothing to fear, and cringing when they have; besides
that, the protection is very frequently extended to most
worthless individuals, merely for the sake of exercising
and maintaining the right; it was relying on this "protection" that made the Zah'leh people so insolent to the
Mooslims, insisting on their dismounting from their
horses on entering the town, and even calling their own
dogs "Muhammad" before the Mooslims — of course
the greatest insult that can be offered to persons who
consider dogs unclean animals, — these facts we heard
from the best authority; they have since been severely
punished, but they most certainly brought it on themselves.

The Maronites are industrious and docile; they are
intelligent and capable of immense improvement: they
are brave, but they have not the *pluck* and fortitude

of the Druzes, nor the support of an admirable organisation, combination, and obedience, which is the very
backbone of the Druze people; nor have they by any
means the high sense of honour which the Druzes
undoubtedly possess, though of course there are honourable exceptions among them. The Maronite, when a
little educated, prides himself on being *rusé*, but his
ruse is a coarse affair in comparison to that of the
Bedouin or the Druze; he is simply dishonest, though
he has just wit enough to try to persuade you that
cheating is the only thing of which he is perfectly incapable: if he cannot succeed in this, he tries to prove
to you that what he gains is in some manner only his
real due, or he assures you *tout bonnement*, that he felt
that to your excellent heart and charitable disposition,
his profit would be equally a pleasure and a grati-
fication.

When the Greek and Latin Churches of Syria forgot
their differences and united in arms against the Druzes,
they were frequently victorious, but their great Druze
Chief, the Emir Fakr-ed-dîn, was so accomplished a
general that the Druzes shortly recovered themselves,
and held up their heads as proudly as ever; this Emir
proved the Druzes capable of becoming active and
thriving in commerce, and he would have probably
made them a great people had he not taken the unhappy notion of going to Europe, where he wasted and
lost both his patrimony and his patriotism.

The dreadful custom of blood-feuds, which exists
throughout the mountains, is of course a terrific promoter of bloodshed. Notwithstanding this, I believe it
is undoubted by all who know the Druzes well, that they
would live in peace and harmony with the Christians if
the Turks would let them; but these latter are un-

ceasingly exciting them against each other, and urging them on to war for their own purposes; never can they be united as long as the Turks stand like firebrands beside both. Of course it is all done in an underhand way, but the truth will out; and no one can be any time in the country without perceiving it.

One day our Druze muleteer, at whose wedding we had been guests one month before, was driving his mule along the narrow path, when another mule, driven by a small Christian boy, jammed up against him. The Druze was a hot-tempered and foolish young fellow, and he immediately thrashed the boy with no moderate arm; the next day, the boy's father, and another man, hid in a large caroob tree, waylaid the Druze as he was going down to Beyrout on our commissions, and fully avenged the boy. The Druze went home with a bleeding head, and a good deal hurt, upon seeing which the women — never slow to join in a fray — took up the quarrel on both sides: they emptied each other's pitchers at the fountain, and finally broke a lot of them against the rocks: miserable trifling squabbles, but from such bagatelles many a grave and mournful tragedy has arisen. We heard that the village priest was trying to make peace between them, and we hoped that there would be no worse results from this, than from a hundred other petty quarrels we had heard of between Christian and Druze.

The week before, an English friend of ours * had arrived in Beit Miry, and taken a house at the same end of the village as our own, but over the brow of the mountain, and therefore commanding the northern view of the valley of El Metn; in the centre, in fact, of the Druze quarter. The moon was now, on the

* The Honourable Roden Noel, son of the Earl of Gainsborough.

evening of the 13th of August, at the full, and we went over to see how gloriously beautiful the valley, headed by snowy Sunnîn, looked in the moonlight from his verandah: this was three days after the muleteer's quarrel. While we were enjoying what was really a magnificent and lovely scene, the mist wreaths, as we thought, which were lying rather thickly in the valley, rose over the moon, and advanced with steady steps, drawing a hard black edge across her face: she was half covered before we perceived that it was an eclipse *, and most curiously beautiful was the effect of the half-obscured light on the mountains: the villagers came out of their houses to observe the phenomenon, and seemed much alarmed by it. "On dit," said our drago-man, "que ces choses portent toujours les grands malheurs, et que le sang va couler tout de suite;" and, as if in sad confirmation of his words, before the eclipse was over we actually heard firing on the mountains opposite, and saw smoke hanging about in various spots — the villages on the other side of the Metn had taken up the quarrel! The Druzes about us seemed very much excited, but as we went home we heard that the Bishop at Madrass had ordered the culprits to come to him on the following morning, and that he would surely induce them to make satisfactory amends to each other.

And early on Sunday morning the good Father did talk very earnestly to both. He desired his Christian son to apologise to the Druze whom he had beaten so unmercifully, which he promised to do; but he stipu-lated that the muleteer, as the first offender, should come to his house to fetch the apology; this the Druze stoutly refused. About 10 A. M. we were at-

* This eclipse, which was total, was not visible in England.

tracted to the window by the sound of loud and angry
voices, and looking out we saw several Druzes collected
on the roof of a house in the village, a few paces on
our left, all shouting and gesticulating at once, and
evidently restrained with great difficulty by some of the
elders; they were all pointing and calling down the
mountain side, where we saw, about a hundred yards
below us, a no less eager crowd of Christians collected
on a projecting knoll of ground on the path to Madrass,
where, with their quick, eager movements, they looked
just like a swarm of bees. We easily discerned similar
efforts being made among them, by the elders of their
party, at soothing and appeasing their excitement,—they
seemed to have formed themselves into a ring, through
which they were determined not to allow any of the more
impetuous ones to break, or to rush up to attack the
Druzes on the summit: when, presently up came the
little party from Madrass with tidings of the conditions
imposed by the Christian upon the apology he had agreed
to make. The words were hastily shouted out to those
above, and in another moment there came the report of
a musket — a Druze had fired! and now, with a rush
on both sides, the restraining elders were unheeded as
the impetuous crowd swept by them — the Christians
ran up the terraces from below, hiding behind the
mulberry trees to fire *up*, the Druzes from above firing
down in answer, — and though numbers failed of their
aim, we saw several deliver its fatal message of death
or torture: meanwhile there was a battle going on
in the middle of the village, the Druzes from one end
meeting the Christians from the other end — but this
we could not see. The ground was so steep and the terraces stood so high, one above another, that on the
mountain side there could be no coming face to face.

It was completely guerilla warfare — each one fighting
for himself, without leaders or plan, picking out any
enemy he could see, and taking aim from behind a
mulberry tree or a bit of rock; later on, a small party
on each side met on the open road and the rocks about
the fountain, and fought for some time vigorously in
the little dell : we saw some fall, and then the rest
escaped through the pine forest close at hand. All this
time, high above the noise of the firing, there arose continually a horrible sound — who that has once heard it
can forget how it thrilled through head and heart!—the
war-cry raised by the women on both sides, as standing
on the housetops, they watched the progress of the fight,
urging on the men, hanging over the edge with eager
gesticulations, or throwing up their arms wildly in the
air, more like frenzied demons than human women;
sometimes there came from one or another a piercing
wail, over the wounded or fallen : while many others
followed their husbands with pitchers of water on their
shoulders, giving them drink ever and anon in the heat
of the burning sun, standing beside them when they
took aim, and every moment shrieking out the fierce shrill
scream which excited every man to do his utmost in
shedding blood. Three of these women were wounded.

The principal Druze houses were, as I have said, on the
little craggy rock exactly above our house; their rifles,
therefore, (and nearly all of them had rifles) were not
more than seven or eight yards from it. Of course their
houses were one of the principal objects of attack; so
every moment the bullets passed over our roof, grating
along the walls with that peculiar sharp *whitzzz* which it
is far more agreeable to hear at a distance than within
half a yard of one's ears; sometimes they passed like
hail across the windows, and the answering bullets from

below as often hit the walls of the house as others fizzed
up over our heads in the open corridor. The Emir and
another man were wounded by stray shots in the little
house next to ours, and in fact there was scarcely a yard
of ground anywhere near us free from bullets. We had
previously agreed with our English friends—there were
two English gentlemen then in Beit Miry—that we
would read our Sunday service together; but now we
earnestly hoped they would not expose themselves to the
flying bullets in order to keep the engagement; but,
afraid that we might need their protection, they never
thought of breaking it, and they happily arrived at our
house in safety and unhurt. Our dragoman wanted
us to immure ourselves in a room lighted only by a
door opening on to the corridor; but the excitement
and interest of the battle was far too great for us to resist
watching it from this open corridor or from the windows
at all sides of the house : we were assured, however, that
this fighting might go on for many days, certainly till
night, and as we could do no good by watching them,
we agreed to read our Sunday service as usual : I do
not think that any of us will easily forget that hour
of prayer, and with what unusual meaning the petition
arose "from battle and murder, and from sudden death
— Good Lord, deliver us," or how we thought of the
same prayers rising at the same moment in hundreds
of quiet churches in England, while our little congregation of five or six persons were assembled here, with
the bullets falling thick and fast around us, and the
voice of the reader frequently drowned in the sharp
click of the muskets, the strange ring of the rifle balls,
and the shrill screams of the women! Fear, indeed,
none of us had ever thought of, nor had we any cause
for it; we knew well that our being English ensured

our safety among the Druzes, and that their respect for us would not fail: a remarkable instance of which was afforded more than once during the battle, when one of us leaned out from a window, and a Druze close by stopped, even in the moment of taking aim, and, lowering his gun, made a salaam to the "Sitt;" and they called to our servants to know whether some buildings on our ground belonged to us or not,—of course we said they did and no one entered them. There was a French family spending a few weeks in some miserable apartments under our house, whereby, happily for them, they were living *under our flag*, and that flag afforded them equal security and safety with ourselves. A number of Christian women, as well as our landlord and his family, rushed into our house when the battle began, the women bringing their gold ornaments, and took refuge in these lower rooms;— not one of them was touched.

About three o'clock the firing suddenly ceased—and the subsequent stillness seemed almost stunning after the tumult and noise: we learned that the Christians had exhausted their ammunition, and therefore fled — the Druzes remaining masters of the field: and then came the saddest part of the day — several wounded and one dead Druze were carried past our house, borne on men's shoulders, bleeding and groaning, and the lamenting of the women was soon heard as they recognised their own beloved ones among the sufferers brought to their houses, — they flung their arms over their heads and sung a wild cry, half Druze war-cry, and half like the Irish *keen*. Druze reinforcements from other villages now arrived, and we saw some of the deserted Christian houses being sacked, and the furniture burned: they said this was done only by the strangers. We opened the hall door, and went out on the steps to breathe more freely in the now still afternoon air, when a venerable-looking, white-bearded Druze, one of their chiefs, immediately came up and assured us, with the most expressive signs and words, that amongst them not only our persons but all our property also, was perfectly safe ;—he said that wherever our flag was unfurled everything would be secure, and added that it was already well known in the mountains: and they afterwards told one of the English gentlemen that they had for three days endeavoured to put off the war on account of the " sitteh Ingleez " who were staying among them : this we heard also in other parts of the country afterwards.

The stillness and silence of the village in the afternoon was indeed a contrast to the horrors of the day : the Europeans profited by it in sending messages to each other, consulting what they should do: the Druzes were, of course, much elated, and as strangers came to join them from other villages we heard that this battle was to be only the precursor of many others, and that they fully hoped to exterminate the Christians through-out the mountains. The other Europeans determined to leave the place at once : one family indeed had already gone : for, in the very thickest of the fight, about midday, these good people had the folly to fly, passing right through the combatants, and of course putting themselves in a hundred times more danger from stray shots, than they would have incurred by remaining quietly in their house : their terror and confusion being too great to allow of a moment's thought of delay, they fled on foot in the burning sun, hatless and bonnetless, carrying their children in their arms, all the way down to Beyrout, a four hours' walk. On arriving in the town their alarm had so much increased at every step and filled their minds with horrible pictures, that they spread the intelligence that all the Europeans had been massacred and their houses sacked; so far from this being the case, we heard afterwards that every single thing from their own deserted house was carried down to them a day or two later, not one thing missing, even the lady's thimble and their provisions prepared for the day included! except, indeed, their grey mare, which they had left tied near the house, and which we saw, poor thing, killed soon after by some three or four stray shots.

I am afraid that the prejudices of some of my readers may be shocked at my confession that my sympathy involuntarily sided with the Druzes throughout the day: of course, in this particular instance they were in the wrong and the aggressors; but apart from the *cause*, the bearing of the Druze, speaking generally, is so much more akin to an English mind than that of the Christians, that one cannot well help such a feeling; the latter were quick and active, but the Druze has a fearlessness and nobility about him — a proud, steady step — a lofty head and eagle eye — a bold athletic form, and a free, open, but perfectly respectful manner, that makes one feel always at ease and safe with them. During the battle it was curious to mark the difference of the ingenious hiding and dodging of the Christian, and the daring boldness of the Druze — it reminded me continually of a battle between a cat and a bloodhound — if such a noble beast would condescend to do battle with a mere cat. The Christians of the mountains are well made, and have a soft, sleepy kind of beauty, set off by gay-coloured dresses: but if ever you see a noble form both of figure and face, full of self-respect and native dignity, and a neatly put on, clean, quiet-coloured dress, be sure he is a Druze, or a Metouaalee (the latter, how-

-ever, have but poor dresses); the dresses of the Christians are more costly than that of the Druze, but the Druze is much the cleaner of the two : numerically, the Maronites far exceed the Druzes, — but the minority of the latter are more than compensated by their courage, coolness, and organisation,

Mr. Noel now left us to see how things were going on in his own house, which he had given up to the shelter of very many women and children, with their little bundles of valuables and gold ornaments; and on going back he found his dragoman had brought in several of the wounded, whose sufferings they did their best to relieve :—that long night was a sad one, passed among the women and children, two of whom were wounded, — the little babies were crowing or sleeping in infantine content, while many of the women were wailing for the dead, amongst whom was the muleteer who had begun the quarrel, and whose young wife had been married but a month before. Mr. Noel came back to us at nightfall for linen rags and medicine — a Druze dodged him in the darkness with his rifle cocked, and was just stooping to take aim when he called out, " Ingleez! Ingleez! " upon hearing which the Druze started up and made amends by accompanying him to our door with many signs of respect, repeating " Ingleez taïb, taïb keteer ! "

A thick fog came up with the night, and shrouded everything from view, but we sat in our corridor watching the moonlight shining in strange brightness down upon the white masses and folds of the fog below us, and listening rather anxiously for any distant firing, fearing lest the Druzes should think of pursuing the Christians in their flight : we heard nothing, however, until, about seven o'clock, the deep silence was broken

by a horrible kind of sound — the Druzes were parading
the village in a band, singing a war-song of triumph —
very wild and simple was the air, and the voices sounded
rich and sweet; but the *meaning* was too well expressed;
and every note thrilled through one with a strange, sad
horror, swelling loudly, and dying away softly, as they
came to and fro : often I think I hear that song still.

The chaunt had scarcely ceased, when we heard, to
our great surprise, drums beating, and the tramping of
horses coming up the road : the firing of the battle had
been heard in Beyrout; those who had fled had given
the alarm, with all kinds of exaggeration, and the Pacha
had, therefore, sent up a body of thirty cavalry to keep
the peace; and at the same time, the various Consuls
had each one sent up horses and mules, to bring down
their respective countrymen, protected by their own
janissaries. In a few hours, all the European families
in the village, excepting ourselves, had quietly packed
up and mounted, and before the sun had risen next
morning, they were all comfortably arrived in their
homes at Beyrout. The English Consul, however, had
sent up no one.

We had brought several letters of introduction to
the Consul, but during our long stay in the town he
had never called, and we had had no communication
beyond a civil note : in this time of danger and need,
however, we fully believed and expected that assistance
would be sent, not only to us, but also to the English
gentlemen then in Beit Miry : so we sat listening for
the arrival of more mules, &c,, but nothing was heard,
and it became a matter of serious consultation what we
should do. The French gentleman, whose family occupied the rooms under us, very kindly sent up to say
he could spare us three horses, if we liked to go down

with them; but we had not the slightest idea of thus
leaving our baggage behind us, having no fears of any
kind for ourselves personally in remaining, while to
leave our things at the mercy of strangers from other
villages was not to be thought of: we knew that the
Druzes had sent to summon their comrades from other
mountains, and it was believed on both sides that a long
and sanguinary war was only then commencing; and
we began to feel that if we remained, we should have no
freedom in the neighbourhood for walking, and, knowing
nothing, alas! of surgery, which we deeply regretted,
we could not be of any kind of use among them. A
minor, but unpleasantly important consideration likewise influenced us: the Christians had carried off their
cocks and hens, their gardens were trampled down, and
it seemed very doubtful that we should get anything to
eat: supplies from Beyrout were easily ordered, but, if
fighting continued, it seemed unlikely that any muleteers would bring them to us; then our men-servants,
being all three Maronites, not one of them could go in
safety even to the fountain to fetch water, though the
cook, braver than the rest, volunteered to go, on condition that we let him carry the flag in his hand! So,
all things considered, we came very reluctantly to the
conclusion that we had better go somewhere else, and
accordingly a note was despatched by one of the descending parties, to beg that mules and horses might be sent
up for us.

We were not, however, uncared for: H.M.S. Tartarus
had arrived some days before at Beyrout, and our
friend, Captain Mansell, becoming alarmed for our
safety, on hearing the terrific accounts carried down to
the town, had gone himself to the Consulate to seek for
assistance; the Consul, and Vice-Consul, the Secretary,

and every one else was away, the Consulate was locked,
and not a janissary to be found; — it was Sunday, and
some hours were lost in searching for them, and then in
getting horses and mules, after which he took upon himself the despatching of janissaries with the animals up
the mountain. And as there are always more kind hearts
in the world than one counts on, we had been remembered by another: a lady had sent out at daybreak to
know if we had come down with the other Europeans
in the night, and not hearing anything of us, and fearing that our Consul had not sent up assistance, she
requested a gentleman belonging to her husband's office
to ride up at once, and invite us to her house; we were
grateful to this gentleman, who readily undertook a long
ride in the burning heat, for persons in whom he had
not the slightest interest; but we were more touched by
the kind thoughtfulness of the lady who had sent him, to
whom we were entirely strangers, and not even country-
women: the life of Madame Broë is, however, devoted
to acts of charity and kindness, and her excellent heart
is ever intent upon succouring those in need: there are
not a few of the poor and suffering in the town, and
many a traveller struck down with fever in Beyrout, who
have had occasion to bless her name.

In the mean time the Turkish Bey in command of the
troop just arrived, sent three of his soldiers to our
house for our protection, and though we were considerably more afraid of them than of the Druzes, it seemed
wiser to accede to the wishes of our servants, and to let
them mount guard in the corridor, where they smoked
and eat cucumbers the whole night long, while we were
packing up our things. We had calculated that the mules
might reach us by 5 A.M., and we were accordingly ready
to start at that hour, but many another wearily elapsed

ere our packages were fastened on the mules, and it
was nearly 2 P.M. before we set off. Our escort was a
large one, made up of English janissaries and some
French kawasses who had been left behind the night
before, I believe for our protection : however, we saw no
one from whom to be protected, and not a creature did
we even meet on the road save a few miserable Christians, who had fled despoiled of everything. That evening, with the war-cries and wailings of the battle still
echoing in my ears, I sat long in the corridor of the
hotel, watching the calm moonlight shining on the little
village, now so far off, and our own deserted but beloved
mountain home, and — strange and striking contrast!
looking at the " crimson and emerald rain " falling in
showers of bright flakes from the rockets and fireworks
of a splendid fête given by Count Bentivoglio, the
French Consul, in honour of the Emperor's birthday.

Early the next morning the two gentlemen we had left
at Beit Miry arrived at the hotel, driven down by the
pangs of hunger ! and in the course of the day we learned,
on the best authority, " that one of us had been murdered
in the battle, and that the other had escaped, with the
maid, into the depths of the valley, where it was confidently expected, both would be immediately shot or
starved to death ! "

The question now was, what were we to do with ourselves ? travelling down to Jerusalem in August was not
to be contemplated by any sane person, while the temperature of Damascus was much higher than that of
Beyrout, where we found the heat so intolerably oppressive that we determined at once to go up as high as we
could into the mountains; it was not likely that there
would be any disturbance in the northern district about
the Cedars, unless the war became quite general, when,

of course, the Metouaalees would join in it, but before
this could take place we should be able to descend to
Tripoli, or to cross the Bekâa to Damascus. Some of
our friends had settled to go to the Cedars for some
time, and as H.M.S. Tartarus was going to Tripoli, the
Captain kindly invited us all to go in her that far, an
offer which we were very glad to accept.

In the mean time a hollow peace was, after a few days,
patched up between Druze and Maronite,—"till the next
cocoons are gathered," we heard said on both sides, and
too true, alas! it turned out to be. A good many small
circumstances came out — the Governor of Beyrout had
strictly forbidden the Christians from purchasing arms
in the Bazaars, but Druzes were allowed to purchase
them freely, and they did so, boasting at the same time
openly in the streets of how many they had killed, and
how completely they hoped to exterminate the Christians
if the war continued; but these spokesmen were, I
believe, the young bloods and boasting boys. From all
we learned at this time and afterwards it was quite
evident that the chief Druzes did not desire war; they
were invited, pushed into it, — they are not men to brook
even a small injury, and they resented it accordingly,
but they would be men of peace if they were let
alone.

It was not only in Beyrout, where it is more difficult
than in most other places to separate gossip and *canards*
from truth and facts, that we learned how completely
the Druzes were favoured by the Government; the unfortunate Christians were seized, imprisoned, fined,
when they attempted to obtain arms for themselves,
while, as I have said, the Druzes notoriously purchased
largely; the Christian mountaineers wherever we went
were provided only with common old muskets — while the

Druze had rifles in great numbers, and many of their Sheikhs had revolvers—only a very few of the Christians, and those only Emirs, had ever seen any of the latter : even the Emir of Beit Miry, but three hours from so large a European town as Beyrout, was astonished out of all Arab gravity at a silver mounted six-barrelled revolver, with which I was one day practising at a mark on one of the trees near his house. He implored me with clasped hands to wait while he fetched a beautiful little boy, his son and heir, to see the sight, and then when I had re-fired it for his edification he solemnly applauded his little son's question, as to whether the weapon came from Sheitân ? I am convinced that the Emir himself believed that Satan reloaded it for me *ad infinitum*.

It is an unquestionable fact that the Turks do, and have always encouraged the Druzes against the Christians : they hate both equally : but their object is plain, — the Druzes are exceedingly warlike and dexterous in fighting, — the Christians are weak in war but strong in numbers — and they therefore try to make use of the Druzes to exterminate the Christians — and when they have done the hard work for them they will come in with a strong hand and get the small body of Druzes into their power. I believe that at least some of the Druzes understand their game perfectly, and see through it ; they are quite willing to be assisted into getting rid of their hereditary enemies, whom the Turks are always representing as the authors of all ill against them, and they think they will take care of themselves afterwards : it will not be a very easy thing to exterminate the Druzes.

The horrors of the following spring completely confirmed all these reports : the Druzes paraded the streets of Beyrout with the Mooslims, the one boasting of the

dogs of Christians they had slain, their boon companions
applauding the deeds : it was reported by a gentleman
who has lived long in the country that he had himself
seen Mooslims ornamenting with flowers the muskets
and knives of those who had killed the greatest numbers.
Wherever the most horrible of the massacres and
butcheries were perpetrated, the Turks edged on and
encouraged the deed : at Deir el Kamar the Mutselim
stood by while the Druzes disarmed the Christians,
and invited the unfortunate 530 Christians into the
Seraï, of which they afterwards opened the gates
when the Druzes came in to slaughter them! At
Hasbeiya the Turkish Colonel collected the Christians
into the Seraï and there disarmed them : he himself admitted the Druzes in to kill the 700 unarmed men,
besides the unhappy women, while his soldiers stood by
looking on at the *battue!* These are but two out of
numberless other cases; at Damascus the Mushir did
everything to invite the Druzes into the town — there
were 5000 of them armed within the walls on the day
before the massacre — and while they did the horrid
work, the Turkish soldiers and Kurds carried off the
plunder, the Mushir sitting at home in the Seraï with
the doors closed against every one.

On the very best authority the fact has been made
clear that, in 1860, the *Christians commenced* hostilities:
the Druze Sheikhs endeavoured by every means in their
power to preserve peace, in all probability because they
felt their own weakness against the overwhelming
numbers of their enemies in the Lebanon : when Kur-
shîd Pacha, *compelled* by the Consuls to interfere, desired the Christian Emirs to send home the fighting men
then assembled, they answered that they were confident
of beating the Druzes, and would beat the soldiers also

if they interfered to prevent them, knowing very well
that the soldiers would do no such thing. So confident
were the Christians, that they were careless — while the
Druzes, fearful of defeat unless joined by their brethren
of the Haurân, made use of all their strength, and improved every advantage they could gain. The Christians
were everywhere beaten, and the Druzes were so much
elated at their almost unexpected victories, that they
pursued the Christians and committed barbarous atrocities such as nothing can justify; although one may
make much excuse for them, remembering their hereditary hatreds, and that the Christians, having sought
to exterminate them, they naturally desired retaliation
and revenge: besides, it is absurd to judge them by the
standard of a Christian or an educated people. At Hhaïffa
and many other places the Christians committed horrible
brutalities, about which nothing has been said; and
while deploring the misdeeds of the wild Druze of the
mountains, it would be as well to remember the acts not
so very long since of many an army of drilled and disci-
plined soldiery belonging to the most Christian countries
of Europe — civilized Europe — and, not to speak of the
atrocities of Austrian, Prussian, Italian, worst of all of
French soldiers, to look back at some of our own in the
unspeakable horrors that have taken place in Ireland,
Scotland, and fair England! Of course the Druze, in
giving loose to his passion, is very guilty, but he is
ignorant and unenlightened:—are we, when our passions
are excited, pious and progressive though we be, much
better? or were the Irish in 1641 or in 1798 one whit
less sanguinary or atrocious in their conduct than the
Druze?

CHAP. XII.

WE were a party of seventeen guests on board H.M.S. Tartarus, and the vessel was so crowded that we were glad to find ourselves in our quiet tents, on the pleasant shore of Tripoli, after twelve hours at sea; we spent the next day, while the horses rested from their journey up from Beyrout, re-visiting the town and mountains. Our tents were pitched in a garden on the sea-shore, close to the Castle of Raymond of Toulouse, and we rode thence by the bank of the Kadisha to the fine ravine behind the town, and through the picturesque streets, till it was time to go home and go to bed, as we were to be up and dressed before 3 A. M.; and so we were, but we did not start till past four, when the sun had risen. We had a very lovely ride of six hours and a half, over a wide undulating plateau with fertile fields, fresh, pleasant woods and purling streams, till the ascent, by a steep and rugged path, to a little chapel perched on the side of a very narrow grand gorge, where we rested for an hour or two; some very pretty smiling girls insisted on our admiring the valley of which they seemed quite fondly proud, and the lovely views of Tripoli, with her rocks and headlands stretching out into the blue sea; they would also make us look at the chapel and their own cottage, the windows of both of which were filled

up with human skulls, looking most dismal — and they
showed us the curved iron bar hung in a tree, on which
a hammer struck the call which served for a church
bell. Then came a tremendous ascent, — disagreeable
enough to mount, but nowhere dangerous — zig-zagging
up between two high mountains of curiously contorted
strata, clothed with the white cypress, with which we
were now to become daily familiar — now and then a
pine, or a walnut, or a pomegranate, and every here
and there tiny gardens perched on narrow ledges, bearing potatoes or cotton, or a few vines. Then, turning
suddenly away from a strange peak, came Jebel Arneto,
which looked as if it had been chopped off sideways,
and meeting the upper streamlet of the Kadîsha again
bubbling by, we crossed the water-shed and followed the
brow of the mountain to the village of Eh'den, a very
large village, nearly hidden in groves of huge walnut
trees. The people crowded round us with equally warm
and troublesome salutations and welcomes, as we made
our way through them in order to choose a delightful
camping-ground under some splendid walnut trees,
perhaps some of the finest trees in the world. As there
was a good bit of ground, all the tents were set up in
the same place, our three grouped round one enormous
tree, with a mountain torrent tumbling and rushing
down between them. The other tents were at some little
distance, and afterwards when another traveller came
up from Tripoli he chose the same ground, retiring to
the back ; nothing could be more picturesque than the
whole group, with our flag in the front, hoisted in a
mulberry tree, and the six or eight horses and twelve
mules picketed beneath the trees with their gay-coloured
trappings and attendants, while round the kitchen tents
there would always be half a dozen gossiping villagers

dressed in the brightest coloured dresses imaginable. The people of Eh'den are remarkably handsome, both men and women, and the children lovely: the women wear a singular head-dress under their veils, made of silver, in the shape of the crown of a bonnet — sometimes with a kind of crescent-shaped horn.

This camping-ground was in fact on a wide terrace or plateau, running the length of the valley along the side of the mountain, which rose almost perpendicularly like a wall immediately behind us, with barely slope enough for the white cedars to grow in a feathery veil nearly to the summit. On the opposite side of the valley the mountain was still more richly clothed with woods, gardens, and villages, while between the two, the gorge — which is called Wady el Kadisha — sunk suddenly down in a deep tremendous ravine, very narrow and very romantic, winding away westwards to the sea, which we saw at the extreme right; while the horizon, from the great height at which we were placed, was apparently some way up the sky. To the left the valley was closed by an amphitheatre of perfectly barren mountains, sloping down in bare terraces*; this was part of the great Makh'mel: on one side, at about half a mile from our tents, a copious spring gushed from the rock, bosomed in a nook of thick woods, dividing itself at once into two streams, one of which flowed down the gorge to the sea, and the other, passing just above our camp, ran down by the Pass we had mounted, into the river Kadisha.

We had intended to have gone on to the Cedars on the following day, and we always *did* intend to go

---

* On one of these terraces there stands a single Cedar tree, not very large, but the only *true* Cedar we saw in the Lebanon besides the famous group in " Solomon's garden."

on "to-morrow;" but the spot was so very beautiful, and
our tents so agreeably placed, and the air so fresh and
cool and pleasant, that we had been there nearly a
month before we really made up our minds to leave it.
We were, in fact, much in need of rest and quiet such as
we found here: the horrors of war and bloodshed had
been witnessed, but, in the excitement of the moment,
by no means fully felt; in Beyrout there was still the
daily and hourly anxiety for news from the surrounding
villages, and the constant listening to the sorrowful
tales of the unhappy, burnt-out villagers who came to
see our servants, and to reclaim the small articles of
their property we had taken charge of; then came the
new journey,— and it was only among the stern and
lofty mountains, and the cool, green groves of Eh'den,
that we began to recover our usual calm enjoyment of
Nature. The peasants of Syria declare that it is
unhealthy to sleep under walnut trees, and the dragomans always advise one not to do so; but the air of
Eh'den is a remedy against everything — though we
all fancied there was some truth in the idea. We were
now 4750 feet above the sea, and though the sun was
excessively powerful by day, and the tents uninhabitable
where they were unshaded, we had plenty of cool resting-places beneath the trees, scarcely any mosquitos,
and such cold nights, that we needed all the shawls and
cloaks we possessed, to keep comfortably warm; never-
theless we managed to be scrambling up the mountain
by 5 o'clock most mornings, and thought ourselves
well repaid each day by the sublimely glorious sight of
the sunlight breaking over the mountain, darting down
into the gorge, and striding with lightning steps over
the valley, bringing out a thousand brilliant colours
which belong only to the gorgeous hues of Aurora,

veiled and mystified by the blue haze and swansdown mists of morning — I could have watched that sunrise every day for years and never tired of its glorious grandeur. There was only one thing better, and this was the sunset: every day it was the same, and every day it seemed to take one's breath away with its sublime beauty, as something too lovely and too glorious to be really of this earth; then the gorge would fill up with haze as blue as the sea, and the walnut groves would turn into masses of shining aventurine gold, and the mountains, yellow and bare by day, would flush over with a tender, transparent crimson glow melting into the golden light, — so delicate, so lovely, and yet so sublimely grand, that no words can describe it, and no pencil imitate its hues.

Eh'den is said to be one of the oldest villages in Syria, and is thought by some people to be the "Eden in Thelassar* " mentioned in Isaiah xxxvii. 12 ; the name is Syriac, and this language was spoken there till lately. It is a fine flourishing village, containing an active and industrious population, hardy and brave; the parish priest told us the boys were very intelligent and quick at learning, but in the Lebanon no girls ever go to school or are taught anything, — even the nuns only learn reading enough to enable them to chant the office in church. M. Regace, the Lazariste priest here, has two or three assistants in his mission, a large school in Eh'den, and one in every village in the valley. The people of Eh'den are well to do in the world — they eat meat always twice a week, and there are really no poor, because those who are richer help the poorer, lending

* Both Schwartz and Jonathan the Targumist consider Thelassar to mean El Ashur, the mountainous part of Assyria, or the country round Adiabené.

money at a good interest which the peasant repays by
the proceeds of his land—he forfeits his property after
some time if he fails to pay, but we were told that this
seldom or never happens. The noble walnut trees are
many of them five hundred years old—they are found
named, their position described, and the quantity of
their fruit recorded in parchments of upwards of three
hundred years old, in the possession of the Emir and
other persons;—some of the trees have passed through
the hands of as many as fifty families; the ownership
of many of them is divided among perhaps a dozen
different families, who collect under the branches, as we
saw them doing at the gathering time, and divide between them the fruit that falls. One of the oldest
families of Syrian *noblesse*, the Dah'reer, once inhabited a village filling up the now barren head of the
gorge, but in a Metouaalee war the village was burnt,
—the family fled to Tripoli, and the soil has lain
untouched ever since. This Eh'den, so famous for its
vines and luscious grapes, and its flowers, and its
summer beauty, is utterly uninhabited in the winter:
it is so cold and so long enveloped in snow, that all the
people, headed by the Sheikh, descend to another village
near Tripoli, where they live till the smiles of spring
call them back to their vineyards; only the poor monks
remain behind, and sometimes a peasant journeys up
through the snow once or twice in the winter to carry
them some little luxury to add to their store of bread,
lentils, and wine.

Eh'den produces excellent potatoes, which are carried
down to Tripoli and sent to Beyrout, for the natives
never taste them, not having an idea how to cook
them; nor do they care to learn, as the Arab eats all
his vegetable food, except bread and lentils, raw; and

s 2

they are disinclined to eat or to do anything but what
their fathers ate or did before them.

It was a pleasure to us to make acquaintance with the
Sheikh, or Emir,—the "pretty boy" mentioned by Lord
Lindsay, now a man in the prime of life; he was the
second son, but as his talents and intelligence were
superior to those of the eldest son, his father gave him a
better education, and associated him with himself in the
business part of his position, and brought him forward
to the Turkish authorities, so as to insure his being his
successor; he speaks Italian and French well, has easy,
pleasant manners, and is both lively and intelligent,
as well as quiet and agreeable in conversation,—in
person he is tall, well made, and very fair. His name is
Yussoof Karrâm,—he is (of course) a naturalised French
subject, and the Turks have made him a Bey: he has
never been much further from home than Beyrout, nor
does he seem inclined to go; he says his duty lies in his
government, which extends to several villages, and he
will not leave it for a day; but his ideas are anything
but *bornées* by the mountains of his native land — he
showed himself thoroughly acquainted with European
politics, and knew the names and characteristics of some
of our Cabinet ministers; he is, in short, much too well
educated for his personal happiness, for, except M.
Regace, he has no real companion save a chance traveller,
and he feels it impossible to marry among the unedu-
cated, illiterate women of his own villages. He came to
see us as soon as we arrived, bringing baskets of grapes
and fresh bread, according to the hospitable custom of
the village,—the only place, by the bye, where we experienced anything of the kind, for though of course we
afterwards made a present to the bearer, the Sheikh
begged us to understand that they only performed their

duty to the stranger, whom they consider themselves
bound to maintain till his baggage arrives.

We returned his visit on the following day; he came
down to the courtyard of his house to receive us, surrounded by some seven or eight persons, and conducted
us upstairs into a large, though low arched room, with
stone mullioned windows — the walls and floor of stones
of two colours in patterns — and furnished with handsome Tripoli carpets and divans. His servants presented *eau sucrée*, then *arrack*, candied sweetmeats,
and lastly coffee; after which came nargilehs for those
that liked them. Of course we spoke of the war — of
the patching up of which he had not then heard any
satisfactory intelligence; he said one must not think
the war in any way depended upon a personal quarrel
anywhere — that was only the opening note on which
others would inevitably follow; and he repeated most
emphatically that the war really depended much more
upon what was going on in the principal countries of
the civilised world than on anything local; that the
real fact was, that, had the news of the Peace of Villa-
franca not been thoroughly spread through the Lebanon,
the war would have been taken up on all sides, and
become fierce and general, and that it was only because
some were not aware of the Peace that it broke out at
all — *else* this one would only have begun and ended a
muleteer's quarrel. The Emir said also that unques-
tionably, did England and France go to war with
each other to-morrow, or the attention of Europe be
thoroughly occupied with some other war, the whole
Lebanon would burst into a flame instantly, and not
only the mountains but the whole of Syria would be
utterly unsafe for Christians and Europeans, as, if anything really serious had once commenced, all the Moos-

lims would undoubtedly join in the fight at once,
while the Turkish authorities would try to exterminate
all the Christians and Europeans in the country. He
dwelt much upon the fact of how much the Turkish
Government secretly encourage the Druzes, hoping to
use them as tools to get rid of the native Emirs for
them, after which the Lebanon would be more easy of
access; but the Sheikh·said confidently their mountain
fastnesses would protect the Christians even after their
leaders had fallen. He told us that during the late
war between France and Austria, the Turks invited all
the Druze and Metouaalee chiefs to a secret conference
in Beyrout to which not a single Christian was invited;
he regretted much the recall of Lord Stratford de Red-
cliffe, believing that no one else could prevent such
things and penetrate the secret, underhand doings of
the Turks; and he lamented loudly and bitterly that the
famous Hatti-Humayoun had ever been obtained, since
it was worse to have it so utterly unused and uncarried
out than never to have had it granted, and he added that
its very fulness of compliance ought to have prevented
the Christian Powers from being deceived into putting
any faith in it, as nothing could possibly induce the
Turkish Government really to fulfil anything of the
kind; the Christians have only been worse off ever since.
Now, when seeking justice, they are always answered,
" You have got your Hatti-Humayoun; what more can
you want? " — although it be but waste paper, serving
but to render the Mooslims more jealous and irritated
than ever. We afterwards heard, both at Damascus and
Jerusalem, exactly the same complaint made, in almost
the same words as those used by the Emir, of the impossibility of getting any justice in the Turkish tribunals
since the Hatti-Humayoun; however, no one does or

ever did expect to find justice in a Turkish Court—well
do they exemplify the Arab description of the Turkish
Government generally, that "The Sultan goes to hunt
gazelles on a lame ass," meaning thereby to express not
merely its insufficiency, but its intentional inefficiency.

The opinions of the Sheikh Yussoof at least deserve
the attention due to a man who, although naturally a
partisan, is a liberal-minded, enlightened person, and
who is, except the Bishops, the *chief* man of influence,
and the only leader of the Maronites. His conversation
wound up that day with the prophecy, only too sadly
fulfilled, that this would be the last summer of peace
in the Lebanon for many a day.

Sheikh Yussoof told us many legends of the Druzes,
currently believed among the Maronites — of how they
worship the figure of a calf made in gold or silver,
and how they have various logs of wood concealed in
their *Khulwehs*, each one named after the God of the
Jews, Christians, &c.; these they take out on certain
occasions and beat, saying that if any of the gods were
true and real, they would save or avenge their types
from these drubbings. But when the sacred manu-
scripts of the Hasbeiya Druzes were scattered abroad, and
an explanation of much of their abstruse and specula-
tive creed thus obtained, nothing of an idolatrous nature
was found in them : had they really worshipped idols,
something must have appeared of it in these books : and
since then a key to various mysterious signs, not understood by all even of the initiated, has fallen into the hands
of Dr. Vandyke, the learned missionary at Beyrout, but
nothing of idol worship appeared connected with them.

Sheikh Yussoof thinks that the Druzes do not believe
in the present existence of God; they say that in the
beginning He created the world and all things in it —

earth, air, sea — and then descended from heaven upon
it; but the great wind, one of these created things,
though small in the beginning, had increased meanwhile
to great power and strength, and, catching the Almighty
as He was reascending, killed Him, so that since that
time there has been no God, and creation has been left
to its own devices.

Hākeem, the founder of the Druze creed, taught, that
on the destruction or death of God, His soul became
incarnate in some other body — afterwards in his
(Hākeem's) own body: that God in the beginning
created a certain number of souls, which number has
always and will always exist — neither increasing nor
diminishing — as, if one person dies, the soul passes into
another about to be born, and thus the original number
always continues somewhere on the earth, to be collected
and restored together at the end of the world. At that
time the Druzes alone will be happy and blessed — the
Christians will be punished for their heresies and
contempt of the Druzes, by having two cantars of lead
hung round their necks — the Mooslims will have two
rotls, and the Jews two ounces, to carry in this uncomfortable manner. They always favour the Jews
above all other people — I know not why. Much of
their love for the English, at least in the present day,
is said to arise from the respect and influence acquired
by Mr. Wood, the late Consul at Damascus, among
them; and then, seeing that the English are neither
Maronites nor Mooslims, they imagine they must be in
some sort Druzes.

More interesting were the stories the Sheikh told us
of the renowned Emir Beshîr, whose ancestors became
Maronites many generations ago; he spoke much of his
greatness, of his unfailing integrity and uprightness —

of his being enlightened so much beyond his age and position, and of how much he managed to effect against all difficulties; but he spoke also of the cruelty and revengefulness which tarnished his greatness, and was so strong a passion in him as sometimes to overbalance his high sense of justice, entailing the most horrible results.

Nothing earthly can persuade the Arabs that the Sultan is not the supreme governor of the world : nor make them believe that his armies can be defeated : or that, if they were, it would make any difference in his position as Sultan over all nations : for instance, the common people in the Lebanon firmly believe that the Queen of England sends some one of her nobles every year to kneel before the Sultan, with clasped hands and many prostrations, to beg from him the favour of being allowed to continue governing her country for another year; and they speak of it as an immense grace and kindness of the Sultan that he receives an envoy instead of herself in person, waiving that duty on her part, because she is a woman, and has children to attend to! They also believe that the Sultan kindly exempted England from paying tribute to him during the time of the Crimean war, because we brought our soldiers to assist his own against his rebellious subjects, — an honour for our armies for which the ambassador had besought the Sultan on bended knees.

We often heard described the immense excitement of the Mooslims all over the country at the time of the horrible massacre at Jeddah ; how they exulted, crowed over the Christians, and kept assuring them that the time was soon coming for extirpating Christians throughout the Turkish dominions : and then, when the news of the bombardment of Jeddah by the English had arrived, how crestfallen the Turks looked, and how

the Druzes went about saying, "Wonderful is the
power of the English! great are the English! we too
are English!"

Some days after we reached Eh'den, the Sheikh invited us to dinner, sending his nephew and five of his
head servants to conduct us in state to his house, where
he came down, as usual, to the courtyard to receive us;
as soon as we were seated in the salon, a silver basin
and ewer were brought, with embroidered towels, and
water was poured over our hands by an attendant
kneeling on one knee. When this had been performed
for each of us, another attendant brought a silver
incense-burner, over the perfumed smoke of which
each guest bent for a few seconds, while another
servant threw drops of orange-flower water over
one's head and hands. Then came trays of apricots
and orange candy, arrack and coffee, and after about
an hour we went to dinner, which was served à l'Européenne, though the dishes were entirely Arab. The table
was set out with flowers and fruit, and the dinner,
which was handed round without being placed on the
table, consisted of twelve courses of meat, prefaced by a
thick vegetable soup, — stewed meats, boiled meats
and minced meats, vegetables stuffed with meats, and
meat stuffed with vegetables, two or three different pilafs
of rice differently flavoured, and then two sweet dishes
— one of square pieces of solidified cream (which, I am
convinced, is the same as the "cream tarts" so often
celebrated in "Arabian Nights"); the other of the
favourite Arab *bakhalāweh*, a very light but rich pastry
made with honey and almonds. These were followed
by quantities of fruit, fresh and dried; besides many
varieties of excellent Lebanon wine. We had coffee

in the salon; and a band of servants lighted us home
with torches and lanterns.

In return we invited the Emir and the French Consul
at Tripoli, M. Blanche, to dine with us the last day of
our stay at Eh'den; there were some other travellers
there at the time, and we made a party of seven persons. M. Regace sent us a basket full of flowers, with
which our tent was gaily ornamented; and our Arab
cook actually managed to give them the same number
of courses *à la Française* as the Emir had given us
à l'Arabe: but our dinner ended with real English
plum-pudding besides, and excellent peach cream-ice,
made by one of the dragomans, and champagne. It is
wonderful what skilful cooks these Arabs are, and how
great a variety of dishes they make out of so few
materials; their *cuisine*, too, being only a pan of charcoal in the open air.

M. Blanche, a *savant*, and a lover of the beautiful
Lebanon, with the geography and natural history of
which he is thoroughly acquainted, advised us to visit
the old Convent of Mar Antoun; so one morning we
started on horseback at an early hour, for it was to be a
long excursion. Our route lay along the Tripoli road
till we came to Jebel Arneto, where we turned off to the
left and commenced descending the side of the valley,
all bright and gay with vineyards, fruit gardens, and
flowers — with the blue sea in the vista beyond — till the .
valley narrowed to a lofty gorge, up which we turned:
it was close by a huge rock, through which an open
arch was cut, bearing a large white cross, — here began
the Convent territory. Through this arch the view was
magnificent, the mountains of the winding ravine
crossing each other at every step, with steep and generally inaccessible sides, covered with woods of low

prickly oak and thorn, with juniper and white cypress;
studded with caverns, and crowned with crosses. Perched
on the edge of one projecting crest, stood the Convent,
se cramponnant against the rock, and seeming to over-
hang the chasm below. The monks ushered us to a
divân under a vine-covered trellis, close to a tiny
chapel cut in the rock, the only part of the Convent
open to the unhallowed feet of women, numbers of
whom come here in pilgrimage to obtain the miraculous
cures for which the spot is famous. The Convent, which
is the largest in the Lebanon, containing one hundred
and thirty monks, has a grand façade of arches built up
against the mountain sides; the large halls and corridors
are chiefly excavated in the rock, and some exterior
buildings seemed to be well and ornamentally con-
structed; but only the gentlemen of our party were
suffered to enter them, except, indeed, the enormous natural cavern, wherein unhappy maniacs are confined! —
fortunately no one was there at the time : the wretched
patients are chained to the rock, and left there in utter
darkness; if they show signs of improvement, the chain
is knotted to a board; when they can undo the knot for
themselves, they are supposed to be fit to return into the
world; — but I should think few of those poor creatures
can ever come sane out of that dreadful place. It is a
fine cavern, with stalactites forming within. On our return to the Pilgrim's resting-place, the monks sprinkled
us with orange-flower water, and gave us a luncheon of
delicious honey, grapes and figs, and two salads, one of
parsley, the other of raw tomatoes. We regretted that
we, ladies, might not see the printing-press, where many
monks are busily employed each day; all we saw of
their occupations were some three or four spinning
goat's hair in one out-building, while in another it was

woven by hand into coarse cloth or carpets. The good
fathers gave us a friendly farewell ere we commenced
our ascent of the far side of the gorge—an ascent fitter
for goats than horses; but very beautiful was the view
looking back on the Convent, and on all the various
colours and forms in the valley below. At the top we
were rejoined by one of our party who had scrambled
on foot up to one of the numerous caverns to visit an
old Hermit, much reverenced for his saintly character;
he, and two others, had once been monks in Mar
Antoun, but, finding that place too comfortable for
their souls' welfare, they had, many years ago, retired
into the solitude of separate caverns, their food consisting only of raw herbs and rancid oil, brought at long
intervals up to the caves. The old man said that his
only occupation was prayer, and that he endeavoured to
entertain no thought in his mind but of God. He bestowed his blessing twice on his visitor with much unc-
tion, besides being very unctuous himself, placing one
hand on his visitor's chest and the other on his back, so
as to insure the blessing penetrating him through and
through : the only thing in the cavern, besides himself
and his goulleh of water, was a copy of one of Liguori's
books translated into Arabic.

We then proceeded along the valley through the
beautiful village, full of fruit and flower gardens, of
Forsraab, opposite to Eh'den, each succeeding view being
more lovely than the one before; and crossing round
the head of the valley, by the picturesque mill and
under the walnuts and willows which overhung the
stream, we scrambled up the other side, and reached
our tents just as the afternoon mist—a very common
visitor—filled the valley. Every one who goes to Eh'den
should take this excursion, which occupies about seven

or eight hours. The thermometer in our tent marked
45° that morning at six o'clock, but the heat in the
midday hours was very great.

One of our favourite walks was to a small but very
ancient convent, Mar Serkis (St. Sergius) — quite at
the head of the valley, by the Source, nestled into a
nook in a wild little gorge of its own; the kind-hearted
old monks always appeared quietly contented and happy
among themselves; the want of comforts seeming
atoned for in their minds by the fine view from their
windows; they were very full of a new church they
were building above the convent, but the one underneath it, said to be upwards of 500 years old, was more
interesting to us; it is almost entirely excavated in the
rock, and is entered by a rock-hewn winding staircase;
it is very venerable-looking and impressive, with its two
or three sombre lamps shining dimly in the utter darkness, and a few Arabic prayers written in the Syriac
character for its sole ornament. The Source was always
a favourite haunt of ours — its ice-cold waters gushing
in full volume at once from the rock, under a pomegranate and some fine walnut trees — on the one side
tumbling rapidly down into a delightful little dark dell
shaded over with white poplars and weeping willows,
where it was immediately hushed into complete silence,
like a child silenced in the midst of its glee, not uttering a murmur till another " fount's young waters " had
crept from under a rock to meet it; then they both
went whispering and babbling and laughing quietly together, over the rough way, till they came to the old
mill, whence their course was a rapid and bounding
one all the way to the sea. On the other side it glided
into the white-cypress wood, and along a half natural,
half artificial channel on the mountain side through

the village, and down the Pass, till it rushed out, the full-grown Kadisha, under the walls of the Castle of Raymond of Toulouse at Tripoli.

THE BROOK AT EH'DEN.

From the blackness of the cavern deep
Where jealous rocks my sources keep,
    Where the phantoms dark
    Who have given me birth
    All my destiny mark
    From the womb of earth,

I come — from under the rugged roots
  Of the ancient walnut tree,
Just where the young pomegranate shoots
  Throw scarlet buds on me:

Then by the monastery old
  Where sunbeams never rest
Till all the west, with liquid gold
  And crimson splendour drest,

Flings back one glorious rosy ray
  To the lonely heart in the rock-cut cell,
Whose only joy in the silent day
  Is the faintly-sounding sweet prayer-bell:

Then I flow beneath the Cypress' shade
  On the mountain's rocky steep,
Where the goats browse close to the shepherd maid
  In the bosky thickets deep:

And I babble under the bright, bright green
  Where the vine a wild wreath weaves,
And I mark how the sunlight laughs between
  All the happy graceful leaves:

And my pebbles shine with lustrous glow
  Where my waters fain would stay;
For a smile of Childhood's bliss, I know,
  Is there thrown across my way.

Then the Night has darkened down, before
    I have reached the trembling stones,
Where I love to feel your steps pass o'er
    And to hear your sweet, low tones,—

So I pause — and lo! the Moon's soft rays,
All in brightest flakes of silvery sheen,
In a tender glory o'er me plays
Like the glow of Angels' eyes, I ween,—

And my lowest drops leap up to meet
    The radiance of her glance,
And my heart is full of joy, as sweet
    As the fire-flies' bright dance:

And I sometimes think, some tiny stars,
Dwelling just without the heavenly choir,
Whose fullest splendour some earth-stain mars
But whose eyes shine bright with holy fire,
Have come down my little wave to kiss,
On my breast their golden gifts to strew,
And my path to brighten with hours of bliss
Like the shining paths the stars pursue:

    No not for *me* this radiant lot:
    They pass along their glorious way
    Though "resting not, yet hastening not,"
    They know no change, they fear no stay, —
    I hasten on, and sudden slip
From under the lovely silvery flakes,
And their sweet bright light my breast forsakes
    As shades of blackest darkness dip
    Cold hands within my stream.
    All sorrowful and mute I go,
    Where village men pass to and fro,
    And lights upon me beam;
    They use me, but they heed me not,
    Nor list my plaintive murmuring—
    The little songs all whispering
    I sing to ease my lonely lot.

    But courage! 'neath the morning sky
    I bravely leap from rock to rock,
    With steady course increasingly
    I triumph over every shock—

THE BROOK AT EH'DEN.

On, on with earnest strength I go
To that vast end that comes, I know;
And oft when Sunlight's fiercest beam
Beats scorching on my limpid stream,
  Some gentle shadowing tree
  Bends lovingly o'er me,
  Cooling my heated wave
  As I the old roots lave —
Some thirsty bank drinks up my dew
And decks herself with flow'rets gay,
Then, mirrored in still tenderer hue,
The flowery portraits I repay.

Now, ere this work of mine is done
And I have earned my long, long rest —
Ere that great Sea hath laid me on
Her grand, eternal, heaving breast,
Beneath her deep, dark folds of blue —
I will look back, — not wasted all
My life —from those whose simple wants and few
I fed within the Convent wall —

From the shade I cooled in morning hours
  Within your own dear Cypress bowers, —
From the bright green vines whose sweet fruit drew
  Rich juices from my freshest dew, —

From the gifts I freely spent
  As passing by the noisy din
Of human care, and wrath, and sin,
  All earnest in my work I went,—

From these — though lonely, though forlorn
  I wander on—yet, as I go,
Sweet blessings all my breast adorn,
  Through all my waters flow.

These all my joy, till—gliding on
  O wondrous Sea, I shall behold thee:
Thy mighty arms, whose home I've won,
  In one grand smile of Death will fold me!

Then mute will be my little song
(Sweet whisperings which to brooks belong)—

For then my voice, in anthems loud,
Will swell the Hallelujahs proud
Of Deep who calls to other Deep,
The Lord's high Name with praise to keep:

My voice, through mighty waves, e'en mine
  The Lord Himself will heed:
Oh flow, flow on, my stream, with speed
  To meet that Love divine!

CHAP. XIII.

SOLOMON'S FRIENDS AND SOLOMON'S WORK.

AT last, after bidding adieu to the Emir, we left our pretty encampment and the merry village with its handsome, gaily dressed people; it was midday when we started, and we had a ride of two and a half hours to reach the Cedars, along a bare, barren road, crossing the low pass between the valley of Mar Antoun and that of Khanobîn; hill after hill of rock without the faintest trace of verdure, till we arrived at the brink of an immense chasm, and, looking over the edge, we beheld the village of Bscherreh hanging on the rocky side of the ravine, embedded in wood and garden; just above the village the magnificent gorge closes round sharply, holding in its curve most weird-looking and fantastic rocks, and the beautiful Falls of the Kadîsha, which tumble down in masses of white foam to the gardens at the bottom,— on the other side of the ravine the village of Hasroun lies on a shelf of verdure and luxuriance. We turned away from this beautiful view, back to the hard, yellow, barren mountains on which the sunshine was pouring in fierce and pitiless rays,— when, in five minutes more, a general shout came from the muleteers, and the saïs beside me called out "Shoof! shoof! ya sitt! el Arz el Arz!"* and I saw in the

* "Look, look, oh lady! the Cedars, the Cedars!"

centre of an immense plateau, lying in the very bosom
of the giant mountain which closes round three sides of
it, a single black patch, so black and dark, I scarcely
believed that this could be the Cedars of Lebanon!
We rode on quickly, and forgot all fatigue and heat and
everything else directly we were under their delicious
shade, half an hour after our first view; it is difficult to
describe the first feeling there, — your head must ache
with the scorching heat, your eyes burn with the unshaded barrenness of the last few hours — you must feel
the soothing coolness of the shade stealing through
your heated veins, you must smell the powerful and refreshing fragrance of the Cedars, and see the venerable
forms around you, before you can understand that
beauty and delight which there sink into your very soul;
it is like passing from the noisy din and world-weariness
of some great city's market-place into the silent aisles
of a vast Cathedral, — only that here the solitude is
more complete, the columns and arches are of Nature's
raising, and the holy hymns are sung by sweet birds
twittering and trilling from tree to tree, while all

> "the forest leaves seem stirred with prayer;"

in the fiery heat of the Bekâa the scorched sands of the
Desert, and the arid mountains of Judea, how often
one's mind harked back to the cool, green shades of the
Cedars, and one began to understand the glowing description of the Beloved whose eyes are like pools of
water, and whose " countenance is as Lebanon, excellent
as the cedars." (Cant. v. 15.)

It was difficult to choose the prettiest among so many
pretty spots for our tents, but we finally fixed them close
to the little chapel in the centre of the grove, from whence

we had a view of the sea: the chapel is but a square
construction of roughly hewn stones, four young cedar
trunks forming the support inside : the altar was hung
with pink chintz and ornamented with a cheap French
print of the Madonna della Seggiola; every morning
at six o'clock an old Maronite priest came over from
Bscherreh, a walk of two hours' distance, and chanted
a short service — sometimes a goatherd or two would
join him, sometimes our servants or muleteers, but
whether alone or not the voice of prayer and praise rose
there every morning at dawn of day, and always sounded
appropriate and *due* on what seemed holy ground, and,
instead of breaking the silence, really seemed to make
the solitude more apparent.

The Cedars form one group or grove covering an
undulating piece of ground not a mile in circumference ;
they are not scattered about, but stand in one dense
mass, after passing the boundary of which, there is not a
shrub to be seen for many miles; there are about four
hundred young trees, in themselves a beautiful and
noble little forest, thronging round the patriarchs or
" Apostles," as they are called by the Maronites ; of these
venerable trees there are yet·twelve, besides another as
old which has been lying on the ground for the last five
or six years past; there is another very old one, which has
evidently been burned, and of which so little remains
that one cannot be sure of its generation; but these
" twelve Apostles " are unmistakable, although the
peasants believe that no one can count them — that
some magic puzzles those who try, and the numbers
ever elude their grasp. The largest of the old Saints
is forty-five feet in girth, the second forty-two —- while
some of the branches we measured roughly at fifty-
eight paces in length ; whether they can have lived three

thousand years, as the tradition avers, I am not called on
to decide, and as the principal trunk of the fallen tree has
been destroyed, it is impossible to find any vegetable
history written upon its rings; but one likes to fancy
the legend true, and to call them, as the Arabs do, the
"Friends of Solomon;" while, involuntarily, one speaks
of them in the language of his father David, as "the
cedars which the Lord hath planted." One great
charm of the encampment here, especially after the
society of the good people of Eh'den, is the utter silence
and solitude: it is such an indescribable comfort to encamp out of the sound of village dogs and jackals, and to
be able to leave one's tent door open, without fear of an
intruder; perchance in the morning a pretty boy or a
rosy-faced girl would lead a couple of hundred goats
down one of the little dells, their bells tinkling softly as
they passed,— but no other sound of man ever broke
the silence; Nature herself, however, was never silent —
the cicale here were extraordinarily loud, and the trees
were full of little birds of the brightest green and gold
plumage, with a sweet, clear note, while thousands of
tiny lizards glided about everywhere: and to lie upon
the soft sand and the dry bed of cedar spines, under the
cool, green shade, listening to all the sweet sounds,
letting one's thoughts wander back into the long ages
of which these trees are standing witnesses, looking out
the while over the hot, barren mountains and down the
many coloured gorge, to the snow-white coast, and the
blue sea twinkling beyond, with the horizon apparently
half way up the sky (the effect of our own lofty position)
—all this deliciousness is recompense enough for any
amount of fatigue and trouble incurred in reaching them.
The place has but one drawback — want of water,
the nearest spring·being three quarters of an hour off:

and also that nothing but the commonest provisions are procurable at Bscherreh.

We were now 6100 feet above the sea, and we had expected to be colder even than we were at Eh'den in the nights, but the Equinox approached, and we were told that it would be warm after that, — and so it proved; the thermometer was at 45° one morning, and at 67° at the same hour on the next day! We had come again to the time of the full moon, and this was indeed the place to be "read aright" by its holy light; night after night we used to wander through the moon-lit glades, watching the light silvering the mountain which stretches its giant arms with everlasting, strong tenderness round the ancient trees, and listening to the owls hooting here and there in the thick boughs. One night we had a still more beautiful and striking scene: it was the eve of the 14th of September, the day on which the Emperor Constantine is supposed to have seen the Cross of fire shining in the sky, in consequence of which miraculous appearance both he and his whole army received the Gospel of true Light, and Salvation through Christ was proclaimed throughout his dominions; the festival is kept by beacon-fires lit upon every mountain-top in Syria, beginning with the Cedar mountain, besides bonfires in every village, handing on the good tidings, as it were, from one to the other throughout the land; it is a fine idea, and on a calm night, it is still finer in reality; the flames of each fire as they rose and fell in the night breeze shining against the deep *azure* sky, were exceedingly pretty, and every here and there a long train of fire was laid up the side of the mountain, like a fiery snake, which, catching the wind now on this side, now on that, seemed really to have caught also the wriggling, gliding motion of a living serpent.

T 4

Layard mentions a curious fact that occurred when he was at Kouyunjik, of a sweet smell proceeding from some wood burning on a fire made by his workmen: they had taken one of the beams from the excavation, just where an inscription on the building denoted that the roof had been made of cedar wood, brought from the Lebanon 3000 years before: this is doubly curious because the Cedars of Lebanon are *not* the Red Cedar so fragrant in burning, but a *white*, which gives out no particular fragrance when burned: in one's encampment there, one's fire is always made of the small branches broken down by the wind; and some of the chips and shavings cut off from one of the oldest " Saints " which lies now upon the ground, were put into ours, but no perfume came from it save that of the fresh resinous smell of any kind of pine-tree wood. Perhaps that proceeding from the cedar wood at Kouyunjik was only this resinous fragrance, which, though very sweet, is not that of the red Indian cedar to which we are accustomed as a perfume.

We wanted to see the celebrated Convent of Kha-nobîn, which, though not the largest in the Lebanon, is the residence of the Maronite Patriarch — so we set off one morning at eight o'clock and proceeded by the same road as we had come, descending to Bscherreh — a large village of very tumble-down houses planted as thickly as possible with mulberries and poplars, but peopled with very plain men and women — a striking contrast to the handsome merry Eh'denites with whom they are always at war — perhaps from jealousy or mortified vanity. Outside the village, built into and under and over the most extraordinary assemblage of insane-looking rocks, is the curious old Convent of Mar Serkis, and a few minutes further on comes the white foamy.

cascade of the Khadîsha rushing down amidst ferns and flowers—indeed this whole valley is smiling with flowers of all kinds and colours. Then we ascended the other side, and passing through the beautiful village of Hasroun found ourselves opposite to Hadshît—so close, as the crow flies, that the inhabitants of one village can speak to their neighbours of the other across the valley, while the splendid chasm between descends, first in green terraces and then in perpendicular walls of blue limestone cliffs, to the depth of a thousand feet. Hasroun is the most luxuriant spot we saw in the Lebanon — every inch of soil is cultivated, and the place is buried in thickets, and forests of thorns, walnuts, planes, poplars, figs and prickly oaks, tangled over and wreathed together with immense festoons of vines, besides those in more decorously-pruned vineyards; white and yellow clematis and honeysuckle were in all the hedges, and real fields of wheat and English-looking grass on all the slopes. Riding on over breezy downs we passed a gigantic cavern in the rocks on the other side of the chasm, and a lofty waterfall, which must be very fine in spring, as it has but one perpendicular fall; and then we looked down, first on the small Convent of Mar Elisha, and then on Khanobîn, to which, however, we did not descend, as it would have taken us five or six hours more; it did not appear to us equal either in size or position to the Convent of Mar Antoun, nor is the valley, at least as seen from above, as varied in outline or as brilliant in colouring as the other. We returned to Hasroun, feeling very much like cinders out of a furnace, and put ourselves to cool under a walnut grove, where the people brought us great baskets of figs and grapes, for which we duly paid some trifle—but if you stop *in* a vineyard you may eat as much as you like, gratis; any, however, that are carried away you are expected to pay for: this is in accordance with the old Israelite rule in Deuteronomy xxiii. 24. We were so much tired that we caught at the offer made by a peasant to show us a short cut to the Cedars—but let all weary travellers beware how they lend an ear to such flattering tales of peasants, who either scramble over tracks where no horses can follow them, or not unfrequently find themselves at fault, and leave you in the lurch: so it was with our guide—he led us for three mortal hours over the most thoroughly atrocious paths conceivable, and then deserted us, leaving us in such scorching heat, that not only ourselves, but even our dragoman and saïs and the two muleteers, who had accompanied us, were made ill by it.

Our last afternoon at the Cedars afforded us the extraordinary sight of what is called, I believe, a false sun: the mist had jammed itself up into dense masses, like a rough sea of ice-pack, filling up and smoothing over the whole valley, and extending over the sea beyond; behind this the sun in due time sunk, — but, ten minutes after, another sun of a flaming blood-colour popped up, and after shining with an awful kind of dark brilliancy for about a quarter of an hour, it also faded away and died behind the mist-clouds,—very marvellous it was altogether.

We took leave of the grand old trees by moonlight, after a week's stay, mounting on horseback before 4 A.M. and began to ascend great Makhmel, or the Cedar mountain.* The path was of course steep and in some

* Makhmel is the name given to this, the loftiest mountain in the Lebanon, by the people of the district of Tripoli; the mountaineers themselves call it always and only Jebel el Arz—the mountain of the Cedars; its highest peak is called, as are *all* the highest peaks through-

places so narrow as to be rather giddy work for climbing, but in no place in the least dangerous, or very fatiguing, except from the violent wind and the rarefied air. Just as it began to dawn we met a troop of goats, the goatherds singing in chorus to the music of a well-played reed-pipe; very sweet and pleasant it sounded, and a very uncommon incident it was in Syrian travel. Nothing could be more beautiful than the changing views at every fresh step in the ascent, the early light telling out the colours in the clearest and loveliest purity, while from each valley and nook wreaths of delicate bright *blue* mist rose like mysterious veils, slowly withdrawing as the dawn advanced. Suddenly the sun lit up the summits of the peaks, bathing each with its own flood of golden splendour, and, resting there, widened in a sudden sheet of light over the valleys below, flying over Eh'den with giant strides as we had so often watched it from the valley itself. The sun had but touched the upper valleys when we reached the summit — or rather very near the summit; our companions ascended the highest peak, but the coldness of the thin air at this height rendered me incapable of going any further, and our resting-place commanded such an ample view, that we did not much regret losing the northern part over the wide plain of Homs and Hamah, bounded by faint blue mountains, which can only be seen from the real summit. We spread our large map and compass on the ground before us, as we gazed at the *living* map beneath — more living than a landscape usually appears, from the swiftly moving light

out Syria, Jebel el Khodib — the *summit* mountain. The height of the Jebel el Khodib here, which is now believed to be the highest mountain in Syria, has been lately ascertained to be 10,400 feet above the Mediterranean; this Khodib is at some distance still further north of the peak our party ascended, which was then believed to be the highest.

of the rising sun, gliding, as it were, with life-giving
beams over the picture — now here, now there — waking
up each portion, till it seemed really living, breathing,
under the rapid, silent changes.

We were seated on a narrow ridge or backbone between
the peaks, — beneath us, on one side, the two rifts of the
Kadisha sloped down to the Mediterranean, their light
blue and grey cliffs contrasting most vividly with the
orange rocks and red soil in the same gorges: they
were divided from the turquoise blue — such a blue!
— sea by snow-white cliffs, sweeping in many a graceful curve along the coast. On the other side of our
ridge the mountain sloped still more precipitously and
smoothly down into a region of sand, beyond which
came a range of hills, picturesque and rugged, of dark
browns and purples, dividing it from the perfectly flat
Bekka *, stretching out in green and brown to the foot
of the opposite mountain range — the Anti-Lebanon —
which was now of course lying in deep dark shadow
against the magnificently glowing morning sky: one
dark spot immediately under these mountains was
Baalbek; and as we looked the sun passed a giant step
across the whole plain, and brightened up the green
plantations of the village, so that, with a telescope, the
Temple could be discerned.   Directly to the south rose
our beloved Sunnîn, from this side a ridge of rosy crags,
rugged and jagged; beyond that, far away, a lovely and
graceful mountain stood quite alone — the blue cone,
precipitous on one side, sloping down gently on the
other, striped with lilac shades — it needed nothing to
tell us that this was Hermon, — Jebel esh Sheikh,
the chief of mountains: to its left, faint blue mountains

---

* From the Hebrew *Bikha*, meaning plain, as this is *the* plain of
North Syria. From the Arabic *Bekâa* the Spanish *Vega* is derived —
signifying a plain between mountains.

faded away in the distance, and these we knew were in the Lejah: to its right one bright blue ridge, ending suddenly in the sea, was Carmel. Then the sunshine shot down right under our feet and lit up the dark shades of the Cedars, and the hard, white, solid little clouds, like icebergs on the sea, expanded and joined the lighter mist-wreaths that had risen from the valleys, and the distances became hazy and the glorious colouring more faint, — in fact for really extensive views in this country, the first hour of sunrise and the last of sunset are the only times of day when they can be perfectly seen; at all other hours the heat has thickened the air and faded the brilliant colouring which is here *the* greatest charm. The view from Mount Hermon is considerably more extensive, as there are no intercepting peaks near at hand: but that from the Cedar Mountain is certainly more varied and beautiful, even if it is not, as one traveller calls it, "the loveliest yet grandest scene that the world possesses," — it is indescribably and grandly lovely.

We had a long, tiresome descent of nearly two hours before we reached our tents, which had been pitched near a clear and very cold source called 'Ain Ata, where we were thankful to creep under some fine walnut trees out of the burning, fervid sun; we had a fine view to look at all day, — Hermon's graceful head towering up in the distance, while close to us lay nestled in a mountain basin, the pretty Lake Yemouni and fiery red mountains speckled with prickly oak rose all round us. This spot is subject to sudden squalls, coming over the heads of the mountains; our tent was not properly secured at first, and was rudely overturned by one of them, and we left behind us a variety of stains on the rocks and ground from the upset ink-bottles, that must have puzzled the goats for many days

after. We were glad of a good sleep that night, but on
the next we mounted at 1 A.M., and started for the
great plain of the Bekâa, the heat of which no one
would willingly encounter by day, in the summer.
The road lay up and down steep glens and vales, thickly
wooded with low trees and shrubs, — pine, prickly oak,
and white cypress—all of them twisted and stunted into
strange, grotesque shapes, which, in the deep shades of
the waning moon and the starlight, assumed most
mysterious appearances : — now an old friar begging
with his arms stretched out and his head thrown back—
now a lady with a long train and a dancing step — now
" bears with ragged staffs " on each side of the path like
constables — now sturdy dogs, and, more frequently,
cocks with or without tails, and their heads perked up
till I half expected to hear the horrid *crow* close to my
ear; and in the lowest glade a gigantic knight on a
charger seemed to approach, his black armour shining in
the moonlight and a white shield glistening on his arm
— but his noble horse suddenly dropped his head, the
knight mysteriously vanished, and the white shield
turned into the white, smooth trunk of an old gnarled
oak ! We stopped for five minutes at Deir el Ah'mar,
which seemed to be a hamlet inhabited by dogs only —
no other living thing was moving; the dawn was
commencing as we arrived at the dead flat of the great
plain, and very pretty it was to watch the light darting
on Hermon and the great mountains we had just left,
colouring the summits into a pink, brilliant as a rose
leaf, above the purple violet and browns of the lower
mountains and the green plain on which we now cast
long shadows behind us. The Morning Star was still
shining with serene beauty, as we turned aside to the
single Column in the plain, about which little or nothing

is known, as neither inscription nor sculpture remains upon it: otherwise it is little injured, — it is of the Corinthian order, standing on a pedestal of steps; the column is not nearly so lofty as that of Diocletian at Alexandria, which is eighty feet high; this one is only sixty, but there is something grand in its loneliness and silent mystery: doubtless our horses thought it uncanny, for they every one shied at it, and could scarcely be persuaded to go round it. The sun was shining brightly on the famous Six Columns of Baalbek as we reached the village at 5 A.M.; we got into a garden on the north side of the Temple, but the heat was very great, and we had all fallen asleep before either our tents or our breakfast had arrived.

As the heat was very great here — 96° in the shade each day — we did not visit the Temple till after dinner: when we thought ourselves fortunate in seeing it *first* by sunset; it is a fine scene in the morning, but no single and incomplete architectural object can be more lovely than the Six lonely Columns standing with such dignity and majesty in the midst of desolation and ruin around them, bathed in the golden glory shed by the setting sun, with the Temple of Jupiter seen through them, a Mosque beyond, and the chain of barren mountains crimsoned into beauty behind them.

Baalbek has been so frequently and ably illustrated, by pen and pencil, in the last few years, that only a very few words are necessary to record the impression made by its graceful majesty upon the traveller; and it is to be hoped that many more generations will see these ruins as they are — so enormous and ponderous were the materials used, that the puny hand of modern man can do but little to injure them — earthquakes are the only destroyers to be feared.

"Time hath not harmed the eternal monument;
Time is not here, nor days, nor months, nor years—
For sure those mighty piles shall overlive,
The feeble generations of mankind. . . . .
A mighty mass remains; enough to tell us
How great our fathers were, how little we.
Men are not what they were: their crimes and follies
Have dwarfed them down from the old hero race
To such poor things as we!"*

Ascending a lofty flight of steps at the extreme east, the worshipper entered a magnificent open portico with a square hall at each end,—thence he passed through a hexagonal court surrounded with columns, into the great quadrangle, four hundred and forty feet long, across which a double colonnade † led to another flight of steps, which gave access to the platform on which stood the Temple of the Sun. This edifice was surrounded by fifty-four columns of seventy-five feet in height; the loftiest, it is said, in the world, and appearing still higher than they really are from their (almost) extreme slenderness — they are but six feet six inches in diameter. ‡ No trace of the cella of this temple remains, and there are some doubts that it was ever built; only six of the fifty-four columns of the peristyle are now standing (although the bases of a great many are still to be seen *in situ*, the present outside wall being built up between them), but these six are the chief beauty of Baalbek —

"Flinging their shadows from on high,
Like dials which the wizard Time
Had raised to count his ages by:"

* Thalaba.

† Destroyed to build a Christian Church, which, in the time of Constantine the Great occupied this court.

‡ The usual proportion of a Corinthian column is $8\frac{1}{2}$ diameters to the height, whereas the height of the columns of the Temple of the Sun are nearly 12 diameters: those of the Temple of Jupiter have 10 diameters.

they tell their own tale by the exquisite carving of
their capitals, which marks the purest Corinthian; the
acanthus-leaves are cut with remarkable freedom and
richness, by no means overloaded, and the abacus is
supported by delicate volutes of the most graceful
design; it is curious to observe the effect of the weather
upon these columns — on the north side almost every
leaf and many of the volutes are perfect — while on the
other they are shapeless blocks.

The whole of this Temple and the Great Courts rest
upon giant walls supported by the Platform of Cyclopean
masonry, justly considered one of the wonders of the
world; in the western end are the three stones — rocks
one ought to call them — from which the Temple was
called *Trilithon* by the Greeks, — two of them are sixty-
four feet, and the third sixty-three feet long—all three
are thirteen feet both in height and in thickness.   The
Platform, of which every stone is gigantic, is supported
by three passages running under its entire length and
breadth, vaulted, and of exceedingly fine workmanship,
the enormous stones nicely and neatly joined,— they
are wonderful places to walk through — handsomer and
of finer finish than the vaults beneath the Temple of
Solomon at Jerusalem.   Of course the beauty of Baalbek is in the Temples, but the Platform was, to me at
least, a still greater interest,— one had the same crush-
ing feeling of the long ages of its past history come over
one's mind, that one had felt in the Temples of Egypt,
— and all in vain — for the shadows of its antiquity
elude one's grasp : it is a relief to seize upon tradition,
and to believe it modern enough for Solomon's workmanship; but one fancies one recognises the Phœnician
(Canaanite) stamp upon its massive simplicity, which
may be called barbarous, but which, in the hands of the

Egyptians and Phœnicians, became sublime also. Possibly Baalbek is much older than Tadmor, and was one of the cities already standing in the country before Joshua marked out the boundaries of the Israelites: it cannot be the Baalath built by Solomon when he built "Tadmor in the wilderness," both of them stone cities, because Josephus distinctly explains that to have been near Gézer, in the tribe of Dan; while that the rocks of which it is built are so much more enormous than anything at Tadmor, may be partly accounted for by the fact, of the quarries at Baalbek being so much nearer to the building than those of Tadmor. Looking up from the exterior of these huge stones, and seeing the Six Columns shoot up skywards with their slender, tapering shafts, they have been not inaptly compared to "Ariel mounted on a mammoth's back!"

Although the ground has filled up the interior of the Great Court to such a height — at least twenty feet — as to render it impossible to form a correct judgment, one can hardly imagine that these beautiful walls were sufficiently high inside for the very great size of the area; the court was entirely surrounded with recesses, having six, four, or two columns in front of each, formed of Egyptian red granite and porphyry, quantities of the débris of which lie all about; each recess contained a number of niches for statues, probably standing above others now buried, in which the priests or worshippers sat; these are all richly sculptured, many with eagles, fruit, &c., but the Egyptian asp spoken of by some travellers we thought very little identical with its supposed original. This temple was dedicated to all the gods, with Baal as supreme, and is supposed to have been built, or at least the greater part of it, in the time of the Emperor Antoninus Pius, A.D. 138—161. I often

pondered where the columns that Sultan Suleymân took
in 1550 from this Temple to adorn Santa Sophia could
have stood; I conclude they were among these small
ones closing in the recesses of the Great Court, as they
seemed to have been the only columns in Baalbek of
coloured marble or of like dimensions.

The Temple of Jupiter is about two hundred feet to
the south of the Temple of the Sun, beyond the grand
Court, and is said to have been built at the same time;
the ground on which it stands is much lower than that
of its imperial neighbour, but it has its own platform : it
is larger than the Parthenon, but, probably from the
very lofty columns near it and the impossibility of
getting a distant view of the whole, it appears considerably smaller, and you have no idea of its real size till you
come to measurements.   Dr. Robinson remarks that nowhere else does it seem so impossible to reconcile the
gigantic size of the fallen stones of the same entablature
or column with those still standing, as at Baalbek; so
perfect are the proportions that neither the size, nor
any other *one* characteristic strikes the eye, in the perfect balance of the whole.   It has another peculiar charm
in its completeness, for although ruined and hidden,
Baalbek still remains *as a whole;* perhaps no Temple
(always excepting the Theseum at Athens, which is six
hundred years older than Baalbek), remains so complete,
nor is the execution of the details surpassed by any
other work of the kind.   The cella is surrounded with
forty-two columns, a triple row at the east end forming
the portico, within which is the famous doorway, whose
sides are formed of single stones forty-two feet high; it
is covered, overloaded, all round with border after border
of the most exquisite sculpture, fruit, flowers, leaves, and
wheat-ears, interspersed with little Cupids and panthers;

but the most interesting of the ornaments is the large
Eagle sculptured on the soffit of this doorway, holding a
caduceus in his talons, and the strings of garlands, up-
held on each side by genii, are twisted in his beak. The
ceiling of the peristyle is equally rich, and as a great
deal of it has fallen, it can be closely examined: it
is divided into hexagonal compartments, each one filled
by a bust or figure carved in such high relief as to seem
leaning out of its frame; the contours of the figures are
very graceful.

These Temples had been built about 800 years when
they were turned into a fortress; they have sustained
several sieges and much rough usage since: the Saracens
and Crusaders built up walls within and without, which
now remain to the extreme discomfort of the traveller:
there is, however, a fine Saracenic palace or castle,
close to the Temple of Jupiter, whose unadorned
architecture contrasts well with the rich sculpture of its
Corinthian neighbours; the walls are strong and
massive, and the octagonal hall in the centre, which is
gracefully vaulted, is remarkably handsome.

At a short distance from the great Temple, standing
alone among ruins, huts, and gardens, there is a little
gem of a Temple; it is shaped like a star-fish, the
seven columns surrounding it being placed in a circle,
and the cella wall receding in a semicircle between
each; it had once a domed roof, and is most richly
ornamented, within and without, with sculpture, the
delicately carved capitals of the fluted columns reminding
one of some of the best things of the kind at Venice;
the whole Temple is only thirty-eight feet in diameter,
and, alas, much destroyed; I am convinced it was intended for a *kiosk* or *boudoir* for the gods, when they
left the Great Temple to take a little recreation.

Then there are the Quarries, to which we rode one

evening, where the famous stone, sixty-eight feet long,
and weighing probably 1100 tons, still lies unremoved;
the peasantry believe that the genii, working amicably
with the men of old, carried these stones for them, but,
being one day offended at something, this stone was
dropped in the quarry, and no human strength has been
found capable of lifting it since; it is said to be the
largest stone hewn for building in the world,—the
obelisk in the quarry at Assouān is, however, twenty-
seven feet longer and nearly as wide. These quarries
point to such gigantic works, that one does not wonder
they have given rise to legends of supernatural agency
— adding the craft of jinns and genii to the might of
the " giants who lived in those days." At Baalbek one
learns to think naturally of the Rephaïm, the Emims,
the Zanzummims, the Zouzims, and the Anakims,
whose fathers, it is said, won from Heaven the reward
of a more than mortal strength, for having given up
solitude and celibacy on the tops of the mountains, and
returned to a life of usefulness among their kinsfolk in
the plains,— the best argument for the " athletic religion" so much in fashion at the present time, that I
have ever come across — Mr. Kingsley should certainly
make use of the legend! The quarries, which extend
over a great distance, are very striking from their
sharply cut cliffs, or clefts, and their deep caverns
(some of which appear to have been made use of, both
as tombs and dwelling-places), some supported by
pillars, others only open-mouthed, and from the strange,
grotesque forms in which the rock has been left,— be-
ides its unusually brilliant colouring,— orange and
white, blue and grey, and a bright coppery green.
From one of these wild mystic-looking nooks, a very
large eagle soared out slowly and calmly; he disdained

to take any further notice of our presence, but settling himself with much dignity on an adjoining point, his mate glided silently out of a hole close to us, and disappeared behind him — they were scarcely four yards from our heads.

One of the questions of interest concerning Baalbek is its name, which still puzzles the learned: it is believed by all to be its original name, or, at least, an ancient one, to which the Arabs, when they conquered Syria in A.D. 630, wisely returned; but if the *bek* is a Phœnician (and hence Hebrew) word, it has not yet been found in the language: some persons think that it may have been derived from the Egyptian *baki*, meaning city, and that the Greeks applied it when Cœlo-Syria fell to the lot of the Græco-Egyptian kingdom, in which case it would be as modern as their name of Heliopolis, and means only the same thing : Dr. Robinson, however, suggests that it is from the later Arabic *bakka*, a throng or crowd, and that it describes the place where worshippers of Baal met in a crowd. Some have tried to derive it from the same word as the name of the plain beside it — Bekaa — (*Bikha*, Hebrew for *plain*) as if to denote " Baal of the plain ; " but this is untenable, as the *k* is not the same letter when used in Baalbek as in Bikha.

A little Wely near the town is shaded by a cypress tree worth seeing : though not nearly as tall as the splendid cypresses of Smyrna, it is so round, so full, and so luxuriant as to make a specimen fit for a picture,— it is said to have been as large and full more than a century ago.

We left Baalbek at 11 P.M., after four days' stay; our dragoman was ill, and we took a guide, who led us for some time, up and down, over apparently barren mountains, but by so good a path, that we did not suspect

we were going wrong : there was no moon, only the
beautiful stars, and one radiant planet near Orion, about
the heavenly birth and parentage of which the saïs told
me a long legend, of which, unfortunately, I took in
only about half. At last we reached the brow of the
mountain, and turned into a tremendous ravine with
a torrent roaring at the bottom ; the road became a
succession of smooth, sloping slabs of rock, and presently
the guide sat down, and coolly informed us that he knew
nothing about the route, and could only say that we
were on a goat-path, where horses never passed, but
which ultimately went down to the bottom of the
ravine : the whole side of the mountain was enveloped
in pitch darkness, so that we could not see one step
before us, and it seemed more than likely that we
should reach the bottom by an expeditious, but not
precisely agreeable mode of descent, as the path was
nowhere more than two feet wide. We were benumbed
with cold and fatigue, and excessively sleepy : however,
there was nothing for it but to go on, trusting to the
sure-footedness of our horses ; we finally reached the
end of the path in safety, but I need not say that the
four hours we were on that mountain side were neither
very short nor very agreeable. Morning dawned as we
emerged into the pretty plain of Surghāya, and the ride
through the smiling green pastures was refreshing, with
the wild craggy summits of the Anti-Lebanon towering
over head, and Hermon filling up the end of the picture.
We got to Zebdāny at 6 A.M., a bright pretty place,
with the hedges covered with sweet white roses and
clematis, and English-looking gates, neatly made and
painted, to the gardens : this plain is very rich and
luxuriant ; Bludan, the summer residence of the Europeans of Damascus, standing perched up, halfway to

heaven, on a green plateau near the summit of one of
the mountains. We resumed our route early the next
morning, passing over the rest of the plain of the Bārada
with its pretty waterfall and light Roman bridge, and
the fine pass of Abila, the modern Souk; the steep cliffs,
which close in with beautiful windings, are covered with
tablets and tombs, some of them ornamented with
columns and carved doorways,—one of the tablets gives
the name of the Roman legate of Syria, by whose order
this road was cut through the mountain. This was the
scene of an immense triumph of the arms of Islam
under Khaled, in A.D. 634, over much more than ten
times their own number of Christians.

The road was most lively with passengers; one troop
we passed was of about two score of Bashi-Bazouks,
going out to hunt, with falcons standing on their wrists
and long spears in their hands; then strings of camels
and Bedoueens, sometimes fifty in a string, and mules
without end. Unfortunately we took a wrong turn, and
instead of following our mules to 'Ain Fijeh, we went
along green lanes and woods and streams till a peasant
told us we were but an hour or two from Damascus, and
we had to go back some miles before we could cross the
river; it was midday before we came to a lovely village,
wherein we rested, for we were faint with fatigue and
hunger, having tasted nothing that day; then we
ascended the hills on the other side, and found ourselves
in the Desert, El Sah'ra, over which the sun was pouring his fiercest rays as we paced along the winding track,
over one featureless hill after another, the wretch of a
guide continually refusing to go any further, and having
to be collared and thumped into obedience and utility:
probably this Desert is green enough in the early spring,
for between the loose stones over which we trod, like that

of a sea beach, most laboriously, numbers of very pale
lilac colchicums were springing up at every step, where-
ever one saw the soil beneath the stones, it seemed as
hard as the stone itself; and one could not help thinking
of the curse with which God threatened the Israelites:
" The heaven that is over thy head shall be as brass,
and the earth that is under thee shall be iron." We
were not of course entitled to the protection of Mooslim
angels, or we should have been very thankful to be able
to say with Muhammad, " The people in Syria are happy
indeed, for the kind angels of heaven spread their
sheltering wings above their head,"—certainly no kind
angels sheltered us.

At last we descended into a fig orchard, and soon came
to the river; all the rest of the way was under the deep
delicious shade of planes, walnuts, and fruit trees, beside
the rushing, tumbling stream whose cool sound was
music to our burnt up ears; and at 2·30 P.M. we thankfully found the tents placed beside that never-to-be-for-
gotten 'Ain Fijeh.

The Temple of Fijeh is thought to be one of those
built for the original Phœnician Baal-worship of Syria,
like that of Afka, to which it bears some resemblance: it is built in front of the living rock, which was
probably cut out to admit of it, and was very simple,
containing only one hall, about 30 feet square, built of
very large stones, between which the trees have long ago
pushed themselves; the Temple stands half on a platform or ledge of rock which has been left bridging over
the cavern, whence, out of darkness, mystery, and silence,
not a gentle bubbling spring, but a full-grown river,
leaps into life, rushing past the rocks with a great song
and bustle of joy for a few yards, when it tumbles head-
long over a rocky ledge in masses of snowy foam; the

trees everywhere crowding down its banks, bending
over its waters, dipping in and playing with the laughing waves which seem to leap up to meet them, and
arching over the broad, full stream in long vistas of
watery loveliness and lanes of greenery. I believe
this is one of the fullest sources in the world, springing
at once, as it does, into a river: it is the clearest water
possible, and singularly bright in colour, in the morning
a full deep emerald-green — in the evening a sapphire-
blue : it was impossible to help thinking of the two
jewels, so exactly did it resemble their clear gem-like
hues by turns. Beside the source, only two or three
yards at one side, there is another Temple, still smaller
than that above the cavern,— its very massiveness and
simplicity telling of its extreme antiquity;—one square
column still stands, and there is a cornice, a bold but
simple cavetto like that we saw at Afka, and afterwards
both at Deir el Ashayr and Rukhleh ; the whole building
is very rough, but a sort of huge, massive grandeur
hangs about the now almost formless stones ; and
the situation is as romantic and poetical as can be
imagined. It must have been in a spot precisely resembling 'Ain Fijeh that Egeria taught the Roman king
those secrets which made Purity a Religion, and Virtue
its own best reward. It is a delicious place — the
valley, scarcely 200 yards wide, cannot contain itself
for joy at its own luxuriance, but flings up orchard
after orchard, vineyard after vineyard, upon the mountain at each side ; and the river goes laughing through
the woods, pouring out lapfuls of richness as it goes,
and merrily bathing the tree-roots that revel in its
cooling stream. We scrambled up part of the mountain to look down on the tangled crowd of trees
below,— the contrast of the beauty below and the

yellow barrenness above is most striking. The village
is a miserable concern, but we were pleased at seeing
two newly plastered Mooslim graves, with a little bed
of bright flowers formed on the top of each,—they
were the first we had seen blossoming over Mooslims,
— but afterwards in Asia Minor it became a common
sight.

We found the villagers so troublesome that day and
the next morning, that we moved off to a delicious little
meadow of real thick springy grass beside the bright
rapid river,— a favourite bathing-place with travellers,
about half an hour on the Damascus road, and settled
ourselves under a rock to sketch : a goatherd politely
brought up a goat, and feasted us on warm frothy
milk in an ancient silver bowl, engraved with Cufic
inscriptions. This spot has not the romance or the
antiquarian interest of the fountain, but it is extremely
pretty, the valley widening enough to let one see the
deep blue-green of the river, and the splendid cliffs
changing from yellow sameness into blue-grey crags,
jagged and broken into rifts of the most picturesque
nature. We had had enough of the Desert, El Sah'ra,
the day before, so we chose to try the lower or river path
recommended by the peasants,— a river path indeed,
for it was chiefly *in* the river, across the windings of
which we waded *nine* times, the horses nearly up to their
middles and scarcely able to keep a footing in the rushing tide; and then pushed through the thick groves,
dividing the trees and hedges as we went, to the immi-
nent peril of hats and legs, and riding-habits that were
already well dipped in the stream. At last we came out
on the barren mountains, where an eagle welcomed us
with a Jupiter kind of nod before he deigned to move
on; and hurrying over the hills we reached Kubbet-

es-Seiyär nearly an hour before sunset; there was a
furious wind blowing, but we found shelter in the pretty
wely, while we sat down to enjoy the famous scene
from which it is said Muhammad piously turned away:
se non è vero, è ben trovato.

The vast plain of yellow sand is bounded on all sides
by mountains,— Hermon on the right (west) towering
up close at hand dark and craggy; — to the south, the
mountains of the Haurān, in all the tender hues of
distance; — to the east, the pass up which the road to
Palmyra winds, joining the craggy Anti-Lebanon upon
which we stood; at our feet, and extending to the middle
of the plain, is the mass — *thirty miles* in extent — of
gardens and groves in all the riches of the fullest
summer foliage, deep and bright green of every shade;
in the midst of which, almost buried as it were under
the leaves, is the city, oblong shaped, but with one
suburb (the Meidân) stretching out a long thin line
to the south, shining with a dazzling, delicate white,
like a city built of pearls, shooting up its tapering
minarets and graceful domes, as if in jealousy of the
poplars around it: truly it is no wonder that the Arabs
who first bore the banner of Islam through the wearisome desert of Arabia, burst into shouts and transports
of joy when they beheld these towers and palaces, rising
among the verdant plains and murmuring streams that
make such sweet music in the air; one might have
thought the pretty buildings, like the walls of Ilion, had
risen to the tune.   One cannot take in a scene like this
in a moment, and we had but just begun to understand it,
and to feel satisfied with feeding on its beauty, when the
sun sunk behind Hermon, throwing one last gift over
the city, of such a crimsoning hue as turned the pearl
into an opal, and lit up the trees into almost metallic

lustre, bathing the mountains in a flood of peach-blossom that really made the whole view one of quite nearthly beauty. It lasted but a few minutes: the glorious dream passed away, the plain dimmed in shadow, and we descended the hill as quickly as we could to reach the gate before it should be closed for the night. It was just dark when we entered the city, and our first introduction to its long, narrow, winding streets, perfectly and entirely dark, save where a *café* or some miserable lantern made the rest of the darkness seem still darker, was not of the pleasantest, certainly the last appellation any one would give them now is the word "straight," unless it meant a passage too narrow or *strait* to turn in; a succession of horrible yells and howls announced, every now and then, that some one had gone over a wretched dog, as we went stumbling on over the dust-heaps in the way. At last we reached a very small door, where our dragoman was waiting for us, and we dismounted at the hotel, which seemed to our tired eyes and after our six weeks of tent-life, like an enchanted place, with its brilliant colours, latticed windows, and lamps hanging between oleander and citron trees, loaded with blossom, and filling the cool night air with fragrance; we went to sleep in good, clean beds to the music of the falling fountain, which splashed gently over the marble basin in the centre of our apartment; with a satisfactory feeling even in our dreams that, at last, we were in Damascus.

CHAP. XIV.

THE FAIR CITY.

"Damascus is the mole on the cheek of beauty—the plumage of the peacock of Paradise—the brilliant neck of the ring-dove—and the collar of beauty." —*Arabian Poet.*

IT is curious that of the four oldest cities in the world — Sidon, Hamah, Damascus, and Hebron,— not one has lost its first original name: Hamah became Epiphania under the Greeks, but retained the name less than three hundred years; Damascus is called by the Arabs of the Desert, *Esh-Sham*, but is known to them also, as to all the world, by the name used for it by Abraham the Patriarch; it is the only large and flourishing city of the four, having 150,000 inhabitants, and immense wealth within its walls: while Hamah, the Syrian Manchester, contains only 30,000. In architectural objects of all kinds Damascus is incalculably inferior to Cairo, but in natural beauty, how far superior! so that although there are quite enough fine and striking buildings to lend variety to the scene, the eye forgets to need the work of man among the enchanting verdure, rushing streams, lofty shades, and beautiful mountains that surround the city. I cannot understand any one comparing the Bazaars of either Cairo or Constantinople to those of Damascus: those of the former have no pretension to building of any kind, besides being much diluted with the garb and features of the West, and

those of the latter are entirely Europeanized, while
Damascus is thoroughly Oriental, containing in its streets
such an endless, indescribable variety of all nations and
classes East and South of the Mediterranean, that it is
impossible to tire of its sights or of its interests, in the
amusement and pleasure of the moment: while looking
backwards in the stream of Time, few places to the east
of Europe can equal it in historical interest.

The Pachalik of Damascus extends up the whole
country to Hamah along the Orontes, and east of the
Jordan down to Petra. There is a large garrison always
kept in the Citadel, and the city is governed by a Pacha
of the highest rank, who is always a Field-Marshal
(Mushir) and — far more important — the Emir el Haj,
or Prince of the holy Mekka caravan. It is a city of
very large manufacture, and there is probably no other
city existing, unblessed with water carriage, with such
extensive commercial trade ; its silks supply Egypt and
travel eastward till they meet those of Persia and Kash-
mir — its cottons and woollens, goat's or camel's hair
stuffs are used throughout the East, and also in Egypt
and Arabia: its gold and silver ornaments and its arms
supply the Desert, Arabia and Syria, while its fruit
is eaten from Tiflis and Baghdad to the shores of Europe.
It is not easy to enumerate a hundredth part of the
treasures that are displayed in the Bazaars of Damascus :
they are mostly divided, as in all Oriental towns, into
classes,— the silks in one bazaar, the spices in another,
and so on : but many booths combine variety enough to
chase away any chance of monotony ; among the finest
and most costly things sold are the golden-wove stuffs
of Mekka, which are very beautiful, and are chiefly used
for the thick stiff cloaks of Sheikhs and Emirs, and are
dyed in rich bright colours, violet, maroon, &c. &c. The

carpets, silks, and shawls of Persia abound every where;
they are of every class and sometimes of great beauty:
from Persia also come finely ornamented nargilehs and
embroideries of all kinds, Kashmîr and Bokhara shawls,
old porcelain of great variety and delicacy, as well as
from China; arms from Baghdad and Kashmîr, and gold
and silver ornaments of all kinds, vases, cups, incense
burners, perfume throwers, coffee services, &c. &c. The
bazaar of made-up and second-hand clothes is particularly amusing, and as gay as the saddlers', which is full
of housings and trappings of horses and mules, from the
richest gold and silver embroidery, enriched with pearls,
on velvet, down to the common but bright crimson
leather saddles, and the many coloured harness of plaited
worsted cords and tassels, decked with rows of white
cowrie-shells and charms; then the preserves and con-
fectionary, gum, spice, and drug bazaars — always
graver and more perfumed than the others, — and the
gay, lively cotton and printed muslin bazaar, full of
colours and combinations of which one thought even
Manchester must be innocent, but which are manufactured for the special delight of the Arab and the Kurd.
Then come the narrow lanes of the red boots or yellow
slippers, which seem numerous enough to shoe the
population of Syria for twenty years; and the car-
pentery bazaar of carved, inlaid, and painted chests, so
barbarously made but so delightfully pretty.

Remembering the extraordinary vicissitudes which
the beautiful city has undergone, it is more a matter of
wonder that *any* architectural objects should remain in
its streets than that there are so few *, — one of the most

* A slight sketch of the history of Damascus in Note 1 may be found
interesting to the general reader.

distant possessions of Rome, farmed out and ground
down for its revenues — the battle-field of Arabs, Saracens, and Christians, overrun by Kurds and Tartars,
burned and destroyed by Timour — it is a marvel that
even the once beautiful church, parts of which are probably older than our era, should be still standing. The
city walls have been preserved for convenience, and they
bear, in some places, every mark of extreme antiquity; it
is, indeed, very interesting to observe the different ages,
which are frequently very distinctly marked in one small
piece of wall, and to see how completely the old form
realises in one's mind the stories of Rahab and the spies,
and the two escapes of St. Paul. The moat is still wide
around them, and in some places full of water, shaded
over by trees; in others it is a dry receptacle for every
kind of rotting filth and abomination; in truth, a ride
round the outside of Damascus is a severe trial at all
times to the olfactory nerves. The gates are mostly
Roman, built over, added to, and altered by the Saracens,
through whose tumble-down towers and broken battle-
ments, the fine Roman arch and bevelled masonry may
still be distinguished; they are all of them very picturesque. The castle looks well, and would appear to have
been once a strong building, and the Serai is handsome.

There is not much variety in the minarets of Damascus, except those of the Great Mosque, which are models
of elegance and delicate beauty, very graceful and rich,
though airy; viewed *en masse* they make a striking
picture. The baths and cafés enliven every street:
both are nearly always painted in broad, horizontal
stripes of scarlet, blue, and white, which, though not in
the least elegant or *recherché* — in fact, it is somewhat
barbaric — yet is very effective and gay. Wherever you
go inside the city, you look, at short intervals, into a

dark cool chamber, in which are men smoking, lounging, chatting, and lemonade drinking; or into a court shaded by delicious trees, with a bubbling fountain or a large tank of running water; or into a larger, airier, lighted hall, gaily painted within and without, where men are resting after the delightful fatigues of the bath, wrapped in white garments, sipping coffee, and smoking nargilehs; the noise that proceeds from both café and bath duly announcing their neighbourhood. Near the outskirts of the town they are still prettier, at least in the evening, when they are brilliantly lighted up with lamps hung in the trees, and always full of people; one, by the Castle, is particularly pretty, with rude wooden platforms hanging over the rushing river, seeming as if slung, like a suspension bridge, by the wreaths of creepers that have flung themselves everywhere, and shaded by innumerable bending trees, another, near the Bab Tuma, where the river is more foaming and its voice louder, — very rickety and wretched, but all the more picturesque for that, — hidden under weeping willows and poplars, pomegranates, and planes, presented an endless variety of costumes by night and by day in the various groups enjoying *kief*. Near the Castle, too, is another sight, a plane tree of which the trunk measures forty feet in circumference, and within which several hermits have lived, acquiring a *green* old age in a solitude they would not find there now (although the little door is yet unremoved in case of another occupant), since it is in the centre of a busy suburb, and always surrounded by crowds of laden mules, donkeys and camels, with their noisy drivers.

Except for the cafés and baths, the streets of Damascus are duller than those of any other Oriental town, and people say they look poor because they expect so renowned a city to look grand; indeed, I have heard persons who have come back from a hurried visit to Damascus, declaring that " the whole town was built of mud — nothing but mud walls everywhere ! " — they had only glanced at the exterior, and did not perceive that there were well-built stone walls beneath the mud, — a strange, anomalous taste in our eyes, but the invariable Eastern custom : as soon as the stone wall is completed, it is covered with a coating of mud, which hides all its solid goodness, and which looks tattered and miserable as soon as it begins to peel. The new houses are being built with handsome projecting windows, opening on to the streets, and the gaily painted and gilt lattices are extremely pretty; but this is quite a modern and un-usual innovation; in general, the long lanes wind about between high or low walls, but all quite blind, except for occasional insignificant doorways, topped with one small bit of carving, and an apology for a window stuck in here and there, seldom anything better than a rough hole or a long slit closely covered over by a ragged wooden lattice.

But stop at one of these miserable little doors (that is, if you are fortunate enough to have so good an intro-duction to the inmates as we found in the English missionary Mr. Robson), and let us see what is within-side. A little room, or half dark passage, leads into a small open court with a fountain and a *leewān* (a recess always on the north side of every court, furnished with a divan, the *salon* used by the inhabitants of the sleeping rooms which surround the three other sides of the court) : this is occupied by the servants of the household; and from this another passage admits you into a much larger court, always paved with coloured marbles, and with one or more fountains shaded by pomegranates, lemon,

orange, and oleander trees; wherever you look, all is
marble, both white and coloured. This court has its
raised *leewān*, splendidly ornamented on the walls and
ceiling, and its divan covered with rich brocades; here
you are generally received, and presented with lemonade,
sweetmeats, and coffee; but in most rich houses one of
the rooms round this court is also a reception-room, of
which the walls are entirely covered with marble mosaic
and gilding, a fountain at one end, a divan at the other;
coloured matting and handsome Persian carpets on the
floor, and near the ceiling a row of windows, latticed
with pierced marble or carved wood in patterns of fairy
intricacy and lightness; the ceilings are always of wood
most delicately carved, painted, and gilt, A closed door
in this court leads by a little passage into a third court
much the same, only handsomer than the others, where
the ladies reside, and beyond which they do not come
in Mooslim houses., The houses are mostly two stories
high, but some have only one, the flat roof forming as
usual the promenade; in Damascus the roofs of the
hareem are generally covered with lattice or torn mats
and green creepers.

One Saturday Mr. and Mrs. Robson were kind enough
to take us to see some of the best houses of Damascus,
which now generally belong to Jews. On this day
they sit dressed in their finest clothes and jewels to receive visitors; at the first house we visited, a large family
were assembled round a widowed mother. The eldest
daughter, who had been married four years, and was not
quite eighteen, was very tall and slender, with a com-
plexion as white as snow: her black hair and large
bright eyes and small mouth made a beautiful face,
though the highly arched eyebrows they all have (a
painted line drawn after the hair is pulled out) add to

the silly, inane expression of their faces. This girl was very lively, and never ceased asking questions and chattering, showing us all her ornaments, which were chiefly diamonds and pearls, on her head, neck, and arms. All the ladies were dressed in Manchester muslin skirts of bright colours, and short silk or velvet jackets embroidered in gold; sky-blue and bright green seemed the favourite mixture of colours. The neck and bosom of each was covered, not concealed, by embroidered muslin, the skin underneath being frequently painted. On the death of the father, the house and all its contents becomes the property of the son; the mother remains there only on sufferance. In this one the master was only a child of twelve years old, but he exacted much respect from the servants (who sat in the room, by the bye, all the time, below the divan, and joined loudly in the conversation), and he was very finely dressed, wearing several diamond and turquoise rings, and an enamelled watch hanging by a pearl chain. He served us with sweetmeats, making a salaam to each before presenting the spoon, which we returned on giving it back : and after he had passed on, each one made another salaam to his mother, the mistress of the house. They took us over the whole house, which is extremely handsome, no portion left unornamented, and all done in the finest inlay of coloured marbles, as delicate as any Florentine table : this is the old and good style — in the new houses this. is only imitated in paint, put on by a pierced form — mere stencilling, in short.

The little son conducted us then to his grandfather's — a still larger and handsomer house, with four or five large courts and splendid apartments. Here also even the upper apartments were very beautifully decorated

which is not usually the case, their ornament being
generally confined to a little painting. The women in
this house were very ugly, but gaily dressed; a troop
of romping boys and pretty girls burst in, however, the
girls wearing very handsome belts of filagree gold bosses
sewed on velvet and set with jewels, — the handsomest
of these come from Baghdad.

But the finest house we visited belonged to a Jew
named Lisbona — a handsome portly man, who was sitting on the divan without shoes or stockings, chanting
Hebrew from a big book on his knee. He was very *jolly*
and talkative, and called to his wife and mother to join
us: they apologised much for not being able to offer us
coffee, as being the Sabbath they could not light a fire;
and then made a close examination of our dresses, &c.
The old mother wore a widow's head-dress, a black *kefiyeh*
thrown over and concealing the indispensable gold coins,
and a huge bunch of short, black ostrich feathers laid
on each side of the head and face; a large black
tassel hanging from the back of her head, below which
an immense number of stout black silk cords and tassels
reached nearly to the ground — making altogether a
heavy and really ponderous affair, only useful as a sort
of domestic portable hearse of the ugliest description —
so unlike our pretty, modest, English widow's cap. They
showed us numbers of pretty things — nargilehs, zarfs,
sugar-stands, &c. &c. — all in the finest silver filagree,
so much better made than anything we had seen in the
bazaars that we begged Lisbona to tell us the maker's
name, intending to buy some; but nothing would induce the excellent Jew to answer anything of the kind
until he had inquired again and again from each of us,
and entreated Mr. Robson to assure him of the fact,
" Have you got money enough to pay for them? Are

you *sure* you have money enough?" and when that was settled, he turned coolly to me and said, "Then why do you wear that common thing on your shoulders? You have got a beautiful dress — why don't you wear a nice shawl too?" My dress was of stout English cotton print; but I had put on a pretty silk shawl which had been given to me in Beyrout, and which, being of native manufacture, displeased his sense of propriety, and made him think I was too poor to have anything better; of course I did not mention that my dress cost about a sixth part of its price, and was intended for use, not beauty; but we took the hint, and never paid another visit dressed in Arab manufactures. These good people took a lively interest in us and our adventures; but the women pestered us with ceaseless questions as to what we had done with our husbands — where we had left them — what could have induced them to let us go so far without them; and I do not think they were ever persuaded that we had none; though, finally, the old woman ran after us, emphatically entreating us, "Oh, maiden! oh, maiden! if you really have not got a husband, *do* let me send for such-and-such a marriage-merchant from the bazaar!"

The prettiest thing in that house was a fair sweet-faced boy in a side room, with one hand rocking a cradle containing a fat pretty baby, and holding in the other a fine Hebrew Psalter, from which he was chanting aloud. The cradle was of polished walnut wood inlaid with mother-of-pearl, and had "Peace and happiness," in Arabic, on each side. Lisbona and all the other Jews, on hearing that we were "Ingleez," immediately inquired after Sir Moses and Lady Montefiore, and, without paying any attention to the answer that we did not know them, sent scores of salaams and compliments to them to be delivered without fail.

Then we went to a much smaller house belonging to a Christian merchant, M. Freije, a rich and excellent man, with a lovely wife handsomely dressed, and wearing a pretty *soufah*, the same head-dress as that worn by the Maronite women of the Lebanon, but still handsomer: she had about 3000 bits of gold fastened to it. She was busy superintending her household affairs, mounted on the pattens, some ten inches high, worn by every Damascus lady, but finding us curious in pretty things, she kindly went to her coffers and brought out several splendid dresses and velvet jackets embroidered in gold, — the embroidery on one jacket alone had cost 12*l.*; she also showed us quantities of antique silver vases, zarfs, &c., and exquisite egg-shell and Persian china. Their house was being newly ornamented—not painted, but an inlay of jet-black marble upon white; it had rather a sombre appearance, although beautifully done, and was very much mixed with mirror and gilding—the present taste at Damascus, but which does not, I think, harmonise well with the marbles. Then we went to see some Mooslims in a beautiful house, known to many travellers from its having been the hotel for some few years; the rooms were splendidly decorated with marble mosaic and incrustation of gilding, and the very large court was made lovely, like another of the houses we had seen, with several small *jets d'eau*, besides the large fountain, and a variety of fruit trees and beds of flowers festooned together with thick wreaths of *convolvulus major*; the divans and hangings in the different rooms were all of the rich Damascus brocaded silk, some of them embroidered with gold, and the doors of the rooms were beautifully inlaid with mother-of-pearl.

Ah immensity of screaming to the unveiled women to get out of the way ensued on our appearance at the door; however, Mr. Robson being disposed of and imprisoned in one of the rooms, we were admitted, and found the lady of the house and a beautiful daughter of fifteen, both enormously fat, attired only in gowns and loose trousers of thin pink muslin, through which their stout brown limbs did look remarkably odd; they were at breakfast, and would take no refusal but that we must sit down too, — so we were placed on little stools round the low *koorse*, or table, on which the tray was placed, and took a few mouthfuls of the fruits, the pilafs looking too greasy to be pleasant for one's fingers.

We spent a good deal of time in the bazaars, wishing to buy many things as specimens of Damascus manufacture, and I never tired, mentally, of watching the endless variety of faces, figures, costumes, and objects in the long, long alleys; then, too, the purchase of each article took as much time as buying a house full of things at home would have taken, — I often wished one's home friends could have had Prince Cheri's telescope to see us, in our English dresses, sitting duly doubled up beside the well-turbaned, richly-dressed merchant, on his little counter, in solemn conclave over the price of a silk dress or a pot of confiture, or refreshing ourselves after the fatigue of each purchase with a saucer of pink ice and a cup of delicious coffee.

Most of the dresses made and sold at Damascus are of cotton, with the pattern thrown up in silk; many of the patterns are Oriental, but some of the prettiest are European, — these are about 2*l.* 5*s.* the dress; those of unmixed silk reach to any price, and are all of them costly; some are beautiful

things, especially those which, like the scarfs, have
silver thread woven in one way and gold thread the
other.   They make some good woollen articles, besides
an immense variety of coarse stuffs of camel's and
goat's hair.

Many of the bazaars are lofty stone buildings, handsomely vaulted; some, less modern and less commodious, are more picturesque, as the Greek Bazaar; but
the most interesting of all are the Shoe Bazaar, the
Goldsmiths', and the Carpenters' Bazaar, in all of
which ancient columns, half obscured by the booths,
and beautiful vistas of arches, meet the eye at every
step.   The finest building in the bazaars is the khan
As'ad, — a model of that graceful, simple energy
of style which is the best characteristic of the pure
Saracenic architecture; the interior is a square of three
domes around a large and lofty central dome, supported
on square piers; these domes are pierced with windows, and the whole building is of alternate rows of
black and white marble — ornament enough in itself;
the goods of the merchants are ranged on the marble
floor round the sides of the square, and a large fountain occupies the centre; nothing can be a finer study
for an artist than the endless variety of bright-coloured
costumes and goods grouped on the ground, contrasted with the grave severity of the black and white
bands, while the slanting lines of sunshine fall in
dazzlng rays athwart the dark shadows of the pillars
and recesses under the nine domes.   The khan is
entered by a splendid doorway, as fine a specimen as
can be found of the rich fretwork and interlacings,
slender columns and mosaics, for which Saracenic architecture has no rival.   This khan is modern, but there is
nothing of pure Saracenic more beautiful in Damascus

Of course the Great Mosque of the Khalif Wāled —
once the Christian cathedral of the city — is the most
interesting and beautiful of all; it is extremely difficult to see, as no Christian foot is allowed to cross the
threshold, and they are very jealous of Christians even
looking in; it would, therefore, be quite incomprehensible without Mr. Porter's plan, connecting the
court of cloisters with the colonnades hidden in the
bazaars; a hasty glimpse in passing by the outer gates is
all the view one can obtain of the inside; of the outside,
likewise, only a few fragments are visible, but these
are beautiful; the upper part of a large gateway can
be seen from the roof of one of the bazaars, which is
delicately executed and in better taste, because not
overloaded, than any of the work on the Temple of
Jupiter at Baalbek; from another roof the capitals of
several columns can be seen — they are in the purest
and loveliest style of Greco-Roman art. Peeping in
through some gates one can see the noble cloistered
quadrangle, surrounded by Corinthian columns, and an
exquisite fountain in Saracenic style in the centre; the
gates themselves are of brass of very good workmanship,
still bearing the figure of the Sacramental chalice, now
placed amid Arabic inscriptions, the additions of later
years. The head of St. John the Baptist is believed to be
really still in existence in the crypt of this church. May
the day come — and that soon — when, in both Santa
Sophia at Constantinople and in this Church of St. John
at Damascus, the worship of Christ shall be re-esta-
blished to endure throughout all generations, when the
mists and veils that now darken the hearts of both Jew
and Gentile shall have been torn away! For two
thousand years the inscription (in Greek) on this portal
has announced that " Thy kingdom, O Christ, is an

everlasting kingdom, and Thy dominion endureth
throughout all generations," — the Arabs believe that
the time is at hand when Christianity will be proclaimed
throughout the land, and Christian governors rule there;
and we, too, look forward to the time when the Lord
shall have "made bare His holy arm in the eyes of all
the nations; and all the ends of the earth shall see
the salvation of our God." *

Standing on that roof, with these thoughts in one's
mind, there was nothing more beautiful in our eyes than
to look down at the crowded bazaar beneath one's feet,
and to see, gliding quickly through the crowd of self-
satisfied Mooslims, dark reserved Jews, wild Bedoueen,
and savage Kurds — the white cap and simple blue gown
of a Sister of Charity : wherever one went one saw them,
generally in couples, hastening along with a basket on
one arm containing medicine and food, administered
alike to Jew, Turk, Heretic, and Infidel; every one who
spoke of them used but words of admiration and respect.
One day we went to see their abode, and found ourselves admitted to an elderly, happy-looking, sweet-
faced Mother, who told us that they had arrived —
six of them — on that day five years in Damascus,
without any house having been prepared for them.
Slowly and surely, with brave and pure hearts, they
had laboured on, and much have they effected in
those few years : now they have a well-built but substantial building † for their Convent, rough but clean
and neat, containing seventeen Sisters, two of whom
are Arabs, and a school of about 150 children,
besides many day-scholars, including Mooslims and
Jewesses, and one Metouaalee. We heard these children

---

* Isaiah lii. 10.   † Now utterly destroyed.

read well and intelligently in some religious book, and saw their excellent writing. They were very clean and tidy, and remarkably well-behaved and happy-looking. Their dormitory, with rows of simple mattresses laid on the floor, their kitchens and play-grounds, were all perfectly arranged. Bread, olives, and thin soup was their food, all of which the children learned to prepare. The upper classes were well advanced in French, and embroidered beautifully — an accomplishment which would insure their future support. It is impossible to see a more pleasing and interesting institution; and, for the first time in Damascus, one felt some hope of anything being accomplished towards the Christianising of the people. Well may English people blush, over-whelmed with shame when we see such self-sacrificing and successful work, and remember that *our* Church has done nothing, absolutely nothing, in Syria.[*] I have said that the French have established missions and schools throughout the country, — but God knows there is work enough and room enough for both to labour, — and where are ours? — a few excellent, hard-working men, sent out by the Presbyterians of Scotland, and Ireland, are all that Great Britain has ever contributed to the land that gave birth to St. Paul and the Apostles. If *they* had stopped at home, what would have become

---

[*] In Palestine a mission has been established at Jerusalem for the Jews; but throughout the rest of the land the English are believed to be destitute of religion, and no sign of their worship appears in the length or breadth of the country to contradict the assertion. Even in Beyrout where Englishmen congregate for commerce, and where numerous English travellers are continually passing and repassing, and where a Consulate (with now a Consul-general) has long been established, there is not a single clergyman to call them together, and not the slightest thing marks the observance of the Lord's day, or their remembrance of Him, in the land once sanctified by His presence.

of us, and how would the Gentiles have found salvation? Has England no yearning of love for the land of
her Saviour? no debt of gratitude to pay back to the
country whence her redemption came, and which lies
now shrouded in mists of thick darkness? Let us imitate the zeal of our neighbours, and take example by the
sagacity and liberality with which their missions are
conducted: it is such poor, pitiful work, to send a man,
single-handed, here, and another there, and bid *them*
"convert the land," while experience has indeed taught
how little (or rather nothing) the most devoted efforts
can thus accomplish here: if anything is ever to be
effected, it must be by an organised body, whose labours
may be directed simultaneously to the wants of body as
well as soul — feeding, clothing, as well as teaching and
civilising the natives: thus, and thus alone, may we,
with God's blessing, look for some results.

The English Consul, Mr. Brant, from whom, as old
friends, we received the kindest possible attentions, lives
in a beautiful house of the old Damascus style, in the
Mooslim quarter; the same house has been occupied for
many years as the English Consulate, and has been over
and over described — perhaps its chief charm is in the
large size of the court and the tank in the middle,
besides the remarkable variety of the trees and shrubs
planted there — several kinds of acacia, orange, lemon,
oleander, Japan medlar, varieties of roses and myrtle
(on the perfumed berries of which I made my luncheon),
besides a great many other shrubs. The large reception-
room is very handsomely inlaid and carved, the cost of
which, even many years ago, the Consul said must have
been 800*l.*— now that everything is so much dearer and
labour so much more expensive, it would cost twice that
sum and be badly done. With all this fine Orientalism

around one, it was curious to see English curtains and
table-cloths, to hear English music on an English piano,
and to eat a thoroughly English dinner two thousand
miles away from home: these things have a value we
cannot understand until we have been out of England
for a good long time: and I confess I was rather surprised to find how much I too enjoyed them.

One special pleasure Mr. Brant was so kind as to obtain for us, was the permission to visit the renowned
Abd-el-Käder *, and we went to his house one day, accompanied by Mr. and Mrs. Brant. We were taken first
into the hareem, where Mrs. Brant interpreted in Turkish,
which the first lady of the hareem speaks. She was
sitting alone in a grand reception-room on a cotton quilt,
with a dress of thick wadded quilting, and loads of white
muslin folded round her head — the only handsome thing
she wore was a gold tissue scarf round her waist. She was
old, stout, and very ugly — but it is said that her husband has a great respect and regard for her, and that,
although he consoles himself for the decay of her charms
by those of many others, he always treats her with much
affection, telling her his plans and consulting her about
what he does: perhaps her being an Algerian Bedoueen,
like himself, is an unfading charm in his eyes. She
was suffering much from rheumatism, and said Damascus was a dreadful place, it was so cold nearly all the
year. The younger females remove into the country to
some of his gardens in the summer, but this one remains
in the city. Her son, a boy of twelve years old, came
in and sat on his heels beside her; she seemed very fond
and proud of him, appealing to him about his father,
of whom he spoke simply as " Abd-el-Käder : " we were

* Which means, " Servant of the Powerful One."

told that they drop the expression of relationship in the case of a very distinguished person. The room was an odd jumble — the Damascene form and fountain furnished with French hangings, and filled with French china and ornaments : so indeed is the whole palace, and nothing can be brighter, gayer, or in worse taste ; the Damascene patterns, so pretty and so suitable in their place, are spoiled by the mixture, and utterly absurd are the French daubs of European ideas misapplied upon the Oriental walls — for instance, the lower part of the walls of one room, which would have been naturally a beautiful inlay of marble mosaic harmonising with the marble floor, was here replaced by painted views of Buddhists' Pagodas, peopled with French shepherdesses and Marquises, placed in the same accurate perspective as appears on the famous willow-leaf plate of long memory. Abd-el-Kāder is greatly, and naturally, blamed by his Algerian followers for having so entirely discarded the Bedoueen in himself, and above all for wearing the dress of a Damascene merchant, — it may be said that it is very fine to see him contented and making the best of his exile, and that it is wiser to "do in Rome what Romans do," but it does seem strange that he should carry the signs and characteristics of his long French imprisonment about with him, and thrust it upon the Orientalism with which he is surrounded, and which is natural to him ; — however, we understood that France is not a very palatable subject of conversation in the house, and of course we did not allude to it in any way.

The old wife appeared to keep up no kind of ceremony or etiquette, though she is said to be a severe and rigid matron over the younger wives ; her slaves were all negresses, dressed in a single garment of pink cotton, and each had a nose-ring with one turquoise passed through the wide flat nostril, looking exactly like a forget-me-not dropped on a bank of black mud; they stood at the lower end of the room, below the divan, chatting among themselves and laughing at our conversation, while they finished the sweetmeats we had left uneaten. We went into other rooms to see some younger wives of the Chief and those of his sons — one of whom was extremely pretty, like a tiny wax doll, with pink cheeks, coral lips, black hair, and eyes that were half closed over by magnificent eyelashes, sweeping the cheek; it is said that he buys a new wife every quarter, and that he once replied to an English gentleman at Broussa, who asked him why he had so many wives, that he did not know how he could better expend *French* money than on such frivolous luxuries ! * They are chiefly Circassians, but all those whom we saw were the smallest, most delicately-made little creatures possible.

After taking leave of the Hareem we joined the gentlemen of our party in a marble-floored hall, daubed round with French figures, and the comfortable Oriental divan exchanged for hard French sofas, on one of which Abd-el-Kader was sitting in European fashion. He came forward to meet us, and we were greatly struck with his appearance : he has a tall, majestic figure, fair skin, grey hair — that once was black — a long, white beard, a forehead and keen piercing eye which could nowhere be passed unmarked. I never saw more intellect marked in the one, nor a more truly eagle expression in the other, — as one of our party afterwards admirably described him : " His every look is that of a prince, born and accustomed to command, acting upon promptly-

---

* He has an income of 4000*l.* a year allowed him by the French.

formed judgment—in one word, a *Leader*—this is
one's first impression ; afterwards you see he is a man of
high intellect, loving thought for its own sake—a Mooslim Athanasius, who would no more brook a mystery
than an insult, but with the keen blade of his intellect
would cut the difficult knot, throwing the whole
weight of his ability on whichever side he took up, and
stopping all discussion on it with the neatness of a
logical formula." Abd-el-Kader is a man of much
learning ; he has written four large and profound trea-
tises on Controversy, Philosophy, and the Cosmogony
of the world; and he himself gives the daily theo-
logical lecture in the Great College at Damascus; his
court is crowded every day and all day with persons
soliciting audience of him, so that it is difficult to find
him for even a moment at leisure ; it is said that his
Algerian followers are daily, but secretly increasing,
round him, and doubtless the last acts of his history
are by means played out; a noble incident of that
life has occurred since the above was written. England
and France will ever remember his conduct during the
massacres in the spring of 1860; it was not love for
France, but the humanity of his enlightened mind and
the fervent respect which he felt in his heart for the
defenceless Sisters of Charity, which made him sally
forth to their rescue, at the head of his own wild
followers ; nor would he have been a whit less forward
to aid and support the subjects of England, if the firm
high character and unflinching conduct of the British
Consul had not been protection and defence enough in
itself.

Abd-el-Kader is regarded as a sovereign, and respected as a man of sanctity, by all Mooslims ; therefore,
when visiting Jerusulem some time ago, he occupied a

small suite of rooms in the Mosque of the Moghrebîns, a very holy place, and, one day when the British Consul was paying a visit to the Pacha of Jerusalem, Abd-el-Kader was announced : the Pacha went to the door to meet him, and bowed down to the ground before him ; he stayed but a very few minutes, and the Pacha accompanied him to the threshold, and there again prostrating himself to the very floor, he kissed the hem of his garment, which Abd-el-Kader did not withdraw, but, lifting up his hand, he stood there and addressed the Pacha in a sort of speech or sermon : "I call upon you, oh Pacha! to remember what a responsible and important position you occupy; never forget how great is your duty, and how immense an account will one day be required of you for all the power bestowed upon you; fail not in any particular of your manifold duties; remember to give alms to the poor, to do justice to the widow, and to succour the oppressed," — and much more, the Pacha standing the whole time humbly before him, with folded hands and downcast eyes, in the attitude of a slave. Considering the high rank of the Pacha of Jerusalem, this scene was a very curious one.

CHAP. XV.

" The hue of youth upon a brow of woe,
    Which men called old two thousand years ago !
    Match me such marvel, save in Eastern clime —
    A rose-red city, — half as old as time !"

                                                BURGON.

PART I. — THE JOURNEY.

THE world-famous ruins of Palmyra are naturally a
common subject of conversation at Damascus, and
although we had never entertained a serious thought of
reaching them, believing it to be quite out of our
power, we made many inquiries respecting them from
the Consul and other people ; and, one day, Mr. Robson,
the excellent missionary, and his wife showed us a port-
folio of drawings, conveying so grand an idea of the
magnificence and glorious beauty of the ruins, that we
were seized with the most intense desire to see them for
ourselves : however, the more we asked about the
journey, the more entirely impossible it seemed for us
to accomplish it; the fatigue and expense combined
made it out of the question.

Now there happened to be some other travellers
staying in the hotel, who were also very anxious to go
to Palmyra, and among them, happily for us, the famous
artist, M. Carl Haag, to whom we recounted the beauty
of the drawings we had seen, and he too went to see
them next day; he came back still more enthusiastic

about the original objects than we had been. "If I am a ruined man all my life, or if I walk there in Bedoueen sandals, I *must* go to Palmyra!" he kept repeating all that evening. So we all agreed to see whether anything could be managed for us, and the following day Mr. and Mrs. Robson took us to see the Sheikh of the Anazeh, who makes all the arrangements whenever any one does go to Palmyra.

It must be explained that the fatigue of this expedition arises from the fact, that no one has been allowed for many years to remain at the ruins more than twenty-four hours; twenty is the usual time: of course you must be almost *inhumanly* strong if you can make the long journey there and back, fifty hours of camel riding, and not spend those twenty hours in sleep or rest,— while, as the ruins are three miles in extent, no one could take more than a glance at the principal objects, even if ten hours were spent in traversing them; and as the fear of Bedoueen *ghuzoos*, and the want of water, necessitate riding that part of the journey nearest to Palmyra at a stretch of twenty-four hours without stop or stay, both going and returning, few persons like to undertake it. Then the fee given to the tribe for allowing travellers to go there with safe conduct, is usually 30l. each. We came, however, at a fortunate moment; the Anazeh tribe were encamped close round the ruins, and there was nothing to fear when once we had reached them. The Sheikh was immensely impressed with M. Haag's eagerness, and with the conviction that all the world would soon know from his drawings what a glorious place Palmyra is; and the Anazehs really love and value the ruins; and so, to cut a long story short, after many days spent in consulting and debating, with various pros and cons, he engaged to let us stay five whole days; and, if all the party in the hotel joined together, at the price of 15l. a head, he engaged to choose good dromedaries for us (on which *all* one's comfort, and therefore strength depend), for which we paid 2l. each extra. It was also a golden opportunity of seeing a real, true Bedoueen tribe in the desert, and we were promised to go among them as the Sheikh's guests, and live upon camel's milk and flesh, &c.

So, to our own infinite astonishment, as well as pleasure, it was really all settled—with two days allowed us in which to make arrangements for our departure, on Friday the 7th October, after the Mosque prayers. Our little dog was consigned to the care of the cook, with the baggage — all unnecessary ornaments safely deposited therein, that no sparkle of gold might tempt the passing Arab; and we spent the morning stuffing our saddle-bags with a change or two of linen, drawing materials, and one book each: stout cotton dresses were put on instead of riding habits, the provisions were stowed in the dragoman's saddle-bags, and we started on foot for the Sheikh's house, outside one of the gates of the city — the Bab Tuma. The Sheikh was ready in his scarlet cloak and mash'lah, and having hooded his falcon — an indispensable companion — he took us to the court, where, indeed, was a scene of Babelar confusion; eleven dromedaries were on their knees, all roaring, and growling, and groaning, as if they were being killed, after the manner of dromedaries the moment they are requested to kneel, and the whole time they are kneeling; all the camel-drivers and armed escort rushing about screaming and shouting — flocks of poultry at one side shrieking, gabbling, and cackling — pet gazelles were hiding in a corner — and a number of beautiful Arab mares were standing transfixed with astonishment at the unwonted crowd and noise. Our minds were soon concentrated upon the art of mounting! quite an ordeal for a novice, and on the first success of which, the Arab prophecies whether you will make a good rider or not, and be worthy of his beloved beast. A couple of men held down each dromedary by standing on its fore-knees, while the Sheikh himself lifted us ladies, each with a sort of flying jump, into the middle of the seat, hastily settling our shawls, &c.; and while directions were shouted on all sides, with such earnest vociferation that it was impossible to understand one syllable of them except to "hold fast!" up jumped the animal, raising his hind legs first, when you go nearly over his nose,—then his forelegs, jerking you as unexpectedly backwards, against the hinder pommel of your saddle, and affording you a knock on your spine that you remember against all future occasions.

By four o'clock we had all streamed in procession out of the gate—a goodly cavalcade of eleven dromedaries, besides the Argeels, their owners, who always accompany the camel, sometimes on foot, sometimes mounted behind the riders. The dromedaries carried our party, including the servants, the Sheikh, and the escort of armed Bedoueens, Anazehs, and others—thirteen men in all; while several Damascus acquaintance accompanied us for a mile or two, after the kindly Arab fashion of leave-taking. Such a noise as we made altogether, for the Bedoueens had a darabouka (a drum) to which they sang lustily, shouting their good-byes on all sides, the whole way through the delightful gardens and green lanes that encompass the city. In two hours and a half we reached the village of Doumah, which stands on the edge of the gardens: it was all alive with men and women gathering the grapes, and spreading them out so thickly on the ground to dry into raisins, that we took them for red carpets; while many were crowding round the fires, by the aid of which they were turning the sweet juice into *dibs*—a luscious sweet in which the Arabs delight, and which is so often mentioned in the Bible, rendered, in our translation, honey. From this we passed out upon the great plain, and presently met the Baghdad postman galloping in at the end of his nine days' journey.

The sun went down at a little before seven; then suddenly the Sheikh uttered a command, and down went all the camels. "This is our halting place for the night," said he. What, here—on the road? Shall we not go a little on one side and look for some shelter?" "Oh, no," said the Sheikh, "this is the best, for here we can see who comes, and we have to look out for robbers!" It did look astonishingly bare and strange for a night's rest; but, in a few moments, the dragomans had arranged our carpets, thick wadded couvertures, cloaks, &c.; the fire was quickly lighted, made of the dry thorns which grew all around us, and the kettle was boiling; cold fowl and hot tea were presented : then the camels were arranged, lying down in an external circle—the falcon unhooded, and placed upon his perch —the saddle frames built up into a wall, and our saddle-bags placed under our heads—the resolution was carried, *nemine contradicente*, that the Desert was both cheerful and comfortable—and before eight o'clock nearly all the party were giving loud and vigorous tokens of a profound sleep. My sister and I, however, were too *new to* sleeping *à la belle étoile*, and on so very hard a couch as that rocky road, to find rest easily : we were amused, too, in seeing one of the camels, every now and then, get up and hobble about with his one leg tied up

close under him, till, finding he could gain but little by
such limping amusement, he would lie down again and
snore. Twice the practised ear of Sheikh Miguel gave
the alarm of thieves, and prevented their approach.

Amongst the Bedoueens, stealing on a large scale, in-
volving danger and risk — such as coming by night into
an encampment and silently making way with the
camels — is not considered disgraceful; but all stealing
from one another's tents, without danger, is considered
entirely mean and bad; so bad that the punishment is
cutting off the hand. The greatest punishment for
grave crimes is beheading with a sword: for all lesser
things, such as stealing a camel, &c., branding with a
hot iron is the usual punishment. False accusations
are always punished by the infliction of whatever
punishment would have been awarded to the accused
if proved guilty.

The Bedoueens can be plentifully cool in their naïve
impudence. Our good Sheikh had a little black negro
boy — a slave — with him, whom he was taking to the
tribe, thinking the winter in Damascus too cold for
him; he had lately been ill, and the kind-hearted
Sheikh got up early in the night, and taking off a cloak
lined with fur, that he had to sleep on, wrapped it
round the child; in the morning it was found that one
of the Bedoueens had quietly appropriated it for himself
as soon as the Sheikh had gone to sleep again. Of
course this Bedoueen was not an Anazeh; our escort
was purposely composed of Bedoueens of several of the
minor tribes and villagers inhabiting this Desert, as the
best security for our protection.

A few words about our friend Sheikh Miguel * may

* Pronounced Midgewell.

not be uninteresting: his eldest brother, Muhammad,
is the head Sheikh of the Mizrâb, one branch of the
Sab'a, a powerful division of the Anazehs; he is himself of equal rank with his brother, but Muhammad
always remains with the tribe, while Sheikh Miguel
does all their business with the Government, and
escorts travellers, for which purpose he lives part of
the year in Damascus.   He is—like *all true* Bedoueens
—a small man, about five feet three inches in height,
slightly made, but erect, very graceful in all his motions, and with a light, easy step; his face is really
beautiful—of a perfect oval—a long aquiline nose,
delicately formed mouth, small regular teeth of dazzling whiteness, and large black eyes that could be soft
and sweet as any woman's, or flash with a fierce, wild,
eagle glance that really made one start.   He wore a
short black beard, and long crisp ringlets under his
kefiyeh, which was of the very finest and brightest
Damascus silk, bound round his head with the pretty
akgâl — a double wreath of camel's hair tied and
tasselled with coloured silks.   His dress was a *kumbaz*,
or long, tight gown of striped and flowered silk, with
wide, open sleeves hanging down to the knee; then his
Sheikh's cloak or pelisse of bright scarlet cloth bound
with black braid, and three bars of broad black braid
across the chest,—this, with the scarlet leather boots,
worn over stockingless feet, and reaching to the knee,
is the distinguishing dress of the Sheikh : over all came
a mash'lah * — a shapeless but very comfortable cloak—
sometimes of thin white cloth, edged with colour—
sometimes of coarse, thick, brown and white camel's-
hair cloth — sometimes of the same material in black,

---

* *Mash'lah* means *to strip off.*

violet, or brown, with a handsome pattern in gold thread woven in upon the shoulders — this latter kind comes from Mekka, and are costly but very beautiful. A silk scarf wound many times round the waist, into which a couple of revolvers and a big knife were stuck, and a sword hung round the neck by a crimson cord, completed his costume. As to his manners the " best-bred " polished English gentleman is not more polished than he, and the Bedoueen chief joins an easy chivalrous grace to his quiet dignified demeanour, which has a double charm. From the moment we left Damascus and became his " charge " till we re-entered the city, his kindness and thoughtful attention never ceased — morning, noon, and night, travelling or stationary, whatever we might be doing, alone or surrounded with Arabs, he had an eye and an ear always ready for every want of ours; whatever little difficulty might arise, the Sheikh was sure to be at hand to help one out of it. His conversation — of course through an interpreter — was always full of interest, and more might be learned from him, I imagine, than from any one, of the ancient histories of the great Arab tribes, of which so little is known: he and his brothers had all been taught reading and writing, but he told us, as people say of vaccination, " they only *took* with me." His Bedoueens and the escort addressed him occasionally with " O Sheikh ! " but most often it was " O Miguel ! " and they talked and joked with him with a freedom that was sometimes rather annoying to us, for they never hesitated to interrupt any of our conversations with him, whenever they had a remark to make. At home in their tents they observe some etiquette; when the Sheikh enters every person rises, and stands till he bids them be seated, and they do not permit him, when encamped, to do any menial work; but out in the plain a Sheikh would be greatly despised who made any difference between himself and his people, or did not attend to his own camel, and eat the same food as the others. The office of Sheikh is entirely hereditary; but a very bad or insane heir is set aside, and either the next of blood, or some one remarkably distinguished by his prowess, is elected in his place.

The Sheikh awoke us all at sunrise on the following morning; our toilettes, which consisted chiefly of shaking ourselves, were soon performed, and our breakfast of fowl, bread, and tea, was likewise quickly despatched. We were all mounted and away by seven o'clock, and soon came to some ruins of an extensive khan and a tower, whence we turned up the low pass of the Anti-Lebanon mountains, called the Bourghaz — or passage—rather slippery and steep for camels. Their movements, either in ascending or descending, are very unpleasant to the rider; they make each step like a stumble, jerking up or down upon it, shaking you all through, and helping you to arrive at the camel's own opinion, when he was asked which was best for him to go, up hill or down, and he answered, "May the curse of Allah light on both! for the flat plain is the only place fit for a beast like me!" We here met a great number of donkeys with long planks of timber lashed to their sides; and as they dragged these loads over the rocky ground, the roaring noise they made was perfectly astonishing, and much alarmed the dromedaries, who are very timid creatures, and are therefore very unpleasant to ride past unusual sights or sounds, or in towns at night. We passed the ruins of a temple, four columns and a sarcophagus, and of some wells excavated in the rock with much care.

Descending on the other side we were *in the Desert,* here narrowed between mountains to a valley of, we were told, ten miles wide. I need not say that our eyes were not of the smallest use in judging of any distance in the Desert; the atmosphere is so clear and so heated that objects at many miles off may appear quite close to you, and it is an ever-recurring marvel why one goes on hours and hours and never seems to approach any nearer to the objects you have been looking at all the time. Another deception, which is frequently puzzling, is the magnifying of distant objects by the heat, so that a few tamarisk bushes look like a grove of trees, a horse seems a tall camel, and a camel looks like a walking tower. The Sheikh had some business to transact at a large khan which had for some two hours seemed under our feet, called Kuteifeh, and we had therefore the advantage of an hour and a half's rest on our carpets in the inner court; he despatched his business and said his prayers in the Mosque, while we ate our luncheon, which was a sumptuous one, for we had nice cool oranges and fine raisins bought in the khan. Senân Pacha built this khan about three centuries ago, a handsome, solid building, with rows of fine arches : some houses have gathered round it into a small village, and there are gardens with pleasant trees, under whose shade we passed in leaving the place. Our course lay now nearly due east, and we soon crossed the track to Aleppo and Homs, which here turns off to the north. Our camels became very troublesome this afternoon, stopping to browse on certain aromatic plants which appeared on the plain, and as you have no particular bridle, and camels are remarkably self-willed, and reluctant to take advice in a language they don't understand, you have to sit still and bear it; but it is a very odd sensation

when their heads disappear entirely under their bodies
and their long forelegs go walking on over their own
heads! after which they suddenly pull up these same
heads, and look round in your face with such a meek
expression of injured innocence, you are obliged to say,
"All right, good drom., only do go on." The drivers
make them go on capitally, either by requesting them
to do so in the politest Arabic, or by enforcing their
wishes with the bakourah (a hooked stick), as they sit
behind you: but when the driver is walking, your
puny efforts of persuasion are ludicrously unsuccessful:
mine were remarkably so, for my heel did not quite
reach the neck of the beast, a good kick upon which
tells him he is to quicken his pace, and no infliction of
my bakourah ever had the faintest effect upon his mind
or legs; indeed, at last it became rather a favourite joke
among the Argeels to see the "little Sitt" beating on
her camel with impotent fury. I had the most charming dromedary, a dear beast, whose sweetness was described in her name, "Helweh" (which means *sweet*),—
she had the easiest, most elastic step, and the most delightful trot in the world; but, to counterbalance Helweh's
charms, my driver was a horrid old man, who would
not walk much, and therefore was always sitting behind
me and continually going to sleep, and, whenever he did
so, his dirty head would drop on my shoulder, and get
very roughly shaken off. He was, besides, the most
garrulous old gentleman, and considered his conversation worth hearing; so, whenever I was speaking to any
one of the party, or that the interpreter was telling
anything particularly interesting, this old man elevated
his hoarse voice and began a speech to another of his
brethren, always choosing the furthest off that he might
shout the louder. One day I was so angry that I knocked

him over the head with my bakourah and told him to
"hold his tongue," having learned to make the request
in Arabic on purpose : I was rather ashamed of myself,
but the other Argeels went into fits of laughter for ever
so long, and afterwards they used often to inquire why
I did not try him again, with many witticisms about his
old head that I did not understand.

My sister's first dromedary was a very spirited, frisky
creature, upon seeing which the kind Sheikh dismounted
and put her on his own, a gentle black animal, called
Simri (black), of which she became very fond, and she
had a good, well-behaved young driver, who used to
teach her the names of the mountains and the plants,
&c., and, when she had repeated her lesson correctly,
would call to all the others to come and hear the results
of his good teaching. She used sometimes to share her
luncheon with him, generally dry bread with a few
raisins, and sometimes provided herself with lumps of
sugar for him, and once, thinking to give him a treat,
she gave him a stick of chocolate, all of which he received with true Arab politeness, and said "taïb, taïb,
kattar-herak*," but he secretly imparted to the interpreter afterwards that she had given him some horrible
stuff made of black earth!—this was the chocolate.
Whenever we gave them anything they always divided
it among the whole set, and seemed grateful and pleased.
This is one of the delights of the Bedoueen—the *true*
Bedoueen—not only that you know you may trust
them, and that they are invariably respectful and polite,
but that they seemed pleased and really grateful for
little kindnesses. The Syrian seldom looks pleased,
and scarcely ever says "kattar-herak."

* "Good, good, thank you."

The falcon-bearer was a true Anazeh, and he always had a good-natured word and an inquiry as to how we felt, whenever either of us came near him : he approved of us mightily because we took to the dromedaries like " ducks to the water," and enjoyed it all from beginning to end. I can well understand the various accounts given by travellers of dromedary riding : the fact is that your liking it depends wholly upon two things—first, the natural pace of your animal—and they all differ in this, more almost than horses; and secondly, the way in which your saddle is settled. The shedād, the sub-struction of your seat, is simply an inverted V of wood, very smoothly made, with a stout back-bone along the top, at each end of which is placed a pommel about a foot high; fastened to the pommels over the top of the back-bone is an open square frame, stuffed with camel's or goat's hair—this forms your seat : across this, hanging down on each side, you throw first your saddlebag, then a carpet, a wadded quilt, two or three cloaks and shawls, and, in short, as many things as you can heap up, —the more the better, since these coverings make your saddle by day and your bed by night. You sit in the middle of the seat with a leg on each side of the front pommel, varying your position according to your pleasure, and you must lean a little forward always, or your back would rub against the hinder pommel. The saddle-bags are two handsome pouches of dark brown camel's hair, adorned with rows of tassels of all manner of bright colours, little tufts of ostrich feathers sewn on here and there, to draw off the " evil eye " from the good things within, and twelve or more long cords hanging from them nearly to the ground, ending in gay-coloured tassels— these keep up a continual swaying when the camel walks, and when he trots they have a very funny appearance.

We had plenty to look at on this our first day in the desert; the mountains on each side were perfectly barren, but they glowed with fine colours,—the ground was riddled with the holes of jerboas and rats whom we sometimes saw running off into safety, and towards evening several pretty gazelles were seen dancing about in the thorns, and among the *hashish el kali* which covered the ground: this is the plant from the ashes of which they make potash for soap — the Damascus and Jerusalem soap being composed only of this stuff mixed with olive oil;—it is the only trade the Desert Arabs carry on with the city, and the smoke from their fires for burning it, is seen curling up in a dozen different directions at once; it is a dry, thorny, ugly-looking plant. We passed also a very large salt-marsh, glistening and sparkling in the sun as if it was a lake: then came the village of Jerood, and after $10\frac{1}{2}$ hours of riding, independently of our rest at Kuteifeh, we came upon the pretty village of Atny — where there was a stream and a good many trees: we got over a low wall into a small enclosure, where our night encampment afforded unlimited amusement to the villagers until quite late: and we spent a pleasant evening, chatting with the Sheikh over our dinner; some time after a party of ten well-armed men mounted on horseback arrived, whose appearance the Sheikh did not much like; and so, to ensure their not attacking us on the morrow, he engaged them as guards extraordinary, from the dangers of the road to Karyetéen. This was not a pleasant resting-place for light sleepers,—the jackals prowled round our little enclosure with the most horrible howls and cries— once or twice they leaped over the wall, and I had to throw stones at them to make them go away, and three times I heard, seemingly quite close to us, the horrid

yelling laugh of a hyena, which I confess made me feel
a little queer.

We had now, too, arrived under the Desert dew, which
fell this night so heavily upon us, that in the morning
the thick shawls above our couvertures were wet through,
and I wrung a great cupful of water out of a bit of
my dress that had unwarily escaped covering in the
night. But the curious thing about this Desert dew is
that no one ever catches cold from it: the Bedoueens
never have rheumatism or coughs from it, and the most
delicate travellers encounter it without harm : one of
our party had a very weak chest and throat, my sister
was very liable to cold, and I to fever, yet we slept exposed to the heaviest dews for fifteen successive nights
without taking any remarkable precautions, and we never
found the slightest evil result from it.

We started soon after sunrise, our ten new friends
accompanying us, making a gay scene in the Desert,
as they scoured the plain, *ventre à terre*, with their
white mash'lahs and gaudy kefiyehs streaming in the
wind behind them, pursuing one another in mimic warfare, then suddenly wheeling round, pursuer becoming
pursued, and sweeping about in quickly changing circles,
uttering their war-cries, and poising their long bamboo
lances as if to throw them at their enemies, quivering
from end to end ; these lances are twelve feet long, and
are ornamented with bunches of black ostrich feathers
at the junction of the bamboo with the long steel point;
at the other end is an iron spike, used for planting the
lance in the ground when the bearer is dismounted :
the horses carry much more trappings than the camels,
and their gay-coloured tassels sweep the ground as they
gallop along, casting up clouds of sand in the air. They
continued this for about a couple of hours, and then,

getting tired of the play, galloped on before us, promising to send back a messenger if they found any dangers
on the road; the Sheikh had judged rightly, however,
and it was fortunate he had engaged them as allies: for
on our return we found they had left us to rob three
laden mules, and the next day they took possession of
the English mail to Baghdad, kept the letters for a time,
and appropriated a large portion of Government treasure.

It was terribly hot this morning, and we all suffered
a good deal from the burning glare on the barren
ground: it was amusing to see how by various degrees,
sooner or later, each of us began to leave off looking much about, and gradually retired into his or her
kefiyeh, becoming, as the heat increased, more and
more transformed into the semblance of mummies; indeed our appearance would have been rather amusing
in Hyde Park. I had a silk shawl folded thickly over
my shoulders, then the white mash'lah, underneath a
very thick, grey tweed cloak with a large hood, and our
huge felt hats were covered with some yards of muslin
hanging down, kefiyeh fashion, all round, the front
part of which could be folded over the face; and in the
middle of the day I always bound a blue veil several
times over my lips and nose, as the only means of preserving them from blistering. Once or twice we tried
to read — easy enough with the dromedary's even step
— but the glare was so dazzling on the white page that
we always gave it up after a few minutes. We put up
two hares, and the Sheikh shooting one, we dismounted
in the narrow shade of a low wall of what was once a
large khan, called el Kharab—the ruin—and made some
coffee while the hare was being roasted whole. Feasting
merrily upon its bones, which we handled Arab fashion,
we rode on after nearly an hour's delay—an hour that

seems very short when it is thus snatched in the middle
of a long day's ride for rest — but we forgot all our
fatigues in the enchantment of the scene around us;
the whole Desert gradually changed into a pale, sweet
blue, looking so like the sea one almost thought it must
be water; then the mountains, with their ever-varying
crags, became dressed in their evening hues of brightest
lilac, purple and violet, tipped with gold, and the deep
blue of the sky paled, as streaks of pink and crimson
stole over its length and breadth. M. Haag went into
raptures, and the Argeels' hearts were evidently soft-
ened, for, as the sun sunk, they permitted us the pleasure of a delightful trot in the cool evening air, though
they had complained bitterly in the morning, when we
wanted to refresh ourselves under the burning sun, that
we should "certainly kill the camels," and that we
"might as well be a set of postmen at the rate we
wanted to go!" The quick trot of a good dromedary
is a delightfully easy, pleasant pace, and a great relief
after some hours of the monotonous long swing of the
walking pace.

The first sight of Karyeteen was very pretty in the
western sunbeams — the bright specks of the white
houses, lying under the mountain side, as they seemed to
be, though in reality a long way from them, and, in the
distance, the faint blue summits of the mountains over
Tadmor — our much-longed-for goal, which was eagerly
pointed out by the Argeels; for, be it well understood,
Palmyra is but the Latin translation for the "Tadmor-
in-the-Wilderness," * built by King Solomon (Tadmor
and Tamar being the Hebrew for a palm), and no one
but the European traveller ever gives it such an appel-

* 1 Kings, ix. 18.

lation; the Romans, indeed, called it Adrianopolis, but
Tadmor has ever been in all the Eastern world its sole
name, and Tadmor, or Tedmor, is it still called by all
the Arabs of the "wilderness" around it.

It was moonlight ere we reached the large village of
Karyeteen, and as we skirted the outer walls we heard
nothing but the loud cries of about a thousand jackals.
We were a very long time threading its lanes before we
arrived at the Sheikh's house and khan — court within
court — each one quickly filled with crowds of his relations and dependants, who came out to see us dismount
in the outer court, and then pressed round us, trying to
touch our faces and finger our clothes, and asking innumerable questions before we reached the large chamber prepared for us; here, we saw in a moment, the
people would be in and out all night — for they were
already packing themselves in, in tight rows, to see us
eat and sleep; moreover, I felt the lively inhabitants of
the mats, carpets and cushions rubbing up their forces
for the onslaught, and we therefore quietly escaped to a
small terrace on the housetop, where, lifted up above
them all, we reposed in perfect silence and quiet after
our fourteen hours' journey. Our ten guards of the
morning had announced our approach, and the village
Sheikh had prepared a banquet for Sheikh Miguel:
from our little terrace we looked down into the guest-
chamber, where we saw the numerous guests crowding
in relays round the enormous *pilaf* of mutton and rice,
a bowl of which was sent up to us with plenty of compliments, from the village Sheikh, on which we made-
a very good supper.

This Sheikh was a very tall, stout man, large-
limbed, and large mouthed, — he was wealthy and prosperous, — but he looked unhappy and depressed: and

Sheikh Miguel soon told us the cause: he had an only
son, the delight of his heart, for whom he bought a
little black slave as a playmate: the two boys, one day,
playing together, got hold of the Sheikh's pistols, and
the slave accidentally shot his master's child,—the
father, in a transport of blind rage, killed the slave, and
was still miserable with grief for his loss.

All Bedoueen Sheikhs have their black slaves, for
they are the only servants they can have; no Bedoueen
of any tribe will hire himself or herself as servant to
any one, and however obliging they may be in lending
assistance on some special occasion, the idea of rendering it constantly, or as a duty, would be most indignantly rejected by them all.   But these black slaves are
always kindly treated, and generally become very much
attached and faithful to their owners: we used to see
Sheikh Miguel giving his little black boy his food with
much care, morning and evening; and the interpreter
told us, that the boy was most affectionately attached to
the Sheikh, and that if his master was to forget him and
give him nothing to eat, he would neither ask for food
nor complain, till he starved.   They are really valuable
servants, and sometimes cost large sums of money: we
heard of one, in Damascus, who was so highly esteemed
by her dying mistress, that she had left all her children
in her entire charge.

The banquet continued long after we had fallen asleep,
— so numerous were the guests to welcome the highly-
respected Anazeh-chief; these feeds are terrible affairs
sometimes to the host, for an Arab invitation includes
" you and yours," and your guest, therefore, brings his
brother and his cousin, and his cousin's cousin; and when
you have invited a party of ten guests you may have forty
or fifty, or in fact, any number arrive, all expecting an

equal welcome, and, what is worse, an equal share in the food.

. We were roused from our slumbers at sunrise, but as the escort were not ready to start till nine o'clock, we might have rested longer: they were baking bread I believe, for their journey, while we stood in the crowd below, baking ourselves in the sun. M. Haag made sketches of the faces round us — some superhumanly ugly, but some remarkably pretty: there was a young son of a neighbouring Sheikh, so pretty and so girlish-looking, that we could none of us agree as to whether he was a boy or a girl,— there not being any remarkable difference in the costume at that age; and when I asked him which he was, he blushed every shade of red, and ran away laughing like a mad thing.

This Karyeteen is a large village with a mixed po-pulation of Mooslims and Jacobite Christians — the Sheikh's premises enclosing a rather handsome Mosque, which seemed ancient, and some well-built houses. There are most copious springs and fountains behind the town, which supply innumerable rivulets and streams in the cultivated ground round the houses; they also fill a circular reservoir — a little lakelet — outside the village, where the caravan camels are all watered, surrounded by wild weeds and flowers. From this lux-ury of water Karyeteen is believed to be the *Hazar-enan*, (village or enclosure of fountains — *enan* answering to the Arabic *'ain*) of Numb. xxxiv. 9, 10, describing the north-east corner* of the "promised land;" and again

* According to Mr. Porter, this much-disputed "border" is very simply described: the Mediterranean forms its western extremity, thence the only real valley opening into the eastern country is that of El-Husn, which separates the great chain of the Lebanon mountains (here called Mount Hor, probably some local name applied to one of

by Ezekiel (xlvii. 17) in speaking of the territory promised at some future time to the children of Israel.
Here Abraham and Lot probably rested on their way
from Haran to the Land of Canaan; and Jacob too,
when he came out of Padan-aram with his wives and his
children and all his property, to return to Isaac his
father; for the natural highway from Mesopotamia into
Syria led by the fountains of Tadmor and Karyeteen.

This was to be our grand day of twenty-four hours'
fatigue, and we were all rather put out at our departure being delayed till the sun was high and burning,
though not high enough to prevent the view of the long
range of blue hills to the south-east from looking lovely
as we emerged from the town: such tender and delicate
hues one *can* only see in the Desert. We were now in
the Wady el Kebeer (the great valley), which we were
told was from twenty to thirty miles wide — its termina-
tion was to be Tadmor, and we looked eagerly on to
the faint blue distance throughout the day. Very early
in the day the Sheikh pointed to a ruined tower on the
plain, and said, " We shall halt there :" it seemed quite
close to us; but hour after hour we toiled on over the
scorched-up, burning, barren ground, where scarce
even a thorn was now growing, and we never, never
seemed to come any nearer. There was no use in ap-
plying to our good Sheikh, for the Bedoueens cannot tell
the time or distance of anything; and he invariably answered " Two hours—two hours," to everything. Before

the northernmost peaks) from the Nusairiyeh hills, which end at
Antioch; this valley leads directly to Hamah, whence the border came
through Zedad and Ziphron to Hazar-enan, "the goings out of it;"
these two places are identified by Mr. Porter, with every appearance of
probability, as Südüd and Zifroun, villages on the direct track between
Hamah and Karyeteen.

we understood this, it was rather trying to have braced
oneself up to hold out the time specified, and then find
it might be two, twelve, or any number of hours. No
Bedoueens have any idea of dates or times; it is the
same with the Druzes and Syrian Fellaheen: "I was
born the year so much rain fell;" or, "That happened
three years before such a Pasha came;" or something of
that kind, are their invariable answers; and in Palestine
a Fellah will tell you, "Oh, my father was quite an old
man — he lived in the time of David!"

At length, near sunset, we found ourselves actually
close to the tower, and some of us dismounted to examine
it, while the dragomans made us a little coffee further
on. This place, el Khasr, is called the Robbers' Tower,
because it is a great place of rendezvous for *ghŭzoos*, or
plundering parties, and many an unwary traveller has
been seized upon here, and dragged within its crumbling
walls. Some fine work is still to be seen on the doorways, windows, and ornamental medallions of the picturesque ruin. The stone of the fallen columns seemed
composed entirely of fossils, and we picked out some
beautiful little shells with our fingers and penknives.
Further on, and in a line with the Robbers' Tower, appeared another, at some distance, still more ruined:
the remains of a circular reservoir and of an aqueduct
are found between them, — the reservoir continuing
filled with water for some time after the rainy season,
adds another attraction to the Ruined Tower for robbers;
our Sheikh therefore kept a sharp look-out while we
pledged each other in spiced coffee, and watched our
own shadows flying out to endless lengths across the
plain, as the sum sunk below the horizon. One has no
idea of the beauty and poetry of shadows till one goes
into the Desert, — there I never wearied of watching

them, and delighting in the new language they talked to me.

The moon rose soon after we mounted again, and the little hasty rest had been so refreshing, that we more than ever enjoyed the night; the camels keep better together than in the day, and the Argeels indulged in a number of wild songs, for the special encouragement of their creatures,— some of the tunes were pretty, wild and sad, though monotonous, and the words poetical, — the chief burden was in the style of "Go on, oh Camel, my love, my beauty, go on quickly, and the prettiest girls of the village shall come out to meet you ; go on, and when you kneel, the maidens will feed you with fresh sugar-canes, and stroke you with their soft hands," &c. ; then they improvised verses about the riders, which elicted great applause and some amusement ; they were chiefly personal descriptions, which we did not, of course, understand, but sometimes we caught allusions to incidents that had happened in the day, or to things we had said to them in our very meagre Arabic. M. Haag, who dressed like a Bedoueen, and was always full of jokes, was a favourite with them, and the chief songs were about him, with good-natured fun about his continually dropping asleep, &c. ; the songs were very pleasant when the singers walked, or when you were listening to your neighbour's Argeel, but one soon wearied of the loud voices shouting in your very ears at the full crack of their lungs, when they twisted themselves up by the dromedary's tail, and arrived behind your own *shedad :* moreover, one was sure to lose, in the row they made, exactly the most interesting part of whatever conversation was going on amongst ourselves, —moreover, whenever one saw two of one's friends engaged in a comfortable chat, that instant one's driver

was sure to send his camel rushing up, rudely dividing
them, for the better arrangement of their own chorus,
and one's apologies for the interruption were all the
more supremely ridiculous, because we each knew that
none of us had the slightest shadow of control over our
own beasts.

The singing one day ceased, on their understanding
that my sister had a head-ache; but, on being told the
same thing the next day, the dragoman overheard them
inquiring from the Sheikh, if the Ingleez women "always had *battal*" that is, good for nothing "heads!"
One must converse, if possible, in night travelling, for
else it soon becomes difficult to keep awake, and a
tumble from a dromedary is not the pleasantest thing
possible; we were not quite enough at ease to twist back
and lie down half behind the pummel as an adept can
do, though of course, not when your Argeel is mounted
behind you, — but, if one could manage this, it would
afford a delightful rest, for the camel's long, swinging,
perfectly even step, is the most sleepifying thing in the
world, and at night, when you have not even your own
shadow to watch, or if you are going eastwards and cannot see it, it really is the hardest thing to keep awake
after a long day's ride.

The dromedary's pace is something under five miles
an hour. One is apt to imagine it slow, for the stride
is so long that they seem tardy, accustomed as one is to
the short, quick step of the horse; but see the quick
pace at which the Argeels walk to keep up with them,
or, better still, dismount and try, and then see if you
don't change your opinion; if one of the party lags
behind or dismounts for only a moment, see how tedious
the waiting for him again seems; or if you yourself lag
a little, how soon your companions disappear into moving

specks, and how long you are in overtaking them. Some of the dromedaries, especially those selected for the post, go at a wonderfully quick rate, but their gallop is a very rough pace; they cannot endure much of it, and die when at all overworked. Their owners are indeed most attentive to and careful of them; the camel becomes very quickly attàched to a kind master, and they are very fond of these their valuable possessions. We found our dromedaries soon became acquainted with us, and would come when called by name to receive chicken bones from our hands; sometimes they roused themselves, and made little observations upon us at night, and at Tadmor I woke more than once feeling my camel gently sniffing at my feet. Their proper food is chiefly barley, but on a journey they ought to have balls made of rice and dhourra mixed up with spices: our men took none of this food with them, expecting to find supplies of it at Tadmor; there was none, however, and except what the poor beasts got in the khans and a few plants by the way, they had nothing whatever to eat, till we returned to Damascus, but the green stalks of the dhourra, which they like, but from which they derive little or no nourishment. Meantime they feed, as the natives say, on their own humps — that is, the humps gradually diminish in size: as long as there is any hump visible the camel can keep on; as soon as it disappears he languishes and dies. Every camel is branded with the mark of his owner and of his tribe, and it sometimes happens an Arab may be travelling among a distant tribe and come upon his own long-lost camel, either stolen or strayed, when the indelible brand proving its original owner, enables him to reclaim it. The most curious thing we heard about the camels and their masters, our interpreter vouched for as a fact, and by no means an uncommon one, that, so acute is the *smell* as well as the eye of a Bedoueen, they will tell, blindfolded, of any track of camels, not only how long since trodden, but even to what tribe the passing camels belonged!

Among the Bedoueens of this Desert the red camels are the commonest and the most esteemed; those of the Nejd (the desert about Baghdad) are generally black. It is of the latter that their tents and ābbahs are made, while the dyed colours are woven into their carpets and hangings, to form the stripes of their ābbahs and mash'lahs. The camel's milk is excellent when fresh and warm, but not when cold; nor is it rich enough to make butter. The flesh of a young camel is as good as beef; it looks coarser, but has no strong taste; and is considered a great delicacy by the Bedoueens.

The night was whiled away in hearing about all these things, and many a Bedoueen tale besides, while the glorious moon rode her course and then waned, and the morning dawn came. It was very cold that night, and we dismounted twice to try and warm ourselves; but in the morning, oh! how broiling hot it was. The low pass which opened into Tadmor itself seemed quite close to us at daylight; but wearily, wearily we journeyed on under the scorching sun till one o'clock; a mirage lent its beautiful deception to amuse us, and for a few moments it was difficult not to believe that we had water to pass before reaching the mountains, which had now swept round to the north-east, across our valley; they deepened into the very darkest violet, while, to the left, they faded into pale amethyst; presently the Saracenic Castle above Tadmor became visible, and we all got more and more excited and feverishly eager as the tombs cut in the rocks became more and more easily distinguished; then, as we began to ascend the pass, a

few more, built like low towers, stood on the summits
of the hill, like grave, silent, patient sentinels, beckoning us on to enter the City of the Dead.

Not all dead, however, for suddenly there dashed up
the path towards us some seven or eight men, armed to
the teeth, brandishing their long lances, shrieking and
yelling and shouting, to welcome our good Sheikh
Miguel: we had been discerned by scouts on the hill-
tops, and they had galloped out to meet us. Thus accompanied we soon reached the finest and best of all
the tombs (called by the Arabs the "Bride's Tomb,"
simply to betoken its great beauty, not because it is supposed by them to have been occupied by any bride), and
we dismounted in order to examine it, and to rest a little
in its shade while the Sheikh heard all the news of
Tadmor. It was very bad news indeed for him, and a
grievous disappointment for us all : the famine was so
great in the land in consequence of the drought, that
the Anazehs, knowing nothing of their beloved Sheikh's
approach, had broken up their encampment and departed only three days before, going towards Baghdad in
search of pasture for their camels. We discussed the
possibility of pursuing and remaining a few days with
them, but the direction of their track was all uncertain;
pasture might or might not have been found in this
hollow or in that; and three days' start in the pathless
Desert made the overtaking them too doubtful and
hazardous to attempt. So there was good-bye to all our
promised plans, and our hopes of living among the
Bedoueens themselves, feasting on camel's meat and
milk, and seeing all sorts of Bedoueen mares and sports :
the Sheikh's new tent, too, which he had promised for
our special use, had been carried off to be "seasoned;"
altogether the disappointment was very great; but to the

Sheikh himself it was much heavier,—he was longing
to see his young sons, and had intended to take them
back with him for the winter, to give them some education in Damascus: now all was frustrated, or at least
deferred to another year.

We bemoaned his disappointment and our own for
some time, and then turned to examine the Tomb. It is
composed of a square tower, thirty feet on each side,
and eighty feet in height, divided into four stories; the
lowest story has three huge blocks of stone in the centre,
lessening in size one above another, through which a
flat-headed doorway is cut, with deep mouldings and
much ornament; above this is an arched window, the
sides of which are formed of human-headed bulls, much
resembling the Assyrian type.   Under this, a recumbent
figure, like a swathed mummy, lies on a projecting slab,
and a tablet, bearing an inscription in Palmyrene, with
a Greek translation, says that it is the tomb of the Ela-
belos family, with a date of the Seleucidæ era, corresponding to A.D. 102; the chamber on the ground floor
is, on each side, divided into four compartments, which
narrow pyramidally as they ascend; a fluted Corinthian
pilaster ornaments each division; these recesses have
several stone shelves across them for the reception of
bodies embalmed and wrapped in mummy cloth, of
which large quantities lie about; at the end of the
chamber opposite to the door, there are two rows of fine
busts, nine in all, standing on shelves, and other busts on
the walls, but the chief beauty inside is the exquisite
ceiling carved in medallions, like that of the peristyle
of the Temple of Jupiter at Baalbek, containing busts,
birds and flowers, delicately sculptured, upon a bright
blue ground; they are somewhat broken, but we thought
we discerned the eagle with Ganymede in one of

them ; a handsome cornice surrounds the chamber.
One of the eight compartments is occupied by a small
staircase leading to the upper stories, which are lighted
by narrow loopholes for windows ; the ceiling of the
second is of elaborate geometrical patterns; the third
had only a pretty cornice; and the fourth was quite plain;
the recesses round this upper chamber are vaulted ; all
the ceilings are of enormous stones laid quite across the
chambers, and like the rest of the building within and
without most beautifully united; the stone, too, is of
the purest white. The general proportions of this
building are charming, and the details are carried out
with such high artistic skill, that it is a perfect gem, —
sad and mysterious it looks, as it stands there alone, in
the middle of the pass, against the deep blue sky.

We were soon remounted, impatient to go on, — only
a few steps further to the very middle of the Wady, and
then — what can be more beautiful, more glorious in all
the world, than the view that burst upon our eyes !
There—like nothing in Nature, but the first time one
sees the wide ocean spread before one, lay the Desert in
its apparently boundless infinitude, glowing in radiant
colours of unnumbered variety; while, like jewels laid
upon her fair bosom, stood Tadmor, though in ruins, still
empress of the plain, majestically grand ! First, though
furthest off, the Temple of the Sun rose up in giant
massiveness ; then as we advanced another step, the
splendid Colonnade, with the Triumphal Arch, its noble
gateway,—and one building succeeded another, each
and all dazzlingly white, save where touched with shining gold or rosy pink—how absolutely interminable
it seemed, as column succeeded column in endless succession, up to the very mountain foot, meeting other colonnades which branched off at right angles and then faded

down in ruins,—lone columns standing up here and there, and those of the Amphitheatre curving round in a broken semicircle, amidst the miles and miles of scattered stones, broken pillars, fallen pediments, and huge blocks, which covered the whole ground! a few dark masses told out from among the light columns; these were the platforms of smaller temples and halls, and one, the palace of poor Zenobia! On the left, above all this, the Saracenic castle looked down very grandly from its lordly height upon the elder ruins below, while green gardens of fruit trees and graceful palms clustered together at the extreme right of the great Temple.

On we went, our armed escort, in triumph at our safe arrival, screaming and shouting, and the horsemen, who had come out to welcome us, careering about on their wonderful horses over rock and ruin, with utter heedlessness of all obstacles, like persons possessed; and as soon as we began to cross the plain and to near the ruins, the townspeople came streaming out in a great mob, shrieking their noisy welcomes and crowding round the Sheikh as if they would pull him off the camel with their impetuous embraces, kissing his hands and knees at every half-step. We rode to the eastern side of the Temple and debated whether to encamp there in the shade, or further off among the gardens,—the crowds of people soon decided the point,—we saw we never should have had one instant's peace near the town. So we went on, the camels starting aside in horror every now and then from the dead carcase of some wretched camel left mouldering in the way, till, down a little descent, we reached a small terrace, secluded and quiet, from whence a very low, ancient stone door, still turning on its original stone hinges, admitted us

into a delicious garden of olives, plums, and pomegranates: the camels were unloaded on the terrace, and we
ladies retired into the thickets of the garden to enjoy
the welcome luxury of a good bathe in the little river
which ran through it.

In spite of our fatigues we wandered out after dinner,
under the irresistible temptation of a full moon, among
the ruins: we had seen Karnak and Baalbek by moonlight, and we were thankful to see Tadmor also with
the Desert around it dipped in molten silver: the light
and graceful Colonnade, and the heavy masses of the
great Temple, are above all things lovely in the solemn
holy light of the moon, and we could have stayed there
all night, had we not known that we were risking a
good deal. We had taken the interpreter with us as our
guard and guide, and we believed all the people to be
asleep, at this hour, within the gates of the town: but,
as we were standing in the ruins of Zenobia's palace,
suddenly voices were heard, — "E Wullah!" and
"Mash'allah!" exclaimed the guide, "if these are
stranger Arabs we are undone! and here they come!"
He quickly motioned us to keep behind him, and advanced to meet them as two Bedoueens came tumbling
over the stones, laughing loudly: they stopped short
when they saw we had an Anazeh with us, and on being
told we were friends of Sheikh Miguel, they made a
rough salaam, and said, "Allah give you peace!" but
we took the hint that there might be others about, and
quickened our steps towards the encampment without
any loss of time; the Sheikh had been obliged to go
into the village to eat *pilaf* and receive welcomes without end, and was much displeased with us for having
ventured so far at night without him. Probably the
Bedoueens knew he was in the village, as they were towns-

people themselves, and had kindly followed us to relieve us of any superfluous articles we might have in wear, but, finding one of the Sheikh's people with us, they did not dare to do so.

The Sheikh's tent having been sent away, we were under the necessity of sleeping here, as well as on the journey, under the unveiled stars; but it was no subject of regret even to my sister or myself: we had become accustomed to our hard couches upon the dry stony ground, with sketch-books and saddle-bags for pillows; here we had the graceful branches of a palm tree waving above us, and we slept well, night after night, in the warm, soft, delicious air.

PART II.—THE RUINS.

THE Temple of the Sun, is, of course, the first thing to be thought of at Tadmor. It is an immense pile of gigantic masonry, enclosing a square of 740 feet each way, one fifty larger than the court of the Temple at Jerusalem, the structure to which it is best comparable; for, unlike the beautiful temples of Greece, which stood with all their charms of light and oft-repeated shafts disclosed to the first and most distant glance of every eye, those of Tadmor and Jerusalem were jealously enclosed in a double row of cloisters, with a high massive wall, the Temple itself standing isolated nearly in the centre of this cloistered court; the whole structure is, like that at Baalbek, raised up on a platform of large stones, surrounded by a broad moat, now nearly filled up, but still distinct. It would be very interesting to ascertain whether there are the same, or any substructions formed beneath this platform, as there are under those on which both Baalbek and Jerusalem stand: so similar is the *idea* of all the three platforms, that it is probable they exist; but, from the filling up of the ground, the entrances are very likely hidden. The surrounding wall was seventy feet high on all sides; the flat surface broken by a row of pilasters, supported on a slightly projecting base, and a few false doors and pediments unsymmetrically placed. The west side was pierced by a magnificent doorway and portico; the latter has disappeared, and been replaced by a strong Saracenic wall with a lofty door. Through breaches in the external wall, many of the columns of the cloisters may be seen, while, above all, the lofty columns of the Temple itself tower up with much beauty and elegance.

As great things stoop to mean uses, this wall now encloses the whole town of Tadmor — the miserable hovels thickly fill up every portion of the court, clustering in the corners round the columns up to their very capitals, hanging on to the carved ornaments like decayed birds' nests, and poisoning the once sacred enclosure with fœtid squalor and indescribable filth. It is almost impossible to get any general idea of the ruins, even as they are, through this horrible swarm; and probably before many generations have passed these people will have succeeded in destroying every vestige of the interior of this once glorious edifice.

The Great Portal was thirty-two feet high, and sixteen wide, standing between two smaller doorways: the sides and lintel were each of a single stone, and all are exquisitely ornamented with bands of carving, in wreaths of fruit and flowers, quite as graceful and artistic as those of Baalbek, but not as deeply cut. One of the great sides of the central door has half fallen from its place, and leans like a tired giant against the Saracenic

wall': all are blackened with the smoke of the fires
which the Arabs, who make a dwelling-place of this
portal, are constantly burning there. Above each doorway are two huge projecting brackets, which look very
mysterious — possibly they once supported statues. A
hundred columns — perhaps more — of the double
cloisters still stand ; but it is excessively difficult to see
the half of them, even though one clambers on to the
tops of some of the Arab houses.

Opposite the portal stood the Temple itself; the
cella was surrounded by a single row of lofty columns
with bronze capitals, all of which have of course disappeared, as the natives even now constantly throw
down the pillars and friezes in order to wrench out the
clamping irons between them. Parts of the beautifully
carved entablature remain ; the festoons of flowers held
up by winged figures or genii are still quite visible;
and when gilded by the rays of the western sun, with the
bronze capitals shining in the light, it must have been
a noble and striking picture, — even now it is one of
the finest bits at Tadmor, when the sun sinks low
enough to illumine the lofty columns only, and the
western wall throws the miserable wretchedness at their
feet into shade. Several fragments are left, both here
and in two small Temples at some distance, in which a
row of short columns are mounted upon others of ordinary size, forming, in fact, a clerestory, like that in the
Hypostyle Hall at Karnak, and, as is shown by Mr.
Fergusson, like the House of the Forest of Lebanon
(1 Kings vii.) at Jerusalem, and the Hall of Xerxes at
Persepolis.

The Sheikh took us into the Mosque, which was once
the Temple sanctuary — a large hall, with a single row
of Corinthian columns on each side ; but one cannot be

sure whether these stand in their original positions or
not, they are so strange a patchwork of various remains
— capitals, turned upside down, now acting as the bases
of some of them. At the north end is a large arch with
much sculpture, which has probably been added by the
Arabs; and at each side are two small chambers with
richly-carved ceilings, one of which has the signs of the
zodiac, with figures of the deities still visible, despite
the efforts of the Mooslims to destroy them. On the
soffit of the arch is the eagle with expanded wings, resembling the famous eagle at Baalbek. A small staircase leads to the roof of this Mosque, whence the view
is as grand as it is extraordinary: such a strange
mixture of crowded wretchedness in the living present,
contrasting with the faded witnesses of the splendour of
the past — the sadness of the broken friezes and prostrate columns, and the nobility of those that still soar
up against the cloudless sky with their richly-carved
capitals, and the graceful rows of colonnades in the
plain outside, leading the eye into the boundless Desert
beyond, dying away on the horizon in its garb of many
colours. It is curious that an earthquake has so shaken
the external wall of the Temple that two sides — the
north and the south — lean very considerably inwards,
without the stones being relatively displaced: it is now
as if they had been so built intentionally to give them
an Egyptian or pyramidal air.

At about 300 yards' distance from the north-west
angle of the Temple, is the grand Triumphal Arch commencing the chief Colonnade: a very curious and
remarkably beautiful piece of building it is. The
central arch is flanked by a lower one on each side;
but between them, on either side, are inserted *two
oblique* arches, projecting southwards, but so as to be

invisible in a front view: taken with the central arch
alone they are gracefully pretty, but then the side
arches cannot be seen at the same time. Flanking the
gateway, on the south, are three columns on each side,
very curious ones,—round and square columns united
together, the square sides facing each other, and the
same with the round,—with *double* capitals placed one
above the other: these capitals are in bad taste, but
all else about the triumphal arch is beautiful. The
sculpture on the inner (north) side is rich and uninjured — endless varieties of wreaths and scrolls, and
bands of fruit and flowers, and fantastic ornaments
gracefully mingled, cut with equal skill to those at
Baalbek, and in better taste, because not so loaded,—
heads are carved on the great door jambs, and beautiful
bits of sculpture lie in half-buried heaps all around.
From this Arch four rows of columns, forming a triple
Colonnade, ran towards the mountains for very nearly a
mile in length!—not quite straight, for it bends slightly
to the north-east, enough to prevent a vista to the very
end. The columns are fifty-seven feet high, formed of
three drums, of which nearly all the lower ones are now
covered up with loose sand, while between the second
and third a narrow stone is inserted, from which a
bracket projects, probably intended to support a bust,
as they are too near the top for statues: doubtless this
must have had a fine effect when the busts stood there;
but at present they have a very singular and awkward
appearance; several of them still bear inscriptions in
Palmyrene, and also in Greek, giving the names of the
persons whose portraits they bore. The capitals are of
richly sculptured acanthus leaves, rather stiffly arranged; and on the abacus is an ornament very common at Tadmor — a row of oval balls with roses

sculptured between each; the columns are united by a
plain architrave, supporting a very rich entablature of
the pine-cone pattern, extending the whole way; above
that came a frieze of billet moulding, with a row of the
egg-and-rose moulding finishing the whole; only very
few stones of this frieze yet remain *in situ.* A double
gateway, one beyond the other, on the west side, ornamented with a broad band of the pine-cone pattern
bent round the arch, and a well-executed moulding of the
egg-and-rose ornament, leads to a row of columns placed
in a semicircle, which is supposed to have been the
amphitheatre: nine of these columns are still upright,
and many others broken off; they have all brackets on
each side, looking, in their present meaningless position,
like the handles on a paviour's pound; a rich frieze still
unites some of the columns, and finely sculptured pediments and other stones are heaped up in huge masses
on the ground.   There is another gateway similar
to this further on, and opposite to it a Colonnade
branched off to the east, or a small Temple may have
stood here, for there are one or two tall slender columns,
and some others supporting a second story of little
columns. Not far from the great Triumphal Arch at the
entrance, are four monolithic shafts, only one of which
is standing upright now,—they are of dark red granite,
with capitals and bases of the ordinary stone: this
granite is said to be Egyptian, and to have been brought
here by Solomon at the foundation of Tadmor,—the tradition may be false, but it is not a bit more extraordinary
than half the facts appertaining to Tadmor and Baalbek.

    Between these two gateways, a little to the west, are
enormous heaps of masonry—one heap is said to have
been a Hall of Justice; the other, to which a street of
columns appears to have led, has time out of mind been

declared the ruins of Zenobia's Palace. It has all the appearance of a palace; and the tradition seems confirmed by the very remarkable quantity of broken ornaments with which the loose sand is filled,—if a stone is displaced hundreds of fresh pieces of glass, sometimes prettily shaped and of every colour of the rainbow, are turned up, with beads of all shapes. Many metal ornaments also, evidently for females, have been found here, and are now worn by the Bedoueen women.

Towards the end of the Colonnade are four large square masses of masonry some twelve or fourteen feet high; and here probably was the central intersection of the city among the royal and public buildings; it is believed that these square masses were the pedestals on which statues or groups of statues once stood, or the bases of a four-sided triumphal arch like that at Latakia and many other places; these pedestals are found still existing at Shuhba in the Haurân, a city of unknown date,— in the centre of the ruins of Jerash,— in the middle of ancient Antioch,— and, I believe, at Bozrah.

About a quarter of a mile to the east of this there stands a little gem of a Temple, almost perfect in form, though the sculpture is sadly mutilated; it is called, by tradition, the Temple of the King's Mother. It is very small, simply a cella with pilasters against the outer wall, and a portico of six beautiful columns and two half-columns, which (if my memory does not fail me) were fluted. The whole building is mounted on a small platform; the stones are, as usual at Tadmor, very finely joined, and the capitals are richly and well carved, preserving their freshness and sharp cutting still; the view from it is perhaps the best of Tadmor as a whole,— it is superb. The little Temple faces that of the Sun, the eye then sweeps up the whole length of the Colonnade, with the distant gardens seen between the columns, then the dark masses of Zenobia's Palace, and interminable columns beyond, up to the fine mountains dividing the Baghdad desert from the Wady Kebeer, by which we had come. (See Frontispiece.) One afternoon that we walked out here is worth a few words of description: the day had been changeable and stormy, but the sunset came with its usual magnificent glow, and the stones of the little Temple seemed literally overspread with burnished gold, contrasting with the crimson and pink splendour of the western sky. Suddenly, and while the sun was still bright and warm, the great silver globe of the refulgent moon sprang up from the distant horizon, throwing an instantaneous flood of blue-white light over the immense plain, *meeting* the sun-glow in which we still stood; and scarcely had we time to observe the peculiar harmony melting into one another, when, with the rapidity of change belonging to an eastern sky, in the Desert especially, a densely black storm-cloud burst suddenly forth from behind the mountain close beside us, and pouring down over our heads came the dark, heavy shower, *actually falling between* the calm and lovely moonlight and the rich glory of the setting sun! It was, perhaps, just one of those moments in Nature which one might live a hundred years without ever seeing a second time; but it was something, once seen, never to be forgotten.

There is no spot like this small Temple for obtaining a general idea of the immense proportions and mass of the Temple of the Sun, with the huge platform on which it stands; but it struck me still more here than even at Thebes and Baalbek how little these magnificent Temples were built for external beauty. Exquisite and splendid as they were, *the* coup d'œil was always *after entering the doorway*, since, in every case, the Temples were shut in by a wall, above which only the most lofty of the columns towered: with the Greeks it was exactly the contrary — the splendour of *their* temples was chiefly on the exterior; and we moderns strive more for external rather than internal effect. One would have thought that the Temple of the Sun above all would have been more open than any others; but perhaps the ancients knew best,— like the surpassing splendour and the golden lining to the House of the Lord in Solomon's Temple, the rays of the sun were collected in the Temples of Baal, between the shadows of the surrounding walls, and thus concentrated the attention of the worshipper on the immediate shrine of the Deity. At Baalbek it is doubtful whether the walls on the west and north sides were ever built, or intended to be built, much higher than the bases of the columns; but I could not help fancying, as I thought over the other examples, that it had been as lofty as the rest, or as it is now. With the idea of concentration, these walls would be less required at Baalbek than anywhere else, for there the view is hemmed in by the lofty mountains that bend round three sides of the Temple; whereas at Tadmor, Karnak, or Thebes, one can imagine the sort of want — almost a necessity — for the mind to feel some arrest or refuge from the boundless infinitude all round, before it anchored on the shrine of the holy Symbol within.

Between the giant and the little fairy-like Temple there is a spring of good water, and a deep hollow which, for half the year, is a little lake: it has been well lined with masonry, and the stream murmurs over the pavement with a pleasant little sound. An aqueduct

also crosses the plain here, which once carried water
from the mountain to the Great Temple. Nearer,
indeed quite close to the Colonnade on this side, are
the remains of the women's Baths; they are much
ruined, and covered over with sand; but two or three
openings are still kept free with narrow stone steps,
where the townswomen come all day to fill their
pitchers; the water is of a high temperature.

Beyond the extremity of the Colonnade, among
heaps of ruins of all manner of beautiful things, there
are several Temples (possibly mausoleums or baths, but
they seem more like the remains of temples): one has
a pediment elaborately sculptured; a portico of another
seems to have stretched across the end of the Colonnade,
some portion of which is still standing,— and a sarcophagus, inside a small Temple near this, sculptured on
the sides with garlands of fruit and flowers held up by
satyrs, is worth looking at. It is perfectly impossible to
describe the details of the immense amount of ruin
closely heaped together in this part — friezes and capitals
and nameless fragments richly and beautifully sculptured with vine and acanthus leaves, fruits and flowers,
wreaths and medallions in endless variety, among scrolls
of geometrical network and fantastic ornaments — all cut
in that richly-coloured stone, which is in itself a beautiful thing: as you hold it in your hand, or step over it,
it is *couleur de rose tendre*, blushing at itself,— as the
sun shines on the vertical mass, it is dyed over with gold,
rich, luscious, and gleaming, — while, at a few miles'
distance, it is of a dazzling white; the buildings of
Tadmor would be beautiful and grand in anything
and anywhere; but they owe much to their material;—
in the stern, grim granite of our cold North, and
in this vast and lonely position, they would be very

solemn and very mournful — a very spectacle of grief:
but in this lovely stone, endowed with such rich and
tender hues, the otherwise human-made thing seems
spiritualised into a solid fancy — a dreamlike fabric of
some delicate thought, congealed by a magician's hand
into tangible stone. Sydney Yendys has a fine simile
of the Colosseum, resembling an old gladiator slowly
dying, crumbling away in mouldering grief — a true
picture of the ruins of the West, where Time flings
funereal garlands of autumn-fallen leaves over her dead:
— Palmyra seemed to me, from the first instant I saw it
stretched out before me in all its investiture of bright
colours, like a fair maiden, a flower-crowned bride,
lying down in a repose that was really Death, though it
seemed only a deep sleep, with her white robes and her
fair flowers still around her, *they* living though *she* was
dead, floating down the stream of time — "the queenliest
dead that ever died so young!" Yes, and even though

"The Crown is withered, yet the Queendom lasts!"

There are countless more ruins of temples, and colonnades, and monumental columns, extending on all sides
— but I spare the reader any more; besides, that I
myself never got so far as to see the half of them.

Tadmor has been a good deal run down by those
who have not seen it, — the difficulties of getting there
are so great, that it was best to find out the grapes to
be fed on when there were sour; then it was thought a
good way of exalting Baalbek, to declare that even the
city of Adrianopolis was not to be compared to that of
Heliopolis: whereas, the fact is, that Tadmor is not
comparable with any single group of temples such as
Baalbek: there is scarcely another city in the world
standing, with its streets and public buildings still dis-

tinctly marked out, without a modern city overlying the
ancient one: it is not only a few temples, but a whole
city, once vast and complete: and thus Nineveh, Persepolis, and Thebes are, perhaps, its only prototypes. I
was once asked whether Palmyra was "not a broken-
down old thing in a style of slovenly decadence?" Of
course, its style is neither pure nor severe — nothing
over which the lavish hand of hasty and Imperial Rome
has passed is ever so: but Tadmor is free from all the
vulgarity of real decadence; it is so entirely irregular as to
be sometimes fantastic; the designs are overflowing with
richness and fancy, but it is never heavy — it is free,
independent, *bizarre*, but never ungraceful — grand,
indeed, though hardly sublime, it is almost always be-
witchingly beautiful.

The union of the square-and-round column in one —
one of the characteristics of Syrian architecture — is
commonly repeated; the chief ornaments employed are
the egg-and-rose moulding and the pine-cone, as I believe it is called usually: here, in the Colonnade frieze,
this ornament is like a succession of pine-apples; but it is
very difficult to see it distinctly, as, though much has
fallen within reach of examination, it is also much worn.
The pattern might be a representation of fish scales,
when it would be in connection with the worship of
Derceto, the mother of Ninus — one of the names of the
sun in Phœnicia, where a fish was an emblem commonly adopted for Baal; or perhaps it is a pattern
formed of the cone, under which form the Syrians
adored the sun, and also Jupiter; as the Paphians
adored Venus, mysteriously representing her in a pyramidal or flame-shaped stone. That the pine-cone was
a religious emblem throughout India and Assyria is
well known; it was sacred to Bacchus for the intoxi-

cating quality of its resin, with which the old Romans medicated their wines — the fiercely-burning, fiery characteristic of its balsam or resin was, it is supposed, used as a type of the life-giving properties of the sun. Of the Phœnicians one cannot help thinking in looking at Tadmor, — that platform chants the same mysterious strain as the platform of Baalbek ; and whether these " great stones, and costly stones, and hewed stones," date only from the mighty hands of King Solomon, or that they had stood there for ages before, when there were giants in the land, they must have had the same origin as those at Baalbek. The Phœnicians, or Canaanites, as they are usually called in Scripture, planted cities in the Haurân and the Lejah — may they not also have had a city here, by the abundant Desert spring, of which Solomon took advantage when he built his store-cities, "Baalath and Tadmor, in the wilderness "? It was, in fact, the bulwark or outpost of the kingdom of Israel, which extended to the banks of the Euphrates (Gen. xv. 18 ; Exod. xxiii. 31 ; 1 Kings iv. 21, 24), and had been built for the protection of his caravans bringing merchandise from India and Assyria.

At the foot of the range of hills we had crossed in arriving at Tadmor, and at the distance of a good mile from the furthest end of the Grand Colonnade, there is a hollow in which a little chasm opens, ending with a cave which is said to go some way underground, but which we could not explore, as we had brought no candles from Damascus. From this cave a stream comes bubbling quietly out — this is the Râs el 'Ain (the head of the fountain) — and from this the little river flows for about three miles before it is lost in the thirsty sand Nothing can be more limpid than this stream as it runs away over the little stones ; it has no other beauty save

TADMOR.

the clusters of brilliant sulphur which cover the rocks
of the chasm, for the water of the spring is saturated
with sulphur, and is of a very high temperature ; it had
cooled, and the taste of sulphur decreased, in the two
miles of its windings, before it reached the spot where
we encamped. Gardens and fruit trees cluster round
its banks, and shade the waters, and certainly the sulphur does not lessen the luxuriance of the trees: we
used to fill a large leathern bag, called a *zemzimeer*,
every morning, and hang it in the branches of one of
the trees — in a couple of hours the sulphur had precipitated itself, and the water was perfectly cold and
sweet. But before we left Tadmor, we thought that
the daily bathing in the hot stream, and the having no
other water to drink, had made us all feel weak and
languid. There were other causes for this feeling, however ; the year had been one of excessive drought and
consequent famine—the Desert pastures had all failed,
and there was but little food of any kind for the camels,
of whom vast numbers had died, and the town was
thickly strewn and surrounded with rotting carcases ;
for where they dropped down, the carcases were left —
the Tadmorites have an idea that the smell is whole-
some, and when they are sick, they go and sit beside
one of the putrid carcases to inhale the beneficial perfume! Inside the town, every one possessing a camel
keeps it, like the Irish pig, with the family in their
tent or hovel, or it lives outside the door, in the lane.
If the poor beast dies, there it stays, as if nothing had
happened ; and unhappily, because one year lately some
dogs went mad, the people shot them *all*, so that now
there are only vultures to do the scavenger's work, so
fearfully necessary everywhere, but especially under
the powerful Eastern sun. There were *scores* of car-

cases within the gates; and as we were walking along
the narrow lanes, especially once when darkness overtook us, it was impossible to avoid stumbling over and
crunching into the disgusting heaps, and stepping not
only over, but through them! It was only among the
ruins that we ever escaped the smell; and in spite of
the opinion of the Tadmor people, and of some French
medical philosophers, I am convinced that we all suffered seriously from the horrible stench — the whole
place was unhealthy. Several of our Argeels got fever,
and lay groaning and shivering by day and by night;
the Arab remedy for which disease—on the homœo-
pathic principle of "like curing like"—was to place
the unhappy patient, without any covering but his
ordinary clothes, to lie in the full blaze of the mid-day
sun! I need scarcely say that we did not observe any
beneficial results from this treatment.

The people of Tadmor are most unmitigated barba-
rians; they are Fellaheen of the lowest order, permitted
by the Bedoueens to live within the town, on condition of
their acting as purveyors for the tribes; the caravans from
Aleppo and Damascus to Baghdad all touch there, and
leave the kefiyehs and mash'lahs, &c., which the Bedoueen
requires: then they tend the groves and gardens along
the stream, one half of the fruit of which the Bedoueens
buy, and the other half they take.   They are a rough,
rude set, and have all the vices of the Bedoueen without any of his virtues. It was a perfect ordeal to go
even for a few moments inside the gates—men, women,
and children would instantly pour forth from their
hovels and mob us, examining our clothes, pulling us
about, trying to feel whether our arms and legs were
made of flesh and blood, like those of the Arabs, or of
some Western substance quite differently fashioned;

while they roared, screamed, and shouted in our ears enough to deafen us. One day that we wanted to climb up on one of the houses to see the view, the Sheikh of Tadmor himself accompanied us, and two of our Argeels, in hopes of keeping the peace—but it was entirely useless; the scrambling process was difficult enough of itself, and with the whole population swarming round us to see the show, not even the whip of the Sheikh, nor the sticks of the Argeels, had the slightest effect in clearing the way; several times they took us by the shoulders, and turned us round to see our faces; and more than once I received a heavy thump on my head — for the purpose, I believe, of ascertaining that I had a natural head under my large brown hat, which was in itself a source of high astonishment to the savages. So it is not to be wondered at that we only thrice endeavoured to see the inside of the town; nor that we turned deaf ears to the numerous enticing invitations from the Sheikh to dinner, as well as to the more serious offers made to my sister and myself. The morning after our arrival, in our first walk out to the ruins, a crowd of townspeople mobbed us in the Great Arch; and several men eagerly begged to know how much our relations would expect for us. In spite of the assurance that Frank women were never thus sold, they continued to bid for us; and after my shaking my head at some of their offers, one man enthusiastically rose to the sum of 10,000 piastres; but, like the fox in the fable, when told decidedly that he could not have me at any price, he turned away and said, " I would have offered another thousand if her eyes had been black ! "

The Sheikh of Tadmor himself held out tempting promises. He had already four wives, who occupied, he explained, one large room in his house, each one with

her family inhabiting a corner; but he was tired of one
of them, and would willingly get rid of her; and he
impressed upon us, with a bewitching air on his coarse,
ill-favoured countenance, that he did so much wish for
an Ingleez wife! he rose to the astonishing price of
nine camels, and added a tenth when he heard I was
a good rifle shot! He was a horrid savage, this Sheikh
Faras, cruel and mean, a very different character from
his brother, Sheikh 'Ali, who was set aside from the
Sheikhship on account of his being lame and deformed,
but who was the friend and adviser, the judge and con-
soler of all the townspeople: he could read and write,
and had a good deal of intelligence and quiet good
sense. A dreadful story was whispered to us of something Sheikh Faras had done a year or two before, when
the Anazehs were encamped round the town, but both
the Sheikhs were away in war: Faras stole about a score
of camels from the tribe, and was manufacturing a story
of how he had got them, prior to bringing them home,
when Sheikh Miguel unexpectedly returned to Tadmor;
and he could not find an excuse for going out through
the camp to the place where he had concealed them.
The war was suddenly concluded, and the Anazehs did
not move; four months after the miserable animals
were found by accident, tethered in a small deep hollow
as the wretch had left them. The poor creatures had
gnawed each other as they stood tied together, and the
skeletons, picked by the vultures, yet remained leaning
against each other, whitening in the sun!

There never had been known such a year of distress
as the present one in this Desert. To the south of
Tadmor, at this season, it is generally green with herbs,
affording pasture to the camels: now it was all parched
and burned up; and though towards the east some of

the ground appeared green and smiling at a distance, the herb was not high enough to be browsed on by any animal. Scarcely any rain had fallen in the preceding winter; the torrent-beds remained dry, and the ground unsoftened: now even the wells and springs were dry also. Another such year, they said, would be absolute destruction to the tribes, and their hearts were very sad and heavy; for the time of the early rains had come, but none had as yet fallen. The Anazehs, as I have said, had gone eastwards, in hopes of finding pasture; but the camels were so weak and so few, from the frightful mortality among them, that great numbers of their women had been left in the town of Tadmor to get on as well as they could till the next spring; those women and children who had gone with the tribe had most of them walked, leaving their "carriages" behind them. These carriages, or *howdahs,* are wooden frame-works, covered with scarlet cloth, and gaily ornamented with ostrich feathers and shells, placed over the back of the camel for the women and children to be carried in; but this year the camels' humps were so reduced that the howdahs could not be fastened on, and the weak legs had to be spared all unnecessary burden. All this distress falls most heavily on the Sheikh; for should one of the Bedoueens lose his camels—their only wealth—the Sheikh must set the example of giving him one of his own, and those who have most contribute in order after him, until the poor man has again as much as he had lost. The Sheikh is essentially the father of his people; and in years of distress, when he has many losses among his own camels, and has to share what he has with those who are poor, he is sometimes reduced really to poverty. In time of war the Sheikh takes, by right, a large proportion of the spoil: at other times

what a man gains by his own prowess he is entitled to
keep, though he generally makes an offering of some
part of it to the Sheikh. One evening, just at dark,
when we were seated round our dinner, a heavy
cloud broke into rain : we hastily concluded the soon-
diluted soup, and retreated under our carpets; but the
Sheikh ran joyfully up the bank, and stood there with
a light heart, watching the clouds, and listening to the
thunder as sweet music, praising Allah for His goodness, and calling out to assure us that we should have
a thorough wet night! We were as glad as *possible*,
under the circumstances — all the more as we had fortunately that day purchased a nice, thick Tadmor
carpet, which, however, did not prevent the rain from
soaking down in little lakes underneath us. But the
next morning all was dry; it had rained but an hour or
two, and the Sheikh was as sad as ever: "Mash-
allah! it is God's will," was all he said, with the submission and acquiescence, not fatalism only, of a really
good Mooslim, "and He knows best!" The very next
day we heard a dreadful story. Some Arabs came in
from a journey they had been making, and told the
Sheikh that not very far from Tadmor, only three or
four days' journey, they had come to an encampment of
black Bedoueen tents. They rode on and on, and were
surprised at hearing no barking of dogs — still more at
seeing no smoke from the cooking fires. Puzzled, and
wondering what it could mean, they reached the tents
— still the same silence, and not a moving thing to be
seen. At last they dismounted, stuck their lances in
the ground, and entered one of the tents, with the cus-
tomary " Peace be to all here : " it was peace indeed ;
for, lying on the ground, were stretched the corpses of
women and children in every tent of the encampment! It

was an encampment of the dead! Their husbands and
fathers had left them, to seek food and water; but they
never returned, and were afterwards found at various
distances, strewn about, as they had dropped by the way,
lying dead beside their dead camels!

We heard while at Tadmor (for he never told us any
stories about himself), two anecdotes, among many
others, of Sheikh Miguel, characteristic of the courage
and daring for which he is so justly noted, — the real,
cool courage, free from all Arab boast or bluster. Some
hostile Arabs of another tribe came down one night
last winter, and stole all the cattle of the Tadmor
townspeople: Sheikh Miguel was staying there at the
time *en passant*, just as he was now staying there for
us; but of course the affair was no concern of his; nor
do the Bedoueens like interfering with each other's
quarrels. So he sat in his tent smoking, not thinking
to be mixed up in it, when Sheikh Faras and some of
the Tadmorites came and petitioned for his help. He
could not resist the appeal of distress, for he is a
generous and most kind-hearted man, and in a few
moments he rose up and mounted his mare. Then
turning round quietly to the Sheikh of Tadmor and
his companions — great blusterers and little doers — he
said, " You can keep in the valley; I will go up yonder
mountain and bring back the cattle." He galloped off,
and before long caught sight of the cattle, collected together, and guarded by seven or eight men. Though
perfectly alone, he rode straight up to them, and demanded in a loud voice, " How dare you take cattle
when I am here?" and fired off his revolver among
them. In a moment the whole set of men ran off,
and the Sheikh quietly drove back all the cattle himself
to the town!

Another time he happened to be quite alone with several camels and a large flock of goats, when a *Ghuzoo* appeared in sight at a distance : away flew the Sheikh on his swift steed directly towards them, beckoning with his hand as if encouraging those behind him to follow, and singing his own war-songs very loud. They recognised him on hearing them, and the whole body turned about, took to their heels, and fled away !

We had not as much of Sheikh Miguel's society during our stay at Tadmor as we should have liked; by sunrise we were all out in different directions — sightseeing, curiosity-hunting, and sketching; and though we took refuge in our pretty shady garden during the mid-day heat, he was then always settling business in the town, or surrounded by visitors and friends who came down to our encampment. The Bedoueens have little curiosity, thinking few people worth as much consideration as themselves; but the townspeople were glad enough of the excuse to come down and stare at the Frank ladies, asking endless questions about everything, and, if they could get an opportunity, feeling our dresses, inquiring how much they were worth, &c. &c.; they also particularly enjoyed seeing us eat, just as we visit the Zoological Gardens at home at feeding time. We fed indeed on much the same food as themselves, — Arab bread, which is always good when fresh, and, morning and evening, a fowl stewed in a basin of dhourra, called *bourghoul*, with sometimes a few dates; but the grand curiosity was seeing us all eat together, — for, with the Arabs, the men and women always feed separately, — besides the astonishing knives and forks that we used. They brought down quantities of curiosities to sell us; unfortunately they have begun to learn their real value, and where they used to ask a piaster they now demand

a mejidi, and as often price bits of natural stone or
pebbles quite as high as the real antiques.　Sometimes
these trifles are of as much value to *them* as the best
antiques; for instance, a black stone marked with a
cross in any way, is called a "luck-stone," and insures
to the fortunate owner the fidelity and warm affection
of her husband or lover as long as she possesses the
stone.　Anything bright or pretty they string together
in long necklaces, with coins, &c., and sometimes they,
unconsciously, possess very beautiful and valuable things
among the veriest rubbish.　Several women had some
beautifully engraved gems and cameos, with which,
however, they would not part at any reasonable price ;
some ancient gold coins, and many small square pieces
of stone, or some composition, with figures impressed
upon them, which are supposed to have been Palmyrene
weights, and have been picked up in great numbers in
the ruins where the private houses of the city stood ;
they have also numbers of coral and agate beads, and
sometimes some good uncut jewels, picked up generally
near Baghdad.　We were always looking out among the
women's necklaces for the small Assyrian cylinders,
some of the best of which have been so discovered; and
one day the Sheikh took us into the town to the house
of one of the richest women to see a cylinder she had,
and which he thought she might be induced to sell to
us.　We made our way into a large windowless room,
full of smoke, in which the mistress was weaving one of
the excellent carpets the Tadmor people make, of
brightly dyed camels' hair, thick and close, striped
with pretty patterns.　Of course we were soon in the
midst of a crowd, with all the women trying as usual to
kiss us — a hobby of theirs, that cost us a great deal of
trouble in dodging round each other and making in-

genious escapes. At last she brought the necklace with
the cylinder of pale pink carnelian, cut with several Assyrian devices, one of them a priest in the act of making
offerings on an altar before the sun. Seeing how much
we were interested in it, she asked *un prix fou*, and
we went off to pay a promised visit to Sheikh 'Ali, the
Moollah of the mosque, who gave us coffee in a clean
nice room — the only clean one we saw in Tadmor — and
insisted on our dining some day with him, enumerating
on his fingers the various dishes he would provide for
our entertainment. He was an intelligent old man, and
seemed respected, for he was able to keep the crowd
from tormenting us; and after some days he induced
the woman to give us the cylinder at a reasonable price.
We had the good fortune to issue from the great gate
of the town just as Sheikh Faras was coming in mounted
on his finest mare, a grey of beautiful and splendid
form. She was considered priceless, and he would not
have sold her for any sum; but Sheikh Miguel said if
any misfortune *obliged* him to part with her, he would
probably value her at 1800*l*. . Very beautiful she was;
and it was as great a surprise as pleasure when, in a fit
of intense and very unusual politeness, he offered one of
the gentlemen of our party to mount her. There was
no bridle of any kind, but he vaulted on her back, and
the fleet creature was off like an arrow, and out of sight
in a moment, over the heaps of loose stones and ruins
without a check or stumble, while the Sheikh stood in
the most amusing anxiety watching for his return and
saying, "Where is he gone? how far will he go?" as if
he thought her rider would run away with the beautiful
creature in the wide Desert: I believe he would gladly
have done so, so delightful was her pace and her extraordinary fleetness. When he came back, the Sheikh

actually offered my sister and me to ride also — a high
honour, which we declined very unwillingly, not being accustomed to a Turkish saddle; but we were much pene-
trated with the compliment, as, among themselves, it is the
greatest indignity for a mare to be mounted by a woman.

The Sheikh's pretty little son, a child of about eight
years old, was riding home another spirited, gentle mare,
with beautiful legs and a fine small head, and some of his
followers were careering about, brandishing their long
lances, while we lingered at the gate of the great Temple
till the sun had sunk and left us in the dark; but this
grand double gateway — one, of the now old Saracenic
work, and the other, the still older structure of Imperial
Rome — always interested us so much that we were apt to
delay beneath its shadow. It was such a curious feeling to
stand here in the very narrow space between the two
lofty walls, looking through the inner one to the Temple
columns towering up within, lighted up with the dying
sun, and to think back over the magnificent processions
of worshippers that had so often gone up here to the
Temple of Baal — venerable priests and eager devotees,
and the kings who reigned here sovereigns of the Desert;
and, in the centre of all, Zenobia, the proud empress,
coming from her palace all down that pillar-shaded
Colonnade, in her jewels and her beauty, entering at this
very portal to bend her knee before Apollo's shrine; —
while all the time our eyes watched the stream of
modern life continually passing through — modern and
savage, yet probably but little changed in appearance
from that of the ancient inhabitants of this Desert, carrying one's mind back, far beyond the proud Roman, to
Scriptural pictures of camels and sheep and goats, and
the Arabs, in their simple and probably unaltered dress,
like the fierce, robber-looking son of Ishmael, plentifully

armed, as though " his hand was against every man,"—
and we, the children of the far West and of to-day,
standing there in the shadow of the Roman and the Arab,
among the desolation of *all* the Past, and the degrada-
tion of the Present, gathering up all in one shadowy
Thought, — the only eternal thing in the whole scene.

And so, thinking over the long past, we will go and
visit the Tombs of Tadmor — very interesting indeed
they are. There are two sets of them : some, far away on
the sides of the mountain, are, like the " Bride's Tomb "
before mentioned, built in the form of towers; the
others are almost entirely underground excavations,
with a few towers scattered among them, now so much
ruined as to be little worth examination : these underground tombs are supposed to be those of the people —
the towers, those of the nobles. They are all built in
successive stories, usually four in number, sometimes
more; the form invariably pyramidal, though in some
cases with interrupting stories, of perpendicular sides.
Inside, in each story, a narrow passage or chamber
runs across from end to end, with three or four compartments or cells on each side, each cell containing
stone shelves for the bodies, which seem to have been
run in on grooves when required, as the shelves were
wanting in many instances. A pyramidal-shaped opening led into a cell at the end of each chamber, originally closed by a stone door ; and in some of the larger
tombs this opened into other chambers. The compartments were separated by pilasters, and in one instance
by fluted columns with very peculiar acanthus-leaved
capitals. Staircases, usually still perfect, led from one
story to another ; and, strangely enough, in some instances, on the second story, where the end cell was wanting, there was a doorway, high above the ground like

those in the Round Towers of Ireland; the stone hinges for the door, and the hollow for the bolt, yet remained.

The ceilings of most of the chambers were richly ornamented with graceful patterns geometrically arranged, and many of them are still very perfect. In one Tomb the ceiling was divided into diamond-shaped compartments, those in the centre contained sculptures of winged genii, and the others held busts in high relief. Very rich cornices surround each chamber, and are frequently employed on the outside of the tomb also. In one there was a handsome variety of the egg-and-rose ornament, with a battlemented moulding above and below; all were delicately but vigorously executed. Each cell has its own loophole for ventilation.

In the inside of one chamber, over the doorway, we saw the sculptured representation of a mummy placed on a sofa with carved legs; the foldings of the cloth, with which the mummy was swathed, very distinctly shown, and the body garlanded with an embroidered band or wreath of flowers. The exterior of another Tomb was distinguished on the second story by a pediment, and on the third or fourth story a tablet for an inscription, guarded or supported on either side by the head of an aged man with a long beard—beautiful heads and finely executed; like old Greek busts of grand, calm, restful, mighty faces — with closed eyes, which one fancied seemed yet silently conscious of the unnumbered ages that have passed over them, and have left there an expression of grief, but also of noble, perfect rest—mingled into glorious harmony "of more than human beauty." Above these, again, were two kneeling figures, much destroyed, whether of men or women we could not tell; on a still higher story two small heads, with wings folded back, perfect and well sculptured; and on the highest story of all, a row of small pillars and a cornice.

Outside the second story of another Tower was an arched recess, with a fine band of vine-leaves and grapes moulded round it. Within the recess lay the figure of a mummy, reposing on a carved sofa; and above that another figure, in a half-reclining posture, with three other figures standing behind it, all in good relief,—the heads had been knocked off every one. A Palmyrene inscription is here carved under the couch; these in-scriptions, containing the names of the dead and a date, are usually placed outside the Tombs, and are very fre-quently both in Palmyrene and in Greek. All that have been found are prior to the date of Aurelian's con-quest, and many of them date about the commencement of our era. The Tombs are mostly lined with white stucco, on which a good deal of colouring remains.

The score of tower Tombs, scattered among the under-ground Tombs in the other cemetery, near the Râs el 'Ain, are believed to be of older date than these; but they are so much ruined, and so much encumbered with sand, that they are scarcely comprehensible — many of them have been patched with more modern construc-tions. In one of them we discovered two headless sta-tues, life-size, represented on one stone — husband and wife, as it were, sitting together—the male leaning back in a carved arm-chair; the female in a more reclining position, as if on a sofa, her left hand on the shoulder of her husband, and holding in her right a pine-cone like those so common in the Nineveh marbles; both are attired in graceful many-folded drapery, with rich bands of embroidery and jewels down the fronts and round the shoulders and necks of the dresses; the drapery is gathered lower down into embroidered boots.

The arrangement of the excavated Tombs is simply that of a passage or passages, with a tunnel vault over-

ENTRANCE

head, usually four cells on each side, and three at the end of the passage. The whole of this hill may be honeycombed with these Tombs, concealed in the long accumulation of sand; those that are known have been discovered by such accidents as that of a camel falling into a hole, which proved to be the hollow before the entrance, or gazelles escaping into the Tomb from the chase of the hunter; many of the Tower Tombs are full of gazelles' bones and horns strewn on the ground. In all the Tombs we saw heaps of human bones, but tossed together—thrown away after the mummy-cloth had been unrolled from the bodies; for the Bedoueens set great store by this gummy cloth, with the old spices still adhering to it, to use as plaisters for their sick horses. We saw no bodies yet lying there, but the Sheikh told us he had seen many; and there is no question but that in numbers of the upper stories, now inaccessible from broken staircases, or in the Tombs below the present surface of the ground, vast numbers of mummies must still lie untouched. The Sheikh mentioned having seen some in perfect condition with bronze lamps on their bosoms; and many gold ornaments have been found in them, some of which are now worn by the Bedoueen and Tadmor women; we remarked,

indeed, how much more elegant and tasteful some of
their ornaments were than the usual run of Arab women's things.

These Tombs are all far away from the ruins and the
town, and stand on the sides of a sand-blown valley.
The dead calm, the lonely silence, and the utter desolation of the place are very striking, — and to the most
thoughtless, sitting there among the dead, and looking
out over that grand and lovely view, a thousand painfully interesting thoughts and questions cannot but be
suggested. The illimitable Desert spread out beyond
the mass of once luxurious Palaces, crowded Temples,
and busy streets, with these Tombs full of fleshless
bones, that seemed no further removed from life than
the now empty, ruined buildings, alike wrapped in the
same mantle of deathly silence — the warrior, the ruler,
the merchant, the prince, and the people — all now
swept away, with only the shadow of the shadow, as it
were, of their earthly glory yet remaining ! Where are
their immortal souls now stored, waiting the great Day
of Account ? And what has He, the All-merciful, in
store for those who knew not His revelation, nor His
gracious Promise, nor even of His imposed Laws ?
What shall be the portion reserved for guiltless ignorance ? The answer of unwavering trust, even in such
unfathomable mystery, came in the wide-stretching
Desert all around us, boundless as His Mercy ; in the
unmeasured sky above, trackless and incomprehensible
as the mystery of Eternity ; and in the all-glorious colouring in which that scene was clothed, by the Hand
of Love that showers Mercy and Blessing alike upon
the evil and the good; and who will one day " bring
the nations " into the city which will need nor sun nor
moon, for the " glory of God " will lighten it.

To make up for our terrible disappointment in not seeing the Anazehs, the Sheikh good-naturedly told us a variety of customs common among them, and one evening we got him to describe their favourite "sabre dance." The men stand close together in a half circle, elbow touching elbow, jerking themselves quickly to and fro in concert with a sideway movement, while a woman, generally the wife of the Sheikh, stands alone in the middle, swinging a sabre rapidly round and round in her hand. From time to time one or another of the men darts forward, and pretends to seize the hem of her dress. If the woman is awkward, or the man not excessively agile, a hand or a finger is cut off, or a wound of some kind given; and these accidents frequently occur, — in spite of which they are very fond of the dance: it requires, of course, great nerve and skill on the part of the woman; but the women of the tribe are not wanting in these virtues. In time of war a curious custom prevails among them. The most beautiful woman of the tribe, or rather she who combines with this most sense and courage, and has therefore most influence among them, is placed on a camel which is adorned with colours, scarlet cloth, shells, feathers, &c. The camel is then led out among the warriors, and placed in the very thickest of the fight, where the woman remains, inspiriting and encouraging them by her songs and her exhortations. At the conclusion of the battle, whoever has fought the best comes to her, and with his sabre cuts through all the legs of the unfortunate camel, when of course the woman is precipitated to the ground. If this valiant man is one of her own people she is his lawful prize and well-earned wife; but if the enemy are the conquerors she is taken away by them, and must afterwards be ransomed. A married woman is very rarely selected, never but when an un-married girl cannot be found sufficiently courageous and spirited ; but this is very seldom the case. While she is thus placed on the field of battle, the rest of the women guard the tents, assisting in the fight as much as possible with stones, which they are most expert in throwing. If their enemies are the conquerors, they are quickly expelled, and their tents plundered and stripped of everything in a moment; but if their own people win the fight, the women instantly rush out to the tents of the defeated and strip them ; it is the women always who are employed as plunderers of the tents.

When the warrior returns from a distant fight, it is the invariable custom that his own tent is the last he comes to, and in this tent the wife must remain : brothers, sisters, every one in the encampment goes out to meet him, but the wife *must* await the meeting with her husband till all the others have seen him. It is sometimes a hard rule to keep, for there is much love among them ; but any deviation from it would be con-sidered a great breach of propriety.

When a woman is newly married, she is, a few days after, dressed out in her best attire, with all her richest ornaments, and taken round by her husband to visit every tent in the tribe, or at least in the encampment, in turn. She has to drink coffee with every one, in token of their friendliness and acceptance of her as a wife among them. Nor is the choice of a wife quite so simple an affair among them as we are apt to imagine. The Anazehs are exceedingly proud, and particular to an extreme degree about descent and pedigree. The rank of husband and wife must be equal; and if marriage with a stranger is in question, there is as much search and inquiry made about the age of the family and the pureness of her descent as in the case of any Spanish grandee; and if every step in the pedigree is not satisfactorily ascertained, the engagement is broken off. We saw one girl at Tadmor, who was really extremely pretty, with soft sweet eyes and long black hair reaching to the ground. She was immensely admired by and spoken of among the Bedoueens who frequented the town; she was of a good station among her own people, and not a word had ever been whispered against her,— but she belonged to a tribe which the proud Anazehs consider inferior to their own, and not a man among them would think of marrying her. The true-blooded Bedoueen, in fact, values no one but one of themselves; and to marry a woman *not* a *Bedoueen*, is considered a grave dishonour, and expulsion from the tribe is almost invariably the consequence; moreover a Bedoueen man of a high tribe, such as the Anazehs and Shemmaars, &c., would think himself utterly degraded if he condescended to dishonour a woman of any other race, blood, or religion but his own; stranger women, prisoners in their hands, would be made to labour and possibly hardly treated, but they would be safe to the last from dishonour or insult. The real Bedoueens are not in the least affected by any display of dress, or ornaments, or riches, or rank in any one out of their own tribes. We were told of a Pasha who had charge of some Government negotiations with one of the more northern tribes, who was exceedingly surprised that no one but those commissioned to deal with him, had the curiosity to come out and look at him. He had taken great pains to attire himself grandly, and to have his standing and rank duly blazoned forth among them; but he had the mortification of finding they did not care one jot about it at all, or value it in the least.

The most flattering description a Bedoueen can give of a woman, is that " she has hair like a mare's tail," and " a neck like a camel's." We wished to have heard more of their love-songs, but translation is very difficult in Arab songs, where much depends upon the play of words, and even of letters ; and it is scarcely possible for any foreigners, however fluent in the language, to enter into the beauties of the verses ; but they are all extremely fond of poetry, and we used to like to listen to them, sitting round their fire every evening reciting and singing song after song, while one of the party ground coffee in a mortar, beating time, as all expert coffee pounders do, with the pestle, in a tuneful cadence. Many a night we went to sleep to that pretty, quiet music. They have as many love-songs as war-songs, and often they recount the exploits and describe the beauties of a favourite mare, sometimes of a camel ; but there is never anything coarse in their songs, as, almost always, in the songs of Egypt ; nor even in the talk of the men among themselves, as they sit chatting together, is there ever a word which a woman need blush to hear.

Unfaithfulness on the part of a wife is immediately and invariably punished by death ; her head is cut off, if not by her husband, by her father or brother; her crime is looked on as the dishonour of her whole house and family, and by them must be wiped out.

The Anazeh women have not good tempers, and the men do not consider them patient or gentle enough to be fit to milk the dear and precious camels; this office is, therefore, always performed by the men. But they are allowed to ride them, and are most expert and fearless in doing; so it is very pretty to see them mount, which they are accustomed to do without stopping the camel; they place one arm on his neck, which he bends down as he walks along, and then, resting one foot for a second on his knee as he crooks it forward, they spring up standing on his neck, and so get into their places, the camel assisting them with a little jerk for the second jump; they are quite at ease when mounted, and think nothing of standing upright on his back, settling their children in the *howdahs* as he strides along. We could not hear that they had medicine of any kind for the camels when sick; and all they do in cases of sores is to burn the flesh round the sore with a hot iron, — an operation we were twice obliged to witness, to our own sorrow.

The dress of the Anazeh women consists of a long robe or chemise of dark blue cotton, reaching from the throat to the feet, and confined by a belt of embroidered leather; over this a *kumbaz* or pelisse of some bright colour in silk or cotton, according to the wealth of the wearer; yellow leather boots if she is rich, and as handsome a necklace of varieties of things strung together as she can obtain; over this a mash'lah of white or striped camel's-hair cloth, which must, as well as her kumbaz and chemise, be long enough to hide her feet, and the sleeves of the blue chemise must also be long enough to trail on the ground behind her; she ties up the ends when busy. On her head she wears, if she is rich, triangular gold ornaments hung at each side of her face, with from ten to twenty short gold chains and coins depending from them; long ear-rings, and, in "full dress," a nose-ring, generally of turquoise; her veil, called the *shembar*, which is placed across her face close under her eyes, and reaches to her knee, is of dark brown crape, and she wears a gay silk kefiyeh over it, bound with a rope of dyed camel's hair prettily twisted up. Zenobia is a common name among them to this day; they pro-

nounce it *Zenobēeah*, which is said to be the original
pronunciation. They have mostly black hair, but the
lighter and redder it is, of course the more it is admired,
and they are always washing it with *henna* to give it a
red tinge. They use *kho'hl* on the eyes, and all the
Bedoueen men use it also; it is considered a great pre-
servative in the glaring sun, and I certainly found it
very cool and pleasant on the lids, keeping them from
blisters. If a Bedoueen woman appeared without *kho'hl*
on her eyes, she would be thought as untidy and un-
dressed as an Englishwoman without shoes, and they
always have a little bottle containing the *kho'hl* close at
hand *: there is a great knack in putting it on; the
eyelids are closed lightly upon the freshly-blacked pin,
which is drawn quickly from between them, blacking
the edges of both lids at the same moment. The use of
kho'hl has been always general in the East: Herod the
Great, we are told, painted his eyes with kho'hl, and
also dyed his beard and hair with *henna;* but it was
considered very effeminate, and St. Cyprian indignantly
denounces it as "the devil's grease."

They are very much afraid of the "evil eye," and the
women wear certain round stones hung to their waist-
bands to preserve them from such a misfortune. They
have generally a number of silver bracelets, which come
from Baghdad, and the name of their husband is invariably tatooed upon the back of the left hand. A line
upon the temples and the chin is all the face-tatooing
in which they usually indulge; and they express great
surprise at our dislike to it, as their idea is that it

* *Keren-happuch*, the name of one of the beautiful daughters with
whom Job was rewarded for his patience, is the Hebrew word for the
little bottle containing the *kho'hl*.

imitates the blue veins showing through the skin, and is therefore a natural ornament.

There was an old hag of a woman at Tadmor, who was much considered by the townspeople, on account of her having twice made the pilgrimage to Mekka; she was in consequence called Hajji Elleerieh—but we called her "Meg Merrilies!" She was the greatest chatterbox woman could be, and had quantities of legends and stories to relate. She was a very successful curiosity-finder, and we used to take her out with us sometimes, when we went hunting along the ground where the ancient houses had stood, in hopes of finding coins, bits of porcelain and glass, &c. One day, when she saw me busy cleaning a pretty little pebble I had found, she began with, "Oh, lady! I have found something much prettier than that; it must needs be a stone belonging to some *jinns*, for I never saw anything like it before." She would not for a long time tell us any more about the wonderful stone; she said she was afraid, and she knew we should not believe her if she told us all she had seen: however, after a whole day's coaxing and flattering, she told us that she had been out, one day, among the ruins of Zenobia's Palace, not long before, about mid-day, when, the sun being very hot, she sat down by a low wall to rest; presently she heard the hissing of serpents close to her, and turning her head to look over the wall, she saw, at a few yards off, two serpents fighting; their heads were curved far back, as their bodies glided and wriggled about, facing each other; and every now and then they would dart like lightning one at the other, each trying to seize his enemy's head. At last one gave the other a mortal bite, and he fell prostrate and bleeding on the sand. Then she made a noise, and the victor glided frightened away, while she went

to look at the dead snake, curious to see for what they
had been fighting. And lo! out of his mouth came the
apple of discord—this little white stone! and she opened
her hand, and showed us a large, round pearl; a costly
one in any place, but doubly valuable in my eyes with
this marvellous tale attached to it, and, above all, for
having been picked up in Zenobia's Palace. The Bedoueens did not know it was a jewel, nor had any of
them ever seen a pearl before; and as it is too fine a
pearl to have belonged to any traveller passing by, I
am morally convinced, and always shall be, that this
identical pearl was dropped off the necklace of the
beautiful Zenobia herself, just before she left Palmyra
— for ever! I need not say that we bought the pearl.
The Sheikh said that, although the old woman was a
great rhodomontader, he did not think the story of the
serpents untrue; it was not a story that she would have
invented, and he had himself more than once seen serpents fighting in the manner she described for some
such article as a bit of stone.

One of the gentlemen of our party was anxious to
get up to the fine Saracenic castle which overlooks the
town, and Meg Merrilies offered to show him the way;
so one afternoon they set off together by a path that she
assured him was quite feasible: she missed it, however,
and after two or three hours' walk they arrived at the
foot of an almost perpendicular cliff. She wanted to go
back, but he insisted on going on, and, taking off his
shoes, he managed, being an expert Alpine climber, to
ascend the rock. She scrambled after him by another
way, a long time after, holding on with her long hands,
which were like eagle's claws. He entered by a loophole, for, though the castle is nearly quite perfect, the
drawbridge and all legitimate entrance is destroyed.

He described it as the gloomiest castle he had ever seen, with numerous vaulted chambers and extensive dungeons, occupying a very strong position. Meg Merrilies most unwillingly followed him, and kept on exhorting and conjuring him "not to be afraid of the jinns," of whom she was herself evidently in mortal terror, and when she came down she gave us a most lively account of all the trouble she had had in persuading him to go on, describing his misery and dread of the awful jinns, and all she had done to soothe and comfort him! She would stop on the way down the mountain continually to gather the potash plant, and when she had got a good bundle in her veil, she addressed him with, "Oh, young man, in the flower of thy blooming youth! carry this load on thy back for me, for thou art young and strong, and I am old, — and then I will *perhaps* give thee part of the profits of my bundle!" He good-naturedly helped her, but her version of the story to us was, that he was so completely worn out with fatigue and terror that she was obliged to carry the "welled "* (who is about six feet high) on her back for a long distance. To this castle, in seasons of drought, the people of Tadmor go in grand procession, dressed in their best clothes, and when there they sacrifice a lamb, and offer up prayers for rain.

Our promised five days had expired, but most reluctant were we to leave the enchanting spot; every day new points of view were to be seen, other tombs to be examined, and fresh sketches to be taken; so we made a joint petition in due form to our good Sheikh for leave to stay longer; he was, as usual, full of kind desire to accede to our wishes. The tribe was indeed

* "Young man."

gone, but he had heard of nothing but peace round the place, and if we liked to stay we might do so as far as he was concerned; but the matter was more difficult with the Argeels,—they earned more per day in Damascus than we gave them, and, the time of our contract having expired, they wanted to go back. We made them a handsome present, however, to be divided among them, as well as ten piasters a day for the food of each camel, and they agreed to stay a few days more.

Our English ideas of the Desert—the expression we use for the *ne plus ultra* of all that is horrible—are so vague and so unlike the truth, that I despair of making any one understand by words alone the exceeding and glorious beauty of the scene around us. At home we think of the Desert like a white sea of gloomy though glaring barrenness *, a wearying monotony of ugliness; instead of which no scene in nature can be clothed in more brilliant, more varied, or more quickly changing colours. In the narrow space between the foreground and the horizon, when laid down on paper, no brush could ever be made to lay in the countless streak after streak of colours filling up that space; in despair of catching them by any other means, I have scribbled down upon the margins of my drawings a score of descriptions of the view at that moment before me,—such as this, beginning with the foreground:—"Brown, dark red, violet, lilac, gold, rose, crimson, pale green, orange, indigo-blue, sky-blue;" these all blending into delicious, strange, incalculable harmonies, ever and ever changing, —every effect seemed the most beautiful, and one

---

* Many of the Deserts of Africa are, I believe, like this: where the sand is loose, and consequently wind-blown, of course nothing can grow; in the Great Desert the sand binds, and much of the varied colouring is owing to the appearance of the thorns, &c., growing upon it.

wished it to last for ever, — when, in another two minutes, all would be changed into something so much
lovelier still, one never knew whether one admired or
wondered the most. Many and many a time, anxious
though I was to draw all I could, my pencil stood still
in my hand while I was engrossed in watching the rapid
and beautiful changes which no brush could copy and
no tongue describe. Then the mountains that approach
Tadmor on one side, would shine out in shades of violet,
purple, and a delicate misty lilac, of such brilliant hues
that one felt startled at the sight; and, late in the day,
the Ruins used to look literally like things built of pearls
set in burnished gold, as they stood against the background of wine-empurpled mountains, or, as sometimes,
on one of the fine dark stormy evenings we had, against
a sky of deep sapphire blue, unlightened by the sunshine
which touched accidentally on their fair whiteness only;
it seemed, indeed, to my fancy, as if the Ruins sometimes
in the very intensity of their glowing colours, found a
silent voice, unheard by the ear, but understood by the
mind that listened to their " eloquent teachings," — as
if they were the clear upper notes, the sweet treble of
the deep harmony evoked all around in the sublime
colouring of Nature. Holy and noble indeed are these
colours, which God has given to clothe and invest his
creation : " of all God's gifts to the sight of man, the
holiest, the most divine, the most solemn,"* and they
who see the fair things in the Desert in their most radiant brilliancy, as though they were fresher there from
the Creator's hand than in any other place, may well
fancy with me that one heard them saying—

* Ruskin.

"Though heedless man might quite forget Thy praise,
We praised Thee; and at rise and set of sun
Did we assemble duly, and intone
A choral hymn that all the lands might hear. . . .
We, the Seven Daughters of the Light, to praise
Thee, Light of Light! Thee, God of very God!" *

I often thought too of the legend, which may be truth, of how Solomon built a palace here for the daughter of Pionkh, King of Egypt, who sighed for her native deserts even among the fair palaces and gardens round about the hill of Zion, and how she dwelt here in the Desert, so like and yet so unlike her own grand, wild, and impressive wilderness of sand; the one grand in barrenness and desolation, the other sublime in beauty and loveliness. The sky, indeed, was the same over both — unclouded and serene, and with that most exquisitely lovely hue that ever earth has seen; and what must not that sky have been to the men of those early days, with simple minds but high thoughts, who, intimately per- suaded that directly behind its slight though ever un- drawn veil Jehovah and all His angels were assembled in awful majesty, "looked upon every cloud that passed as literally the chariot of an angel, and every ray of the morning and the evening as streaming from the throne of God!"† No wonder, in truth, that they worshipped that sun, from whose light and warmth all generation seemed to proceed, as God, or at least the chief token of God; more wonder if they had not done so; and no wonder either that, when they raised such buildings to His honour, and filled them with the shining gold and the ivory, and the gems and the incense, and all that could intoxicate and enchant the senses, the rough and rude-minded son of the Desert asked no question and

* Maynard.   † Ruskin.

wondered no more, but fell prostrate in awe-struck adoration before the shrine of Baal!

Here, too, most probably came the Magians of old, passionately craving after and yearning for light — a light more tangible and nearer to their hearts than the purely spiritual religion they had been taught to follow — with their pulses beating high, and their hearts big with expectation and hope, which the Divine spark was working out within them, as they followed the Star which their science had told them must have brought a message to them — a high and holy and solemn messenger, which they reverently followed, not pausing in their sacred journey even at this famed and beauteous shrine; but, laden with the best that they had, the poor outward symbols of that which was better within, they followed steadily on till the beautiful angel of the Lord (as they in their simple creed believed that Star to be) stopped above the low hills of Judæa, and, with the unquestioning, childlike humility of the true philosopher, they, the great priests, the Wise Men of the East, knelt down with exceeding joy before the little Child, and recognised in Him the Divine Man, the day-spring of a new and brighter day, which should give light, not to the children of Abraham only, but to all those who "sat in darkness and in the shadow of death," and would "guide their feet into the way of peace."

M. Haag's beautiful sketches proceeded with great rapidity: the people molested him very little, and I am certain some of those who did see him at work, believed that his drawings were done by magic. It was a great thing to get out of the way of the rude curiosity of the townspeople; for though we always had a man of the town or one of the Argeels for our protection wherever we went, they bored us dreadfully whenever we were

within reach. My companion was generally a fine
young Bedoueen, so very black, but so erect and handsome, that we called him " Black Adonis." He used to
lie on the sand close to me while I drew, twisting up
and smoking cigarettes; but after a day or two he began
to be interested in my performances, and got nearer
and nearer: at last I was very much amused to find
him gazing intently over my shoulder, looking up when
I did, and watching my pencil as it moved. I doubted
that he really understood the picture, and, to prove him,
I made a long line which did not exist in nature, when
a deep grunt just at my ear startled me into a sense of
my error : I rubbed it out, and was rewarded with a
" taïb, taïb;" and for the next three hours that young
savage sat there, forgetting to smoke, looking on with
the deepest attention, keeping up a running accom-
paniment of grunts, and rebuking me with an indignant
"la, la " (no, no), when I put in a figure that I had
seen sitting there the day before, but which was not
there now. At last I gave him a bit of paper and a
pencil, and said "ente amel soora" (you make a picture),—he burst into a long, low, grave chuckle, and
said "Anazeh fingers too big;" but we were fast friends
ever after: and I heard him relating my invitation to
his fingers, with much gusto, that night round the evening fire.

One afternoon my sister and I went out together, with
only the guide, a Tadmor man, to carry our sketch-
books, and stationed ourselves at the Temple of the
King's Mother. Beyond this neither man nor woman
of the town would go alone after dusk; they said the
place was full of jinns,—but the jinns were of flesh and
blood: stray Bedoueens of small tribes might be, and
were almost always, lurking about to plunder any thing

or person they could find, and they were gentlemen not
to be lightly adventured with. We had plenty of time,
as we thought, before us, and we settled quickly to
work, my sister choosing a fallen capital for her seat,
which the guide was moving a little into position, when
a serpent of deadly venom darted out from behind it,
with head erect and hissing tongue: fortunately the
guide had a huge stone in his hand at the moment, and
the creature was crushed at once. The man said it was
an evil omen; but he lay down beside us, and was soon
fast asleep, and we sat drawing, and never looking
round, till, all of a sudden, we saw two mounted Bedoueens not very far from us, and coming in the direction from Baghdad! It was rather a startling sight at
this distance from protection, and we wakened the man,
who immediately seemed in an awful fright, and hid
himself in the inside of the Temple. It was too late to
hide, we knew, and moving would be more likely to attract their keen eyes than keeping still; but I am free
to confess that for once my heart did beat uncommonly
quickly (though we both assured each other there was
no danger whatever), remembering very well that we
were two miles from our people, and that the sun was
fast sinking behind the mountain. But, to our immense
relief, the men passed on without seeing us, and as they
skirted the town, and turned down towards our camp,
the guide pronounced them Anazehs.

So they proved to be, as we found when we got back
to the camp, and bad news they brought, viz. that they
had seen hostile Arabs on the way — at some distance,
indeed, but possibly scenting us from afar. So the
Sheikh issued his decree at once, that off we must go
at sunrise the next morning. We ate our last dinner,
much to the joy of the Tadmorites, who had sent down

a formal message that morning to the camp, saying
that they did hope we would soon " move on," for that
we had eaten nearly every cock, old and young, in the
town, and they could not supply us with any more!
We were, indeed, aware we had eaten the *old* cocks, but
were all unconscious of having ever tasted a young one.
So we had to make the best of our departure, and to
believe it was time to leave : we were all feeling ill and
languid, from the heat, our overtaxed strength, the
sulphur, and the carrion; and the camels were evidently
getting weak from want of proper food.   A centipede
had emerged from under the pillow of one of the gentlemen the night before, and a deadly serpent been
killed in the mash'lah of one of the dragomans on the
same day.   The precious sketches were packed up, we
made our last notes by starlight, filled the saddle-bags,
took a farewell bathe in the sulphur stream, and lay
down for our last sleep in the air of the warm sulphur-
scented stream.

THE RETURN.

PART III. — THE RETURN.

THOUGH brightly still shone down the moon's soft ray
Upon the hard rough pillars where we lay,
The wary Bedoueen watched her orb decline,
And waked the sleeping camp from dreams divine.
Then, one by one, each prostrate figure rose,
Around his head the gay kefiyeh throws,
And as the bright light reddened into morn,
And flushed with crimson hue the sand and thorn,
We bade adieu to that strange resting-place,
And tow'rds the West again we turned our face.

But first our way we slowly paced beside
The warm-breath'd stream, where maid and stripling tried
'Mid thirsty beasts the hideous skins to fill;
And by the mighty Temple Wall, where still
The lingering shades in cool grey masses hung,
And gazed aloft, where early sunbeams flung
Their light upon the carven columns tall
Which tower up above the huge, grand wall, —
Across the plain, by many a look delayed,
We passed beside the long, long Colonnade, —
All solemnly serene those pillars stand,
As some fair forms uprisen from the sand,
Which, ever gathering round their long-hid feet,
Pays thus with jealous care its homage meet.

There, lost in boundless blue infinitude,
The Desert lies with every colour hued,
Bright orange streaked with grey and glowing red,
Then violet soft o'er all the distance shed,
While, over all, the last faint shades of night
Dispersed before the morn's triumphant light.
And there the Temple, all her grace displayed
By bright Hyperion's first and latest rays,
Gives back the mute response of golden praise
Which pitying Time upon her stones hath laid!

Then past the stone heaps, once the Palace fair
Of her whose feet in jewelled sandals bare
To worship proud within that glorious fane —
Imperial Princess of the Desert plain!

Oh! slowly then we clomb the barrier hill,
Where stand a hundred tombs of ancient story,
With one long gaze regretful eyes to fill —
Fit place of farewell to Palmyra's glory!

Here stood the sad dethronèd Queen, and wrung
Despairing hands where golden fetters clung, —
Here stood to upbraid those mountains stern and great
She deemed sure guardians from the younger world, —
Here gazed upon the splendid home where late
The widowed Queen her own proud banners furled, —
Now — o'er Palmyra, Roman eagles wave, —
Her Temple courts profaned — her Queen, a slave!

But yet, I trow the anguish of that gaze,
Dwelt less upon the pride of brighter days,
Than on the Tombs — now of their treasures reft —
Where thrice four hundred years of honour slept;
And half in envy burned as she descried
The Tomb of that first Queen — th' Egyptian Bride,
(For whose delight, 'tis said King Solomon raised
This home, more lovely far than that she praised
On mighty Egypt's shore of still unrivalled fame);
And thought how calm she slept — untouched by shame, —
With those proud hearts that Death alone could thrall —
Closed eyes that wept not for their Daughter's fall!

'Tis said Zenobia made another home,
By Tiber's banks, in stern ungrateful Rome,
That on her brow — divinely calm — there reigned
The impress of serenest peace unfeigned:
Not such the mark that guilt or shame confers, —
Nor chains nor fetters could that soul degrade, —
Erect, she bore the vassal's sign — and made
The shame Aurelian's — and the triumph hers!
Yet oft, I ween, when Evening's golden haze,
In clouds of sunlight wrapped her wondering gaze,
Rome's cruel walls no more the heart enthralled,
By memories fond to that loved home recalled;
Beneath the shade of waving palms she dwelt,
Before Apollo's sacred shrine she knelt,
Her homage paid as fancy saw again

The crimson glory flood the Desert plain,
The pearly columns shine with roseate hue
Against the violet hills and deepening blue,
And cried, "What though my voice no more I raise,
This ceaseless beauty offers up glad praise!"

And we too turned away—our last look bent
On those old Tombs,—while, like a bright dream spent,
The wild, free life upon the Desert plain,
The beauteous and sublime infinitude,
The gorgeous-coloured ocean, rainbow-hued,
Those rosy Temples with their golden stain,
All lovely things we shall not see again,—
Sunk down behind the barrier hill, which closed
From view the living Tomb where calm reposed,
In marble letters writ upon the sand,
The dim but yet proud story of the land:—
And happier far than they who here adored
Mysterious gods, and their dark aid implored,
We lifted up our hearts in mute appeal,
To that true Son of God whose righteous Heel
Hath trodden down the Serpent's sinful head,
O'er Death's dark shades His healing radiance shed,
And spread from north to south, from east to west,
The Faith which makes both Jew and Gentile blest!

Then passed we to a narrow vale, among
Dark violet mountains, where light mist-wreaths clung,
Gazelles and jerboas bounding through the thorn
Brush off the sparkling dew-drops of the morn,
And, dancing lightly on the path, the bird,
The camel-lover's * little note is heard.
So slowly paced the camels one by one,
So, one by one, each long, slow step was done,
Each measured footfall's swinging cadence sung,
As higher sunbeams shortened shadows flung:
The wild fierce rays seemed scorching every brain
As all around they scorched the barren plain;

---

* *Habeeb el gemmal*, the lover of the camel: a little black and white bird, that is always dancing on the path, about a yard before the camel, as he paces along, especially in the morning.

And then on either hand th' unbroken walls
Of purple crags grew streaked with shades of red,
And darkening browns upon the lilacs spread,
As blazing up the midday sunshine falls.

And still the same slow step went calmly on,
And, one by one, th' unmarked hours were gone,
Till, blessed sight! blue waters coolly lave
The purple mountains' feet with rippling wave,
Delicious creeks and little bays appear,
And seem our hot and burning eyes to cheer,
And all th' horizon gleams with shining lakes —
When lo! they quickly vanish like the flakes
Of snow that fall beneath an April sky, —
And all the Desert seems more hot, more dry; —

At last, the boundless, unflecked dome of blue
Deepens behind us into sapphire hue
While radiant westering floods of brightest gold
In warm embrace sweet rosy clouds enfold:
Dark hues of plum upon the mountains shed,
And on the Desert plain a ruddy sea is spread
O'er which the long blue shadows fleetly fly;
Then darkening clouds were all around unfurled,
And sank the sun into another world,
Whence long, long after o'er the eastern sky
Sweet pictures of bright pink and gold he flung —
The evening echoes of the hymn he sung
At break of day, — like Farewells floating back
From lips unseen upon a winding track.

A moment on the soft, warm sand we lay,
And drank the fragrant cup and longed to stay,
But as the deepening night around us came
A distant spark revealed a hostile flame,
And quickly quenched was ours, and we had gone
With that slow footstep calmly striding on,
And aught but whispered tones the Sheikh forbade,
Lest we by tell-tale winds should be betrayed.

For now the night-breeze fluttered o'er the plain, —
Now fragrant with sweet-scented herbs it came —
Now whistling with a hard and rustling tone —
Now sighing with a low and tender moan, —

Anon a swift and savage gust would rise,
And with a solemn fury sweep the skies;
Then hush—and softly clinging round the face
A sweet and balmy breeze with loving grace
Would breathe—most like a cloud of rosy hue,
Alone and matchless in a heaven of blue ;
Or, like the memory bright of one sweet day,
Shining throughout the weary life-long way.

So with the same long step we glided on,
And, one by one, th' unmarked hours had gone, —
No change came o'er the darkened way,
Save where the stars moved on in bright array,
Or flung themselves athwart the gleaming night,
And fell with glittering glances out of sight.
So, ever " ohne Hast und ohne Rast,"
Till since the dawn full twenty hours had past,
And by the Robber's Tower we glided fast,
Lest lurking Bedoucen the troop descry,—
When, suddenly, the red Moon leaped on high,
And, in black masses mingled on the ground,
The silvery beams our shadows all confound,—
Dismayed we thought discovery sure at hand,
And listened for the Arab's rough command ;
But all around unbroken silence spread,
And nought disturbed us as we onward sped ;
One enemy alone appeared, unsought,
With whom we each with painful efforts fought,—
While every hour he more victorious grew,
Sweet sleep! unwelcome then, but friend most true !
The pitying Sheikh the camels bade to kneel,
That we a hasty hour of rest might steal,
And in a shallow wady on the ground
All soon were wrapped in dreamless sleep profound.

While there we lay and wearily reposed,
Th' eternal eye of every star was closed,
And night's cold grey had turned to ruddy morn
When we awaked to find the Desert thorn
Was bending o'er our heads its little arch,—
Then hastily we rose—resumed our march,
And chased our own blue shadows flung before
The rising ray,—no living thing moved o'er

Th' unchanging yellow sand, till formless shade
And quivering air the midday hour betrayed;
When lo! a cloud of moving dust appears,
And to our little band it quickly nears,
    Now circling round in front and flank,
    Then swerving off as though they shrank
    With pity from our little troop,
    Then turning back with sudden swoop,
    In narrowing circles wheeling round,
    And hoofs scarce lighting on the ground,
    With tightened bit and poisèd lance,
    With savage shriek and fiery glance,
    With angry words and hostile mien,
    On, on, they came, wild Bedoueen!
    Our guns were fired—and quickly they
    Reined up,—and then we guessed the play
Which welcomed us in Desert style to share
Their homely shelter from the scorching glare :
With kindly toil they led our beasts to drink
Delicious draughts within the lakelet's brink,—
This done, our steps to Karyeteen we pressed,
And in the spacious khan at last found rest.

We were not destined to find much repose at Karyeteen, as we were obliged to keep in the shelter of the
guest-room from the heat of the sun, and no entreaties,
coaxings, persuasions, objurgations, or anything else
could keep the people out of the room. They made us
very comfortable upon cushions and mattrasses; but,
seating themselves beside us, if we closed our weary
eyes for one moment, a finger stole up to feel our
cheeks, or stroke our hair, or pulled at our dresses to
see how they were made: so we gave up trying to sleep,
and retired into another room for the still better refreshment of a good bath; our dragoman standing outside the door *en garde*, about forty or fifty women
crowding round him and abusing him for keeping them
out and preventing their climbing up to the windows
to look at us. "I tell you the Sitts are bathing!"

" E wullah! isn't that what we want to see?" And at last they tried to break open the door. We then returned to the guest-chamber, where fresh and fresh relays of people came in to inspect us as we lay on our cushions; my sister patiently answered as many of their questions as she understood, while I amused myself with writing the foregoing lines, as a history of our return ride.

Towards sunset they brought us a banquet of meat and rice in various shapes, with vegetable-marrow and lentils, ending with a huge dish of fine dates stewed in butter, or rather oil, smoking hot; very good it was, but one could eat but a very little of it. It was rather a picturesque scene, for the room was a large one, and the whole town seemed crowded in to inspect the Franks feeding. The dinner was placed on the ground, and lighted up by two brass candelabras, each of them five feet high and handsomely made, which threw bright lights upon the swarthy faces ranged around us, with the many-coloured kefiyehs of the men, and the gold ornaments of the women. Some of the men were very handsome; and they were highly delighted when M. Haag made a hasty sketch of one or two.

We mounted as soon as it was dark, a large caravan of camels and donkeys accompanying us out of the town, as they had asked permission to benefit by the Sheikh's escort. The donkeys seemed like so many mice running beside the camels, but the long strings of baggage camels, tied in dozens and scores, were very troublesome, for our dromedaries were continually getting entangled among them; and as there was no moon and the night was very dark they fell very often. It was so cold by midnight that, coming after our many

sleepless hours, we were all continually falling asleep,
and at last the whole party got down to walk, so the
Sheikh said we had better have tea, and we lit the fire,
and then Sheikh, Argeels, and all went fast asleep, and
we slept till near sunrise, to the Sheikh's great annoyance, for the night's halt had been quite unintentional,
but a very great relief.

Our journey back was not so pleasant as the journey
there, for the camels were so weak they would lag, and
we had the sun nearly all day in our eyes, which is
much harder to bear than when it is behind one; moreover we were ourselves pretty well tired out. But we
had a lovely view all day of the snowy mountain range
reaching up to Homs, a beautiful feature in a Desert
view : the snow had fallen while we were at Tadmor,
but, curiously enough, although it had been very thick
on Hermon as we left Damascus, it seemed to have
almost quite melted away as we returned. We were
joined in the course of the morning by an armed Arab,
mounted on horseback, who would answer no question
as to where he was going, or to what Tribe he belonged.
The Sheikh looked grave, and after some time offered
him a piece of the bread he was himself eating, but the
Arab declined it — and there could not be a more un-
friendly sign. After an hour or two the Arab was suddenly missed from among us, and the Sheikh became
anxious, still more so when at dusk he was descried at
a distance waiting for us with two other Arabs, — of
course there might be two dozen concealed. So we
were desired to close in a compact body and to ride on
quickly, the Sheikh advancing in front, and we got a
little excited, and some of us hoped to see a little
"fun;" when, on reaching the men, the Arab's companions turned out to be two of our own escort, who had

ridden on while we had delayed to let our camels feed
on some tamarisk bushes we had happened to find : the
stranger wished us good-bye soon after. There is no
doubt that he intended mischief, but if he belonged to a
Ghŭzoo, he probably told them we were too strong a
party to attack ; and so ended our last attempt at an
adventure.

We rested that afternoon at Atny, and, starting
again when the moon got up, mistook our way into
Jerood, and got into an encampment of Bedoueen tents,
setting all the dogs into a chorus of furious howls ; a
great annoyance, for they run at and bite your camel's
legs, and make him wrathful. The camels stumbled
and fell a great deal, but the night work was pleasanter
than the very hot days ; indeed, I always enjoyed the
night journeys, both in the Desert and in Syria (when I
was not sleepy), almost as much as those of the bright-
coloured day. The night was so clear and light, and
the sky so *blue* instead of black, that one can still see
something of the scenery, although the contrast of the
silver moonlight and the densely black shadows are de-
ceptive : and then one can think so quietly and uninterruptedly, with one's head cool, and one's eyes unscorched,
while truly there was always food for thought around
one, above all in the full, softly-glowing, God-created
lamps of Night that shone in the sky. In the far East
it is easier than in our gloomy skies to understand how
naturally the men of old turned to them for worship ;
and how they yearned for the changeless purity and
Eternal Order they saw there and nowhere else. Often,
too, I thought of the child with his pure heart so fresh
from the Hands of God that he saw Him everywhere,
and asked if the stars were not " gimlet holes to let the
glory through," and felt how fully his innocent eyes

had seen, in spirit, the glory revealed in their beauty, which, like the miracles, manifested through the simplicity of His human life, the Divine Glory within it, revealing the Light which was already shining in the darkness of the world that comprehended it not.

It is beautiful to look out at any moment of night upon the glowing stars, but you cannot read their meaning clearly, unless, night after night, you have watched " the bright procession " move " down the gleaming arch," till you have seen the whole " celestial army " sweep across an " endless reach of sky," and pass out of our poor human sight to rise in other skies, and till you have learned the bright lesson of the " marshalled brotherhood of souls*," moving calmly, silently on, held up in the Hand of God the Father of all, " binding " their " sweet influences † " into one harmony, as He permits the souls of some to ride in majesty through the world, and others to shine meekly and dimly, but oh ! in His sight not a whit less radiantly. If there was one thing more in my mind than another, by night and by day, in all my long rides through the Desert, it was the oft-repeated words, " Heaven and Earth are full of the Majesty of Thy Glory ! "

These are some of the thoughts that occupy one almost unconsciously in the long silent hours of Eastern travelling; and difficult as it is to carry the mind of one's reader along with one in descriptions, and hopeless as it is to paint in words the scenes that met our eyes for theirs, it is really impossible to make them enter into trains of thought that arise from the accidents of the atmosphere and the silence and the beauty around one.

We found the Bourghaz pass perfectly stifling, and

* Buchanan Read.   † Job xxxviii. 31.

were thankful that the good Sheikh ordained a rest, for the sake of the camels, under the shade of the thick lofty trees about Doumah, which had seemed hopelessly far off. My sister's camel, the dear Simri, had lagged latterly very much, and she dismounted, hoping thus to relieve the tired beast, but within a few yards of Doumah the poor thing knelt down on the road side, and lay there till she died two days after. We had a most refreshing meal of grapes and delicious fresh leben (sour milk) under the trees, before we remounted; my sister was given a very fine white dromedary, and we all set off racing each other at a brisk trot.

We had a grand entry into Damascus; about two hours' distance from the town we met the beautiful and almost priceless mares of the Sheikh, out exercising, and he immediately mounted his favourite and galloped wildly and gaily all round the cavalcade. The dromedaries knew very well how near they were to home, and they went merrily along while the Argeels brushed them up, re-arranged their own kefiyehs, and then burst out into choruses of songs, screaming and shouting, and some of them standing up and dancing on the camels' backs amid peals of laughter, while the darabooka played unceasing rub-a-dubs of the noisiest description. Very merry and bright it was; the road was lively with people, to whom the astonishing fact of our long stay at Tadmor was again and again related, and a thousand welcomes were shouted to Sheikh Miguel as one after another recognised him. Most cool, refreshing, and delightful did the green trees overhanging the rough paths, the bright gardens, and thousand rushing streamlets appear to our Desert-used eyes. I need not say how still more welcome the excellent hôtel beds felt to our wearied bodies as we sank to sleep to the music of the fountain in our room, after fifteen days' absence. But I may add that, for my own part, I would willingly undergo *twice* the fatigue again to re-visit that magnificently lovely Tadmor.

ZENOBIA. (Written in Palmyrene characters.)

END OF THE FIRST VOLUME.

LONDON
PRINTED BY SPOTTISWOODE AND CO.
NEW-STREET SQUARE